THE

BANKS

OF

CERTAIN

RIVERS

THE

BANKS

OF

CERTAIN

RIVERS

JON HARRISON

LAKE UNION
PUBLISHING

Published by Lake Union Publishing, Seattle

www.apub.com

Amazon, the Amazon logo, and Lake Union Publishing are trademarks of Amazon.com, Inc., or its affiliates.

ISBN-13: 9781477825235
ISBN-10: 1477825231

Cover design by Eileen Carey

Library of Congress Control Number: 2014938157

Printed in the United States of America

for Margie Lynch

W hen Christopher was still in middle school and not yet so big, my employer, the Port Manitou School District, frequently sent me off to education conferences. I'd just finished my master's, and as low man on the administrative totem pole I became the selected emissary for our district. Most of the events were pretty dull: technology trends in education, new media for science teachers, and so on. Holiday Inn banquet rooms in Lansing, Detroit, Grand Rapids. I'd go alone, suffer through, and report what I'd learned to the board once home. But every once in a while I'd be sent somewhere fun: Chicago, Denver, a city like that, and if I could work it, I'd arrange for Chris and my wife, Wendy, to come along for a mini vacation. We had good times on those trips.

The autumn that Chris entered the eighth grade, not long before he turned fourteen, I was directed to attend a conference in Wisconsin called "Engaging Teens in Science and Math." The topic seemed interesting enough, but the locale was most intriguing: a hundred-year-old hotel on Lake Michigan owned by some storied Milwaukee brewing family. It seemed to me like the sort of thing Chris would love, and Wendy was all for it, so I used our frequent-flier miles and got tickets for the three of us.

The hotel, we discovered upon our arrival, was ancient, rambling, and totally charming. Painted yellow outside with peeling white trim. Additions built over additions. Exposed pipes, shared bathrooms, and not a level floor in the place. There were screened-in porches for each room with splintery Adirondack chairs facing the lake, where Wendy could read from her stack of paperbacks, and sea kayaks and Sunfish sailboats pulled up on the beach for Chris to mess around in for hours on end. They both loved it.

Unfortunately for me, the conference was a complete bore. Not that I disagreed with the topic; I was entirely for it. I'd just heard it all before. I was lucky enough to run into a friend, Anne Vasquez, an elementary school librarian from downstate; she'd been sent out on the conference circuit too, and we made a point of meeting up when we could to mitigate our boredom.

Anne and I sat together on the last day, Sunday, to listen to the final speaker in a giant ballroom on the southern end of the hotel. Chandeliers hung above us, and tall windows opened out over a broad grassy lawn to the lake. We were both tired, and it was hard for us to pay attention to anything being said up at the podium. Anne kept elbowing me and pointing to a young woman and toddler out on the grass. The little guy was just learning to walk, and for whatever reason it seemed very funny to us each time he lost balance and toppled. The more we watched, the harder it became not to laugh, and I started to feel like one of my own students, goofing off, pushing it, waiting for someone to scold me.

Anne nudged me again. She wasn't laughing this time; a man in a suit was urgently shooing the woman and her child off the lawn. Anne looked back at me and shrugged. A moment after that, the room filled with a loud thumping noise, and every head in the place turned to see a blue medivac helicopter ease from the sky down to a spot on the grass as gently as a butterfly lights on a twig. The woman who had been speaking up at the lectern stopped, and we all watched as some medical personnel hustled a rolling gurney toward the chopper. One of the flight nurses held an IV bag aloft as he trotted alongside, and a mechanical chest compressor pounded away at the strapped-down form on the stretcher.

"Whoa," Anne whispered. "Somebody got it bad."

They hoisted the gurney up into the helicopter and shut the door, the engine throttled up again, and the rotors began to turn. A piece of paper was blown over the grass. I felt the vibration in my chest as the machine shuddered and lifted, a deafening presence in the room. The chopper flew away, and the room was silent.

"Well," the woman up front said into her microphone, "there's our excitement for the afternoon." People laughed awkwardly, and just as I started to wonder where my son was at that moment, the same man in the suit from the lawn entered the room with two policemen and everyone stopped laughing. The man in the suit held a clipboard in his hand.

"Mr. . . ." He paused, staring at the clipboard, struggling with the name he was trying to read. I went cold through my face and chest and fingertips, like the blood had gone from my body, and I stood up before he said anything else. I saw the word trying to find shape between his lips. I knew it was me they were looking for.

"Mr. Kaz . . . Kazen . . ."

"That's me," I said. Anne put her hand over her mouth.

"Can we have a word with you?" I knew. Everyone in the room knew. I think Anne started crying when I told her I'd be right back.

She knew I wouldn't be right back.

They took me outside. "There's been an accident," they told me.

"Was it Chris? I need to know. Where is my son?"

"It was a terrible accident. She was in the pool."

"My wife? Where is Christopher?"

"Is this your son, Mr. Kaz—?"

He was by the fence around the pool when they brought me to him. He was still just a boy then. He was seated on the ground, shaking, and someone had wrapped him in a tan-colored blanket. A woman in a hotel uniform knelt next to him and rubbed his back.

"They wouldn't let me help her," Christopher said.

"Her finger got stuck," one of the policemen said.

"I was ready to help. I know CPR."

"Jammed tight. Maybe two minutes before we could . . ."

"I know *how* to do it, Dad. They wouldn't let me."

"She's being flown to the university hospital. We've got a car to take you there."

"We'll get your things together for you," the man in the suit said.

They'd been diving after a pebble. A polished agate Chris had bought in the gift shop. Taking turns. My son in his baggy yellow trunks, my wife in a black Speedo one-piece. Chris had thrown it, a high lazy arc—plunk!—and Wendy followed, diving through the sun. She kicked herself down and felt over the bottom for the pebble. The pool was old. The grate was old. Her middle finger wedged tight in the grate; they didn't think about those things back when it was cast.

I don't know if anyone else was watching. Anyone watching would have seen how her kicking changed, how it became frantic. They would have seen how the air bubbled out of her, and how most of the life bubbled out of her too.

"Why wouldn't they let me help her, Dad?"

I dropped to my knees and put my arms around my son.

"Christopher," I said. "Christopher."

-------- ———————————— -----

CHAPTER ONE

One humid night at the beginning of summer, while jetliners rumbled overhead and fireflies winked green along a far-off row of brambles, my best friend and I sat by the fire pit out in the field behind my house. It was almost midnight and the fire was nearly finished, and as we drank away the last of an unexpected bottle of scotch Alan had brought over as an end-of-the-school-year gift, I tried to explain a recurring dream I'd been having.

"So it's like, I'm running," I began, the words thick in my mouth.

Alan tipped his head back and closed his eyes. The fire popped, and a log tumbled into sparks.

"In this dream," he said.

"Yes. I'm running. On a plain, a plateau, or something. Endless, right? And I'm just running over it."

"Away from something? Are you being pursued?"

"No. Not at all. It's effortless. Almost pleasurable. And it goes and goes. I run, but I don't get tired."

"Understandable," Alan said. His eyes remained closed. "For a guy like you."

"I know. That part's not so remarkable. But after a while I come to this mountain, and I don't stop. I don't need to stop. I go up and up, and it's just as easy. Potential energy, right? Sometimes it gets steep, but that's no problem; I scramble, use my hands, but I never slow down. It's almost like I get faster. I want to keep going. But then . . ."

"But then?"

"I run out of mountain. I just sail over the top and into the air. And below, there's this river, but I can't get down there."

Alan opened his eyes and sat up.

"Like you start to fly?"

"Yes, but—"

"Flying dream," he said, leaning back and nodding. "Yeah."

"But I want to keep running. I need to get down to the river for something."

"Mmm." Alan sipped his drink, sighed, and closed his eyes again. "Flying dream. I get it. I totally get it."

The thing was, my friend didn't get it at all. We were in no state for me to try to explain it once more, and, having told him about it, I never had the dream again.

I'm thinking about that dream now. With a bloody lip and my ass hitting hard on sun-faded pavement, I think of it for the first time in months. There are stars around my head, cuckoo clocks and canaries, and close to my eyes I see my own red fingertips, foamy with hemochrome spittle.

If I'm not mistaken, I've just been hit in the face.

But there's that dream too. Before the skinny elbow connected with my lip, before the whole of my body went down to the ground, *before everything changed*, I'd been running. Just like that dream. We had been running, my girls and I, effortlessly, all of us.

Effortless. That, as I sit here trying to put things together in my head, is what I know. Effortless running, blood-red fingers, and a lone dandelion leaning up through a crack in the asphalt before me. And that's about it.

Putting my mind to it, here's what I can piece together: our feet fell and fell; piston legs, bodies like engines. There were no mountains. Our first long Friday practice of the season, and we were cruising on autopilot. Flying. My kids are twenty years or more younger than me, and I'm not sure who was more amazed: me for keeping up with them, or them with me. But there we were: together, schooling like fishes, gliding footfall after footfall. Pouring down streets finally emptied of their summer tourist throngs. A school of runners breathing easy through the streets. Ages indeterminate, unnecessary, erased.

The weather was sublime. Not necessary for a perfect day, I know, but a nice bonus. The chilly rain we'd had over those first days of September—an abrupt onset of dreariness that seemed to signify an end to our mostly gorgeous summer—had vanished, leaving behind warm, puffy-cloud days and cool nights tailor-made for autumnal bonfires. And while I have no scientific evidence to say so, experience suggests a long Indian summer should follow. A breeze from the lake—rich with the smell of fishy sea grass and outboard gasoline—came up through the buildings, through the mostly empty streets, and seemed to push at our backs no matter which way we turned. Pushing us along. Urging us along.

I know it couldn't really have been that way, but right here on the ground, reconstructing it all, that was how it seemed.

The first week of school had been completed, and I have to say there too, I had no complaints. I'd been scheduled to teach one regular physics class in the mornings, along with a third-period Algebra II class (filling in for a long-open vacancy in the math department), and almost all of the kids turned in my first homework assignment. While I hadn't yet looked closely enough to gauge the quality of the work, the fact that so many of them made the effort to get it back to me on time seemed to bode well for my prospects of happiness this fall. My afternoon class, my dream class, was Advanced

Placement Physics, populated by seventeen motivated upperclass-men with little apparent propensity for drama or slacking. All signs pointed to a very enjoyable semester.

We were breathing easy.

Kevin Hammil, the district's brand-new, fresh-out-of-student-teaching high school biology teacher, had joined us on our run. He's from somewhere in Texas, was an All-American middle-distance runner in college, and so far seemed to be a pretty good guy; he's soft-spoken with perpetually knit eyebrows and a Grizzly Adams beard that offsets his lean runner's form. He'll be assistant coaching boys' track in the spring, and he'd offered to help the cross-country coaches with stretching and weights this fall. I was glad to have him along, and my runners seemed glad too.

To my side as we trotted down Pine Avenue and onto the bike path along the northern bank of the Big Jib River, flowing through the guts of our empty town, I caught a smirk from one of my AP seniors, Cassie Jennings.

"I heard they fed the python yesterday, Mr. Hammil," she said, trying to keep a straight face. Cassie finished sixth overall at the state cross-country championship last season, and having seen how comfortably she ran today, I didn't think a top-three finish was unreasonable to expect from her this year.

Kevin swung his head side to side like a sad dog. "They fed him, all right. You know what the best thing to do with that snake would be?" He spoke in an earnest drawl, staring ahead through his gait. "Y'all know what we should do with that snake?"

It's all coming back to me. Trees bent through a short gust off the lake. Leaves rattled and fell into the river, gulls wheeled in the air. We were flying.

Jenny Cohn, a new sophomore who apparently hadn't yet heard any of my new colleague's vocal complaints about the ten-foot-long rep-tile sharing his classroom, took the bait. "What's that, Mr. Hammil?"

"We should have him made into a nice pair of boots. Snakeskin boots. No, come on now, don't give me that look. A gorgeous pair of—"

"Ew," one of the girls said. They all laughed, and I heard Jenny call, "It's just a stupid snake!"

"All right, just a snake. You take him, then. Any one of you. Take him, put him in your room for a while. Lying around all day, looking at you with that mean snake face. Gives me the willies every morning. And what's-his-name, that goofball, snake wrangler, whatever he is, butting in on my class to throw a damn chicken in there—"

The girls laughed harder, and I interrupted them with a wide left turn. "This way, guys," I called. "Over the bridge. Down Lake Street." I sensed the growing mirth over Mr. Hammil's genuine discomfort displacing the wonderful rhythm we'd established; funny or not, I knew I needed to squash it right then.

"Let's pick it up a bit for the last mile," I said. "Cassie, pace us in. Once around the athletic fields. Amy?" I looked around for Amy Vandekemp, a junior who seemed to have exchanged last year's knock-kneed gawkiness for a much-matured stride and an overserious demeanor. "Amy, get up front and bring us in with Cassie."

There was a collective snicker as Amy came up through the bunch of us to take her place at the head of the group, and as she passed, I saw why: a gull had scored a direct white-and-green hit down the back of Ms. Vandekemp's tee shirt. She seemed oblivious to the laughter (and bird shit), and I wondered if I should ask Cassie after practice just what the rest of the team thought of this kid.

The girls quieted down with their increased effort, and we heard nothing beyond the collective rasp of harder breathing over the wind and leaves. "Pick it up, pick it up, *pick it up!*" I called from the end of our accelerating column. Kevin rose into an easy sprint to fly ahead of the group in the last couple hundred yards before circling around us as we loped into the student parking lot.

"Nice job, ladies!" he hollered, oblivious to the look I shot him for stealing my line.

"Very nice run," I said, clearing my throat. "Thank you all for the great effort." I meant it too. One of my sophomores bent over gasping with her hands on her knees, and I patted her shoulder as I passed. "Keep moving, Sarah. Walk through it." Kevin nodded at me, happy with the workout, and I nodded back. I hadn't had the heart to tell him that, less than a week into the school year, he and his beard had already acquired the campus-wide nickname of Hammil the Mammal. I didn't think I could keep a straight face if I told him anyway.

We gathered in a loose bunch around the open hatch of Cassie Jennings's old Subaru wagon—one of the few cars remaining in the student parking area—where a big Igloo cooler filled with ice water sat on the weedy cracked pavement. A low laughing sounded from the row of cedar trees at the other side of the lot, and I glanced over to see a group of what I assumed to be football players horsing around after their practice. They must have been junior-varsity players, I figured, because most everyone else involved with football had convoyed away hours earlier for tonight's big away game in Grayling. Kevin clapped his hands. "All right, ladies, I'm doing a voluntary weights session in—" I raised my hand to him and shook my head, and he made a mock-chastened face.

"Hold up there, Mr. Hammil. Settle down." The girls giggled, and it dawned on me that my new twenty-something, VW-camper-van-driving colleague might be the object of some crushes. I'd have a word with him on this later, but I was sure he already got *that* memo. "Couple things before we go. Again, great job today. Thanks. I want you to get out for an easy day tomorrow if you can, and take Sunday off. Rest day. Mr. Hammil"—another giggle—"has offered to help us out with some strength training. Totally voluntary, but I'd encourage you all to take advantage of it. Have a great weekend, be safe, take it easy if you're driving over to watch the game tonight. I'll see you all Monday afternoon." The girls began to chatter, some said goodbye to me, and Kevin started jogging in place.

"Girls!" he shouted. "Auxiliary gym! Ten minutes! See you there!" He clapped his hands again—one, two, three times—and ran off.

Most of the team followed Mr. Hammil in a gossipy shuffle, and I hung back to wait for a chance to chat with Cassie while she loaded the cooler back into her car. Amy Vandekemp stayed behind too, looking like she wanted to have a word with me as well. But I wanted to talk to Cassie alone, so I started to suggest to Amy how *beneficial* weight training might be for a developing runner like herself. Before I really had a chance to say anything, though, a cloud came over us from the other side of the parking lot: a sudden aggression, a barking shout, from the group of boys whom I'd mostly forgotten. They'd circled up around a scuffling pair, or maybe it was three of them; in any event, their lusty chant of "*Fight! Fight! Fight!*" showed they'd obviously forgotten about me too.

"Guys!" I shouted, taking off in a run toward the little mob scene. "Hey! *Hey!*" It took a couple long seconds to cross the lot, and the circle parted for my entry just as one of the kids—a chubby, freckled little punk—lifted himself from the adversary he'd been pinning to the pavement. The freckled kid merged into the bunch, and I held up my hands. "Let's cool it down," I said, turning to see them all, keeping my voice level. "Bring it down a notch. Okay?" They were all underclassmen, and I didn't recognize a single one. Their expressions ranged from frustration at interrupted bloodlust to worry that they were somehow in serious trouble. None of them seemed very eager to talk.

"So?" I asked. "What's going on?" I knew about scuffles; they weren't in any trouble. I'd make them think they were, at least for a little bit, then send them off with a warning.

One of them started to speak, but stopped. "What's that?" I asked. Nothing. "Nobody wants to tell me what's up?" They mostly stared at their shoes, except for the one on the ground: he looked up at me, panting, all spindly limbs and pimples, with a torn shirt and a dusty scrape on his forehead. I took a step forward, grabbed him by his shirt, and hoisted him up to his feet. He twitched like he wanted to scurry away, but I kept him in place with my hands on a pair of bony shoulders that lifted and dropped as he worked to catch his breath.

"Guys," I tried again, "I need to know what—"

"Tater's a pussy, that's what," came a sneering, unidentifiable voice from the circle, followed by sneering laughter; they were all laughing. And with that, the kid I held fast with my hands—presumably Tater, the pussy in question—began to shake with fury before spastically windmilling his arms as he sought to escape my grasp. Watch the elbow. *Watch the elbow!* I didn't let go quickly enough, but I watched the whole time, and even though I ducked to the side . . .

Pow.

That's what I recall. Like dreams and real life, potential energy becomes kinetic. Order is followed by chaos. And if anybody should understand how one crumbles into the other, it's me.

From: xc.coach.kaz@gmail.com
To: w.kazenzakis@gmail.com
Sent: September 7, 12:43 pm
Subject: gchat

Wendy-

So, fourth-period lunch, and I'm hiding out in the gym office because Beth Coolidge thinks, somehow, I'm willing to volunteer to construct a homecoming float for her this year. I'm not, so I'm avoiding her by concealing myself in this office with no computer. Negative side: it stinks in here. Positive side: I'm getting good practice typing on the phone with my thumb.

If I can sneak out to the practice fields after seventh period this afternoon without Coolidge seeing me, I'm home free.

A story for you: The district computer guy was fixing something in my room today and he asked me if I knew about the chat thing built into gmail. He opened it so I could check it out, and I nearly (no joke) fell out of my chair when the contact list popped up with your name at the top. Your status was "offline," but still, it was a big surprise to see you there.

-Neil

CHAPTER TWO

Feet pound behind me, more than one pair; all cuckoos and stars have fluttered away. The foot sound is accompanied by Cassie Jennings's voice. "Mr. K.!" she calls. "Mr. K.!"

The boys are all gone, scurried off to who knows where, and suddenly I'm unsure if they were ever there in the first place and *what the hell just happened here?* Something's happened, though; the blood on my fingertips when I touch my hand to my face is proof, as is the jab of pain in my mouth and the Tilt-A-Whirl spin that the parking lot takes when I make an effort to get up. I slump back down and remain seated, and turn my gaze back to that dandelion wilting between my feet. *Poor guy*, is all I can manage to think.

"What happened? Oh my God, his face."

"I'm fine," I say. "Seriously." The stars have cleared from my vision, but my upper lip has begun to throb in a way I imagine to be visible, like a hammer-banged thumb in an old cartoon. I check to make sure that my front teeth are still firmly planted in my gums, first with my tongue and then with my fingers. Everything is where it belongs. Cassie and Amy Vandekemp stand over me, and I shoo their hands away when they try to help me to my feet.

"Come on, Mr. K.," Amy says. "Stand up."

"I'm fine," I repeat, as if a second time will make it true. I rise, and the girls hold out their hands like they're expecting me to topple. The world has stopped spinning, but the looks on their faces might be the most unsettling thing of all.

"Your face is really bleeding."

"Who were those losers?"

"There's ice in the cooler . . ."

We walk back to Cassie's car, the three of us, and even though I feel perfectly steady on my feet, my two star runners look ready to catch me at any moment.

"I mean, girls, come on," I say thickly through my fattening lip. "I've taken shots before. Harder than . . . it's nothing." Their lack of response suggests I've only thought this, and not actually managed to speak it out loud. "I'm okay."

"Sure," Cassie says. We're back at her car, and I take a seat on the rear bumper as she digs through the detritus covering her backseat. "I've got a bag somewhere."

Amy stands back a bit with her arms crossed, peering over in the direction of the teachers' parking lot by the school. "Where's your car, Mr. K.?"

"Not here. I was running home tonight." This has been my routine ever since Chris has been old enough to drive: catch a ride to school with him in the mornings, and have an easy, head-clearing run home at the end of the day. It's only a little more than three miles, and with the good weather, I've been able to do it every night so far since school started.

"Can you run with your face like that?" Cassie asks. She hands me a crumply plastic grocery bag with a handful of ice cubes inside. The whole mess is wrapped with now-soggy paper napkins, and when I press it to my face some icy water dribbles down my front and makes me jump.

"I'll find a ride," I say, glancing down at my wet and blood-spotted running shirt.

"Sorry," Cassie says, wincing at the sight of the dark mess on my chest, before hesitantly adding: "I could drive you home?" She chews on the concept for a moment, struck by a flash of protomaturity, before stating it again with a little more resolve. "I'll drive you home."

"Amy has to come," I say, muffled by the bag, and the two girls look at each other. "Can you get her home after you drop me off?"

"What do you mean, 'Amy has to come'?"

"I mean, it's a district policy thing. You can't have a teacher and student alone—"

"Yeah, yeah, whatever, but there's bird crap on her shirt."

"What?" Amy says, trying to look over her own shoulder.

"I don't want bird crap on my car seat!"

"Cassie," I say. "Have you noticed the condition of your car's interior recently?"

"It's probably carrying some *disease*."

"Shut up, Cassie," Amy says softly, but her tone more than makes up for any lack of volume. "Seriously. Shut up." Then Amy Vandekemp does something that actually makes Cassie's mouth fall open: she takes off her shirt, turns it inside out, and puts it back on again, avian stain and all, before I even have a chance to look away. "Let's go. I need to stop at my locker on the way out." Then she takes the passenger seat up front, closing the door behind her with a suitably dramatic slam. I bet her arms are crossed in there too. Cassie looks at me and nods like nothing just happened.

"Amy and I will take you home," she says, smiling like it was her plan all along.

--------- ⸺⸺⸺⸺⸺⸺⸺ -----

On the old highway north of town, past the scrub grass and summer houses on the Lake Michigan shoreline, a sharp turn inland marks the southern end of the Olsson Dune Orchard complex. In 1924 my wife's paternal grandfather, a very tall Dane named Nils Olsson, bought eighty-nine lakefront acres bounded by the Little Jib River to the north and the highway to the sawmill to the south, where he grew sweet cherries for nearly forty years before turning it over to my father-in-law, Dick, in the early sixties. Dick was the youngest (and tallest) of the three Olsson sons, and the only one interested in taking over the farm; he ran it—profitably, I should add—right up until the heart attack that killed him. That was nine years ago. Since then, the working part of the farm has been leased out to some small-time operators; it's still mostly cherries, but a couple of guys from Chicago have started making some almost-palatable wines from a vineyard they put in on the southeast corner of the property not long after Dick passed away.

A couple guys from Chicago. They all seem to be coming up from Chicago lately, buying old houses, fixing things up, tearing things down. Building condos and tee-shirt shops. There are deals to be had, and vineyards to be put in. A lot of my friends—self-identified locals all—feign anger at the changes, resentment toward the new development and remodeling projects. I don't mind it so much. I know they don't either. It's easy enough to knock the tourists, but things have really been looking up in town; shops and restaurants are busy and the people who own them are doing well. People who own property are doing *very* well. Let them fix up the town, I say. Look at how much better off we are than everyone else downstate. This place—the pinky finger of the mitten-shaped peninsula I call home—is one bright spot in a generally dismal state economy. Let them come up and remodel all they want.

Besides, on the tip of that little finger, we've got the orchard. They can build all around us, but my wife's family's orchard is just one of those immutable things that will always *be*.

Rolling along over the Old Sawmill Highway, the interior of Cassie's car goes dark as we veer eastward away from the lake, and the trees along the road close over us. Textbooks with shattered bindings mingle with crumpled papers down around my feet, and on the seat next to my backpack (Amy grabbed it for me when she went in to get her things) there's a polyester work uniform of some sort wadded up in a pile. I'm thinking up a million different explanations for why the engraved nametag on top of the clothes says CARRIE instead of CASSIE, but I don't ask why, because asking would mean having to listen to an answer, and my head hurts enough already.

The girls have been thankfully quiet for the duration of the ride, as if they sense the headache blossoming in my frontal lobes. Amy has the window open, which is fine, welcome even, and they've mercifully kept the stereo off. I tell Cassie to slow down as we approach my driveway, and direct her to make the turn. The jolt as the car comes off the pavement onto gravel makes me smack my face with the ice bag, sending a new trickle of cold down my front and a zing of pain up through my teeth.

I'll be fine. I will.

As we roll up the drive, I smile—reflexively, if painfully—when I see Lauren Downey's brand-new Prius parked in front of my mother-in-law's garage. I didn't think she worked on Fridays, but, as the most senior of Carol's in-home caregivers, she can call her own shots, scheduling-wise.

"Nice car, Mr. K.," Cassie says, nodding to the bright red Toyota.

"Not mine. My place is over there. Keep going past these trees."

We roll through the leafy shade into a clearing with my house at the center. It's low and gray, single-storied and tidy with white trim and a deck that wraps from the front to the back, where I sit many evenings to watch the sun drop behind the dunes. My home. I'm perplexed for a moment by the sight of a large shrink-wrapped dark object strapped to a wooden shipping pallet in front of my garage door; as Cassie rolls to a halt in front of it, I realize it's the new fireplace I ordered back in May. On the plastic wrapping, in coarse block letters, someone has scrawled:

N. Kazenzakis, Port Manitou, Mi.

This was supposed to have been delivered while I was home so I'd have some help bringing it inside, but what the hell, I've waited long enough. At least it's finally here.

I clamber out of the backseat as soon as the car stops and hold the sopping ice bag away from me, letting it drip on the ground as I grab my pack. Cassie leans over to talk through Amy's open window.

"You can just throw that back in on the floor," she says. "I'll take care of it later."

"I'll put it in my trash," I say. It's possible that the introduction of moisture could encourage the growth of some horrible life-form in there. "Thanks for the ride."

The girls drive off, the sound of gravel beneath tires giving way to the sawing drone of insects and a far-off lawn mower. I drop my pack and the ice bag to the ground next to the pallet, and lean my hip into the fireplace to gauge its weight for moving. The substantial mass does not budge.

My house seems dark and stuffy inside, and I leave the front door open behind me to encourage the circulation of fresh air. It smells of sawdust and new construction, plaster and cool stone, the evidence of my perpetual remodeling project. A knotty oak floor laid down last spring. An empty slate hearth Chris and I built last winter. How we'll manage to shoehorn the fireplace in there I'm not sure, but I'll worry about it later.

Back at the altar of my bathroom mirror, my lip doesn't look as bad as I'd imagined it would. A little swollen, fuller than usual, but pushed out from beneath by my tongue, the split in my flesh looks nothing more than superficial. I draw my bloody running shirt over my head and drop it into the sink under cold running water, and bring my hands to the sides of my face, blinking as I press my fingertips in circles against my temples. Here I am. Aside from a fattened lip, I haven't at all changed since this morning, the last time I looked over myself. Complexion and nose: faux-Greek and stately. Eyes: green as they've always been. Hair is still short, still no less gray and still suitably dense. My shirtless torso is neither bulky, nor scrawny, nor fat, just like the rest of me. A lifetime of running has been pretty good for that.

At thirty-nine years old, I could be seeing something much worse, I suppose.

I grab a clean shirt and change into some jeans, and down a couple Advil with a big glass of water in the kitchen (the one part of our home that feels decidedly complete) before walking across the field to check on my mother-in-law and catch Lauren before she takes off for the day. It's still breezy and warm outside, but the dry leaves whirling on the old concrete barn slab—now a basketball court for my son—say summer is just about finished.

I let myself into Carol's house through the garage. Lauren's working on something in the laundry room, and she barely glances up when I say hello.

"Are you home early?" she asks, and when she finally looks to me for a reply, she lets out a tiny shriek. "Oh God, Neil, what happened to you?" Lauren covers her mouth with her hand, maybe in shock, or maybe because she's trying to conceal laughter. She reaches for my face, and I jump back.

"Don't touch it!"

"Don't be a baby. Come on, stand still. I'm not going to hurt you! Big baby." She manipulates my lip, smirking the whole time, and it's not so bad. She is a registered nurse, after all. A professional. "Oh, you're fine. Put ice on it when you're back at your house." She takes my hand. "Really, what happened? Let's go show Carol."

"Broke up a fight. Nothing. Stupid. Which Carol do we have today?"

"Fairly lucid Carol. But it's about 1964."

My seventy-six-year-old mother-in-law was in fine shape and mentally sharp right up until two winters ago when she slipped on some ice on New Year's Day and broke her left shoulder blade. The fracture itself shouldn't have been such a problem, but the infection she picked up in the hospital sure was, and the pneumonia that settled into her lungs after that *really* was. She's been on so many different medications since then I can't even keep track; some make her weak, while others leave her confused or just not there. Most of the time she's hardly the same person anymore. There are glimmers of clarity once in a while; we wait for them and encourage them, and when they're slow in coming, the revenue trickling in each year from the orchard is enough to pay the nurses who come and keep her going until she perks back up again.

It's a shame, her decline, because she was a lot of fun and we always got along well. I really loved her. I mean, of course I still do. But it's different now.

In the living room, Carol leans to her side in an easy chair that seems absurdly large for her withering form. There's an afghan draped over her legs, and a clear plastic line strung from her ears across her wrinkly white-pink face to bring oxygen to her nostrils. My wife Wendy's high school senior portrait—braces, bangs, and all—hangs in a frame on the wall behind her. A talk show plays on the TV, and the volume is so high that I nearly have to shout.

"Carol, how are you?"

She turns to me with her wet, red-ringed eyes, takes in my lip with a blink, and returns her gaze to the talk show.

"Arthur, you're going to kill yourself on that motorbike," she mutters.

Arthur is Carol's younger brother. And if my memory of family lore serves, Uncle Art sold his motorcycle just before leaving for his first stint in the Vietnam War.

Lauren puts her hand on my shoulder. "It's Neil, Carol. Your son-in-law."

Carol stares at the television and coughs. "There's something wrong with the fuse box still," she says. A wadded-up tissue is clutched between her brittle fingers. "That's three boxes of fuses Dick's had to buy this summer."

"I'll take a look, Mom."

"Fix it, will you?"

"I'll see what—"

"Just fix the damned thing!"

To the best of my knowledge, Carol never, ever used to swear.

Lauren pulls me out to the dining room and frowns. "She wasn't so cranky earlier," she whispers. "Are you going to look at the fuse box?"

"This house hasn't had a fuse box for at least twenty years," I say. I'm leaning in close as we talk, which is ridiculous because—even if the TV wasn't on at maximum volume—Carol is so deaf now she wouldn't be able to hear us anyway. Lauren still has her hand on my arm, and she's looking up at me.

"You should take a look just to make her feel better."

"There's nothing to look at."

"Sure there is. Tell her you're going downstairs to take a look. I'll come down and hold the flashlight." Lauren smiles and bumps her knee into my leg. She's still gripping my arm.

"No way. What is up with you lately? *No way.*"

"Yes way. I need to. Now." Lauren is still smiling up at me, looking at me, nodding her straw-colored ponytail into a bounce. "Now, now, now."

I shake my head and suppress a laugh, and peer back into the living room. "Going to check that fuse, Carol," I call. No answer. Lauren grabs a flashlight, and when I click the light switch at the top of the ancient basement stairs, Lauren snaps it right back off again. This time I let myself laugh.

"Fuse box, Neil," Lauren says, jabbing me with the flashlight from behind as we descend.

"Is that what we're going to call it now?"

"Shut up." She nudges me, through the cobwebbed dimness under heavy sawn beams, toward a sagging couch at the far end of the basement. Raw copper pipes and electrical wires run between the joists above. I sit, and Lauren, standing before me, head cocked and half smirking, undoes her pants and lets them drop with her underwear to the floor. She kicks her feet free from the clothes, and shakes her head when she sees me glance beyond her to the stairs.

"Carol's not coming. She's not going to see." Lauren props her hands on her bare, slender hips, pale skin glowing in the next-to-nothing light.

"Just what is it that she's not going to see?"

Lauren rolls her eyes as she straddles me on the couch. "Do I have to say it? You really want me to say?" She reaches behind her head and, with a serpentine movement of her neck, frees her hair from the elastic tie that's been binding her ponytail. She presses her forehead to mine, spilling her hair over both of us, and when I flinch as she starts to kiss me, she draws back.

"Shit. I'm sorry. Did that hurt? I'm sorry." She brushes her fingertips over my mouth, quite a bit *less* professionally this time, before reaching down to unbutton my jeans. I bring my hands there to assist, changing myself from passive observer to active participant. Equally culpable.

"I'm sorry," she says again, eyes closed, and in a way that seems out of place in a situation that already seems far too brazen for the Lauren I thought I knew, she presses her lips to my ear and says: "We're safe now. Safe. You want me to say it? Okay. Let's fuck, Neil. *Let's fuck.*"

And, for a lack of anything better to call it, that's exactly what we do.

From: xc.coach.kaz@gmail.com
To: w.kazenzakis@gmail.com
Sent: September 7, 4:01 pm
Subject: poppies

W-

Thought you'd like to know that even though Chris managed to accidentally mow them down to nothing last spring, those orange poppies you put in on the west side of your mom's house are THRIVING. Beyond thriving, even. Every year they seem to grow more indestructible. Anyway, they're ready to blossom a third time this season, and my fingers are crossed they don't get zapped by an early frost. I know how much you love them. I think of you when I see them.

-N

CHAPTER THREE

My mood is not the only one brightened when Lauren and I go back upstairs; Carol is smiling too when we reenter the living room.

"Hi kids," she says, fiddling with the oxygen cannula under her nose. I'm not sure if she knows who I am now, or where she is in space and time, but I don't want to disrupt her perception of things from before.

"Checked the fuses, Mom," I say with a little too much cheer. "Everything looks fine."

"Wonderful, terrific," she says. Then, with no pause: "That black man came by again."

"Excuse me?" I'm searching my memory for any family stories that might fit, and coming up with zilch. It's odd to hear her say too; I'd never known Carol or Dick to be racist, but a person's skin color is just not the sort of thing she would have pointed out before she got sick. "Who came by?"

"That man, you know him, he stopped in . . ." She waves her hand at nothing. "I told him I was too tired to talk."

"Just now?" Lauren asks. "Right now while we were . . ."

"Downstairs?" I finish for her.

"No, no. Dick had a word with him, I believe."

Old memory. Whew. Lauren shrugs, her face lit with relief, and my mother-in-law offers nothing more. Just another phantom from years past, in and out of her world like that. I tell Carol that Christopher will check in with her tomorrow, and Lauren walks out with me through the garage to the driveway.

"Jesus, she had me scared," she says with a nervous laugh. "I mean, I didn't *hear* anything upstairs . . ."

"We can't do that over here again," I say. "Ever. That was really stupid."

Lauren pokes me in the stomach. "Jerk. You didn't seem to think it was so stupid at the time."

"You didn't give me much of a choice. What is up with you lately?"

"Nothing's *up* with me lately." She pokes me again. "Did I tell you I got almost fifty miles to the gallon coming back Tuesday?"

"No kidding?"

Lauren's three-quarters of the way through studying to become a certified nurse practitioner, and has to make the four-hour trip down to Michigan State's main campus in Lansing and back once a week this semester for coursework. Her old Astro van was a drivers' ed film waiting to happen, and after weeks of my urging her to upgrade to any vehicle of a recent vintage (and offering to loan her the money to make a down payment), she finally settled on a new Prius. So far, she seems to be quite pleased with it, even if now I bug her about the possibility of unintended acceleration.

"It's great. And that was with a thousand pounds of IKEA stuff in the back." Lauren grins, nodding toward the car, and I notice now that the back seats are folded down under a pile of cardboard boxes. "Bookshelves. Which I'll coerce you into assembling, if we can get them up the stairs." She glances down the long driveway, then takes my hand and starts to pull me back to the garage. "Come here," she says.

"What, again?" I'm laughing, but still. "And you tell me nothing's up."

"Stop it. I'm not . . . you jerk. Come here." We reenter the garage, and Lauren throws her arms around me by the trunk of

Carol's old Buick. "Come here," she says again, pressing her face into my shoulder. "Nice surprise. I didn't think I'd get to see you until tomorrow."

"I was pretty happy to see your car when we drove up," I say. My arms are around her too, and we're rocking, barely, from side to side. "Chris is gone 'til late tonight, if you want to coerce me into bookshelf assembly. Or anything else."

Lauren looks up at me, shaking her head. "Too late. Going to a movie with Danielle. Shelving must wait. And I need to get back inside to finish up with Carol. Like now."

"So I'll have to wait until tomorrow."

"Tomorrow." She presses her face back to my chest and sighs. "Tomorrow. It's good I got you for a little bit today. It's too hard to wait for Saturday sometimes."

----- ———————— -----

Back at my house, I find Alan Massie's old balloon-tire bicycle leaning against the new fireplace. It's rare for a day to pass where I don't see him at least once.

"Alan!" I call as I approach my open front door.

"In the kitchen," he calls back, and we meet in my living room. Alan is shorter than me, on the muscular side of stocky, and has kept his thinning hair in the same crew cut he had when he was flying as a captain for United Airlines.

"I was leaving you a note," he says, waving a piece of scrap paper before noticing my face and lifting his eyebrows. "You take an elbow to the lip?"

"Yep." I learned long ago not to question Alan's near-mystical way of just knowing things. If nothing else, it's a nifty thing to see him show off at parties.

"Thought so." He grabs me by the chin and turns my face from side to side. "You're fine."

I'm expecting him to make some nonchalant reference to my recent sexual relations as well, but he says nothing. He probably knows *that* too. Alan crumples the paper in his hand. "Wanted to see if I could borrow your truck tomorrow," he says. "Do you need it?"

I laugh at this. My friend's use of "borrow your truck" here is in fact shorthand for "get a ride to my destination," while "Do you need it?" means "Are you free to take me?" Three years ago, Alan lost his pilot's license after suffering what looked to his coworkers like an epileptic seizure during a layover. He hasn't had anything like it since (he swears he just dozed off in the terminal), but as part of the process of getting his medical certification reinstated, he has to show that he can remain convulsion-free—without medication—for some arbitrary period of time. And because he insists it will show the mercurial Federal Aviation Administration how seriously he takes his noncondition, Alan has voluntarily stopped driving cars as well. Thus the need for my chauffeur services.

"I haven't talked to Chris," I say, "but I don't think we have anything planned. Where am I taking you?"

"Lumber yard. Does early work?"

"Early works. But—" It dawns on me that the fireplace is completely obstructing my truck's exit from the garage. "We need to move something first."

Alan follows me out to the shipping pallet and prods it with his toe. "No problem," he says, rubbing his chin. "We can move it." He examines it from all sides. "You *might* have a problem fitting it into that space you guys built."

"Don't tell me this now," I say.

We stare at the fireplace for a couple minutes at least, plotting our moves or maybe wishing the pallet would sprout legs and carry the whole load over to the doorway on its own. But it doesn't, so Alan and I crouch down and begin to shuffle the thing from side to side toward my front door, crunching driveway gravel as we go.

We're stopped almost as soon as we begin, however, by a growing motorized buzz off to the south that snaps Alan straight upright.

"That son of a bitch," Alan says, shielding the sun from his eyes with a hand to his brow. "He got the 210. Son of a bitch."

"The 210? Who got what?" I rise and look in the direction he's gazing, toward the growing sound.

"Leland Dinks got another airplane. He was talking some shit about getting a new Cessna last week."

"Son of a bitch," I say, as it dawns on me that *Leland* is very possibly the black man who paid Carol a visit earlier. Just then a small blue-and-white plane roars over the trees and buzzes my house, passing so close over our heads it seems like I could hit the windshield with my spit. The plane circles over the field out back and comes over again, prompting Alan to give the aircraft—along with Leland and his pilot—the finger as it screams over us.

"Beat it, Leland!" he shouts. "Go crash in the lake!"

"Alan, jeez." I know he doesn't mean it, but still.

"That guy . . ." His voice trails off with the fading sound of the plane, and he shakes his head. All that's left in the air is the buzz and rattle of insects in the tree line.

"Let's move your thing," he says.

Alan throws himself back into moving the fireplace with extra vigor. I understand his frustration; Leland Dinks owns the chunk of property immediately to the north of both of us, and has been pressing us to sell him our land for the past couple years. He's in the early stages of building a lakefront condominium and golf course development, and each new offer to buy seems to come with increased urgency at an increasingly higher dollar amount. Every time, we've refused. Leland's been coming at me with kid gloves, though; I've got the beach frontage he covets, more than a mile of it, and he doesn't want to piss me off. He doesn't care so much about Alan, though, and has accordingly built a parking and maintenance area for his big construction machines just beyond the river demarcating their shared property line. Worse still is the airstrip he's put in over there, the final approach of which brings the private planes of Leland's prospective buyers and investors buzzing right over Alan and his wife, Kristin's, house. Alan has a right to be mad, I think.

It takes us another ten minutes to get the pallet to the foot of my front porch steps. Just as we're trying to figure out the best way to move the thing up the steps and inside, we're interrupted again, this time by a shiny black Ford truck with tinted windows coming up my drive. The truck loops around and comes to a halt in front of us, the engine cuts off and the door swings open to reveal Leland Dinks inside. He's wearing dress pants and a white button-down shirt, the lower buttons just barely showing some strain at the belly.

"What, bothering us in that plane wasn't enough?" Alan says, dusting off his hands on his pant legs. Leland ignores him completely as he jumps down from the big truck.

"Leland," I say as we shake hands, "were you over at Carol's house earlier? Bugging her about—"

"I was just checking in to see if anything had changed."

"The only thing that's changed is that all the paperwork's done, I'm handling Carol's stuff now, and if you need to talk about the orchard, you can talk to me. Not her."

"Well, let's talk then. And what the hell happened to your face?"

"Not important now. I'm telling you, like I have a thousand times before, there's nothing to talk about. We're not . . ." I stop myself, and look at the fireplace. "Wait. I'll make you a deal. We can talk about it."

Leland's expression brightens. "Really?"

"Really. But you have to help us move this thing inside first."

He laughs, rapping the top of the fireplace with his knuckles. "That's all? That's nothing. Let's see where you're putting it."

He follows me inside, with Alan behind, and I shove the couch and chair to the sides of the living room to give us a clear path to the hearth. Leland looks around the room.

"You've been doing some work, Neil," he says. "Looking pretty good in here." I realize, as he says it, that it's been years since Leland Dinks has been inside my home. We used to run together, back when our kids were little, and he and his wife, Sherry, would come over for dinner once in a while. Our sons were close friends then, all up through middle school, and we saw them a lot. Then Leland got more wrapped up with his real estate dealings, all my stuff happened, the boys stopped being friends, and we stopped seeing each other. Things change like that. Especially when you have kids. You don't really mourn the difference, you just accept that things have changed and move on.

"It's a never-ending project," I say. "Chris and I need to nail up the trim next. Maybe this winter."

"I can get you a break on materials," Leland says, turning slowly to take in the room. "You should call me. I'm set up with a bunch of suppliers."

Alan snorts at this. "You want to help him fix up his house so you can tear it down to build condominiums? That makes a ton of sense."

Leland holds out his hands and shakes his head. "You guys need to hear me out. I'm not asking to buy everything this time. You can keep your houses, keep a big piece of your property, and I'll still give you both a deal on a condo. We've got it all mapped out. I can show you the drawings right now—"

"Fireplace," I say. "Let's get it in here, then you can tell us everything."

"Right," Leland says. The three of us move the thing inside easily (only after Alan and Leland take a moment to bicker over whether or not it will fit through the door), and come back outside to hear Leland's pitch. It doesn't take long for him to become very enthusiastic, waving his arms over the set of blueprints he's rolled out and weighted down flat with rocks over the hood of his truck. He's offering as much money as he did the last time, a sizable amount of it, but for only half the land; he wants roughly to split the orchard diagonally to take the northwest corner (including all of our beach and the old Olsson guest cottage), along with the northern half of Alan's farm.

"And to top everything off, I'll throw in a timeshare for both of you," he says, smiling broadly. "Use it whenever. Rent it out if you want. And let me tell you this. I don't want to hear your answer right now. You guys take a week to think about, and I'll—"

"I don't need a week to think about it," Alan says, picking his bike up from where we moved it to the ground. "I can give you my answer right now: no. No, no, and no." Leland shakes his head as Alan mounts the bicycle. "I'll see you in the morning, Neil!" Alan calls, riding off down the drive.

"Can you talk to that guy?" Leland asks, watching the bike clatter away in a cloud of late-summer dust. "Are you able to get through to him?"

"I don't think there's much of a point," I say. "And honestly, I don't think there's much of a chance that I'm going to change my mind either."

Leland claps his hand on my upper arm. "I told you, I don't want an answer yet. Give it some thought. Some serious thought. I'll come by sometime next week, and you tell me then. That okay?"

"Fine," I say.

"All right," Leland says, rolling up his plans. "Next week sometime. All right."

Inside, after Leland has gone, I unpack my bag, and when I fish my cellphone from my work pants pocket, I find I've received a text message from my son.

Just got to Grayling, it says. Like most of the other kids from

Port Manitou, he's gone with his friends to watch tonight's game too. I tap a message back.

Have fun. Let me know when you're headed home.

A moment passes while I stare at the phone, and finally it sings and hums in my hand. The screen says: Will do.

I take a water bottle from the pantry and fill it from the tap; our water is drawn from a well and is rich in sink-staining iron. I can taste it when I take a long sip. Glancing back at the pantry, I consider for just a moment how nice it would be to fill a glass with some of our mineral-rich ice cubes followed by some decent whiskey from the dusty bottle in the pantry I have stashed away for special occasions, but I've set a (mostly enforced) rule that the only alcohol consumption I do anymore is in the company of friends. This occasion, a night alone, is not so special. Water will suffice for now.

I step through the dining room and past the sliding door to the back deck. Insects still drone over the dry field, and now and again a gust of wind whistles through the pines to move the long yellowed grass in waves.

A text-message sound dings from inside the house, and I need to wander around for a moment to find where I left the phone on the bookshelf. I'm expecting another text from Christopher, but instead I'm notified that a message awaits from EL DEE, my shorthand for Lauren Downey. Slide to unlock. Tap to read.

Movie plans canceled. Project shelf assembly is a go. Can we call a meeting?

I dial Lauren's number, and she's quick to answer.

"A meeting?" I ask. "Like a meeting meeting? Or a meeting to assemble IKEA shelves sort of meeting?"

"What would be your guess?" I can hear her smiling. "Doesn't matter what it's for, really, let's call one. Do you want to grab something for us to eat?"

"A meeting," I say again. "I'll be there in a little bit."

From: xc.coach.kaz@gmail.com
To: w.kazenzakis@gmail.com
Sent: September 7, 5:50 pm
Subject: IKEA

Something reminded me just recently of the trip we took to Philadelphia the year Chris was in 6th grade. Our son only wanted to see the Liberty Bell, and you only wanted to see the first US IKEA store. I'm sure you remember the little argument we had about that. I thought it was kind of stupid to go in there, and you did not; we went back and forth, back and forth, and finally I said fine, fine, we'll go in the store. We didn't talk the whole time we were in there. Chris bopped around from display to display, oblivious, and I clenched my teeth and swore I would not be the one to give in to speaking first. I don't remember which one of us did.

Of all the stupid things we could have bickered about, right? Of all the regrets I could possibly carry around, can you believe that one memory hurts as much as any of them?

Anyway, there's one of those stores in Detroit now. I haven't been there yet to buy anything myself (I don't know if I could bring myself to do so), but these Swedish products keep making their way up to PM.

-Neil

CHAPTER FOUR

A meeting. This is our shorthand, our shared private language. It defines for us something I am not quite ready to say in a more formal voice. Lauren would say it, she *does* say it, but in deference to my reluctant self a code word is employed. The meeting is called, and I'll happily go.

I find my canvas tool bag in the garage and check to make sure it has at least some screwdrivers, pliers, and wrenches, the sorts of things I anticipate I'll need for the assembly of prefab furniture. The bag is tossed in on the passenger seat of my decade-old truck, and I make one last trip into the house to grab the book I've been reading, one of Murakami's early ones (sent to me by my brother Teddy; he and some of his friends started up a dudes-only book club last year and he keeps bugging me to participate sometime via webcam).

There are evenings like this, meetings like this. We get together when we can. Two years, almost, of Lauren and me spending time in each other's company and saying nothing really about it. Over the course of this unspoken but seemingly real pairing, some standards have evolved. During surprise blocks of mutually free time, carryout is usually ordered, and if we're meeting at my house, films are often viewed. Lauren has a strange affinity for the Brat Pack movies of the eighties; they carry a sort of novelty for her, and this novelty seems to be increased by the knowledge that more likely than not my brother and I saw these films in the theater upon their original release. Viewing *Pretty In Pink* once in 1986 was enough for me, but since Lauren seems to love it so, I'll tolerate repeated showings.

If we're at Lauren's, where there's no TV, we'll usually end up eating and talking and, almost always, reading together on her college-era futon with our feet twined together under a tangle of blankets. She'll have a couple nursing textbooks stacked in her lap along with a highlighter clenched between her teeth, and I'll have some novel propped up on my chest: one of Teddy's suggestions, or one of my own corny genre adventure-on-the-high-seas tomes. The Titanic will be raised, the world will be saved.

In either place, if time permits after reading and eating and movies and wine, our clothes are often shed and our bodies come together. The tone of the meeting becomes something more serious. Sometimes (at my house) the act is conducted noisily, and other times (her condo has thin walls) it is a more silent congress of bare skin. Recently this has become more frequent. More and more frequent.

In my truck, I cut through town to the new pizza place we discovered a couple weeks ago. I phoned in our standard order before I left home: a small cheese and olive for me and Greek salad for her (though history suggests I'll sneak bites of the salad and Lauren will end up eating nearly half of the pizza).

Lauren lives in an older condominium next to the Big Jib River spillway where it flows into Lake Michigan, just south of Port Manitou's public beach and municipal marina. I cross the bridge over the spillway into her complex and pull in behind the Prius parked in Lauren's open garage, and as I step out of the truck with our food balanced on top of my tools, I'm heralded by the sound of sailboat rigging pinging against masts in the still-strong wind. Up the stairs to Lauren's living room, and I manage to not drop our meal.

The room is a mess of torn-open boxes and broken slabs of packing foam. Instruction sheets and cream-colored shelving boards are spread over the floor, and Lauren, in a sweatshirt and torn jeans, is seated cross-legged on her futon.

"I tried to get started," she says, smiling. "But I realized I should probably wait for you."

"This . . ." I look around the room. "Is kind of a disaster. Do you know what goes with what?"

"Not really." Another smile. "But the pieces are all labeled. We'll sort it all out. How's your mouth? Your lip's still pretty swollen."

"It feels a little better. How did you get everything up here?"

"Malcolm and his new boyfriend. They were leaving just as I got home." Malcolm Rice, Lauren's next-door neighbor, is a former student of mine, and was the first out-and-proud gay high school kid I ever knew. You see that more frequently now—it's not such a big deal anymore, at least not at the high school—but ten years ago it was pretty impressive.

"They insisted," she says. "Really, they had everything upstairs before I could say no."

"That sounds like Malcolm." I set the food on the coffee table and use my foot to clear a space on the floor to sit. "New boyfriend is a good guy?"

"Very good guy." Lauren goes to the kitchen to get plates and paper towels for napkins. "Quiet guy. He's going to tune up my bike."

"Uh huh," I murmur. I'm looking over one of the instruction sheets, and as I scan the debris around for something matching "Part A" on the diagram before me, I see one flat, unopened parcel leaning against the wall that makes me pause.

"No," I say. "You didn't." Printed on the side of the long box are the words 42" LCD TV. Lauren holds her napkin over her mouth with both hands and raises her eyebrows.

"I did!" she squeaks.

"This is the refuge, though—"

"It was on sale."

"—our place for reading!"

"I'm not getting cable," she says. "It's only for movies!"

"Are you going to take all the John Hughes movies from my house if you have a TV now?"

"Are you saying you watch them?"

"I'm not . . ." I can't keep myself from smiling at the question. "I don't watch them. I'm just saying maybe I like the reminder of you in my home."

"Chris doesn't ask about them?"

"We have a million movies anyway, so I don't think he even notices them there. He did watch some, I think. I'm pretty sure he saw *The Breakfast Club* at the end of the summer."

"Did he like it?"

"I think he liked it. I also think he felt it was a little dated. It maybe hasn't aged so well."

"Unlike other things around in the eighties."

I make a noise like "Psh!" and swat the top of the pizza box down on Lauren's hand as she's trying to grab a slice. "I'm not the only one here who was around in the eighties," I say.

She flings the top back up and says "Psh!" in return. "You're the only one here who remembers them."

We work for the next hour, sneaking bites of food here and there, finding pieces, aligning them, driving fasteners home. A dent is made in the mayhem on the floor, and Lauren shuttles a stack of flattened, empty boxes downstairs to her garage as I stand one of the shelves up and slide it against the wall. It partially covers one of two colorful orangish, modern paintings she has up in her living room. They were made by her ex-boyfriend, and I hate them.

"You'll need to move your *artwork*," I call as Lauren climbs back upstairs, putting a little unfair emphasis on the last word. I pull the painting in front of me from its hook and angle it to examine the rough dabs of acrylic pigment.

"We can move them right into your house," she says. "I don't know why you have to be so nasty about them. I mean, I do know, but still. I like them for what they are, not for the person who painted them. And you know that he's not so—"

"We don't *really* need to talk about the person who painted them," I say, and I hang the canvas back up where it was.

"You're acting like one of your kids," Lauren says.

"Oh?"

"For such a measured man, maybe this is the one place where your job rubs off on you."

"Rubs off on me how?"

"You're being petty. Like a teenager. Jealous."

"So you have to be in your teens to be jealous, you're saying."

Lauren gathers a pile of books from the floor next to her futon, and she gently elbows me aside to arrange them on the top tier of her new bookshelf. "It's a more raw emotion at that age," she says. "Everything is more raw then."

Lauren had grown up in a suburb of Cleveland. A Midwestern kid, not unlike me. She had a little brother, two years younger, and two working parents who loved each other, except for the year that they lived apart when she had been a junior in high school. When she talks about that, she laughs. It's not like they stopped loving each other, she says, but maybe they needed a break from it. It was a raw time for her too. It was a raw time for all of them.

That was her rebellious time, the year her parents split up. She laughs about this. She laughs about all of her childhood, like it was a ridiculous ordeal that could have been borne only through laughter. Upon her parents' separation she buzz-cut her long hair with clippers in a friend's garage. Short and spiky—she giggles at the memory of it, giggles when she shows me a photo—looking like an otter's fur. Her mother gasped when Lauren came home to show her. Her mother gasped, and cried. Lauren thought this was an overreaction at the time, but she hadn't known her little brother had been busted earlier that week for selling low-grade marijuana in their school parking lot. That was *his* rebellion. There were raw feelings all around.

Her father came back home at the beginning of her senior year. Not that he'd really ever been entirely away; he'd been around every weekend for the duration of their separation to mow the yard and ensure that the systems of the house were in good functioning order. It was just a trial, her parents said later. They needed some space. In the end, they decided they liked being together more than they liked being apart.

Before all that, though, before parental separations and otter-fur haircuts, there were pigtailed summers with a two-week vacation spent each July in Port Manitou, Michigan. Their family had no real ties to the place; Lauren's father read about it in some travel magazine, they visited for two weeks, and they liked it so much they came back every summer after that (on the year of their separation, her parents split their visits over the first and second weeks of the trip). Lauren came to love it. My family was visiting then too, and we've tried to figure out if our trips ever overlapped. I'd wager they did, even though we can't pin down the dates. I wonder sometimes if I ever would have recalled seeing her and her brother out of the thousand or so kids I ever saw building sand castles on the beach. I have no memory of it. I was focused on other things.

Port Manitou figured into Lauren's choice of colleges. She wanted to be close, relatively, and ended up studying nursing at University of Michigan. She would make the drive up north to stay with her family on their summer trips, and after a while she started coming up on her own. She made friends here. She met a guy. After graduation, Lauren went back to Ohio to work in a hospital near her hometown for a few years, but when she learned of an opening for a nurse at the Port Manitou Urgent Care Clinic, she moved up and stayed. It didn't take her long to discover that the clinic, a satellite operation of one of Northern Michigan's big hospital systems, was mired in operational politics and general staff misery, and as soon as she found work elsewhere, at a little hospice and home healthcare business, she left.

Lauren was one of Carol's first nurses when my mother-in-law returned from her hospital stay. I worked pretty closely with all of the nursing staff then; I was over at the house frequently, moving Carol's things to her new bedroom downstairs, building a ramp for the step down into the living room, doing all of those projects that needed to be done for her to live comfortably in her new situation. Downtime was frequent. Carol was pretty medicated, and the nurses stayed a lot, Lauren most of all. I couldn't do loud work while Carol was sleeping, so Lauren and I would chat. Insignificant topics were discussed at first: what movies had we seen recently, funny stories about my students or her patients. Little things.

I found myself over at the farmhouse more and more. I didn't even realize I was doing it, I don't think; Lauren was easy to talk to, and quick to laugh at my stupid jokes. I liked being with her. Over time, our conversations began to dip into more personal territory. She learned where I was from, about my siblings, and the circumstances of Wendy's accident and current state. She told me about growing up, going to school, visiting Port Manitou with her family as a kid like I had.

She was dating a bicycle mechanic/multimedia artist at the time. They'd hung out when she was in college and kept in touch when she was back in Ohio. He loved painting and music and bikes, and he seemed to love her too, somewhere along with his other passions. She hinted to me at times that the relationship wasn't going anywhere, but I never pressed. She also hinted that she loved being a nurse but was considering going back to school to widen her opportunities. I never pressed too much about that either. I hoped she wouldn't move away.

I'd bring lunch sometimes. I'd tell stories over the dining room table, and she'd laugh her easy laugh.

One day things shifted, a tiny seismic tilt that realigned our interactions. I came over to the farmhouse to find Lauren in tears, nearly inconsolable, and she managed to tell me she'd just gotten a call from her mom; her little brother had been in a serious car accident and it looked, at the moment, like he might not survive his injuries. She came to me, and I put my arms around her shoulders, and she cried against my chest for what seemed like a very long time. I knew about that sort of loss. When she calmed down enough, I drove her to her condo in town and told her to let me know if she needed a ride to the airport, or anything else.

She called me later that night.

"He's going to be okay," she said, letting out a long breath. "Okay. Okay. They're pretty sure he's going to make it. It was really iffy at first, but he's stable now."

"Do you still need to get back home?"

"I'm going to wait a few days. He's going to stay with my parents while he recovers, so I'll help out."

"Right up your alley."

"Lucky for my mom and dad, right?" She paused. "Can I ask something?"

"You want me to bring you your van from Carol's house?" I replied. Lauren sniffed and laughed.

"Well, yeah, I guess I do, now that you mention it. But I really wanted to ask if I could take you to dinner when I'm back from Cleveland."

This was maybe the last question I was anticipating, but I smiled.

"I'd like that very much. But there's one thing I need to tell you right away."

"Yes?"

"I need to be sensitive to how Chris is going to feel about anything like this." I knew how *I* felt about it; my heart was pounding so hard I could feel my pulse in my neck and fingertips.

"I understand," Lauren said. "I think I can work with that."

And that was how it started.

It doesn't take us as long to get the next shelf assembled, and when it's complete we stand it upright and shuffle it over against the wall. Lauren starts arranging things on it—books, candles, framed photos—and I get to work on the final piece of furniture. This shelf is smaller, shorter and broader than the first two, and it goes together quickly.

"Where are we putting this one?" I ask as I gather up some torn plastic bags and leftover screws from the floor.

"That's for the office," she says. The condo has a master bedroom on the main floor above the garage, and Lauren has the upstairs loft arranged as an office and guest room.

The piece is heavy, but not too difficult to carry upstairs. I go backward, slowly, stepping cautiously on the smooth wood treads with my bare feet while Lauren looks up at me saying, "Careful, Neil. Be careful. Three more steps. Two. Let's put it over there. Right there. Whew! Good."

We sit on the bed to let our breathing come back to normal, and I squeeze my fingers where they were crimped by my awkward grip. It's dark up here, barely illuminated from the living room below, but neither of us bothers to flip on a light. It's nice in this darkness. Lauren rises to unlatch the skylight on the pitched ceiling, and when she swings it open, I can hear the waves washing in from the lake and the continual low grumble of the river flowing over the spillway. She returns to my side and lets herself drop back to a reclining position with her legs dangling off the bed.

"Thank you," she says, stroking my back. "That was heavy."

I listen to the sounds of the night. Some kids are laughing out on the beach, and when the wind gusts, the papers on Lauren's desk tremble. The breeze carries the smell of autumn. It's easy to let myself fall back to lie at Lauren's side, my feet dangling just like hers, and when I close my eyes and draw in a long breath of that end-of-summer air, her hand finds mine and our fingers weave together. The room seems darker and there's nothing but the outdoor noises. Waves, river, kids talking. I imagine two kids, a boy and a girl, teenagers, walking on the beach. Talking in low voices. Fingers together, just like this. I'm that boy. There were so many walks in the sand by the lake.

"Don't fall asleep," Lauren whispers. "Neil."

I open my eyes. "I'm not asleep."

"I wish you could fall asleep. I want to watch you sleep."

"I can't," I say. I turn my head to look at Lauren. With her free hand she's drawn a hank of hair across her face, under her nose. She looks at me and blinks.

"Have you ever thought of growing a mustache?" she asks.

"My father has always had a mustache. He still does. I doubt I'll ever grow one. Why are you asking me this? And why are we whispering?"

"It's good to whisper in the dark," she says. "Please don't ever grow a mustache. Come up here." She tugs my shirt to move me higher on the bed, then clambers on top of me and presses her face to my neck.

"No, no, no," I say. "We can't. Tomorrow. I need to get home. Chris will be . . . I need to get home."

"I know." Lauren sighs into my collarbone. "Just pretend we can fall asleep like this. Ten minutes. Then you can go."

"It's not like I want to leave—"

"Shh. I know. Ten minutes." She sighs again. "Don't really fall asleep. Just pretend you are so I can watch."

I close my eyes and breathe. Ten minutes. It isn't really long enough at all.

Even with a stop for gas on the return trip, I'm home well before my son. And this is good: there's always been something troublesome to me about the idea of him coming to an empty house at night. I like to be there waiting for him; I like to hear about what he did, or where he went, or how he's feeling. My motivations aren't nosy, not usually, though from time to time it is necessary to engage in parental intelligence gathering. But most of the time I just want to hear what he has to say about things. And I guess I want him to know he's always got someone to come home to.

I could have stayed longer with Lauren, but I think she understands why I needed to go.

I put away my tools in the garage and go inside to check for messages on our machine; there's nothing. When I pull my cell from my pocket I'm surprised to see a five-minute-old text from Chris waiting for me. I must have been driving when it came in.

Leaving now, should be home before 1, the message reads, and I tap the screen to call him back. I'm not really expecting him to answer, only wanting to leave a fatherly "be careful" message, but Christopher answers on the second ring.

"Dad, what's up?" It's funny to me that I'm still so surprised to hear—especially over the phone—how deep his voice has become. He'll be eighteen in two months, so I should be used to it by now, but it still gets me.

"How was the game?"

He laughs, and I hear his friends talking in the background. "We lost. Those Grayling guys are pretty big."

"I heard they were tough. Back around one?"

"Should be. Maybe sooner. We're hanging with the buses on the way back. Slow lane." This is exactly what I want to hear. Not drunken, not fast. Slow. He's a good kid.

"You'll call me if it's going to be later? Or if you need anything?"

"Dad, come on."

"I know. My job to say that. Right?"

"Right. Are we still going to see Mom tomorrow?"

"I'm helping Alan in the morning. And we can't let the field go another week without mowing—"

"I'll get the field. Don't worry about it."

"That's what you said last week."

"Dad, I'll get it tomorrow. I swear."

"All right. We'll go see Mom after we finish our stuff. Take it easy driving, okay?"

"I will." I hear a happy commotion on his end, young shouts and laughter, and Chris says, "Gotta go, okay? See you later. Bye." And he's gone.

I like to think I'm not overprotective. I also like to think I give my son appropriate freedom and room. He's shown himself to be mature and responsible—as a person who's spent his professional life corralling individuals his age, I think I'm a pretty good judge— and as those traits have shown themselves in him and grown, so too have his freedoms expanded. But here's a funny thing: every time Christopher is away like this, and we say goodbye on the phone, I actively say to myself, "I wonder if that was the last time I'll say goodbye to my son?" or, "I wonder if that was the last time I'll hear his voice?" It sounds insane, and maybe it is, but here's my crazy logic: think of every time you've seen or read about the tragedy of a lost loved one, think of the wounded souls left behind, always saying, "I never got to tell her I loved her," or, "I never got to say goodbye." They never thought it could happen to them. I know how it happens, though. By thinking about it, I jinx it. And by jinxing it, Chris comes home.

I wonder if that was the last time I'll say goodbye to my son?

I wonder if that was the last time I'll hear his voice?

The night is quiet. With the cable news muted on TV, I write a couple emails on my phone. The news is meaningless to me, so I turn it off and try to read my book and consider Leland's offer from earlier. There's not much to think about, enticing as it may be, because I've promised Carol, and I know just the thought of it would have broken Dick's heart. My answer, when Leland returns, will be just the same as Alan's, just the same as it ever is: no.

I try to stay awake so I can say hi to Chris when he gets home. I always try this, and I often fail. It's a quarter past one when I feel a hand on my shoulder and hear my son's deep voice saying, "Come on, Dad, get up. You should go to bed. What happened to your lip?"

I sit up, and the book that was open across my chest tumbles to the floor.

"Broke up a fight after school. No big deal." I blink and rub my eyes. "So we lost, huh?"

"We got crushed." My son smiles and pats my arm. "Go to bed, Dad. Maybe put some ice on that. I'll see you in the morning."

It really does work. Chris comes home every time.

From: xc.coach.kaz@gmail.com
To: w.kazenzakis@gmail.com
Sent: September 8, 6:20 am
Subject: envelope

W-

Do you recall a student, when I first started teaching, named
Jake Martinez? He was super nice, played varsity soccer, and
for some unknown reason all the kids called him Envelope
Martinez. Even I started calling him Envelope at school.
Everyone else did, so why not? He didn't seem to mind. I
think he even signed his schoolwork that way. I remember
asking a couple people how he got the nickname, but no one
seemed to know.

ANYWAY, I found an old padded mailer in one of your boxes
in the garage last night. It totally surprised me because it
had your name written on it in that loopy, high-school-era-
Wendy handwriting, not the straight, grown-up-Wendy style.
I thought I'd seen all that stuff too, everything there was
to see, but every once in a while something new turns up,
like artifacts uncovered by a retreating glacier. I was sort of
reluctant to open the thing, to tell the truth. But I did, and
inside I found:

  - Four paperclips, one of which had been opened up and
  bent into a circle

- A photograph of your dad (wearing his orange hunting hat)

- A photograph of two Labrador retrievers playing tug-of-war with a stick (Uncle Art's dogs, maybe?)

- A half-depleted lined stationery pad (with FROM WENDOLYN OLSSON printed over a rainbow at the top)

- Twenty-eight opened letters, from me to you, bound with a rubber band. Seven were written when I was fifteen, eleven more when I was sixteen, and the remaining ten when I was seventeen. ALL were painfully embarrassing to read (indeed, some of them included poems/song lyrics I'd written for you)

And finally:

- One sealed, stamped, but unsent letter in a light-blue envelope, addressed to me from you and thick with folded paper inside

I didn't open it. Part of me just didn't want to, and part of me wanted to save it for later, for when the glacier melts away and stops spitting out artifacts for good.

-N

CHAPTER FIVE

Christopher sleeps in the next morning while I make coffee. It's still early, not yet eight, and through my kitchen window I'm watching the day come over the world to turn the orchard from monochrome to color. Mist burns away. Across the field, under one of our twisted old apple trees, two deer nose at rotten fruit down amid the bent, dewy grass. They spring upright and freeze—cautious, ears turned forward—and bound away when Alan Massie and his old bicycle come rattling around the curve of my drive.

Alan leans the bike against my deck and shuffles in through the side door like he has a thousand times or more over the course of my knowing him—silently, a stainless-steel travel mug in one hand and a half-eaten bagel in the other—and takes a seat at my kitchen table.

"Could almost see my breath out there," he says, settling into a chair.

My arms are crossed as I continue to stare out the window. "It's coming."

"We'll get rain next week."

My coffeemaker hisses to completion, and I top off Alan's mug before filling one for myself. I leave a note for Chris on the whiteboard on the fridge (*Gone to town w/ Alan, back by 11, don't forget to mow the field*) and we quietly make our way to the garage to climb aboard my pickup truck. Alan and I hardly speak again until we're almost to the city limits, when my friend directs me to take a detour.

"Hold up, hold up," he says, pointing at an upcoming turn. "Go through Old Town." Old Town, as the name might imply, is the oldest part of Port Manitou; a strip of nearly-hundred-year-old Victorian-style homes along the harbor with our long-defunct rail depot turned brewpub, and some overpriced tourist shops at the center where the cannery once stood. Recently deemed a quote-unquote "historical district," it is also ground zero for the latest wave of gentrification spreading across our fair incorporated burg. I turn off the highway and Alan cackles as we start down Main Street.

"Have you seen that fucking house they're working on?" he asks, suddenly animated and leaning forward in his seat. "The one they painted—"

"You mean the purple one?"

"Yes, the purple one!"

"My girls call this 'Purple Street' when we run it now," I say.

"Here we go," he says. "Slow down. Will you look at this shit?"

We coast to a stop in front of a narrow house; tidy behind scaffold boards and clad in shocking purple siding, its perfectly restored gingerbread trim has been painted an equally vibrant lavender. Some painters are gathered around a work trailer, and I wonder what their thoughts are on the color choice, or if they've left all their scaffolding erected because they know they'll be forced soon to climb back up and cover their work with more sane pigments.

"I can't believe anyone in the town approved that," Alan says. "Someone's going to make them paint over it."

"You say so."

One of the workers has noticed that we've stopped, and the way he shakes his head suggests we're not the first gawkers he's encountered. I let off the brakes and we roll away down the street. The guy watches us as we go.

"I don't know," I say. "At least it has some character."

"You're kidding me, Neil. That place is beyond tacky."

I laugh at this. "I don't think I'd be so quick to judge—"

"Don't start with me!"

"—considering that thing you have in your yard."

Alan shakes his head. "My thing is different. It's so different. Mega-Putt is a mission rooted in *principle*."

I knew, without needing to ask, that this morning's trip to the lumber store would be in material support of Alan's most recent obsession: the construction of an eighteen-hole miniature golf course along his bit of property adjacent to the highway. This is not a labor sprung from some deep love of golf on Alan's part; Massie Mega-Putt is a project rooted almost entirely in spite. At the beginning of last summer, not long after Leland Dinks established his heavy-equipment storage lot in full view of Alan and Kristin's back door, Alan went over to ask if he'd maybe consider relocating it. Leland repeatedly said no, tough luck, that was the area most out of sight from the resort and it made no sense to put it anywhere else. As the story goes (and I've heard it more than once), Alan said something along the lines of: "Christ, Leland, what if I had a bunch of excavators parked right out there in my yard for everyone coming by to see? Or what if I had some tacky bullshit like . . . like *a mini-golf course* right there by the entrance to your development? That's how much it sucks to have to look at your stuff. What if all your buyers had to see some garbage like that before they pulled into your stupid resort?"

To this, Leland simply replied, "Well, thank goodness they don't."

Alan had eighteen holes plotted out on graph paper and a backhoe rented before the week was done.

Thanks (or maybe no thanks) to the lack of zoning or building regulations beyond town limits, Alan's creation is over the top. It's beyond over the top; it's a Gaudi-esque fever dream of leaning concrete towers, spouting jets of water, sneering gargoyles, and general obnoxiousness. I'd call it brilliant, in a madman sort of way. I have no idea if it's fun to play (Alan, to the best of my knowledge, hasn't let anyone try it out yet), but I do know it's achieved its primary goal: through the small-town gossip telegraph, we've heard that Leland has approached our elected officials more than once to see how he might legally force it to be razed to the ground.

The home improvement store is in a strip mall complex on the east side of town, and the place is already crowded when we pull into the lot. There seem to be many retiree-types out at this hour: dogged faces pushing loads of plumbing supplies, circular saws, and light fixtures.

"So what are we getting today?" I ask, threading the truck through carts and shoppers to a near-enough parking space.

"I shorted myself on light posts last week. Why don't you ever park any closer to the store?"

"Why don't you ever get enough supplies to begin with, so I wouldn't have to drive you out here every Saturday morning? Then my proximity to the store wouldn't be an issue."

Alan laughs as he climbs down from the truck. "Frugality, Neil. This period of unemployment has led me to become a frugal man."

"Right," I say, and Alan shrugs and tells me he'll be right back. Truth is, through cleverness and good luck, Alan and Kristin are well off enough that neither of them really needs to work at all. About ten years ago, when I first met him, Alan was working—during long breaks between flying international routes—on a tennis-simulating contraption, a clunky device involving blocky sensors and accelerometers pulled from several cars' airbag deployment systems that he'd strapped onto a tennis racquet. With the whole assembly wired up to a pair of computer servers, Alan claimed it could perfectly detect how the racquet was being swung through three-dimensional space, and after applying for patents on the thing, he shopped it around to a number of sports companies as a potential training aid. There were some flickers of interest, but the contraption was pretty ungainly, heavy as a sack of bricks, and dangling bundles of wires, and after striking out on who knows how many sales pitches, Alan gave up on it and turned his attention once again to flying. He'd given it a good shot, and was not left embittered. A device ahead of its time, we called it.

Ahead of its time, that is, until a year or so later when chronology aligned with Alan's mad science and four impeccably dressed Japanese businessmen showed up at his home. They were from a certain entertainment company, they explained, and wished to engage in discussions about his tennis racquet invention. Those conversations led to two of his patents ending up in the Wii videogame system, and a whole bunch of money ending up in the Massies' bank account in the form of licensing fees and continuing royalties.

The money didn't change them. Al kept flying planes, and Kris kept on with her dental practice. They stayed the same, but it was an awfully nice score for both of them.

-----————————————-----

On the way back to Alan's place, with a quiver of ten-foot posts sticking out from the back of my truck, I get a text from Lauren. The shelves look fantastic, she writes, and she wishes I could have stayed all night.

"That from Lauren?" Alan asks, peering over at the phone in my hand.

"Yep." I'm angling the screen away from him, but what's the point? He knows.

"Things are going well with her. You guys were screwing yesterday."

"Alan."

"I could tell. I mean, her car was there, you were over there, it's pretty obvious what—"

"Enough. *Enough.*"

"And the look on your face after. Even with the lip. Which looks much better today, I should add. But man, Carol's house? Ballsy, Neil. Ballsy move."

"Okay. Yes. Okay. Ballsy. Whatever. It was stupid. Stupid, stupid. I know we can't . . . I told her we can't—"

"Neil."

"What?"

"Stop."

"I'm just telling you."

"No, I mean stop the car. Right now. Pull over. Right here."

I pull off to the side of the road and put the truck in park, and Alan turns and grabs me by the shoulder. "Will you listen to yourself?" he says, shaking me. "Listen to yourself. You're a grown man, and you're talking like a kid. You need to just suck it up, and get it out there. And Christopher—"

"God, Christopher."

"He's going to take it just fine."

"You say that."

"He's a smart kid," Alan says. "The smartest kid I know. Solid. After everything, solid. He's going to take it just fine."

"But Wendy, the way he feels about her . . ."

Alan crosses his arms and stares forward. "It's an admirable thing you're doing. Maybe. But maybe it's stupid too. And maybe it's unfair. Unfair to yourself, and unfair to Chris. Maybe you're not giving him enough credit."

"Hey, hold on a second. That's not—"

"I said maybe. Maybe. This is just my opinion, Neil. I don't like you beating yourself up. I don't like seeing it. Maybe get it out there."

"*Maybe* I don't want to talk about it right now."

"Fair enough," Alan says, and I put the truck into gear to bring us back up onto the highway. I don't look over at him for a while as we drive, because I know he's right. I don't say anything either, but it isn't long before Alan starts up again.

"Besides," he goes on, "I'd say you have a pretty good thing going. I mean, look, here we have an older guy, a very decent guy, he likes a younger woman—"

"I'm only five years older. Well, six—"

"Like I'm saying. And she reciprocates the feeling."

"It's not that big a difference."

"They like each other, these two. A good thing. Capital *G*, capital *T*. Good Thing."

"It is a good thing."

"A genuine affection. These two are truly *fond* of each other."

"We are," I say.

"You and I have been friends for a long time, Neil. It makes me happy to see you this way. It makes Kris happy. We're all having dinner tonight, the four of us, like we do, and you have no idea how much we are looking forward to it. We look forward to it every week. You're like a new guy."

"I appreciate that."

"But," Alan says, raising his eyebrows, "we're getting tired of being the only ones in Port Manitou in on the secret."

"It's not . . . it isn't going to be that much longer."

"Fine then. Get it out there. Tell Christopher."

"I'm going to tell him. Really. I am."

"When, though?"

"After graduation. Okay? When Chris is done. That's when."

"Is that really fair to him? Or Lauren, for that matter? This isn't as big a deal as you're making it out to be. Your son is going to know about this, somehow. Why not get it out there on your terms?"

I throw my head back and groan. "Leave it, Alan. Please?" He is right, and it's infuriating.

"Okay. I'll leave it for now." We turn into Alan's drive, and he points over to the left, toward Mega-Putt. "Take us right over the grass." I drive across his lawn and park next to a hole featuring something like an Aztec pyramid in miniature, and help Alan unload the posts. Then I start off without saying goodbye—maybe I'm just a little miffed at him still, or flustered—but Alan waves me to a stop and jumps back in, reminding me he's left his bicycle at my house. I don't say anything about it. Coming up my drive, we see Christopher buzzing around Carol's yard on our riding mower, his ears encased in massive headphones and his head bobbing away to some music. He grins when he notices us and waves as we go by.

"Tell him he can mow my yard whenever," Alan says.

"I'm sure he'll get right on that," I say.

"He'll get free passes to Mega-Putt."

We park, and I head out back to check if he's made it to the field yet. Alan follows as far as the fire pit, picks up a stick, and pokes around in the barely smoking ashes. Chris must have made a fire last night.

The field is still not mowed.

"Your son needs to do a better job at destroying his evidence," Alan calls. He hoists aloft a charred beer can dangling from the end of his impromptu spear right as Chris rolls by on the mower. Alan wags the can at him, and my son pretends not to see.

"What is that?" I shout, knowing he can't hear me. "Chris? Where did that come from?" He can't hear me as he bounces past, but I'm sure he knows *exactly* what I'm saying, and I see him smile as he rumbles off toward the tall grass of the field.

"He needed a hotter fire," Alan says, dropping the can back into the ashes. "Aluminum won't melt until it gets up to about twelve hundred degrees."

"Jesus, Alan," I start to say, but I can't come up with anything else.

From: xc.coach.kaz@gmail.com
To: w.kazenzakis@gmail.com
Sent: September 8, 10:23 am
Subject: slam dunk

One other thing: remember the overnight basketball camp
Chris and Steve Dinks used to do on Saturday nights in
seventh grade? Christopher is actually on the staff there
now, a camp counselor I guess you could call him, and I
think he's genuinely enjoying it. He's certainly not doing it
for the money; Parks & Rec hardly pays him anything, but he
keeps going back to coach the games and chaperone the
sleepovers. I suppose there is a sort of compensation for
him in the form of free pizza. Our son's appetite is a force of
nature.

Seriously though, I bumped into the guy who runs the
program last week, and he told me how much the kids love
Chris. He's a natural with them. And they're in awe of his
ability to dunk a basketball. I know he loves the job. It's fun to
see him so into something (besides cooking).

See you in a bit.

CHAPTER SIX

In the kitchen after Alan has gone, I find signs that Chris has been to our local farmers' market this morning. It's a new thing of his, an interest in cooking and locally grown produce, encouraged by my celebrity chef brother, Michael. You'd recognize Michael; he's that bald chef from Chicago with the hoop earring and the weird last name, the funny one with a couple restaurants who cooks once in a while on *Good Morning America* and does a guest judge bit on that chef reality show. Chris adores him, and every time he comes up on one of his frequent visits, Michael teaches my son some new technique in the kitchen. The seeds of culinary art have taken root in my home.

Fueled by this expanding base of knowledge, Chris cooks for us at least one night a week now, and usually he makes something surprisingly good. I've never been too inventive in the kitchen myself, but I do all right, and I'd like to think I've done an okay job nourishing my son over the past few years. His height—six feet six and counting—would suggest I've nourished him pretty well.

He won't let me come with him to the market. It's something he would have done with his mom, and I don't want to intrude on that. I imagine him there, my lone teenage boy, sniffing produce and thumping melons, coming up with some idea for dinner, or thinking how he'd impress Wendy or Michael just by *being* there.

On our kitchen table there are a couple brown paper bags. A

peek inside reveals fresh tomatoes, some herbs, and what looks like a chunk of some sort of plastic-wrapped cheese. There's also a long bundle of hydrangea stalks lying on the table, covered in a riot of deep blue blossoms. He got these, I'm sure, for his mother.

Chris roars past outside the kitchen window on the riding mower, and I take a look in the fridge to see what else he might have picked up. Staring me in the face from the center shelf is a six-pack-minus-one of Budweiser beer. I glance behind it for anything else, and lift it by the empty loop just as Chris barges in through the door from the garage.

"Chris," I say. He stops when he sees what I'm holding, composes himself, and smiles.

"Dad."

"Is this yours?"

"Well . . . yeah."

I drop the cans with a *thunk* to the table and look up at my son. As Christopher is in full inheritance of the Olsson height gene, I do my best to create an effect of being eye to eye with him during disciplinary moments like these.

"Where did those come from?" I ask, crossing my arms and raising my chin to speak with him. I rise up on my toes a little bit too.

"Does it matter?"

"If you're bringing them into *my* house, then yes, it matters a lot." There's an interesting distinction here: When we're working on a project together, it's our house. When I'm enforcing rules, it's mine. Right now, it's my house all the way.

"Dad, I'm almost eighteen, I should be able—"

I hold up my hand. "Two things. First, you're not eighteen yet. Second, even when you are eighteen, it still won't be legal for you to—"

"Will you just let me finish?" Chris slouches a little as he says it, making my job of appearing taller that much easier.

"Fine. Go ahead and finish. But can you dispute those two things?"

"No . . ."

"Okay. Finish, then. What were you going to say?"

"I was *responsible* about it. I waited until I was home, I just had one. I sat by the fire pit and had one. *One*. I just needed to think about some stuff. Okay? Don't you think if I'm responsible about it, I should be able to—"

"Chris, what I think doesn't matter here. What does matter here is the law, whether I agree with it or not. And if you got busted for minor in possession, what would happen with basketball?"

His shoulders fall, and he stares at the floor. "I know."

"And how would it look for me? My job?"

"Okay, I *know*."

"Be smart, Chris."

"Okay."

"Now," I say, working to keep my serious expression, "get them out of here. I don't want to see them in the fridge, or anywhere else."

My son furrows his brow. "Wait, you aren't like dumping them out or anything?"

"I'm going to *trust* you to take appropriate action with that beer. I don't want to see them. I'm sure"—I clear my throat here—"you'll do the right thing. So take care of them, and then we'll go see Mom."

Christopher's face brightens and he rises up to his full height. "Yeah, um, I'm . . . I'll get rid of these right now!" He grabs the cans and trots off down to our basement. When he comes back upstairs, he dusts his hands together, holds them up empty, and with a wide-eyed, completely earnest expression says, "They're all gone, Dad. See that? *All gone*."

We take Christopher's car, an older Volvo wagon that he saved up to buy from Alan and Kris, over to see Wendy. I'm planning on running the seven miles back home, so I've got clothes to change into in a bag in back. It's about a fifteen-minute drive over rolling hills lined with woods and farms, and Chris seems distracted.

"So," I ask, "what stuff did you need to think about last night?"

"Nothing really. Just stuff."

"Stuff like . . . Jill?" Christopher's old girlfriend left a few weeks ago to start her freshman year at Cornell, and my son has been in a minor funk ever since.

"Nah."

Jill Swart was great—smart, a middle-distance runner and lacrosse player—and she graduated in the spring. She and my son dated for almost two solid years, and I know they talked about trying to keep things going after she left for school, but Chris has been surprisingly realistic about the situation. Even though he's pretty reluctant to discuss it, I've managed to put together through various conversations with him that he's told Jill he's okay if she starts dating other people at college. I'm proud of him for being so mature, but I also know how much it hurts him.

"Is it school?" I venture again. "Are you worried about next fall?"

A pause.

"I dunno."

I take this response as an affirmative, but I'm not going to push it. Chris has been offered a basketball scholarship at Western Michigan, and he's having second thoughts. The scholarship is a good deal, and Chris knows it, but Western isn't his first choice in schools, and now the cooking bug has got him too. Michael has offered not only to write Chris a letter of recommendation for culinary school, but to grant him a coveted internship at his flagship restaurant as well. I know my son is tempted. What I don't know, however, is whether or not he's genuinely serious about cooking, or if this is a passing phase. I'll probe more later, and I know just the time and place to do it.

"Hey, I talked to Mrs. Mackie last week," I say. "She told me we can take her boat out tomorrow if we want."

"I'd be into that," Chris says, his expression brightening. After cooking, his other love is sailing, and the assistant superintendent of our school district, Peggy Mackie, has been letting us take her boat out on the weekends. Aside from just being a good time, I've found that sailing with Chris is one of the best ways to get him to talk about things.

"I'll call her tomorrow and set it up," I say. Tomorrow we can talk more.

--- --------------------- ---

We're quiet for the rest of the ride to Wendy's. It's pretty nice, as these places go; the buildings are new and well landscaped, and the staff seems happy and motivated to do good work. There are three wings, each with its own parking lot: the Living Center (for the Alzheimer's people), Hospice & Palliative Care (for the dying people), and Long-Term Care (for the vegetables). We park at Long-Term. Chris brings his things from the farmers' market, and I have the pack with my running clothes over my shoulder. Inside, I'm happy to see the head nurse, Shanice, seated at the main station. Of everyone I've ever met working here, Shanice is my favorite.

"Hi, Mister K.," she says with a broad smile. "Hey there, Christopher." She peers over her glasses at him. "Looks like you brought some things for your mom. You bring those gorgeous flowers for your mom?"

Chris grins, saying nothing, and reaches over the desk for a pair of scissors. He clips off one of the hydrangea stalks and tucks the cluster of blossoms into a pen-filled mug in front of Shanice, causing her mouth to fall open in an exaggerated expression of surprise. Chris bites his lip, like he can't believe he's just pulled off this crazy-smooth maneuver, and starts to blush as he slinks off to his mother's room. Shanice lets out a low whistle as he goes.

"Damn, Mister K.," she says. "You're raising that boy right!"

It's dark inside Wendy's room. The sounds are there, the sounds I've tuned out: the beeping machines, the wheezing machines, the gurgles, and the hisses. They're just extensions of the body at the center of it all, and you ignore them after a while, just like you ignore the sounds of your own living form.

The body at the center. Wendy. My wife. Her mouth hangs open in the dark, and her eyes stare at nothing above sharp cheekbones. Both fragile wrists are curled from atrophy, and her left middle finger, eternally bent backwards from the break it endured when it was wrenched from the pool grate, points up at the ceiling.

Christopher has pulled a chair to the side of his mother's bed, and he leans close to her and whispers things I can't hear. There's a new donated quilt covering her bed, and Chris straightens it out before placing his paper bags on top of it. He pulls a tomato from one of the bags and holds it under his mother's nose.

"Smell this, Mom. Tomato. Smell it? I got it at the farmers' market this morning."

I rub Wendy's bony ankle and grab her chart. I've gotten pretty good at reading it. Caloric intake, normal. Bilirubin elevated. Bedsore on right lower flank almost healed. Weight as of yesterday: ninety-two pounds. And so on. It's like a conversation. Through these statistics, my wife manages to speak to me.

"This is rosemary, Mom. The herb. You can smell it better if I rub it between my fingers like this."

It's impossible to miss the similarities between the boy leaning forward and the woman in the bed. They have the same rounded faces, the same fine, dark hair. Chris got his mother's brown eyes, but not her fair, freckled skin. Instead he carries my almost-olive cast, quick to darken in the sun, and the contrast is evident as he brings his face close to hers.

I peek through the window blinds into the courtyard between

Long Term and Palliative. A young man is out there, talking on a cell phone with a hand to his forehead like he's trying to shield his eyes from the sun.

"This is cheese. I forget what the guy called it. It smells good though, doesn't it? Here, I'll try some and tell you how it is . . ."

And so on.

I step out of the room and walk down the hall. I want to give Chris some time alone with his mom, but also, to be honest, I can't always handle seeing them together like this. It can be too much, so I decide to take a lap. It's a pretty busy day in Long Term, Saturday morning and all, and many of the rooms are populated by ambulatory visitors. I recognize some of them and we smile and nod to each other. That's as close as any of us get; there's a distance we maintain in this place. Outside one of the rooms, a man stares at me with a stunned expression, like he's astonished I could be so casually strolling along. Family member of a new resident, obviously. He hasn't learned the drill yet.

Lesson number one comes from the name of the wing: *Long Term.* Settle in, buddy.

He'll figure it out soon enough.

Just beyond the man in shock, one of the new aides, Irina, a tiny bleached-blond woman clad in pink scrubs, is typing something into a computer on a rolling cart in the corridor. I greet her as I walk past.

"Hello, Mr. Kazenzakis," she says, my last name rolling off the tip of her Eastern European tongue. "Mrs. Kazenzakis is looking very good today, yes?"

I smile and nod. The man in the hall stares at us like he can't believe this is actually happening to him.

Sometime after Wendy's accident, when Chris was a freshman and I'd finally gone back to work, I overheard a conversation between two girls by the lockers outside my classroom door. One of them was talking about an electronic diary she was keeping; it was, she explained, nothing more than an email account she'd had her aunt set up with a password she wouldn't be able to find out until sometime in the future.

"It's great," the girl told her friend. "I just send it anything. What I'm feeling, what I'm mad about, whatever, right? I mean, I'll probably open it up when I'm in college or something and totally cringe at what a dork I was."

The next time I saw Cory, the district's overworked computer tech, coming down the hallway, I called him into my room.

"Problem, Mr. K.?" he asked. While many of our past IT guys had been pasty with black tee shirts and stringy hair, Cory brought a clean-cut sincerity to his job that reminded me of a Mormon missionary.

"No, nothing's wrong," I said. "Just a question. If I wanted to set up a personal email account for myself—"

"That's easy!" he said.

"I know that, I have one already. But if I wanted to set up a second one—"

"Like that forwards to your main account? That's easy too."

"No, hold up, let me finish. I don't want it to forward to me. In fact, I don't want to be able to open it. Basically I want it to have a password that no one knows. Not even me."

Cory screwed up his face. "Well sure, you could do that, but what's the point?"

"You could say it's like . . ." I considered my answer for a moment. "A diary. I want to be able to just write to myself. In the moment. It's not important that I see them later."

"Ohh," he said, nodding. "Like a therapeutic thing."

"I guess so."

Cory watched over my shoulder as I set up an account with Wendy's first initial and last name. He didn't say a word. Either he didn't know anything about her, or, like the best computer guys, he simply kept a blank face and acted like he didn't. He instructed me to turn my head while he reached over me to fill in a password and complete the form.

"There," Cory said. "Now you'll never be able to get in."

"But you know the password."

"You think I'm going to remember what I typed there?" he asked, shouldering his gear bag to leave. "I can't even remember the passwords I'm *supposed* to know."

It was a few days before I could actually bring myself to try it. I was, admittedly, pretty self-conscious about writing messages to the address at first. Was I afraid I'd receive a reply? I started out with "Hi." Letter *H*, letter *I*. Pause, think, Backspace Backspace. Try again. *H* followed by *I*. Hit Send. Type some more. Hit Send again. I typed and hit Send over and over again, and soon enough, weeks went by, and spilling my guts to an unconscious woman became habit. *I miss you. I'm lost.* Months passed and I slipped from confessional to quotidian. What did I wear that day? What did I eat? What were my stupid thoughts? Do you really want to know?

Dear Wendy: Do you want to know my stupid thoughts today?

I'll tell you. I'll tell you and hit Send.

In hitting Send, somehow, I felt a little better.

Chris is waiting, looking perplexed, outside his mother's room when I return.

"You okay?" I ask.

"There's makeup on Mom's face," he says. "Someone put makeup on her."

I frown and follow him into Wendy's room, where I turn the control on the wall above her bed to bring up the lights. Sure enough, she's wearing lip gloss and eye shadow, and her nails have been painted a subtle glossy cream color. I check her feet and find her toenails have been painted too.

"It creeps me out," Chris says. "I don't like it."

"I don't either. Hang on." I head out to the nurses' desk.

"What's up, Mr. K.?" Shanice asks. She can see it in my expression.

"Someone put makeup on my wife," I say. "I'm kind of—"

Shanice scowls, an unusual look for her. "Must have been Ukraine," she says. "I'm going to have a word with Ukraine." She emphasizes the first syllable, like YOU-kraine. Even in this moment, it strikes me as funny that she refers to her employees from the former Soviet Bloc by their country of origin.

"She was just down the hall," I say. "I'll talk to her."

"You don't need to, Mr. K. I'm very sorry about this."

"No, no, it's nothing, she didn't know. I'll talk to her."

I find Irina farther down the corridor. She's set up at a new location, typing something into her console again.

"Irina? Did you put that makeup on Mrs. Kazenzakis?"

She looks up at me. "You do not like it?"

"I do not. Please don't do that again."

"She does look very pretty, I think. She is very pretty woman."

"Thank you," I say, "but I'd appreciate it if you didn't do that again. I'd appreciate it too if you'd clean it off her. She never wore makeup when she was alive."

Irina's face goes hard. "She is alive *now*, Mr. Kazenzakis." She turns away and stomps off down the corridor, pushing her computer cart ahead of her.

I suppose I understand her indignation. But I'm beyond the point where I could care.

From: xc.coach.kaz@gmail.com
To: w.kazenzakis@gmail.com
Sent: September 8, 12:03 pm
Subject: Sorry.

You know what I meant by that, right?

Right?

CHAPTER SEVEN

On the highway home, running, I'm having a hard time finding any sort of rhythm. Normally when I'm out like this, alone, away from everything, my mind goes blank in a trance of white noise, and my body goes on autopilot. I don't think about anything, and it makes me feel alive. A lot of my students run with iPods; they ask me why I never do. The simple answer is I just don't like it. But it's something more than that, really: any sort of music would barge in and ruin that blank-slate feeling I'm chasing after.

There's no blank slate today. I changed in the nursing home restroom and said goodbye to Chris, and we made plans to catch up before he leaves tonight for his overnight basketball gig. Then I went running. I can't count the times I've followed this route home, but today it's like the first time I've ever been on it; almost thirty minutes out and no rhythm. I'm stumbling over my own feet, bristling at the few cars passing me on the road, critical of my form, critical of my thoughts.

The real reason, I know, is Irina. What I said to Irina. Just what does it mean to be alive, anyway? You'd think, with the past few years to dwell on it, I'd have some sort of answer to this question. I don't. Am I alive because I can run? I feel alive when I run, sure, I know that. But the best running for me is when I'm not thinking. Does this mean that being alive the most means thinking the least?

If this is the case, Wendy—the blankest of blank slates—is more alive than any of us, and Irina was right to be angry with me.

It's confusing, for sure.

Wendy, though, cannot be confused by any of this. I've got that on her. After the accident, she stayed in the university hospital in Madison for a few weeks while we waited for the impossible, waited to see if she'd recover at all. Maybe it was four weeks. Things were a blur then. I slept in a hotel just off campus while her condition was most tenuous; at first it didn't look like she'd make it past the first few days. Chris was there, Carol was there, my brother Michael was there and gone, there and gone. My older brother, Teddy, responsible Teddy, angling for tenure at the University of Chicago at the time, dropped everything—his family, his job—to come and make all the official things happen. He pointed to the places on the medical paperwork I needed to sign. My sister, Kathleen, showed up. My parents came from their retirement complex in Florida. All a blur. And Wendy at the center of it all, purple-faced and bloated from the drugs, unrecognizable with tubes like snakes emerging from her nostrils and mouth, with oily hair framing her swollen features, with medical lines taped crisscross to her cheeks and arms.

Days passed in Madison. People came and went. It became obvious over time that Wendy was not leaving us, but she wasn't coming back either. Stuck somewhere in-between, and the doctors—they were such good doctors—explained that as long as we provided her with nourishment she would hang on, she would linger. Like a reflex, like breathing, she would take things in and pass things out, but she would never think again. There was another option, a passing discussion, the denial of nourishment; mentioned once and not discussed again. She would linger, we decided. We decided this by deciding nothing at all. We would need to find a place to facilitate these lingering functions. She would need to be moved.

We found a place not far from home. Kathleen and Carol did most of the groundwork; Teddy handled the paperwork. My state insurance through the school district would cover it all. And Michael, Saint Michael, blasted up on his motorcycle from Chicago week after week to cook for us, to feed us, to keep our home clean, to keep Christopher going to school.

It's still hard for me to admit that I had fallen apart.

Why should I think about this now? I've dwelt on that shame enough. Now is now, I need rhythm and white noise, but it isn't coming. Another mile, and I might as well be running in clown shoes.

I stop and wait on the shoulder for a car to pass, check both ways two times, and jump up and down, mashing my feet into the gravel of the shoulder. "Damn it, damn it, *damn it!*" I shout with each stomp. Then I put my hands on my hips and double myself over to breathe, pursing my lips to make a *whoosh* sound at each exhalation. Like I could purge all this from me so simply. It's worth a try.

I start again, thinking anything, thinking nothing. I manage about fifty yards before coming to a sandy pair of tire ruts headed off through the pines toward the lake. I'm just about at the northern end of Leland's resort, and there's a chain strung across with a NO TRESPASSING sign hung from it like bait. I veer off the road and jump the barricade.

In the trees, in the flashing blades of light, there's quickly a sort of rhythm. I push myself, the soft track gives resistance, and it's not long before my breathing comes harder. Before I know it, I know nothing at all. Irina is gone. I'm through the trees and over a dune, and now I'm running, panting, nearly sprinting along the beach.

I run along the edge of the water, where it's easy in the firm, damp sand, skipping between scalloped terraces demarcated by pebbles, seaweed, and the occasional gull-pecked fish carcass. To my right is Lake Michigan, the mighty inland sea, a deep greenish blue all the way to the horizon. North Manitou Island is out there too, a verdant hump poking up through the whitecaps in the distant haze. And to my left, rising from behind the dunes as I close in on Leland's resort, is the red-girdered skeleton of some new building, abandoned by its workers for the weekend, left with only a silent bulldozer and a couple Port-A-Johns for company. Ahead, there's a man talking animatedly on a cell phone. He's maybe ten years older than me, wearing shorts and leather sandals and a watch with a thick stainless band. He's a little higher up on the bank, and he stares right at me as I approach him.

"Hold on a second," he says into the phone. "Hold on." The man holds his phone down at his side, and I notice a cigar in his other hand.

"Hey!" he calls. "Runner guy! I used to be just like you!"

I can't help but smile as I go by him; I think, *really?*

"All the time I was like you! Don't take things so serious, runner guy!"

I raise my hand in a wave as I pass, and he starts to chatter away again on his phone. Do I look so serious? Does it show in my face?

Past the cell phone man, farther south on the shore, I'm into the more finished part of the resort. A pair of three-story condo buildings frame what looks like a clubhouse or restaurant; out in front there's some sort of nautical pennant flapping from a tall pole stayed like a ship's mast. A gardener is working, but that's the only other sign of life I can see nearby. It's a perfect day, but all the decks and patios are empty before dark sliding-glass doors; are any people living up in those places?

These thoughts are easy. They're nothing. They go perfectly with running; they're just what I need. Farther down the beach now, and I'm at the Little Jib River, the muddy waterway marking the boundary between Leland's development and the northern end of the Olsson property. It's a minor river, more like a big creek, really, and three more NO TRESPASSING signs face over the streambed into the orchard's parcel as if, perhaps, Leland thinks I might be assembling a band of marauders to come and raid his little village. I think for a second it would be funny to stop and turn the signs back so they're facing him, but I don't. I can't threaten this hard-won rhythm.

Little Jib is barely flowing this late in the year, and I shuffle down the loose bank and manage to hop across from cobble to cobble without wetting my shoes, before bounding up the opposite side and setting off again at an easy pace along the lakeshore. There's a feeling of wildness at this end, the northern end, of our beach. The brush seems heavier, the shoreline more littered with driftwood. Like it's been for years. Tiny plovers chirp and scatter over the sand as I approach, resisting flight as long as they possibly can before I'm too close and they're forced to lift off in a chittering frenzy.

Another half mile and I'm at the beach house. Carol's brother, Arthur, has been staying here this summer, as he has for the past few years. He takes care of the cottage, he and his latest wife, and he checks in on Carol. He's good backup for me. Uncle Art's car is gone, but I see he's pulled the shutters out from under the deck to get ready to board the place up for the winter. I'd stop to go in, but there's rhythm to be lost, and anyway, going inside can make me react in unexpected ways. The beach house is heavy with memories.

I glance at the windows as I pass, and run on.

----———————-----

My family started renting the Olsson cottage when I was twelve years old, the summer after Michael and I finished sixth grade. One of our father's colleagues from the Economics Department at Michigan State turned him on to it. It was just about a four-hour drive from our house in Lansing, and we rented it that first summer for two weeks and again for four weeks every July after that until Mike and I graduated from high school.

Our explorations of the dunes those first two summers stayed close to the beach house. Mike and I would swim, shoot cans up in the sandy brush with the pump-action BB gun we found under the deck, or argue over who got the top bunk in the back room where we slept. A couple times a week we'd spend the day with our big brother, Teddy, heaping driftwood into a massive pile on the beach; if the weather held into the evening, our father would spritz the bleached wood with charcoal lighter fluid and set the thing ablaze, creating an inferno we imagined to be visible all the way across the lake in Milwaukee. Sometimes Dick and Carol Olsson would come over and the grownups would chat up on the deck, mixing cocktails while we kids ran circles around the flames.

The third summer we came up, the summer before Michael and I entered high school, our explorations expanded. Teddy had turned eighteen and wanted less to do with his two little brothers; he'd made some friends his age in Port Manitou and wasn't around very much. As it was, we were pretty good at getting into trouble on our own. Michael and I explored Little Jib River, sending branches floating off in its current toward the great lake, or ambushing each other from hiding spots along its banks. Our father at some point informed us that "Jib" was a shortening of the tribal name "Ojibwa," and we spooked ourselves by imagining we were being spied upon through the cedar woods by hidden Native eyes.

Not far from where the river disgorged its roiled waters into Lake Michigan, Michael and I discovered a cinder-block pump house half-buried in a dune up the shore. A corner of its corrugated metal roof was missing and it was filled with rusted iron pipes and valves. Inside, someone had scrawled the word PUSSY on the wall with the end of a charred stick. Aside from confusing us somewhat, the graffiti gave a daring credibility to the space that our fourteen-year-old selves loved. The pump house became our base of operations.

One day, in the second week of our stay that year, Mike and I were running past the cottage when our mother called to us from up on the deck.

"Boys! Mrs. Olsson has some linens for us. Can you pop over and get them for me?"

We said sure; the Olssons' house was more than a mile away, and Mike and I had never made the trip over the dunes and through their orchard by ourselves. It would be an adventure. My brother and I took off at a run, making a race of it. I left Mike in the dust. I remember how the cherry trees, arranged in perfectly straight rows, smelled like summer, and how I swung my arms and shouted taunts at my brother. Mike's a slowpoke. Mike sucks. I came through a pine wood and out into a large, mowed field. I ran, laughing, shouting, "Mike sucks!" over and over while grasshoppers sprang forth from the cropped stubble ahead of me.

Then I stopped in my tracks.

A girl my age stood with a soccer ball at her feet next to a red pole barn at the far edge of the field. She wore blue athletic shorts and a baggy yellow tee shirt, and had knobby knees, short dark hair, and a splatter of freckles over the tops of her cheeks and the bridge of her nose. She stood there, staring at me, and I stared back. Mike ran up, panting, and stopped to stare at her too. The three of us looked at each other, saying nothing, before Mike finally elbowed me, and we continued on around the barn to the Olssons' house.

"Who was that?" Michael asked in a low voice as we slipped away from the girl's stare.

"No idea," I whispered back.

"Why didn't you say something?"

"Why didn't you?"

We climbed the front steps of the farmhouse, and Carol Olsson greeted us at the door. She loaded Mike's arms with a pile of folded sheets and mine with a cardboard box.

"There's stuff for the kitchen in there," she told me before sending us off. "Be careful with it now, some of it's glass."

We nodded and thanked her, and started back. We passed the pole barn slowly this time, peering around the corner. Now the girl kicked the ball into the wall of the barn. She stopped it with her foot when it bounced back, and kicked it again. She didn't seem to look at us as we continued by.

"Hey," she called without looking up. We froze. "Do you guys play soccer?"

"I do!" Mike said, his voice maybe an octave higher than usual. He dropped the sheets to the grass and ran over to her, and she passed him the ball. "I'm going to play varsity next year." He dribbled the ball around her, showing off, before passing it back. He was really good at soccer. I was not.

"What grade will you be?" the girl asked him.

"Freshman. What about you?"

"Same."

The girl tapped the ball to me, and I—still holding a box of clanking kitchen utensils—kicked it with about as much finesse as I would have used to put my foot through a rotten pumpkin. The ball sailed over my brother's head and off into the pine trees.

"Nice one, jerkoff," Mike said, and my face went hot. He started after the ball, and the girl walked over to me.

"What about you?" she asked. I was glad she didn't call me jerkoff too.

"Me? I don't really play soccer. Not like my brother does, anyway. He goes to the camps and everything."

"I used to go to the camps. This is the first summer I haven't. But I mean what grade will you be in?"

"Oh!" My face went hotter. I clutched the cardboard box against my chest. "Ninth also."

"Are you guys twins?"

"No. He's five months older."

She cocked her head. "How does that work?"

"I'm adopted."

"You guys look so alike, though."

"A lot of people say that."

"Well, if you don't do soccer, what do you do?"

"I . . ." I was flustered by the sudden change in subject. Maybe she sensed my discomfort, but I was grateful she didn't press. I wasn't so good at explaining it. "I run track. But I don't know if I'm going to do it next year."

"You should. Because I run too." She smiled, and I held the box tighter. "Four hundred and eight hundred."

"I'm more of a long-distance guy," I said. Mike dribbled the ball back to us across the field, and nudged it over to the girl, with the side of his foot.

"Way to go, you totally got it stuck in a prickle bush," he said. He held out his arms to show us the scratches covering them.

"Aw, did Super Soccer Guy get all scratched up in the bushes?" the girl said. Now Mike's face flushed.

"I think we need to get back," he said, gathering up the tangle of linens from the ground and looking away so she wouldn't see his red cheeks.

"See you," the girl said. She went back to kicking her ball.

Michael tried to smooth out the stack of sheets as we crossed the field. When we got back into the pines, he asked, "So, what's her name?"

"I don't know," I said.

"Why didn't you ask?"

"Why didn't *you* ask? And why did you have to go and call me jerkoff, Super Soccer Guy?"

"Shut up. I'm sorry."

"All right."

A week passed without us seeing the girl again. We didn't talk about her, Mike and I, but we did keep asking if there was anything else our mom needed from the Olssons. After making the tenth or maybe the twentieth query on this, our sixteen-year-old sister finally called us on it.

"They just want an excuse to go see Wendy Olsson," Kathleen crowed from a folding deck chair, sneering from behind her trashy paperback.

"We do not!" I managed, while Michael simultaneously exclaimed, "You know her name?"

"You're busted," our sister said.

We were busted. And now that she had a name, it seemed that we could discuss her openly between ourselves. We'd walk along the beach, trying to top each other, Wendy this and Wendy that. Mike liked to remind me that Wendy loved soccer, and I'd remind him she ran as well. Despite these two facts being pretty much the only concrete things we knew about her—aside from her freckles, dark hair, and bony knees—we did everything short of outwardly professing our love for her.

One night, a bonfire night, we were astonished to see that Wendy Olsson herself had accompanied her parents over to the beach house. She took a seat in the sand down next to Kathleen and proceeded to completely ignore us. The two of them sat together most of the night as Mike and I lurked around the fire, and when she left, she didn't even say goodbye to us.

After, while we got ready for bed, our sister poked her head into our room. "Way to go, dolts," she said. "I mean, hello? She was there, waiting, for like two hours. You could have done something more than stare. Are you guys idiots?"

We returned to our plotting, spending long strategy sessions in the pump house up the beach. Our father had turned a blind eye to Teddy buying beer that summer, and we'd sometimes pilfer a can from the stash in his room to choke down over our planning. They always seemed to affect me more than Michael, and he'd often mention how red my face would turn over our scheming. And how we schemed. Should one of us ask her to take a walk? Did we dare try to kiss her? Michael said he wanted to try to bring Wendy to the pump house to "do it"; I said no way, that wouldn't be classy at all. In truth, I'd had the same idea, even if I wasn't entirely clear on all the mechanics involved if I were to try to "do it" myself. Those things could be figured out when I came to them.

The next time Wendy showed up, a week or so later, we made more of an effort. We grabbed badminton racquets from the back closet in the cottage, and the three of us swatted a shuttlecock through the settling dusk by the lakeside. Wendy, laughing, lobbed the bird out into the water, and Michael, ever eager to please, rolled up the legs of his jeans to wade out and fetch it.

"So are you going to run next year or not?" she asked me as my brother tiptoed into the water.

"I don't know yet," I said. "I haven't decided."

"You should make a list of pros and cons. That's what my mom always has me do when I can't decide something. Is there something about track you really don't like?"

I pondered it. "Not that I can think of."

"Are you any good? Do you win races?"

"Yeah, I guess so. I won a couple races last year."

She smiled. "Sounds like a pretty easy choice to me."

I figured this exchange—and the smile that completed it—had given me an edge in the unspoken battle with my brother. I decided I'd wait for darkness to fall and take a seat next to Wendy by the fire. When the time was right (and her father wasn't paying attention), I'd ask her if she'd like to go for a walk. I didn't make any plan for after that. I didn't want to assume anything; really I just wanted to talk to her more. But my plans were crushed when, as I came back from fetching a sweatshirt for Kathleen, I saw Mike lean down to say something into Wendy's ear. She shrugged and nodded, then hopped up and followed him as he sauntered away along the water's edge.

My throat went tight as I watched them go, and I looked down and pawed at the sand with my foot. Teddy saw it. Kathleen saw it. The adults, laughing among themselves up on the deck, saw nothing. My sister patted at a spot on the blanket next to her.

"Come here, kid," she said, showing some uncharacteristic sympathy. I sank down next to her and let my head droop. "Just because she went off with him doesn't mean anything, okay? Someone's really going to think you're a catch someday."

Her kindness, even if sincere, did little to elevate my mood, and I kept looking over my shoulder down the beach. Nothing. My only consolation was that they'd gone opposite the direction of Little Jib River and the pump house; at least my refuge wouldn't be sullied by the thought of the two of them in there doing whatever it was they'd gone off to do. I looked down the beach again and again, and Teddy punched my arm and let me sneak a couple swallows of his beer.

My father was shoveling sand over the fire by the time I finally gave up waiting for them to come back. I went inside alone, got myself ready for bed, turned out the light, and climbed into my bunk. I waited for what seemed like a very long time before I heard the creaking old floorboards in the hall and the squeak of our bedroom door. I listened as Mike got into his bed below me, and let another minute pass before I brought myself to speak.

"Well?" I asked.

"Well what?"

I swallowed. "Did you do it?"

"No."

"Did you kiss her?"

"No. I didn't kiss her."

"Did you do anything?"

"Just shut up about it, okay? We didn't do anything. She went home like three hours ago."

Three hours? I sat up. "Where the hell have you been?"

"I took a walk on the beach. That's all."

I thought about this, and even felt a little guilty for the way my spirits were lifting. "Did you guys talk about anything?" There was a long, long silence. "Mike?"

"She doesn't like soccer players," Michael finally said from below. His voice was muffled, like he was talking into his pillow. "She said she likes runners better."

And for nothing more than this, I decided to keep running.

From: xc.coach.kaz@gmail.com
To: w.kazenzakis@gmail.com
Sent: September 8, 1:50 pm
Subject: One Letter

It's funny, out of all the things of yours that I've saved, letters
and pictures and everything else, the one thing I wish I had
most of all is that first letter you wrote me before ninth grade
telling me I had better do track again. I'd already decided
by that point I was going to run; I even signed up for cross
country, but then that letter came and it was like "Well, I
guess I really am doing it now." I never told you this, but I
threw it out! I was so terrified of Mike finding it and making
a big deal that I kept it under my mattress for a while, but
even that was too radioactive for me, so I tore the letter and
envelope into little pieces and pitched it.

Did your mom give you my address after we'd left that
summer? I can't believe it would have been your dad.

Tonight I'm going to have dinner with Alan and Kris. Like
we used to do, like we did so many times, but different.
Obviously different. So many dinners, when Chris got a little
bigger, and you didn't feel so bad about leaving him with a
sitter. We weren't seeing Lee and Sherry so much, and the
Massie girls did tag-team babysitting in our own home—no
driving necessary, no definite time to return—and we could
eat, drink, and drink more. God, we had fun. I think of that
night we ended up sleeping in their basement. There are
maybe three times I remember you really being drunk, and

that was one of them: we were two hundred yards from our house but you couldn't manage even to walk the little path in the dark. Usually I was the one to take it a little too far, but you were on that night, *on*, so why go home? You wanted to soak in the hot tub, you wanted more margaritas, you tried to kiss Alan, you called the margaritas "trouble." Thank goodness the kids were back at our house. Kristin called the kids to tell them to lay out sleeping bags and pop another movie in the VCR, and when she hung up the phone you shouted: "Mix us up some more trouble!" And we did. God, that night we did. Captain Alan barked "Here we go!" with his finger on the blender button, and away we went. We were soaking in trouble.

In the morning you covered your face with your hands and groaned for me to close the blinds. They were closed already. Kristin and Alan laughed from upstairs, and I laughed and walked home to find the kids slumbering together in a knot on the inflatable mattress on the living room floor. I made them breakfast, waffles in our wedding-gift iron, and when Kris called to check in, I heard you retching in the background. We decided you could use a little space for your recovery. I took Chris and the girls to the beach for the day, and the whole time our son was under the impression you had the flu. An easy enough deception. When we got home late that afternoon, and Chris found you green on the couch with a wet washcloth on your forehead, he knelt at your side and asked if he could make you some soup. You laughed and laughed.

My nights are measured now. I caromed down that path, bouncing off everything, so many times after you were gone, certainly more than three times, and finally I reined myself in. Things came apart, but I pulled myself together. Captain Alan would let me know, I think, if I started down that trail again. I trust him to watch out for me, and he does.

Things don't get out of control anymore. I promise.

CHAPTER EIGHT

B y the time I make it home, I'm ready to declare my run a success. The proverbial slate has been wiped, and I'm pleasantly tired out. I down a few big glasses of water at the kitchen sink, and find a very gourmet-looking sandwich that Chris has made waiting on our little breakfast table. The sticky note reading *Try this dad*— comically adhered to the sandwich itself—leaves no worry that I'm going to consume something not intended for me.

Chris's fabrication is pretty good. There's arugula, dried cherries, and some pungent melted cheese in a sliced baguette, all stuff from the farmers' market, I'm guessing. I remain standing to eat it, out of the concern that my post-run legs will stiffen up if I have a seat.

Over the table, on the corkboard on our kitchen wall, there's a picture of my father and Dick Olsson. They're laughing in the picture, probably over the fact that they've swapped hats: my father's Greek fisherman's cap is too tight on Dick's head, and Dick's safety-orange hunting hat is so big that it's nearly covering my father's eyes. This was Wendy's favorite picture of her dad; she always said she didn't really know of any others where he was smiling. I'd have to say it's one of my favorites too.

My father, a diminutive, prematurely balding, wisecracking hippy economics professor who had been part of the 1968 protests in Chicago, and Dick Olsson, a towering autodidact who could persuasively argue that Nixon had received a bum deal and kept a portrait of Ronald Reagan over his workbench, formed a most unlikely friendship. Even after all of us kids went to college, before Wendy and I were married and my parents had retired and moved to Florida, my mother and father would still come up to visit the Olssons a couple times a year. The four of them even took a cruise through the Caribbean back when I was in school; by all accounts it was a fantastic time. Carol and my mother always got along well, but it was the peculiar friendship between Theodore Kazenzakis and Dick Olsson that really cemented things.

They remained close up until the end. There are two times in my life I recall ever seeing my father cry: the night the Detroit Tigers won the 1984 World Series, and seventeen years later at Dick Olsson's funeral.

Dick's passing was the great sorrow of my father's life. I guess he was lucky to have just that one.

I finish up Christopher's sandwich and dust my hands over the sink. I consider taking a shower, but through the kitchen window I see Chris shooting hoops on the barn-slab court, so I head outside instead.

"Want to play?" Chris asks me, and I laugh.

"Maybe something like 'horse,'" I say. He passes me the ball and I take a shot that misses off the backboard with a loud *clunk*.

"We'll play to twenty. I'll give you five points."

"You'll still kill me."

"I'll keep my right hand behind my back. You'll beat me if I play left-handed."

I say fine, and he lets me have the ball first. We dance around; he goes easy on me. It's fun to watch him move so well, so confidently, even when he's blowing past and stealing the ball right out of my hands. I manage to hang on, barely, keeping one point ahead of him until it's 15–14. Then in a blur Chris dunks on me, twice, before sinking an unbelievable three-pointer from the middle of the court to finish me off.

"Nice game, Dad."

Panting, doubled over with my hands on my knees, I manage to say, "Nice game."

-----————————-----

I spend the early afternoon grading papers out on the back deck. The work is from my morning physics class and nothing too mentally strenuous: check yes, check no, *100%*, *A+*, *Great work,* and so on. The kids made an effort. Christopher ducks his head out the door to say goodbye, and I tell him to be careful and say hi to everyone at the rec center for me. When I ask him if he needs any money, he shakes his head and says he's all set.

It's a date night, of sorts, so I take a long shower and spiff myself up in a dark gray button-down shirt and some newer jeans. Lauren is planning to check in with Carol before we go, and she'll leave her car parked over there for cover in the unlikely event that Chris makes an unexpected (and unannounced) return home. I've got a few minutes before Lauren is supposed to show up, so I stroll over to the farmhouse on my own.

I find Carol in her room, propped up on a pillow in bed with a months-old issue of *Cosmopolitan.* She's not wearing her oxygen line, and her eyes look bright when she sees me leaning in the doorway.

"Did you have a good day?" I ask.

"Really good day, Neil. Chris came by earlier."

"He said he was going to."

"Sounds like you boys had a nice visit with Wendy." The wrinkles in her face turn to something like a smile. "Chris is such a good boy. You've done a good job."

I smile back, as much at the compliment as at the pleasure of having Carol return from dreamland for a while. "I got pretty lucky with him," I say. "He's all right."

"He is all right, Neil."

The sound of the side door stops me before I can say anything else, and Lauren calls, "Hi, Carol!" When she comes down the hall, she acts surprised to see me.

"Oh, hello there," she says with a smirk.

"Hi, Lauren. How have you been?"

"I've been very well, thank you." She nearly keeps a straight face through our forced formality. "Carol, how are you doing today?"

"I'm just great," she says. Behind the doorjamb, where Carol can't see, I give a big thumbs-up, and Lauren nods.

"I'm going to leave you two," I say, and Carol waves goodbye. "Have fun tonight, Neil."

"I—" Have fun? Does she know I have plans? "Thanks. I will." Lauren tells Carol she'll be right back, and walks me to the door.

"She's doing good? She looks good," Lauren whispers.

"She seems great. Does she know we're doing something tonight?"

"Yes. I told her." My mouth falls open, and Lauren rolls her eyes and pokes me in the ribs with her index finger when she sees the look on my face. "No, of course I didn't tell her. What are you thinking?"

"That 'have fun' thing she said, I don't know . . ."

"It's Saturday night. It's traditional in this country for people to have fun on a Saturday night. So of course she sent you off with good wishes. Don't be so paranoid, okay?" She pokes me again. "Can you run over to your house and grab a bag or a pack? Something to lug our wine in."

I say sure and Lauren sneaks in with a quick kiss. "I'll meet you over there," she says. I head back through the dusk and find a canvas shopping bag in my front closet, and go back out to wait on the front steps. The day is nearly gone and the moon, waxing almost full, is just coming up over the trees. I'm watching a pair of bats circle over the yard when I hear Lauren walking back from Carol's, and I have to peer at her for a moment in the darkness to discern that she's got three bottles of wine held in her arms against her chest.

"Here," I say, getting up to take two of the bottles from her.

"God, I wish she could be like that all the time," Lauren says with a sigh. "Poor thing." She holds the last bottle out and as I take it, she leans forward and kisses me, fully and with no intention of pulling away. I bend my knees just enough to put the wine on the ground and rise back up to slip my right hand around her back. My left hand slides down Lauren's hip, over her jeans, between her legs and up, and as I start to press against her, she lets out a breathy laugh and bites my chin.

"You can't you can't *you can't*," she says. "We have to get over there. I don't have a change of clothes. Neil, we have to. You're going to make me a mess."

"We could go inside and take off your clothes," I murmur into her hair. "Mine could come off too. The problem would be solved."

"We cannot." Lauren places her hands against my chest like she's going to shove me away, but she stops and wraps her arms around me. "Later. Kris and Alan are waiting."

"This is some unexpected restraint," I say, kneeling down to put the third bottle in with the others. "Seeing how you've been lately. But fine, fine." I let out an exaggerated sigh. "It's fine, I guess. I'll just save myself up."

"You save yourself up, pal," she says, and she gives my rear end a smack as I pick up the canvas bag and start away. We set off down my drive, and the moonlight shines in our faces. There's a path along the road to Alan's house, worn smooth by feet and bicycle tires, and I let Lauren go ahead of me when we come to it.

Some lights are still on in Carol's house as we cross her broad front yard. I put timers in there a year ago to create the illusion of activity; it makes Carol feel better if we make it appear that she's getting around easily in her home.

"You really didn't say anything to her about us having dinner?" I ask, and Lauren swings her head.

"Why would I even bring it up?"

"I don't know, you spend a lot of time over there with her."

"So do you. Maybe *you* let it slip?"

"Yeah, right." I maneuver the shopping bag's straps up to my shoulder, and the bottles clank together inside.

"Yeah, right. Neil, I *know*, okay? I get it. I'm not going to let anything slip. No one's going to know anything until you're ready. I'm fine with it."

"I don't get how you can be, sometimes."

"You know why. I tell you enough. You just never want to tell me back, though. You don't like to say it."

"That's not true. I do say it."

Lauren laughs. "Okay, say it right now, then."

"You're putting me on the spot. It wouldn't be meaningful."

"Just say it. You don't even need to mean it."

"I do mean it, though."

"Mean what?"

"You're trying to trick me."

"If you mean it, if you feel it, saying it shouldn't be such a big deal. But I'm not going to force you or anything. Just remember to tell me once in a while. I like to hear it. And not just when we're messing around."

I think about this; is that really the only time I tell her I love her?

The thing is, I do love Lauren. Wildly, madly. I really do. It's hard to love things, though. It's especially hard to admit it. In my experience, the minute you admit that you really love something? That's just about the time it decides to go away.

----- ———————— -----

After her brother's car accident, Lauren spent nearly a month in Pennsylvania. Before she left, I told her to text me if she needed me to take care of anything for her while she was gone. I didn't really expect to hear from her, thinking she'd be pretty busy back home, but hardly a week passed before I got a message from her. I'd been expecting her to ask me to water her plants or something, but instead that first message said:

God, I forgot how much I hate this place.

The rest of her messages were similar in tone. There's a strip mall at every intersection, she'd write. There's an Applebee's in every mall. I miss Port Manitou. I want to come home. I'd type a message back asking what I could do, asking how her brother was doing, and she'd simply write back: no, nothing, all set, he's doing fine.

I want to come home.

Three days before she did come home, she called me to let me know when her flight would be arriving. Could I pick her up? Would I, she asked, if it wasn't too much of a bother? Of course I would.

"Dinner probably won't work that night," she added. "I'll be too tired." She laughed. "You didn't really think I forgot about it, did you?"

After she'd been back a couple days, we made our plans. Conveniently, Christopher would be spending the night at a friend's house, and Lauren suggested we go to a restaurant she loved in Traverse City. I didn't know if she really wanted to go all the way out there because she liked the place so much, or if somehow she sensed how concerned I was over the possibility of the two of us being seen together in Port Manitou. Not that I was worried about it for my sake; I just wasn't sure how Christopher might take it.

We had a good time on our date. What surprised me the most was what an effortlessly good time it was, especially on the twenty-minute drive there; I picked her up and there were no forced moments or awkward silences. She caught me up on her brother's condition, told me anecdotes both funny and aggravating over our meal about his rehabilitation, her family, her hometown. When we made it back to her place, we talked for nearly half an hour while my truck sat idling.

"You could just park and shut the car off, you know," she said. "We could keep talking inside, and you wouldn't waste fuel or irritate my neighbors."

"I didn't want to be presumptuous," I said.

"Oh, look at you. A gentleman!" She pointed at the keys. "Just shut off the engine."

"But also . . ."

"But also what?"

"But also I want there to be a second time," I said. "After this time." I had to laugh at myself. "Look, I'm sorry." I shook my head. "It's been a while since I've done anything like this."

She peered out over the hood, into the condo lot, and smiled. "Park over there," she said, pointing. "Then let's go upstairs and talk."

There was a second time. A second, and a third.

And as the weeks went on, there were more times after that.

--------- ———————————— -----

The faint buzz of a jazz saxophone—one of Alan's Coltrane albums on vinyl, I'm betting—rolls out through the screen door of Alan and Kristin's house as we come up through their front yard. I hear Kristin say, "They're here!" from inside, and she meets us at the door. She's a tiny woman, barely five feet tall, and she looks young despite being almost fifty with defiantly white hair.

"I think it's safe," she says, *sotto voce*, making a show like she's looking for spies out in the darkness before she ushers us in. "No one followed you over, did they?"

"Didn't hear anyone," Lauren says, smiling at the ribbing I'm getting.

I give Kristin a squeeze and a kiss on the cheek. "You can both stop it now. Really."

"I'm teasing. Your lip doesn't look bad at all. And here Alan had me thinking you were going to look like a monster."

"Neil, come here!" Alan calls from deep in the house. I head back to his study, and find my friend seated before three enormous flat-screen monitors—two more than the last time I was in here—across his desk. The walls of the room are lined with books, mostly aviation books, along with pictures and mementos from his time as a pilot.

"Check this out," he says, angling the center monitor toward me. "Watch this guy." He starts an online video of a jumbo jet approaching a runway at an impossible angle, straightening out at the last possible second to make the landing. "YouTube," he says, shaking his head as he shoves the monitor back into place. "Who came up with this thing? I could watch those crosswind landings all day. Sometimes I do."

On the desk next to the keyboard is something like a steering wheel that Chris might have for his video game console down in our basement.

"What is this?" I ask, picking it up. It's surprisingly heavy.

"Ah ha, it's a control yoke for the new flight simulator." Alan points under the desk. "We have rudder pedals too. The realism in this software is amazing. Especially with the extra monitors, it's like a panoramic view. Want to see me fly it?"

"Not particularly."

"Come over sometime and try it. It'll make your palms sweat. I need to stay current. Keep up on my instrument approaches." Alan pauses for a moment, looking at the setup. "I need to be ready for . . ." He stops himself again. "You know."

"Yeah," I say. Alan shuts down the system, and I follow him out of the study. There's a picture of him, hanging just inside the door to the hallway; he's standing in a Jetway in his pilot's uniform: hat, epaulets, a pair of silver wings pinned to his chest. He's relaxed in the photo, a wry half smile on his face, a briefcase down by his feet. I see Alan glance at the picture as we pass it, and I feel bad for him.

Kris and Lauren are chatting on the living room couch when we come out, leaning close and laughing. Kristin nods and raises her eyebrows when she sees us.

"Did he show you his new video game?" she asks me.

"It is *not* a video game," Alan says. "You talk like it's a child's toy. That software is a highly sophisticated training aide. Used by professionals. Like myself." He grabs me by the elbow and pulls me to the kitchen. "Come on. There's work to be done. Ingredients to be prepped. And wine to be drunk."

"Now you're talking," I say.

"And after the meal is consumed and the wine is drunk, I have something else for us in the form of a bottle of ouzo sent by Nicole. A nod to your heritage."

Nicole—the older of Alan and Kristin's two daughters now both away at college—is now somewhere in Europe for a junior semester abroad.

"You forget this heritage is in name only," I say.

"I forget nothing. We'll drink to your adopted heritage. We'll honor your name." Alan presses an onion into my hand and points to a cutting board with a chef's knife on it. "Chop. Coarse chop is fine."

In his spare time—and he does have a lot of spare time now, Mega-Putt construction notwithstanding—Alan also keeps an incredible garden, the abundance of which often spills into my home and Christopher's cooking experiments. Peppers, beans, corn, squash. Varieties of melons and heirloom tomatoes. And onions, like the massive one I'm cutting up right now.

"So things are good?" Alan asks as I chop and begin to squint and cry from the onion. "With Lauren?"

"Just as good as they were this morning," I say, wiping my eyes with the backs of my wrists.

"You still want me to drop it, I can see." He places a bowl of gigantic homegrown tomatoes next to me. "Break these down when you're done with that onion. Coarse chop as well. Look at you crying. I should have given you the onion last. Didn't your famous chef brother ever teach you the right way to use a knife? I won't be held accountable if you lose a finger in here. By the way, Leland slowed down to check out Mega-Putt today. I watched him from up here."

"Just tell me what I need to cut," I say.

With Alan directing, the two of us work our way through a pile of ingredients (along with a pretty nice bottle of cabernet) to make a cioppino. Renaissance guy that he is, Alan has baked loaves of bread too, and we slice them up and brush them with olive oil before toasting them under the broiler. The women have put a pretty big dent into a bottle of wine themselves, and when the four of us come together to sit at our meal, the room is filled with jovial talk and laughter. It washes over me, the wine and the food, and especially the company, and as I laugh with my friends and hold Lauren's hand under the table next to me I am filled with a sublime joy.

Kristin gets up at some point to check a cobbler she's put into the oven, and I lean over and kiss Lauren's cheek. Alan gives me a look: a little knowing smile, a raised eyebrow. Telepathically, through the alcohol and the camaraderie, I know he's telling me, *You could be like this all the time if you wanted, Neil.*

Now Kristin's back with oven mitts and dessert; she orders Alan to grab ice cream and some bowls. He comes back with a bottle of wine instead, one of their own.

"Have we gone through those other three bottles already?" Lauren asks.

"Just be glad he didn't bring out that grappa," Kristin says.

"Ouzo," Alan corrects her.

"Ouzo, whatever. We'll regret it in the morning, whatever it is."

Later, after more laughter and ouzo and Alan's repeated refusals to give us a tour of Mega-Putt, Lauren and I start back home, taking the long route back through the orchard. The moon is high now, casting sharp shadows and lighting our way, and with the anise-flavored spirits thick in my veins, I'm holding Lauren's hand and taking care with every step. She still needs to drive home, so she paced herself after that first bottle of wine, wisely skipping Alan's multiple toasts to my adopted ancestry.

"I love you, Neil," she says, giving my hand a squeeze as I hold a branch out of our way. "I really do. You make me so happy."

I take a breath to answer, and she stops me.

"I wasn't just saying it so you'd say it back, either."

"Why do you think I was going to say it back?" I say, and I hope there's enough moonlight for her to see how I'm grinning. "You're assuming I was going to say it." I hope she can hear the wink in my voice. I'm floating on the fine evening, and I want her to know it.

"Meanie," she says, but I see she's smiling too.

"I love you," I say. "I love you. Lauren. I love you."

We walk along silently, holding hands.

"I know you do. I know you have a hard time saying it. All this stuff, everything, I know it's—"

"I talked to someone," I say. I'd been waiting to tell Lauren this, waiting to be absolutely sure. I really should wait, but once it starts tumbling out of my mouth I can't stop it. "A guy my brother knows. Last week. There's a thing I can do where I basically become her guardian. Our marriage is annulled, but she stays on my insurance. It's pretty straightforward."

We walk, and our shadows are framed by sparkling dew. The air is chilly and I puff out my breath to test if I can see it.

"Do you really want to?" Lauren asks. "Maybe now isn't the best time to discuss this. You're in a state. I can hear it in your voice."

"I do want to do it. I do. I need to consider how Chris will take it, but I love you, and I want to do this. We should get married, I think."

I hear her draw a little breath. "Later, later, later, Neil."

"You're saying you don't want to?"

"I didn't say that," she says in a small voice, still gripping my hand. "I didn't say that at all. Just walk with me. Let's go to your house. I need to warm up before I go. I love you."

We come through the pines and into the field, and the moonlight illuminates a low mist floating over the open space. My house is dark from afar, sharply shadowed by the moon, and Christopher's car is not there. Lauren and I enter through the side door and start to kiss in the kitchen without turning on the light. There's breathing and the sound of clothes, the sound of me pulling her shirt up to run my hands up her sides to her breasts, the thudding sound of something knocked over on the counter. We move without speaking to the couch, she is undressed, I am undressed, clumsily, laughingly, she is seated and I am kneeling before her. Lauren drapes a blanket over my shoulders.

"You must be cold," she whispers. "Come here. I'm cold. Cover me up too."

Still kneeling, I come forward, I'm so hard now and her hand goes down to guide me easily inside her. I bring myself forward and her legs go around me, and our breathing lifts to growls and sighs, whimpers and moaning. I am floating, and her body is firm and warm and perfect below me. Faster, *faster*, her legs up on my shoulders now and she tells me don't pull out.

"Don't, Neil." Her voice is whispery, nearly a cry. "Don't pull out. It's safe now. Come inside me. Now, Neil. Now!"

Shuddering, collapsing, it's over. My face against her neck and her pulse throbbing on my lips and it's over. Together, her arms and legs around me, she whispers "oh, oh, oh" and our breathing returns to us. All over.

I love you, Lauren. I really do. And this isn't the only time I want to say it.

From: xc.coach.kaz@gmail.com
To: w.kazenzakis@gmail.com
Sent: September 9, 2:37 am
Subject:

_____

its kind of hard to typ on these screens sometims i kind of think the screen is bright in the dark especiallly its dark here in the bathroom you probably never even got to see a phone like this ever did you?

alan watches out for me, you know. he doesnt let me go to far.

CHAPTER NINE

I blink my eyes open to full daylight in my bedroom and stretch; the sound of Chris opening and closing the front door has awakened me. I stretch again, thankful that my regimen of running and frequent hydration has granted me a sort of immunity to hangovers. If I do feel crummy later today, I'll just go and run it out of me. As it is, I'm feeling pretty fresh. I roll to my side to check the time on my alarm, and freeze; Lauren is staring back at me—here, naked, in my bed, with my son just returning home—fearfully wide-eyed with her hand covering her mouth. In the instant it takes me to blink and process this information, I feel the expression on my face changing to a similar look of terror.

"Oh shit," Lauren whispers.

"Get out, get out!" I hiss, pushing her out of the bed. "Into the bathroom. Start the shower!"

"The shower?" She frantically gathers her clothes from the floor and holds them wadded against her bare front.

"Get in the shower! Say . . . say you spilled something on yourself at Carol's!" I push her along into the bathroom, throw her shoes in behind her and yank the door shut. I find some shorts and a running shirt and pull them on, and straighten the duvet over my bed as the sound of running water starts. The bathroom door opens and Lauren peeks out.

"My bra, Neil, where is my bra?" I look around my feet in a panic, imagining Chris finding it out on the couch. Lauren points at my bed. "There, right next to the pillow," she whispers, waving her finger. I grab it by a black strap and fling it across the room; Lauren snatches it from the air and disappears again.

I find Christopher out in the kitchen mixing one of his sports drinks in a tall glass. The spoon makes the glass clang like a bell as he stirs, but the sound doesn't cover the rumble of the shower coming through the pipes.

"Hey," I say. "Fun night?" I get a glass of water for myself, and the shower still howls.

"Yeah, sweet. Full house. Thirty kids. They were great." He looks at the glass in my hand, and holds up his own. "You want some of this? It's a recovery drink."

"Sure," I say. "I could use a little recovery right now."

Chris takes my glass and scoops some of his powder into it, and as he stirs—*clink, clink, clink*—I peek into the living room to check for anything out of order. Sure enough, one of Lauren's socks is right there in the center of the floor, and I manage to scurry over and kick it under the couch just as Chris brings out my drink.

"Thanks," I say, and the sound of the shower only seems louder. "Thank you."

"The taste is kind of crappy, but it's good stuff."

"You're probably wondering why you can hear the shower running," I say. Better for me to bring it up, I'm thinking, than him.

"Huh?"

"Lauren Downey is in there. Your Grandma's nurse. Something spilled on her over at the farmhouse and she needed a shower."

"Grandma's shower isn't working?"

"Something's up with her hot water. I'll take a look at it."

"Uh, okay?"

"I'm tired," I say, just to say anything. "Had some rocky sleep last night."

"Oh man, don't even get me started. The seventh graders stayed up 'til almost two. I am *so* tired. I kept telling them they needed to settle down. I felt all like an old guy. I felt like you!"

"Ha!" I say, too loud. I hear my bathroom door open, and Lauren enters the living room from the hall. Her hair is wet, and I see she's not wearing any socks with her shoes.

"All cleaned up?" I ask.

"Yes. Thank you so much. Hi, Chris!"

"Hi, Ms. Downey."

"I knocked over a can of something in the laundry room and it got—" She raises her arm up to her nose and sniffs the sleeve of her shirt, then holds it out to Christopher. "Can you smell it? It's like paint thinner or something."

"No," he says, shaking his head. "Not at all."

"Oh good. How's senior year going? Classes all okay?"

"It's been awesome so far."

"You're in my friend Ashley's American History class, I heard."

"Ashley?" he asks. "Oh, you mean Ms. Burns. She's cool."

"She is cool. Don't mess with her, though. You don't want to see her angry. Just kidding. Hey, I'm going to get back over to Carol. There's a mess in the laundry room. Thanks again, you guys."

"I'll come with you and take a look at that water heater," I say.

Lauren nods so convincingly I could almost buy this thing myself. "Good idea," she says. "Bye, Chris!"

"I'll be right back, Chris."

We're halfway between my house and Carol's before I can speak.

"Holy shit," I say.

"Holy shit is right." Lauren shakes her head. "Oh my God. I'm sorry. I'm sorry! Way too close."

"Some performance, there. Paint thinner?"

"It worked, didn't it? I'm missing a sock. Could you see my hand shaking when I had him smell my shirt?"

"No," I pause, and stop in my tracks. My stomach feels close to turning. "I just totally bullshitted my son."

"It's okay." Lauren touches her hand to my upper arm.

I twist myself away from her and start walking again. "It's not okay. I feel like shit. I feel like I need to puke."

"No, no. Come on. Don't, please. That's not the way you want him to find out. Right? You need to tell him at the right time. That's what you've said. When you're ready. He didn't need to find us that way. God, I'm sorry. We did the right thing."

"I still feel like shit. Hiding things from him. I can't believe I just . . . how did we end up like that, anyway?" We're outside Carol's garage now, and I keep glancing back at my house.

"You fell asleep on the couch. I wanted to get you to bed. We kind of, we just cuddled for a little while. We never get to do that. I fell asleep. It's all my fault. I'm sorry."

"Don't apologize. I should have been . . . fuck."

"Please don't beat yourself up about it. Please, Neil. We did the right thing."

"Right," I say. "Yes. Right." I turn to the door. "You're right. I suppose I'd better make a token check on the water heater."

We go inside and greet Carol. She's out of bed and sitting in her big chair with her walker in front of her, but she seems groggy this morning.

"Are you checking it?" Lauren asks me back in the kitchen, raising an eyebrow. "It's in the basement, right?"

"You have got to be kidding me," I say. And even though I know I shouldn't, even though I know the risk, the memory of last night on the couch fills my head and I let Lauren follow me downstairs.

A short run helps dissipate my guilt in the early afternoon even though Chris joins me. He runs like a puppy at my side, silently, all floppy limbs and big feet. I gave up a long time ago on trying to correct his form. Anyway, it's not like he's trying to go fast; he really doesn't care. There's something reassuring about him galloping along at my side.

Back home, we get cleaned up before heading down to go for a sail in Peggy Mackie's boat. The towel Lauren used this morning hangs from the doorknob in my bathroom, still a little damp, a small reminder that makes me cringe. I toss it into the hamper and shut the lid.

Christopher drives us down to Port Manitou and the municipal marina. I run over to let old Ollie at the gas dock know we're taking Peggy's boat; he's heard we're coming and sends me off with a wave. Chris, meanwhile, has opened up the cabin and is pulling off dark green canvas covers and organizing lines when I get there. It's a handsome boat, about twenty-seven feet long with brass ports and fittings and the sturdy feel of something that could safely carry you across an entire ocean. Peggy and her long-term partner, Lisa, had planned to sail down the eastern seaboard after they retired, but then Lisa developed lupus-like symptoms a few years ago, and the plan was put on hold while Lisa gets her health back in order. Meanwhile, their boat remains tied up at the marina with a more or less open invitation for my son and me to take it out on weekend afternoons. Peggy likes to know it's being used and taken care of. It's awfully pretty, with the name TABBY, and PORT MANITOU, MI underneath, painted in dark green letters on the stern.

"You want to take us out today?" I ask.

"You're the skipper," he says. "But sure, I'll take us out." Christopher has his own little library, in his room, of books about sailing: technical books, charts, and tales of solo voyages around the world. He uses nautical jargon with a total lack of self-consciousness, and bellows things like "Ready about!" and "Hard a-lee!" when we're aboard as if he grew up on some schooner two hundred years ago.

Wendy used to sail. She had a little daysailer growing up, and she raced while we were in college. We made a deal during those high school summers where, if she went running with me, I had to go sailing with her. Seeing as she ran already, and I knew nothing about sailing, I'd say she got the better side of the bargain. It wasn't like I minded. I had fun on the boat, and I never got seasick. Most of all, I liked being with her. We'd go out as often as we could when my family was up on vacation, and she taught me how to do it. Wendy was a patient teacher and I caught on pretty quickly.

She taught Chris too, years later, starting early with him on the same little dinghy we'd sailed when we were kids. I got rid of that boat the summer after everything happened; in hindsight I really wish I hadn't. There are all sorts of small regrets.

Chris starts up *Tabby's* engine and asks me to cast us off. I undo the dock lines and toss them to the deck, and I jump aboard as Chris pushes the throttle and sends us puttering away. My son stands at the wheel, peering intently toward the lake; it's a gorgeous, cloudless day and there's just enough wind coming from the south to work up some whitecaps beyond the breakwater. He steers us past the Port Manitou Light, and *Tabby* starts to gently roll as we head into the swells. I lean back and stretch my arm out along the cockpit coaming and watch my son steady himself against the motion of the waves like an old salt.

"Why don't you get the main, Dad," he says. "I'll head her up into the wind."

I grab a winch handle and scramble up onto the cabin top to raise the mainsail with a ratcheting effort. Once it's up, Chris turns the boat across the wind and cuts the engine, the sail fills with a pregnant belly of air, and we're left with only the sound of the breeze and the rhythmic *swoosh, swoosh* of waves passing under the hull. We let out the foresail, a big striped genoa, and Chris whoops as the boat takes the wind and lunges along through the water.

"We're really moving!" he shouts, as if I hadn't noticed it myself. The boat heels over in the wind, far enough that I can reach over the lee side and touch my fingers to the cool water.

"We're hauling the mail," I say.

Chris has donned sunglasses, and he can't seem to stop grinning. "You know it," he says. He has so many friends with motorboats, jet skis, fast things like that, and I have plenty of friends whom I could borrow those things from if we wanted. But *Tabby* on a weekend here and there seems to be all he needs. He is, for sure, his mother's son.

"So, Dad," Chris says, after we've gone along for a bit, "did you talk to Mrs. Mackie about me taking her overnight?"

"I brought it up," I say. Chris has inquired about taking *Tabby* out—solo—for an overnight stay. He used to take Jill Swart out once in a while for a quick afternoon trip, but now that she's away I don't think I need to worry about him using the boat as a hook-up palace. If it were up to me, I'd probably let him do the overnight, but Peggy is hesitant.

"I won't take her far," Chris tells me, even though he knows I could recite his talking points verbatim. "Just out to South Manitou, and back the next morning."

"I know," I say. "I know you can handle the boat just fine. I don't think it's the trip Mrs. Mackie is worried about so much, it's the anchorage over there. Maybe she'd feel better if she came out with us sometime to see how well you take care of the boat."

"Maybe. Did you read about that girl?"

"What girl?"

"The one who sailed around the world alone. She set a record for being the youngest, I think. Man, I'd love to do that."

I might be ready to let Chris sail to an island I can see from my house, but a trip around the world is another thing entirely. Even if he is almost eighteen. "That's ah, a pretty big trip," I say. "And expensive. Even before provisions. Just getting a boat would be an awful lot of money."

"You could do it on a boat like this, I bet."

"With the right gear, maybe. I think that kid had a ton of corporate sponsorships."

"Maybe I'll talk to Mrs. Mackie."

I laugh, not in a discouraging way. "Mrs. Mackie might be a little reluctant to let you take her boat around the world."

"I don't know, Dad. We sail *Tabby* more than she does. She could be a sponsor too."

"I'll tell you what. You go to school for a year, a full year, and if it isn't your thing, we can talk about you doing a trip like that." My logic here is that, if he tries one year, he'll just keep going and I won't have to worry about it.

"Are you serious? No joke?"

"I am serious. But a year."

Chris is quiet for a while.

I trim the sheets to pull the sails tight as Chris points the boat a little higher into the wind, and spray carries up and hits our faces as the boat lunges forward.

"Porter James is going to drive out to Colorado after graduation," Chris says out of nowhere. "He's going to get a job at a resort and be a ski bum."

"Does Bill James know his son is planning to do this?"

"Porter says he's fine with it. He asked me to come with him."

"There's no way in hell you are driving to Colorado after graduation."

Chris frowns. "What's wrong with it? What's wrong with going to be a ski bum?"

"There's nothing wrong with being a ski bum, as long as you're a college-educated ski bum. Look, this may sound harsh, but absolutely not. You go out there right after high school, and you'll lose all your momentum. But like the other stuff, if you do one year at school, and I mean really applying yourself, you can go do whatever you want. Colorado, sailing, whatever. I'll help you out with it, even."

Chris doesn't speak for a long time. He lets the boat fall off the wind and we ease out the sails; the sun is at our backs now and the motion of the boat calms as we run with the breeze.

"What about culinary school?" he asks after a while.

"What about it?"

"Well, do you define it as something cool and fun that I can only do after a year of college? Or does it count as college?"

I smile at this. "That, I think, would count as formal education. Don't tell your Uncle Mike that I ever said that, though."

"Would you help me out with that too? It's expensive."

"Of course I would help you out with it. If it's really what you want to do, we can figure something out. There are loans and things like that. Financial aid we can look for. Mike would help you too."

"It's in Chicago . . ."

"Are you worried about that? It's not right in the city, but it's close. It's a pretty good place. And you've got your uncles there, so that would make everything easier."

"Should I do it?"

"I cannot say, Christopher. This one's totally up to you."

"If I could just take a break and go somewhere," he says, "to figure things out."

"No." I shake my head. "One year. You have to make a plan and give it a shot. It's not so long."

Tabby rides along with the wind for a long time, creeping up the backs of waves, and rushing down the fronts. Aside from minor communications regarding the trim of the boat, my son and I don't speak to each other for nearly an hour. My son at the helm: a tall young man with strong arms and big hands gripping the broad chromed wheel. How do you tell someone what you're feeling, how do you explain to him that sometimes "No" has a place in the bigger picture, that "No" has a place in the greater compartments of your heart?

"You know, Chris," I say, pausing to search for the right words. "*Tabby's* got a pretty fine crew today."

I think he understands, but my son looks away, out over the water.

We sail a while more, saying little to each other. The wind fades in strength as the sun eases down in the west, and when Chris finally turns the boat toward home, the sails curve above us, filled with golden autumn light.

How *do* you say it, really?

From: xc.coach.kaz@gmail.com
To: w.kazenzakis@gmail.com
Sent: September 9, 8:50 pm
Subject: Rudderless

Chris and I took Peggy and Lisa Mackie's boat way north today. It was an easy run, the wind was coming out of the southwest, which makes sense because it's supposed to start raining this week, so I think low pressure is coming.

Going so far north made me think of that time you took me out (summer between sophomore and junior year? Or the year before that?) and I talked you into letting us beach your boat up the Little Jib River. I think I sold it to you as a picnic or something (I didn't even bring any food), but really I wanted to make out. More than anything I wanted to sneak my hand up your shirt. I desperately wished to unhook your bra and touch my fingers to your bare breasts, but you stopped me again and again and again. Soon, you told me. Soon, Neil. You said it wouldn't be much longer, you said you wanted to be ready, you wanted to be sure. *I* was ready, though, I was impatient, and I said (not so sincerely) fine, I understand, it's okay, let's get going. Then back under way with me at the helm, and the rudder broke off, cosmic punishment for me being a jerk, for me being an impatient teen boy, and we were helplessly blown about a zillion miles up the lake before we finally limped it over to the beach to stop ourselves. I think you'd forgiven me by then. I think you even felt a little bad.

Remember that guy who towed us back down to PM with his trawler? Funny thing: I actually met him a few years ago; he owns the car lot where I bought my truck. I looked at the guy for about an hour wondering "How do I know you?" before it clicked. When I told him, he totally remembered, and we had a good laugh about it. Of course, he didn't know anything about what happened before he rescued us.

Chris looks so much like you in his face. Especially when he's sailing.

-N

CHAPTER TEN

The nameplate on our mailbox is crooked when Chris and I drive past on our way to school Monday morning; I tell him to stop for a second, and I hop out of the car try to straighten it out. Long and weighted with so many letters, the thing won't stay level, so I jump back in and ask Chris to remind me to fix it that evening in case I forget.

So many letters: Kazenzakis. It's a substantial name, clumsy in the mouth and almost too big for things like mailboxes and school ID badges. There have been plenty of nicknames to replace it through my life—as a kid, as a teacher, as a coach. I can't blame people for wanting a shortcut. Kaz, Mr. Kaz, Mr. K., Coach K., Coach Kaz. In middle school I was Special K. Who among my friends *ever* called me Neil back then? Christopher gets them too, the same ones I had and more: C-Kaz, Kazenizzle, K-Zak, K-Hole (yes, I'm aware of the meaning of the last one; yes, I discouraged him and his peers from using it).

This was not my name by birth. I was well into my childhood before learning I'd started my life under a different one; ten years old when my parents told me of my adoption. I guess I'd never considered it odd that Michael was only five months older than me, or if I had, maybe I'd rationalized it by thinking my short gestation was somehow something unique. It was Christmastime when they told me, and I remember my father calling me into his and my mother's room. Mom couldn't have more babies after Michael, he explained, but they felt like they had more love to give, and so I was brought into the family just before my first birthday. They understood it was big news for me, a lot to absorb, and if I ever had any questions, they told me, I shouldn't hesitate to ask. It was normal, they explained, for me to wonder about my birth parents. I shouldn't feel bad about it; they'd love me just the same.

The thing was, I wasn't really troubled by it at all. At least not then. I was pretty happy in the family. I looked like my siblings with their vaguely olive complexions (so much that sometimes I wondered if they'd somehow adopted a Greek baby to make things easy). I revered my older brother, respected my sister's advice, shared my every thought with Mike. I had no real reason to want anything else.

There was that mouthful of a name, however. Some nights, lying awake while Mike snored in our room, I'd wonder about the couple who'd produced me. Not what they looked like, or where they lived, or why they'd had to give me up, but *what their last names could have been.* Was it something simple like Smith or Clark or Miller? Brown or Jones or anything containing two syllables or less?

I chewed on this curiosity for a couple of years, and finally, at the age of twelve, told my mother I'd like to view my birth certificate. She took the request easily, almost happily, as if she'd been waiting for the day I'd ask, and set to work finding out how we'd track down the document. She never asked me why I wanted to see it, and I never offered.

She determined we'd need to go to the state bureau of records, and pulled me out of school one day to do it. I gave my name, signed a form, and while my mom waited out front, I was led back into a cool, vast room with low ceilings and row upon row upon row of gray shelving units. I felt like I was floating as I watched the woman flip with incredible speed through a drawer, her hands a blur, and suddenly—*fwap!*—present with a quick flourish the coveted document. And there it was, typed in all caps beneath the embossed and gilded seal of The Great State of Michigan:

NBM VAN LEEUWENHOEK

"Van Leeuwenhoek?" I said. At least I tried to say it; I didn't have the first clue how to go about pronouncing it. After that shock wore off, I scanned over the document. My mother's name was Crystal Many Lightnings, age sixteen, ethnicity given as Sioux. My father's name was Marty. A white male, age seventeen. I looked it all over again and nothing changed; that was where I came from.

"You all right, honey?" the clerk asked. This was obviously not her first time dealing with a dumbstruck child. "You want me to go grab your mom?"

"I'm . . . I'm fine," I said. "What does 'NBM' mean?"

"New Born Male. Your birth mama and your daddy hadn't picked a name yet. Maybe you came along a little faster than they were expecting."

"Oh," I said.

"Why don't we go get a copy of this made for you."

"I don't think I need one."

"You sure?"

I nodded. She returned it to its place in the file drawer and I followed her back to the lobby and I've never seen the thing since.

-------- ------ -----

Van Leeuwenhoek. Another mouthful. Years later, while getting my teaching certificate in physics, I learned that a Dutchman named Antonie van Leeuwenhoek perfected the microscope in the late 1600s. A Renaissance man. A scientist! I smile to myself now when my classes come to the optics unit and I get to teach that fact; maybe I'm somehow descended from the guy. I suppose it would be fitting.

My first class Monday morning is an exercise in lethargy. While last week the kids seemed energetic, even excited by the new school year, today they're duds, as if this fine weekend we've just had has only served to remind them that summer is really over. I compliment them on their work, return their pages, and spend the next fifty-five minutes trying to rouse them from their collective stupor. I'm not so successful, and I won't have optics or van Leeuwenhoek to perk things up for another six weeks, at least.

In the halls after my class I pick up some general chatter about Steve Dinks running an interception for a touchdown in Grayling, apparently the single bright spot in the 34–6 drubbing we took last Friday night. I have an open period before I have to teach algebra, so I visit the teacher's lounge to check my quaint (and still frequently used) mail slot. There's a guy I don't recognize, reading a flyer, and he greets me like I know him.

"Hey, Coach," he says.

"Hey?"

The guy laughs and strokes his chin. "It's Kevin Hammil. Shaved the beard."

"Kevin! Jeez, you look . . . you're like a different person." Walt Binger stops by, Port Manitou High's special education teacher, Nordic ski team coach, and general comedian, and he gives me a raised-eyebrow look as he points at Kevin's face.

"Didn't recognize the dude, did you?"

"I didn't."

Walt has a weird hyena laugh, and he lets it loose right now. "Bet you were tired of being called the Mammal, *heh heh heh!*"

"Naw, listen, I'll tell you why I did it. You ready? Saturday night I asked my girl if she wanted to get married." Walt breaks in with a

"Hey!" and slaps Kevin on the back. Our young colleague smiles sheepishly. "Yeah, yeah, we've been dating almost three years; I got here, got the job, figured it was about time. She said sure, but the beard would have to go if she was going to say yes. And I really like her, so—"

"Congratulations," I say, shaking his hand. "Wait, she said yes, right?"

"Oh yeah, I shaved, didn't I?" Kevin strokes his chin, grinning. "I did okay, had the ring ready, got down on my knee, and the whole bit."

Walt pats him on the shoulder. "You did it the right way, there, Kev. Way to go. Remind her of the proposal whenever she's pissed at you. That always works with my wife." Beth Coolidge comes in, and I turn subtly away from her in fear she's going to say something to me about her homecoming float. She doesn't have a chance, though, because Walt is on a roll.

"Hey, Cougar-lidge!"

"Goddammit, Walter, you know I hate it when you call me that—"

"Yeah, anyway, Cougar-lidge, did you hear Kevin asked his girlfriend to marry him? And she said yes? You didn't even have a chance to ask him out!" Since her divorce a few years ago, Beth has gained a reputation for pursuing our single (and sometimes not-so-single) male colleagues, especially the new ones.

Beth's eyes narrow. "Go fuck yourself, Walt." She storms off and Walt follows her, continuing to egg her on. Kevin looks horrified by the exchange, but I just laugh.

"The kids can't, uh, hear us back here, can they?" Kevin asks.

"No, no, they soundproofed it years ago." The look on Kevin Hammil's face suggests he completely believes me. "I'm kidding," I say. "I doubt they can hear anything. Even Beth Coolidge screaming."

"Hey, Coach, I have a question for you, sometime . . ." Kevin turns the barest shade of red, especially apparent with his newly shaven face. "You're a good guy, I've liked hanging out with you and every-thing. You're married and all that, your son's a great kid, so like . . . how exactly do you do that? I mean, how do you stay married all those years, keep it going, and raise such a great kid? You really seem like you have your act together, is what I'm saying."

I waver for a moment over whether or not I should tell Kevin the whole story, or, in the spirit of Walt Binger, string him along with a tale of fidelity and marital bliss. Walt himself solves this dilemma for me by hollering from the office, "Hey, Kev, come here, you gotta check this video out."

"I'll talk to you about it this afternoon," I say, and Kevin leaves to another burst of hyena laughter.

Peggy Mackie breezes by, probably on her way to some disci-plinary meeting, seemingly her greatest function in the district.

"Good time on *Tabby?*" she asks, barely slowing as she passes.

"Great time, thanks. Fuel's topped off."

"Call me whenever you want her," she says, leaving with a wave. She halts, remembering something, and turns back. "Actually, do you have a second, Neil? Come with me."

I follow Peggy to her office. She's narrow-shouldered and tall, taller than me, with curly graying hair, and she walks with a pur-poseful stride. "Shut the door," she says. She takes a seat at her desk, and flips a paper facedown before I can see it. "I think I asked you a week ago if you knew Denise Masterson." I nod. "You had her—"

"Last year," I say. "Sophomore. Good kid. Is something up?"

"Sexting."

"No." My stomach drops. "You're kidding me." I've known Denise since she was a baby; her mother Jo was one of Wendy's closest friends. She's a dedicated student, a nice, polite, and quiet girl. Her dream is to attend the Coast Guard Academy after gradu-ation, and last fall she shyly asked me for a letter of recommenda-tion for her application to join the JROTC. So much for that, I'm thinking. This news is a shock, and I know her parents won't take it very well at all.

"Not one hundred percent sure yet. A couple boys got pictures from her ex. Typical breakup revenge thing. No face, but the police computer people downstate are taking a look. I guess there's a chance it's not her, but for now I'm assuming that it is. We'll confront the boyfriend when we know either way. Next day or two. I know you know the girl's family, so will you help if and when we need to talk to them?"

"Of course I will. I know them well. Do I know the boyfriend?"

"Did you ever have Cody Tate in any of your classes?"

This name does not ring a bell. "Nope. Does anyone on staff know yet?"

"Only a couple. It doesn't seem to be out in the student population yet either. The boys who got the photos have kept themselves quiet. It will probably get around like wildfire eventually, but keep it to yourself for now."

"I can't believe Denise Masterson would do that. Her parents are going to be—"

"No one ever believes a kid would do that, Neil. But they do. Please don't say anything to her family until I ask you to." Peggy slides the facedown paper to the edge of her desk. "Anyway, you and Chris had a good day on the boat?"

"Perfect day. I'm supposed to ask you again if Chris can do an overnight."

Peggy laughs. "He already cornered me about it this morning in study hall. Someday, Neil. Not yet."

"I'm in no rush," I say. "How's Lisa doing?"

"She's in Sedona for two more weeks," Peggy says, rolling her eyes. "Some New Age healing thing. I believe crystals are involved. I'm scared she's going to want us to buy a house there if she stays any longer. But she wants you and Chris to come over for dinner when she's back."

"I'd like that too," I say.

"I'll let you know." She glances up at the clock above her whiteboard. "And I'll keep you posted about the Masterson kid."

I say goodbye, and head back toward my room. In the science wing hallway, a few minutes before the bell ending second period, I see Steve Dinks at his locker. We normally don't interact so much, but he looks at me—stares at me, really—with an expression so puzzled I can't help but say something.

"What's up, Steve? You okay?"

"What? Oh yeah, how's it going, Mr. K.?"

"Not too bad. Thought I'd see you in AP Physics this year."

"I had to choose between that and calculus. Sorry."

"Come on, no big deal. Sounds like you had a pretty good game in Grayling?"

"I tried, Mr. K. It was a crappy night."

The bell rings and the hall floods with kids, and I don't even have a chance to say goodbye to Steve before he's washed away in the crowd. He's popular, smart like his dad, really smart, and most likely going to Northwestern next fall. I'm sincerely glad he's having a good last year before college. It's hard to hold a grudge against a kid for too long.

Steve Dinks and Christopher went to the same preschool together, a Montessori run by an aging hippy out of an old house inland from Port Manitou. That's how I first met Leland; we both dropped off our kids on the same days of the week. It was a hectic time; Wendy and I were living with her parents while we were building our own house in the field next door, and during that summer vacation I'd drop Chris off so I could return to the orchard, put on tool bags, and work on the house with Dick.

I say sometimes now that I built the place myself, but really it was my father-in-law who knew what he was doing. I just did what I was told.

Wendy made friends with Leland's wife, Sherry, too. Leland and Sherry kept suggesting we all get together for dinner sometime, they had just moved up from Chicago and didn't really know anyone yet, the boys got along well and why not? It's funny to remember that we found excuses to not see them for a while. Not because we disliked the two, but because we were too embarrassed to admit we were living in Wendy's parents' basement.

We got over it, though. Soon we were hanging out with them pretty regularly, promising we'd have a housewarming fete as soon as our place was done. Leland and Sherry even helped us paint before we moved in, joking that they wanted to get the job over with so we could have our party sooner than later.

Leland was getting started out in real estate then. He worked for a brokerage at first, just an agent, and though he only obliquely talked about it, it was clear sometimes that people reacted negatively to the color of his skin. Someone asked for a different broker to list his property, he'd tell me, or a different person to show him around. They needed a *local* agent, they'd say. A coded request. That was as much as he'd discuss it; he'd act like it was no big deal, but obviously it troubled him. Sometimes I'd say sorry, without even knowing exactly what I was apologizing for, or why. He'd just wave his hand and say, "Ah, forget about it, Neil." I always wanted to ask him more about it, but I guess back then I didn't really know how.

Here's what Leland was: he was smart, and funny, and personable, and most of all shrewd in business. By the time the boys were in the fifth grade, he was running his own brokerage, as well as owning a Laundromat, a car wash, and part of Port Manitou's touristy seafood restaurant in Old Town. We didn't see him and Sherry as much as before, but Steve and Chris stayed best friends. The boys played together, and they did sports together. They did *every* sport together, it seemed: Pop Warner football, Little League baseball, basketball camp, indoor soccer, the whole deal. They were rough together too, the way boys are, tumbling and scratching like a pair of lion cubs, fighting one moment before bounding off together to try something new the next.

In seventh grade the boys joined ski club. We used to have a little ski hill nearby; it's out of business now, but it was less than twenty minutes from my house. There were a few rickety old chairlifts and a rope tow, and the school would send a bus full of kids on Thursday nights to exhaust themselves under the stark night-skiing lights. Leland and I would chaperone sometimes, and the kids—all the kids—would howl with laughter at our knock-kneed attempts at the sport.

The winter of eighth grade for Chris, not so long after Wendy's accident, his therapist suggested we try ski club again. Routine was good, she told us; we were just shooting for something close to normal then. Christopher *seemed* normal, most of the time, but every so often in those first months he would explode with rage. Lamps were knocked over, holes were punched in walls. This, I was assured, was normal too. We'd work through it. Chris could find a release for his anger, and I, on extended administrative leave, would continue numbing myself to the mess of it all with gin, tonic, and Xanax.

The ski club did help. One night that year some other school district from downstate had bused up a big group, and the ski area called and asked for parent volunteers as it was going to be a very busy, and possibly unruly, evening. I wasn't ready to try something like that, wallowing in my new normal, and didn't even consider going.

By that point the boys were pretty good skiers, and they liked to bomb down under the chairlift, showing off to their friends or attempting to impress girls. Chris had a problem with his ski binding that night, and on one run, a couple turns from the top, he and Steve stopped so Chris could try to clear snow from his boot. Up above, on the lift, one of the blue-jeans-clad downstate boys saw them.

"Look at that!" the boy called with a sneer. "Check it out, a nigger on skis! You ever seen that before? It's a nigger on skis!"

Maybe they talked like that all the time. Maybe they didn't, and thought they'd get lost in the crowd. Steve took a deep breath, shrugged, and shook his head. He said nothing. Chris, however, looked up, made a note of the chair number (it was, he told me later, number twenty-four), and actually *ran uphill* in his cumbersome ski boots to beat the chair to the top. As it approached the crest, the two boys on board watched Chris with expressions of awe and terror as he pointed at each of them, asking, "Was it you? Or was it you?"

Chris walked up to the chair as the two boys tried to get off. They were older, but he was bigger, and he grabbed both of them and pushed them, tripping over their skis, to the ground like a pair of dominoes. He punched the one to his left in the mouth and the boy cried, "It wasn't me, it was him!" So Chris turned and punched the other boy's face again and again until the snow around him was flecked red with blood.

Chris stood up from the guy and backed away, maybe realizing the state he'd slipped into. The lift operator had run over while other people had started to gather around, and Chris stepped back as the kid picked himself up off the snow.

"It's cool," the kid said through his bloodied lips. "Everything's cool."

Chris staggered away, through the crowd that had gathered to watch and down the hill to his skis. Steve Dinks had left; he'd skied down quietly, called his dad, and got a ride home. I got a call too, from the manager of the ski area telling me that my son was not welcome to return, ever, and I'd better come and pick him up immediately.

Christopher burst into tears on the ride home.

"What did I do?" he kept repeating, wiping snot from his upper lip with the sleeve of his ski jacket. "What did I do to that guy?"

I told him everything was okay. The manager had explained to me what had happened; there was no need to push Chris on it. I didn't think what he'd done was right, necessarily, but I felt a bit of pride over him standing up for his friend like that. I didn't want to send mixed signals, so I kept my mouth shut.

I told Chris he could stay home Friday; we'd get the therapist over for a long talk. He nodded, eyes and nose red from crying, and went to bed. I fixed a drink, and Leland called me not long after that.

"We need to talk about what happened," he said.

"I know. I mean, I've raised him to use his words before his fists, but in this case, maybe there was a place—"

"Neil," he said, stopping me. "Neil. There is never, ever a place for that. Ever. You have no idea. You should know, you've seen how I've tried to bring up my kids, how I've told them no matter what, no matter *what*, they need to hold their heads up and let that roll off them. That . . ." I heard a tremble in his voice. "Ignorance, Neil. It is pure ignorance, and stupidity. You show them that it's meaningless, you show them that it's stupid, you do that by letting it go. You don't dignify it, you don't glorify it, and you don't martyr an idiot and harden his views by *beating the shit out of him!*"

"Whoa, wait a minute, Leland—"

"Is this how you've raised Christopher?"

"Leland, how long have we been friends? How many times has Chris slept over at your house? You know he's a good kid."

"Look, I understand what you guys are dealing with right now. But I am . . . I'm furious."

"It's like you're blaming me for this."

"Maybe I am. You know what? If this hadn't happened, what that kid said would be a nonissue. Or, okay, maybe three other kids heard it up on the hill. Maybe they say something about it later at school. But then when they ask my kid about it? He says nothing. He doesn't dignify it, Neil. He lets it go, because it's stupid. And it goes away, and everything is as it is. But now, now, you know what's going to happen? Every kid at school is going to be talking tomorrow, and over the weekend, and over the week after that. This is going to be humiliating for Steve. He's going to have to live it over and over. I came here to raise my family away from all that. Do you understand? Can you see why I am agitated?"

"What are you asking me to do here? My son reacted strongly to a racist asshole. Am I supposed to tell him he should have done something different?"

Leland sighed. "You're not getting this at all, Neil."

"Maybe I'm not," I said, and I hung up.

We didn't talk so much after that. I didn't really notice the erosion of our friendship as it was happening; I was blinded enough already by the shot my life had taken in the fall. Truthfully, I wasn't noticing very much at all back then. The boys stopped hanging out too, and I didn't notice that change either.

Sometime in the spring, with only a few weeks to go in the school year, Chris was in Home Economics class, his last class of the day. Steve Dinks was in the class too. In the past they'd have sat next to each other, but as things had become, Chris sat toward the front with Steve a few rows behind him. The teacher informed the room that they'd be starting a fruits and vegetables unit as part of the nutrition section of the class.

"Vegetable unit?" Steve said softly, but still loud enough for everyone in the room to hear. "What are you going to do, bring in Chris K.'s mom as an example?"

People who were there have described to me how Chris lunged at Steve. In an instant, with no warning, he vaulted over two rows of desks and students, twisting through the air, and took Steve to the floor with an arm hooked around his neck. They were an even match, equals in battle—all those times they'd scuffled, all those times one had used his best moves against the other—and maybe that primal understanding ended it quickly. They rose to their feet—panting, glaring—without anyone having to separate them, and never spoke to each other again.

After I came to the middle school and was told what happened, I couldn't bring myself to even look at Steve Dinks while he waited for his father in the office. I took Chris home, and told him it was okay. And after Chris went to bed that night, I *could* have called Leland, *could* have asked him if that was the way he raised his kids, but I did not.

For what it's worth, Leland didn't call me either.

I ended up pulling Chris out of school for the rest of the year. He needed more than just counseling once a week. We got him a tutor for over the summer, and he made progress with therapy. He started school with no problem the next fall.

From: xc.coach.kaz@gmail.com
To: w.kazenzakis@gmail.com
Sent: September 10, 3:55 pm
Subject: Proposal

Even though it was kind of a formality when I proposed, you'll recall I did get on my knee (because you just do that when you're proposing, right?), but I never told you that the real reason I wanted to get married so soon wasn't so things would be official, or because of my whole adoption thing and I wanted the baby to have a proper father on his birth certificate (though that was pretty important to me), it was because I was completely freaked out about the thought of having an infant at the wedding. Now I know it's no big deal, that no one would have cared, your mom didn't care, my parents didn't care. No one cared, but I sure did.

CHAPTER ELEVEN

At practice Monday afternoon, I find the girls on the cross-country team seem to have been affected by the past weekend as well. They whine through our stretches, whine through our warm-up, whine when I tell them our plan for the week. So I make them run sprints to snap them out of it. I'm not above punitive measures. Just after I've sent them off for the second time, Kevin Hammil shows up, looking ashen.

"Jesus, Kevin, are you all right? Did your girlfriend have second thoughts about the engagement?"

"Coach," he says. "I am so sorry."

"Sorry for what?"

"Walt told me."

"Walt told you . . . what?"

"About your wife." I wait, and watch Kevin's newly bare Adam's apple rise and fall as he swallows. "About how she's not well." In this, in the way he says it, the real anguish set in his eyes, I am reminded that Kevin Hammil is still a very young man, and not yet so experienced with the weight of the world.

"It's the reality of my life," I say. "You don't need to be sorry about it at all."

"It's not that. I'm sorry for coming up and asking you for marital advice when I didn't have a clue about it. I feel like an asshole."

"Come on, if you were really an asshole, you wouldn't feel so bad about it," I say. "You wouldn't even consider it if you weren't a good guy. And you are." I hold up my left hand to show him my wedding band. "And if I wanted to avoid it, or pretend it never happened, I wouldn't be wearing this, would I? In a way, I'm kind of asking for it."

"Well, I'm real sorry that it happened, Coach. I'm sorry that happened to your wife."

I nod and thank him. In a strange way, this exchange is the most positive thing I've experienced all day.

After everything happened, as more time passed, I got better at finding those positives. If I found enough of them, I discovered, they could be assembled into something resembling a normal life. There was a rough spot for a while—a very dark time—for me and Christopher both, but we shouldered our burdens and worked at accumulating positives. Chris got serious about basketball and made good friends through his sports, and I blinked my eyes open and rededicated myself to teaching and running. I met Lauren, and we began to see each other, secretly, more and more. Al and Kristin became part of the secret, eventually, but I wasn't ready to tell Christopher yet. I didn't think that disclosure would be much of a positive for him.

Once, after nearly a year of Lauren and I spending stolen time together, I was over at Carol's house working on installing a new disposal in the kitchen sink. Lauren was there, but busy, and we quietly went about our respective jobs. When I slid myself out from the cabinet beneath the sink, I found my crypto-girlfriend sitting at the kitchen table.

"Hey," I said, dusting myself off.

"Shh. Carol's asleep in her chair. Let's go outside."

It was late fall, I remember. A cold day. Rainy. We stood outside the garage door and I, without my jacket, hugged my arms to keep myself warm. Lauren's eyes looked tired.

"You okay?" I asked.

"My neighbor, Marilyn," Lauren said, watching me for a sign of recognition. "You've met her. She drives that old Corolla. Anyway, yesterday, she had a total stroke. Right in front of me. She was putting some crap in her trunk when I got home, I said hi, she said hi, regular chitchat. I run upstairs and come back down, and she comes over in a panic, talking gibberish. I mean, literal gibberish. Complete aphasia, right? She couldn't speak. Lost all her words. She's almost laughing, like . . . panicking, but laughing, and trying to talk to me, putting her hand in her mouth to try to make her tongue work the right way. I'm trying to get her into my van, but she wouldn't get in . . ." Lauren sighed. "I finally got her over and got her admitted at critical care. But then it's like, back home, I'm in her house, trying to figure anything out, *anything*, insurance, family, whatever. Her son's a fucking deadbeat, worthless. So, you know, dealing with that."

"Can I do anything?"

"No, I've got it. Really. Malcolm's helping too. Will she be able to live at home again? Will she be able to drive? Who knows? I'm worried about her. She's not even sixty, Neil. I worry. Then I come here, and it's just . . . I just want Carol to have one good day, you know? One. Can't she pick up, just once? Can't the sun shine on her for just one day?"

"How is she doing right now?" I asked.

"Confused. Very confused. Rough day, like they all are lately. No sunshine. I am glad she's finally getting some rest."

"I'm sorry," I said, and Lauren shrugged.

"Some days are better than others," she said. "We need to talk to the doc about her meds. How is Wendy?"

"Same as always," I said. "They thought she maybe had an infection last week, but it turned out to be—"

"Can I meet her?"

"Can you meet . . . who?"

"Can I meet Wendy? Will you take me to see her? I understand if that's too strange. But I'd like to meet her. Someday. If it's okay."

I didn't know what to say. "Let me think about it."

It seemed, in that moment, not proper somehow. But I considered it for a couple days, and it became hard for me to come up with any real reason to say no. Why shouldn't I take her to make an introduction of sorts? I didn't want Chris to know about it, though, so I confirmed that he'd be at his basketball camp one Saturday, and I checked to make sure that Shanice would not be working that night. If there was any way it would get back to my son, I figured, it would be through some innocent comment made by her.

The day we went to Wendy's place was cold and clear. We took Lauren's van to get there. Once we arrived, I glanced inside first to double-check that Shanice was not in, then waved for Lauren to follow me inside. Wendy's room was dark and quiet. I leaned down and gave her a kiss on the cheek.

"So," I said, kneeling next to the bed and touching my wife's shoulder, "this is Wendy."

Lauren nodded, but said nothing. She seated herself on the opposite side of the bed, and took Wendy's wrist in her fingers. At first I was surprised by the intimacy of the gesture, but then realized—given her vocation, maybe it was just habit—that Lauren was feeling for Wendy's pulse. Lauren kept her fingertips pressed there for a long time.

"This is Wendy . . ." I repeated, trailing off.

What could I say? If my old love could meet my new love—truly, coherently—what would even be discussed between the two? Would Wendy approve? Would Lauren approve? Would they argue? Would they caution each other, suggest I was toxic, suggest that the other should consider not getting involved? Perhaps my worthiness would be discussed. Or maybe they would simply talk about the weather.

I stood up. The whole situation seemed too absurd. "This is just . . . I'll be at the van." I went outside and stood in the chilly air. Why did I agree to it, really? Maybe I'd imagined some sort of absolution, or some sort of direction toward the proper path going forward. But there was nothing of the sort, and I stood in the cold and stewed about it. Lauren took longer than I thought she would to join me, at least five minutes, maybe it was almost ten, and I was nearly shivering when she came back out.

"Okay," she whispered when she rejoined me, and she unlocked the car so we could get inside. She didn't speak again until we'd been driving for a bit.

"It's a very nice place," she finally said.

"Yes, it is." I stared ahead at the road.

"And a good staff?"

"Yep."

The van rolled over a series of hills, and Lauren started to cry. "God, I'm sorry, Neil. I should have never—"

"It's fine," I said flatly. "How is your neighbor doing?"

"Stop it," she said. "Stop. Don't be an asshole, Neil." She shot me a look with her red-ringed eyes. "I like you so much, but please don't ever be that way. I just never really understood." She wiped her eyes with the sleeve of her jacket. "I never understood how it had to be for you, I mean. The whole thing, all of it. I'm sorry."

------ ———————— ------

After the girls finally stop complaining enough for us to complete a long workout (notable for no mention of my nearly healed lip, for no one being crapped on by a bird, and for the way Cassie Jennings and Amy Vandekemp seem to have bonded since last Friday), I have a surprisingly invigorating run home. There's a nice breeze, it's cooled off a bit, and my legs feel fresh. In my body's effort, the drudgery of the day is washed away, and the news about Denise Masterson is, at least for the time being, forgotten. I find Chris has beaten me home when I get there, and he's talking to someone on his phone in the living room.

"I tried to flip it in the pan," I overhear him saying. "Wait, I swear I did it exactly like you showed me. I did! I tried it and it was like, complete disaster. I was scooping noodles up from *everywhere*. I don't get . . . I don't get how you can do it with your left hand too. No, I did not throw it out, I had it for lunch. I was hungry!"

He talks for a while more while I sit in the kitchen and tap out a couple emails on my phone. I hear him say goodbye, and he comes in to join me. He has to sit at our kitchen table at an angle so his long legs can stick out into the room.

"Hey," I say. "Was that Uncle Mike?"

"Yeah."

"How's he doing? You talk to him more than I do, now."

"He's good. He said there might be a little scholarship if I want it. Emphasis on the word little."

"Do you want it?"

"Dad," he says dramatically, rolling his eyes and throwing up his hands. I laugh.

"What? I'm serious! This is your call."

"I'm not *ready* to make this call."

"When does Mike need an answer?"

"The deadline is November thirtieth."

"That gives us a little time. Are you cooking for us tonight?"

"I thought I would. Do you want to know what I'm making? Or do you want it to be a surprise? Uncle Mike emailed me the recipe."

"Let's make it a surprise," I say.

I head back to my room to clean myself up. On my phone I find that Lauren has texted me a single word: LOVE? The question mark is intriguing. I don't think of it as needy, really, but it doesn't seem like Lauren. She's often more assertive. Maybe because I'm feeling so invigorated by my run home, I send the word "love" as a reply. No question mark. A simple confirmation. An instant passes, and my phone begins to buzz with an incoming call from EL DEE.

"Hey," she says. "Thank you for your text."

"So that counts as saying it?" I ask.

"I think it counts." A pause. "Good day?"

"The kids were in a daze today, but it was all right. Summer's over. What about you?"

"Studying. Drank too much tea. I'll be up late."

"Test is Wednesday? In Lansing? Or Thursday?"

"Wednesday. Making the drive tomorrow morning. But I'll stop to see Carol before I go."

"I wish I could see you before you go," I say.

"I don't think you can. Not tonight, and how would you be able to come during the day tomorrow?"

"You'd probably want me to go check the utilities in the basement if I showed up."

"You can say no whenever," she says tonelessly.

"Go study," I say. "Get rest for your drive tomorrow."

There's a small sound, an almost-sigh, and Lauren simply says, "Goodnight, Neil."

I'm feeling just a little unsettled after the odd conclusion to our conversation, and I sit on my bed for a few long moments holding my phone between my hands, before the rich aroma (and off-key singing) coming from our kitchen draws me back out into the house.

My brother Michael's new, latest, soon-to-open restaurant on Chicago's South Side is a French-Vietnamese hybrid, and his current menu planning is seriously influencing his young disciple in my home. The house is filled with the smell of chili, cinnamon, and anise, and Chris warns me not to come into the kitchen lest I ruin the surprise.

"This is a quick one tonight, Dad," he says. "Too much homework for a major production. Keep out of here!"

Our landline rings while I wait. I'd like to get rid of the old phone and go cell-only, but I hang on to it and a listing in the phonebook so my students can get in touch. The caller ID says UNKNOWN, but I answer anyway.

"Hello?" I say. There's no greeting in return, no sound on the line, so I say hello again. There's nothing, so I end the call and return the handset to its charging cradle. I take a step toward the couch, and the phone rings again. Once again: UNKNOWN.

"Hello?" I say slowly. Now there's a little sound in return, almost like suppressed laughter.

"Not cool," I say, and hang up.

About thirty seconds later, the phone rings again. I'm ready to shout something into the handset when I pick it up this time, but I don't, because the ID says Samples, which is the last name of a pair of identical twins in my AP class.

"Hey, Mr. K.?" A young but confident voice greets me. "It's Ross." The twins, Ross and Justin, are practically indistinguishable from each other.

"Ross, what's up? Did you just try to call me?"

"Nope. But hey, Justin is having some test done on his liver Wednesday morning, and he was thinking you could—"

"Whoa, wait up, is he okay? Is he going to miss class?"

"Oh no, he's fine, he's just having this thing where they use radioactivity to test his liver. He'll be back in the afternoon. We were thinking it would be cool if you used your Geiger counter on him."

"Are you messing with me? Is Justin there?" There's a pause, and a voice more or less the same as the first comes on the line.

"Hey, Mr. K."

"Justin, why is Ross telling me this and not you? Are you okay?"

"I'm fine. I was just busy. Do you still have the Geiger counter from regular physics? We could play like, identify the Samples twins through radioactivity."

"Justin, is your mom or dad there?"

"Hold on."

A moment later Susan Samples comes on.

"Hi, Neil, how have you been? Did you and Chris have a good summer?"

"Sue, is your son okay?"

"Oh, it's nothing. He's fine. They think he has an infection in his gallbladder. His liver enzymes were messed up. So he's getting a test. No biggie."

"Is it a biggie if the rest of the class knows about it, and if I check how radioactive your son is with a Geiger counter? I think I'd need your approval to share something like that with the group."

"Sure! That sounds terrific." Sue Samples is a complete free spirit, a literal product of the original Summer of Love.

"Let me talk to Justin again." The phone is handed off once more. "All right," I say, "if you're okay with it, we'll do something fun. Maybe you guys could dress identically."

"Right on, Mr. K."

I laugh after hanging up, both at the ridiculousness of the exchange and the sudden interesting possibility of having a radio-active individual in my classroom. I could graph how "hot" he was over the course of the class (which, I'm sure, the girls would find pretty funny), or, if he's game, he could hide in a locker somewhere in the science wing while we try to find him with the counter. I'll chew on this one.

Chris calls me into the kitchen to a great bowl of steaming broth framed by chopsticks and little bowls of Asian-looking condiments. Chris keeps a vast stash of Mike's "secret ingredients" stored in a red plastic milk crate in our pantry, and many of them seem to be on display over our table now.

"It's pho, Dad," Chris says, making sure he's correct in his pronunciation. *Fuh*. "South Vietnamese. Uncle Mike calls it the original fast food."

I've had pho before, but never like this. Whatever Mike calls it, Christopher's rendition is incredible.

"Okay," I say between slurping bites. "This is going in your greatest hits. You are making this again."

"Serious? You'll tell Uncle Mike? I don't think he believes me when I tell him stuff came out good. It was actually pretty easy to make."

"Of course I'll tell Mike. This is awesome."

I clean up the kitchen while Chris chips away at homework out in the living room. The landline rings again, and though I'm expecting it to be Ross or Justin calling back, Chris hollers, "Unknown name! Should I pick up?"

"Let it go." I turn off the kitchen faucet as my answering machine greeting plays, so I can hear better, and after the beep, my house fills with a raspy older woman's voice.

"That was just despicable," the voice says. "You deserve what you have coming. They shouldn't just sue you, they should have you arrested!"

I freeze while I listen and the machine beeps again, and it takes my son's laughter to snap me out of it.

"What up, wrong number?" he says. "I kind of wish I'd answered."

"Jeez, you think she was mad about something?" I say, shaking my head while I step over to tap the Delete button on the machine.

"Maybe just a little. You didn't piss anybody off lately, did you, Dad?"

"Not that I can think of." I start to laugh too. The woman sounded furious. "What about you?"

"No," he says. "No one I know of."

I go back to cleaning the dishes. When I reach to flip on the light over the sink, the light burns out: *pop!* An instant later, Chris peeks in through the entryway.

"Light go out?" he asks. "I'll get you a bulb."

When Christopher was little, around six years old, he developed a terrible fear of the dark. Seemingly out of nowhere—it had never bothered him before—he refused to enter any room that wasn't first illuminated. Bedroom, bathroom, basement, garage; if he needed to go to one of those places, it was always, "Mommy, can you come with me?" or "Daddy, will you turn on the light?" I think of this fondly now, but at the time it was really sort of a pain.

Bedtime was the worst. I felt the easiest thing would be for us to just leave a light on for Chris out in the hall, or put a bright night-light in his room, but Wendy thought it was necessary for Chris to tough it out and get over it. This was a real reversal for us: Wendy was usually the softie in questions of parental direction, where I always seemed more ready to be stern. I guess if I think about it, I probably was just exhausted by being woken up by our son's nightmares every night. But, as I often did, I gave in to Wendy's wish. We'd push Christopher through it.

My wife developed a little script for when we put Christopher to bed. She'd sit next to him to tuck him in, and she'd offer to tuck in all of his demons as well.

"Now," she'd say, "it's time to tuck you in, then we're going to turn off the light, okay?"

"No," Chris would reply, shaking his head. It went almost the same every night. "I want the light on."

"There's nothing you need to be afraid of, Chris."

"There's a shadow. It's a scary face on the wall."

"We can tuck that shadow in. Here we go." She used her hands to arrange the covers next to Chris. "Goodnight, shadow!"

"My jacket looks like a ghost the way it hangs."

"Let's tuck that ghost in. There. He's not so scary. Goodnight, ghost!"

Chris would start to smile, in spite of himself. "What about mean skulls? Or monsters?"

"Mean skulls and monsters are pushovers for a big guy like you. Let's tuck them in too. There. Ready for lights out?"

Our son would shake his head. "I don't like the darkness."

"The darkness is good, Chris. It's like a soft blanket that lets you sleep. I'm going to tuck the darkness in too. Here we go. We'll tuck the darkness right in." She'd draw the covers up tight under his neck and give him a kiss, and I, standing by the door, would flip out the light. "There. Now everyone is cozy. Are you cozy?"

"Yeah."

"Goodnight, Chris."

"Goodnight."

After a couple weeks of this, or maybe it was more, the darkness was no longer an issue. The routine didn't stop, though. Not for a year at least. Even when he was a little older, and far past his fears of the night, Wendy would ask if he needed her to tuck the darkness in before he went to sleep. He'd only say yes if I wasn't around, but she'd tell me about it after.

I couldn't do it for him. I didn't have the right touch with the darkness. I lacked the proper delivery. And after Wendy went away, there was no one to banish that darkness for either of us.

Following Wendy's accident, after weeks of restless nights, I gave in and put a night-light out in the hallway. It's been there ever since.

While Chris settles in to work on his homework, I return to my room to try Lauren once before I go to sleep. The night-light in the hallway flickers as I walk past. I dial, and the call goes immediately to voice mail.

"Hey," I say, "you're probably studying, give me a call if you get the chance, okay? That was . . . sort of a weird goodbye we had earlier." I end the call and sit there, at the foot of my bed, staring at the phone like a zombie. I almost call her once again, but instead I send a text:

Call me when you can. Love.

Why is it so much easier to express it that way?

From: xc.coach.kaz@gmail.com
To: w.kazenzakis@gmail.com
Sent: September 10, 11:08 pm
Subject: No Reply

I wait and I wait, Wendy.

Shouldn't I be pretty good at waiting by now? Shouldn't I be an expert?

CHAPTER TWELVE

In the morning, after a night of fitful rest and several more hang-ups on the landline, there's no reply—text or otherwise—waiting for me from Lauren. Her upcoming exam is a big one, I know, and she takes her studies very seriously, so I guess it's not too unusual that she hasn't had the time to get back to me. There's that good-night, though, that strange goodbye that's been bugging me, really troubling me; there was a gravity to it that threw me off.

What the hell. I am getting myself wound up over nothing.

Chris and I share our ride in to school, and he seems chagrined by the fact that I have not packed any leftovers from his outstanding batch of pho for my lunch today.

"It's mostly liquid, Chris," I say. "The thing would probably come open in my pack and get all over my stuff."

There's no text waiting when we get to school, and there's not one before the first bell of the morning, either. I have a strict no-gadgets-in-class rule for the students, and I adhere to it myself, so I keep my phone stashed deep in my pack, no matter how much I wish I could sneak over to check it. The kids' attitudes today are not so different from how they were yesterday: a foggy mix of boredom and shell shock. Isn't this academic *ennui* supposed to start a few weeks later in the school year? At least, as far as I can tell, there is no audible gossip about Denise Masterson. I try my best to keep my first-period class engaged, and I do manage to score some points toward the end of the class when I let them know we'll be watching a movie tomorrow.

No texts come during any of the early class periods. Now I'm starting to worry that something might actually be wrong, and, knowing that she's going to be driving this morning, I'd like to be sure that's not the case.

I know it seems stupid, but was it something I said?

I leave a message at lunchtime, and another during my open afternoon period. And one more after that for good measure. Good luck on your test, I say. Drive safe to Lansing. Call me when you get there? Is everything okay?

Really, is everything okay?

I have an open period in the afternoon, and after going over some homework assignments, I check my district email. I'm surprised to find that, instead of the six or so messages I usually have waiting for me in there, I have more than eighty, all coming from a different random Yahoo! email address. Beth Coolidge got burned and unleashed a virus on the school network by opening something like this last year, so I delete them all without looking and make a note to myself to mention it to Cory the next time I see him.

AP Physics serves to lighten my mood. The Ross twins keep straight faces when I make a few comments about Geiger counters—without giving away our plans—as a setup for my expected radioactive student tomorrow. Cross-country practice is not so bad either; a welcome break from a day of stupid anxiety. No punitive sprints are needed, and the girls and I have a long, easy run through town, down along the Big Jib River bike path to the waterfront and back. We pass Lauren's condo, and I see that her upstairs blinds are closed.

After practice, there's still nothing waiting on my phone, and my anxiety begins to tilt toward exasperation.

I run home through another afternoon of glorious, temperate weather. Dazzling sunshine at my back on the highway north, cool shade embracing me as I turn through the trees. Sprinting around the last bend, breathing hard and pushing myself, to the gravel of my drive and . . .

Lauren's car is parked at Carol's.

This is peculiar. I take a step toward the farmhouse, but stop myself; maybe she carpooled to Lansing with one of the other nurses? Two of her coworkers are in the program with her; that would make sense. I could stop in and see if she's there, find out just what in the world is going on, but if she wanted to let me know what was going on, maybe she would have called me back last night and *maybe* I'm feeling just a little pissed off about this right now?

Thinking about it, I don't feel like I've done anything wrong.

I continue past Carol's house to my own; Lauren can be addressed after I'm cleaned up and composed. I take the side door into my kitchen, where I drink some water, looking around for the canister of Chris's magic recovery powder. That stuff was pretty good. I find it in the pantry, on top of his crate of secret ingredients, and mix myself a batch before going to the living room to check the answering machine. The glass nearly falls from my hand when I enter the room, however; Lauren is sitting on my couch, staring at the floor.

"What . . . what are you doing here? Shouldn't you be downstate?"

She's slouched forward, with her hands folded over her knees, and her bag is slumped on the floor between her feet.

"I'm late," she says, in a voice barely loud enough to hear.

"I would say so. Why are you here and not at your exam? And does it have anything to do with why you wouldn't call me—"

"I'm seven days late getting my period. I've basically skipped my period, Neil."

"Oh," I say. I sit down on the arm of the couch, with my back to her. "Oh."

"That's why I'm freaking out. That's why I didn't call you back."

"I see."

"I didn't know how to tell you. I didn't know what to say. And when I started to think about everything, I mean, really think about how this whole thing is, you and me, I really freaked out. I thought, what am I doing?"

I twist and slide down to take a seat next to her.

"Do you think you're pregnant?" I ask. Lauren opens her mouth as if to say something, but she doesn't. Instead she leans forward to reach into her bag, pulls out a handful of chocolate-bar-sized foil wrappers, and drops them with a clatter to the floor in front of her.

"What are those?" I ask.

"Pregnancy tests. I got them from my office. We have boxes full of them."

"Have you taken one yet?"

"No."

"Are you going to?"

"Do you want me to?"

"What are you doing, telling me not to pull out, when you—"

"I was in my safe time, Neil, I was supposed to start any minute!"

"Jesus," I say. I'm trying to mentally tally all our recent unprotected encounters, and I'm losing count. "Why didn't you tell me?"

"I was waiting to start! I've been a couple days late before while we've been together."

"This late?"

"I didn't tell you because I didn't want you to worry about it. And now . . . oh God, I don't know, I don't know! And you know what scares me the most? Do you want to know?"

I'm pretty sure I'm going to find out regardless of what I say, so I keep quiet.

"Sometimes I feel like you're more dedicated to a woman who's *not even there* than you are to me."

"Yes, take the test," I say flatly.

Lauren picks up one of the foil packs and tears it open as she stomps to the bathroom in the hall. The door stays open. I hear the trickle of her urination, I hear the toilet flush. I wait, and wait, and I hear my own blood rushing in my ears. Then another sound: the sound of a sudden, choking sob, Lauren sobbing, the sound of her feet running back down my hall, the sound of my front door swinging open and hitting the wall.

The sound of her car driving away.

I rise to my feet and go to the bathroom, but I already know what I'm going to find. On the edge of the vanity is a shiny beige plastic form with the words "Positive if Second Line/Single Line Control" printed beneath a little window sculpted into the material. I grab it with shaking hands and hold it up close to my eyes.

The window is painted with two unmistakable blue lines.

Clutching the test, I sink to the edge of the tub, bend over, and put my head between my knees.

I run to Alan's house, barge in without knocking, and head straight to his study. He's seated at his desk, reading now, not flying or watching videos, and he pushes his glasses to his forehead as he peers up at me.

"You look a little rocky, Neil."

I pull the test from my jacket pocket and toss it to him, and Alan lets out a low whistle as he examines it.

"Did Chris get someone in trouble?"

"I got someone in trouble. Lauren is pregnant."

Alan says nothing. He places the pregnancy test next to his book, and pushes his chair away from his desk.

"Sit down," he says. Alan leaves the room and comes back with a glass of water. "You want a sedative? Klonopin? Kristin has some. You're looking pretty—"

"I do not want a fucking sedative! What I want is for this to have not happened!"

"Well, it did. Unexpected things come to us, Neil. You know that. Probably better than anyone."

"Fuck," I say. "Fuck!"

"Drink," Alan says, pointing at the glass. "Come with me." I down the water and follow him back outside, and we cross the lawn to Mega-Putt. Alan unlocks a shed with a key from his pocket, ducks inside, and emerges with a pair of putters. "Come on," he says. "Front nine, seven wonders of the ancient world." He takes a golf ball from his pocket and delicately places it at the tee. I'm nearly shaking as I watch him. "Plus a couple from the new world the classical historians missed. Number one is the Hanging Gardens of Babylon. It'll look much better next spring when I can grow some flowers. You go first."

"Are you shitting me? This is happening and you want me to play a fucking game of Putt-Putt?"

"I'm giving you the first turn," he says calmly. "Go."

I shouldn't be so stunned by this latest turn of events. I've been in this situation before. Wendy and I dated all through college, with one moderately bitter, brief interruption suggested by me our junior year to "see other people" that ended up with us deciding we were pretty happy seeing each other after not seeing anyone else at all. We were comfortable, we knew each other's habits, and, while we never overtly discussed marriage, we knew without saying it that we were probably headed in that direction. Probably. It was a novelty for our friends that we'd been long-distance high school sweethearts, and it became something we sort of subtly boasted about. We had about us, perhaps, a mild air of superiority.

Our senior year at Michigan State, against her parents' wishes (and with some objection by my mother), we moved into an apartment together. Our neighborhood was made up of mostly graduate students, established couples, some even with children, and the friendships we made with our older neighbors seemed to cement our superior fantasyland self-image. It was as if we were playing house, playing grown-ups like we'd skipped over some vast, unnecessary area of adolescence. We'd never known about it, and never really missed it.

I was studying physics, and had been accepted into a master's program in Kyoto, Japan, to do research work with the possibility of continuing for my PhD. Wendy, a linguistics major, was looking into English-teaching programs through the university there. We were excited—*so excited*—for this adventure, for making a home overseas and learning a new language and meeting new friends and building on our superior image of ourselves.

Then, in the early spring, Wendy missed a period too.

She'd been taking the pill since our first clumsy encounters our senior year in high school when we'd started having sex, and decided after a few years that she didn't like how moody it made her feel. To be honest, I didn't care for it either, and I was happy for her to be through with it. She felt her moodiness might have even been responsible for our brief breakup, and she didn't want something like that to happen again. So she quit. After that we used condoms—usually—and eventually she was fitted for a diaphragm, which we also used, when we remembered it. Did it fail some night, or had we simply been lazy? It could have been either.

Everything changed. Everything. Japan was out of the question. Maybe we could have handled a baby overseas if we were older, if we were actually as mature as we believed ourselves to be. But we were really just kids, and didn't even want to try. Wendy suffered with terrible morning sickness at first, and missed many of her classes. I knew I'd need a job, quickly, and found there were some grants in the state to help with getting a teaching certificate. The state needed science teachers, and doors opened pretty easily for me in that direction.

An abortion seemed out of the question too. How could we consider it, really, when I'd been born to someone in presumably far worse circumstances? The very fact that I was living made us feel obligated to deal with the consequences of what we'd done, and the fact that my parents had gone to the trouble of adopting me and making me part of their family only strengthened our decision to follow through with it. Do I think differently about it now? I'm fine with anyone who needs to make that choice. I just couldn't have done it myself back then. Wendy couldn't have either.

And anyway, I love my son.

My parents were incredibly supportive. Whatever help we needed, they told us, they'd do what they could. I think they were impressed that we were going through with having a baby. To us, maybe, after the reality of it sunk in, it just seemed one more part of our grown-up illusion.

We drove up to Port Manitou over spring break to tell Wendy's parents. Wendy was less nervous about it than I was. We'd planned the trip weeks before we'd known about the pregnancy, and Dick and Carol had no idea what was coming. We told them at dinner the first night. Carol cried, and Dick just stared at me while Wendy squeezed my hand under the table.

Despite Wendy being pregnant with our child, they still made us sleep in separate beds that night.

Dick asked me to go for a walk the next morning. He brought a shotgun along, broken over his shoulder as was his habit on walks we'd taken in the past. It had never seemed quite so threatening before.

"So what will you be doing for work?" he asked me, picking his way through some underbrush.

"Teaching," I said.

"My mother was a teacher, did you know that?"

"I didn't."

"Like your father. A teacher. I have a great respect for what he does. And for his intellect. It's good that you've taken after him."

I didn't know what to say, so I followed without speaking. We worked our way up through the just-blossoming cherry trees to the cedar woods, and silently went on through the low green scrub until we reached a sandy bank of the Little Jib River, broad and murky with spring runoff.

"My brothers and I played here," Dick said, nodding. I wasn't sure if he was looking for a reply, so I said nothing. "Right here." He nudged some dead leaves and earth with his toe and they splattered into the water. "Once when I was little . . . oh boy, I was tagging along behind Charlie and Ed, my big brothers, just being a pest, really. They were trying to get me to go home, and I was hiding from them, right here where we are now. And what do you know, I slipped off this bank and fell into the river when they weren't looking. It was springtime, like now, the water was running just as big. Maybe even bigger. I tumbled in and went right down to the bottom of this eddy." He pointed to a spot in the water. "I couldn't swim, you know. I was just a little guy. I remember going under and looking up, I remember water going over me, branches floating over and the way the light came through it all . . . I wasn't scared, not at that moment. It seemed peaceful, the way I recall it." He adjusted the gun on his shoulder and gazed into the creek. "Well, who knows how long it took them to figure out what was going on, but after what seemed like a long while Ed hopped in and grabbed me, it wasn't so deep for him, he yanked me up by the collar so I could get myself some air. Charlie bent down—right here—and pulled us both out. It sure did scare me then, Neil. After they got me out, it scared the daylights out of me. Charlie was white as a ghost. I guess I didn't realize how close I was to being a goner. He knelt down and shook me, I was all wet and he shook me by the shoulders 'til I started to cry, and he said, 'Good lord, Dickie, don't you ever pull a dumb shit thing like that again. And whatever you do, don't tell Mom or Pop!'"

Dick shook his head and smiled a half smile, saying nothing else. I kept quiet. He resumed walking along the riverbank, along through the brush and with the current toward the lake, and I followed. He spoke again, more softly now, almost impossible to hear over the rumbling spring current and the twigs snapping under our feet. "It sure did stick with me, Neil," he said. "But I never said a thing about it to my parents, and my brothers and I never did discuss it again." He lifted a fallen branch from the ground and tossed it underhand into the water, and we watched it float away. "Later on, I never, ever let Wendy come up here if I could help it. Even when she was old enough to handle herself, I still worried. I know it was awfully silly of me. All the things she did, all the ways she could have ended up in trouble, just driving in a car, you know, or a thousand times in that little boat of hers. But this place, this river, it scares the hell out of me. I know it's foolish, but it's my own fear, and I put it on to her. What would you do if your own child drowned, Neil? How could you live with yourself if you could have done something to help it?"

We turned south and pushed our way through the brush beneath the cedars until the growth opened up into a rising dune. We climbed up and looked back east over rows of blossoming fruit trees toward the field, and beyond that, rising over the newly leafing treetops, the roof of the farmhouse. Behind us, Lake Michigan spread blue green to the horizon.

"If you can get a job in Port Manitou, if you can save up some money, you and Wendy could build a house here on the property."

"That's very generous, Mr. Olsson. But I don't really know any-thing about how to build a house."

"I'll give you a hand with it." He looked at me. "You'll always watch out for my daughter? You'll take care of her, and your baby, no matter what?"

I nodded. "I will. I swear I will."

"I think you mean what you say." He turned back to the orchard and put a hand on my shoulder. "That's good enough for me."

I don't really have the patience or disposition to be playing Mega-Putt right now, but Alan gently urges me on, calmly giving me a guided tour of his project.

"Hole number three, Lighthouse at Alexandria. Tallest man-made thing in the world for centuries. Anyway, what are you going to do? About this thing with you and Lauren."

"I don't know. I really don't." Putter gripped in trembling hands, I tap the ball, and miss widely. "She took the test, she broke down crying, and she drove away. We didn't even talk about any-thing. I'm hoping she comes back. Before Chris comes home. He won't be done with his stuff until later tonight—"

"Hang on a minute," Alan says, leaning his club against some concrete statuary to draw his cell from his pocket. "Give me just a second." He punches his finger on the pad, and holds the phone to his ear. "Kristin? Hey, sweetie, listen . . ." He turns away from me and walks circles in the grass while he talks. I take deep breaths while I watch him. He swings back in front of me and stops.

"Uh-huh," he says, nodding. "Yes. Okay. Talk to you soon."

"What's up?" I ask him.

"Kristin is going to give Lauren a call, then she'll call us back."

I take another deep breath. On my next turn putting, I miss again.

"But I'm serious here, Neil. What are you going to do? Do you love Lauren?"

"Of course I do, you know that."

"Does she know that?"

"Yes."

"Do you tell her?"

"I think I . . ." I look off across his yard to the orchard. "I kind of suggested we get married when we were walking home from your place."

Alan nods. "You two were a happy pair that night. Did you mean it when you asked her?"

"I think so," I say, and Alan raises his eyebrows. "No, I really did."

"Next question then. Are you ready to raise a child with her?" He nudges my ball into the cup with his own club. "That was close. I'll give you that one."

"The thought of a child is so . . ." I clench my fists around the handle of the putter. "*Another* child. It's not . . ."

"It's here, Neil. This is happening." He places the ball at the next tee. "The Mayan pyramid at Chichen Itza. Obviously Herodotus would never have known about it when he was compiling his list of wonders, but it was certainly magnificent. Go ahead."

"Fuck me," I hiss. I stand at the ball and give it a quick angry swat, and it jumps across a wooden barrier into another vignette. Alan nods.

"You weren't supposed to go for the Colossus of Rhodes."

"Fuck the Colossus, Al! Jesus fucking Christ!" I throw the putter with a sidearm toss so forceful it flies through the air with a helicopter sound, reaches the highway, and bounces across into the opposite ditch. "Are you missing what's going on here?"

"My trying to help you out is what's going on here."

I shake my head, let out a guttural cry of "*Augh!*" and run to the road and south toward the orchard. When I come to the trees, the sheltering regular columns of trees, I turn into them and sprint as hard as I can. It seems possible sometimes, if I press myself with enough physical effort, to forget about everything. But that mechanism in my running, or in my head, does not seem to be working. Taking in air with great sucking gasps, remembering *everything*, I come through to the field and sprint for my house. Alan rides up the drive on his bike as I get there.

"What the hell?" I shout, throwing up my hands. "Can you give it a rest?" I can't get away from anything, it seems.

"I thought the mini-golf would calm you down," he says, panting.

"No." I stagger, and brace myself with a hand against my house. "No. It did not have that effect." I drop to a seat on the steps to my side door and hold my head in my hands.

"Obviously. I bet throwing the putter felt pretty good though."

I look up. "Alan?"

"You destroyed it. So, what about Wendy?"

"What do you mean, 'what about Wendy?'"

"Are you ready to let go a little bit?"

"What are you talking about?"

Alan's phone sings with a ringtone that sounds like a fugue, and he holds up his hand. "Just a second. Hi, what's up?" He nods with the phone to his ear and says "uh-huh" maybe fifteen times. "Okay. Okay. We're at Neil's house now." He gives me a paternal sort of smile. "Kristin tracked down Lauren. She's going to Lauren's place, and they're going to talk."

"Okay," I say, feeling relief wash over me like a cool running river. "Thank you."

"She's upset, but I think she'll get over it. She's emotional. Give her some time." I nod. "Now, Wendy. There's paperwork you'll need to do."

"I've looked into the paperwork."

"Christopher has let go, Neil. He's beyond it."

"I don't know if—"

"He has. Now it's your turn. And one more thing. This is not a question. It's a command, and I'm stating this to you in the most serious way."

"Okay? What?"

"You need to tell Chris. Everything. You need to tell him tonight."

I nod, and return my head to my hands.

From: xc.coach.kaz@gmail.com
To: w.kazenzakis@gmail.com
Sent: September 11, 4:18 pm
Subject: UPDATE

_____

W-

Everything is fine here.

Really, everything is great.

-N

CHAPTER THIRTEEN

Alan encourages me to clean myself up, and he stays at my house while I go back to my room to shower and change into some regular clothes. Just this transformation is an improvement; I feel already like I'm better equipped to deal with things. When I come back out, I find Alan has made coffee and cleaned up my kitchen.

"Thank you," I say, and he holds out his hands in a supplicant's pose.

"It's nothing. Your landline rang a bunch while you were in the shower. No one left any messages, though."

"I get that sometimes. Beginning of the school year. Kids playing pranks. Little shits." I take a seat at the kitchen table. "Were your kids planned?" I ask. Alan offers me a cup of coffee, and I shake my head to decline. I'm wired enough as it is.

"As planned as they could be, I suppose. We actually had a pretty hard time getting pregnant. Both times. You'd think it would have been easier, for the amount of practice we got—"

"Stop it. Really."

"You need to lighten up," he says. "So how will it start? The talk, I mean. With Christopher."

I tap my fingers on the tabletop. "I'm going to try to be as direct as I can be. I mean, I do this with kids all the time at school. I just need to think of it that way. I'm actually pretty good at this stuff, you know?" This is good. If I can view the whole situation with some sort of professional detachment, maybe I can cope with it.

"I know you are," Alan says. He pulls his phone from his pocket to check the time. "When does he get home?"

"He's usually home by now," I say. "But he's got a leadership thing this week after school. Student council—" I'm interrupted by a ringtone, and Alan lifts his hand to stop me talking.

"Hold on. It's Kristin." He steps into the dining room, and I hold my breath. "Hey," I hear him say. "Uh-huh. Yep. Okay. See you in a bit."

"Are they coming over?" I ask as he returns to the kitchen.

"No. Lauren is staying home for now."

"But what—"

"She's calling you in a little bit. She's okay. She's calmed down. You guys are going to be okay."

"Thank you."

"Don't thank me, thank Kristin." Alan peers out the window over my sink, leaning forward so he can see down my drive. "Do you want me to hang around?"

"You don't need to. Thank you, though."

Alan takes his jacket from the back of the chair where it's been hanging. "It's nothing. You'd do the same for me. Of course, I wouldn't be in a mess like this in the first place."

"Jesus, shut up. Don't you ever take a break?"

Alan shrugs. "You know I'm just messing with you. To lighten your mood." I throw up my hands, and he points at me. "Look, it's working!" I shake my head. "Call me after you tell Chris. I want to know how it goes." Alan exits through the kitchen door, and I hear his bike bell as he rides off. I take my own phone from my pocket and check the display in the event I've somehow missed Lauren's call already; there's nothing. The battery shows just a hair more than half a charge, so I plug it into its charger by the answering machine and pace through the house, passing by to check the phone maybe every thirty seconds or so. After who knows how long—maybe just five minutes, maybe a lifetime—I'm too worried I'll miss the call, so I take a seat in the living room recliner and stare at the phone on the shelf. My body will not remain still, though. I get back up, unplug the phone, and pace some more. Ten more minutes pass before vibrate mode shocks my hand. It's Lauren, and I nearly drop the phone to the floor pawing at the screen trying to accept her call.

"Maybe you should come over," she says. "Right now."

I rarely speed while driving, but for this trip, I do. Many of the children of Port Manitou's police forces have been students of mine, and I've been teaching long enough now that some of the cops themselves passed through my classroom when they were younger. If I get stopped, I figure, I've got enough pull that I'll be able to talk my way out of it. Pull is not necessary, though; I tear through town and over the spillway bridge unmolested, and park behind Lauren's open garage door. I bound up the stairs two at a time, and Lauren rises—red-faced and grasping a handful of tissues—from her futon couch as I enter. We come together and I close my arms around her, and we stand that way quietly for a long time before Lauren sighs deeply.

"I think I'm calmed down," she says into my chest.

"Why didn't you call? You should have called."

"I was scared. I was freaking out."

"How did this happen?"

"You can't blame me for it."

"I'm not. I just want to know how."

"It happened, okay? It's not my fault, and it's not your fault. It just is. I'm not ready, and I don't think you're ready, but it happened, and here we are. Right?"

"Okay," I say. "It happened. What do we do? Do you want to be with me?"

She nods, and sniffs. "Yes. I do. Do you?"

"Yes."

"Okay." Lauren wipes her eyes with her fingers.

"All right. Are we going to have the baby?" Lauren gives me a shocked look, her mouth open, when I ask this, and I shake my head. "I'm not saying ending it is what I want. At all. But we need to talk about this. All of this. Do you want—"

"If we end this pregnancy," Lauren says, "that's it. That ends us too. We can't *be*, anymore, if we end this."

"Okay." I say.

"Okay what?"

"Lauren," I say, before taking a long breath to keep myself together. I'm staring straight ahead at a bookshelf I assembled only days ago. It feels more like an age. "If we can't be . . ." I draw another breath, and reach for her hand. "I couldn't take that. It would break me. I would break. Sometimes I feel like I am barely holding myself together. Most of the time I'm okay. But other times . . . if you weren't there, that would finish me off. I'd break."

"It would break me too," she says, in a voice I can barely hear.

"Let's not break."

She nods, and whispers, "Okay." She sniffs again, turns to reach into her bag on the futon, and lets out a half laugh when she straightens back up with a handful of pregnancy tests. "I guess we should get a second opinion," she says. "I need to pee anyway." She clutches the tests with both hands and crosses the room, but stops at the entry to her hallway.

"Come on," she says. "Don't leave me alone for this one, okay?"

I follow her and stand outside the door while she goes to the bathroom; she laughs at me and says I can come in, but I wait in the hall until she flushes. We lean together over the sink to watch the test. The control line is there, solid and obvious, and we wait and wait with me looking over her shoulder until, like an old developing Polaroid, we see the second blue line come into view.

"There's our second opinion," I say.

"I guess we're having a baby," Lauren says. She laughs, and starts to cry at the same time. "I don't know if I'm ready! I don't know what to do with a baby."

"We'll be fine." I wrap my arms around her from behind. "You love them, and take care of them, and hope they turn out okay. That's all you can do."

"You love them," Lauren says, and she turns around and kisses me. "And all this time, have you loved me? I'm not just some secret of yours?"

"I really do. You know I do."

"Okay. We'll be fine then. What about Chris?"

I step back from her, and my throat tightens. "I'm going to tell him."

"When?"

"Soon. Sometime soon. Tonight, I think. I really should tonight."

"Do you want me to be there when you do it?"

"I don't think that would be a good idea."

"I understand. Do you want me to move in?"

"What, you mean now? Today?"

Lauren laughs and sniffs, and gives me a poke in the chest. "No. But soon."

"Yes."

"I can wait, a little, if that would be better for Chris. Oh my God, we're going to have a baby."

"We are." My stomach is tight, partially with excitement, but mostly with terror.

"And the paperwork with Wendy . . ."

"Stop. Can't think about it right now," I say. "I can't. Let's get out of the bathroom."

I step out and start down the hallway, but Lauren grabs the back of my shirt.

"Come lie down."

"You're kidding me."

"No, not for that. Let's just lie down."

Lauren tugs me into her room, and I ease myself back on the bed. She climbs on top of me and presses her face into my shoulder.

"We're having a baby," she whispers. "I'm glad I didn't drink so much Saturday night. We'll have to put all our things together. Will this be our bed? It's not as big as yours. Most of my furniture can stay here—"

"Can the paintings stay here?"

"Stop it. I'm being serious. I'm thinking out loud. We should keep this place. We can rent it out. We should hang on to it. Can we set up your spare room for the baby?" She lifts her head to look at me. "I'm sorry, do you want me to shut up? I'm thinking all over the place."

"It's fine," I say. Like her words, my own thoughts are jumbled. Lauren's weight feels nice on me, not suffocating, and I drag my fingers up and down her back. "We'll figure it all out."

"I should call Kristin," Lauren says, and I cock an eyebrow. "She wanted me to let her know that everything was okay."

"Is everything okay?"

"I think so," Lauren says. "It is. Other than some slight remorse over blowing off my clinical chemistry exam." She smiles. "Yes. I think everything is okay. Are you ready to tell Chris?"

I close my eyes. "I'm ready," I say. But I'm not quite certain that I am.

Racing back up my drive, I curse and smack the steering wheel when I see Christopher's station wagon already parked in front of our house. I wanted to be home first. I wanted to make myself prepared. I also wanted to make sure the pregnancy test wrapper was gone from the bathroom trash. I can't imagine he'd be rooting through the garbage, but then again, who knows what could happen? I don't want him to find out that way.

My son looks up from his homework spread across the kitchen table when I come through the door. He smiles and says hey, but he also looks perplexed by my arrival. Can he sense how nervous I am? Is it obvious to him?

"Had to run an errand," I say. "Your grandma needed something." I hate how easy it is to lie sometimes.

"There was no note," Chris chides me, reaching up to tap the blank whiteboard. "I felt abandoned."

"Stop it. There will be no abandonment."

"What's for dinner?" he asks.

"What's for . . . you aren't cooking?"

"Your night, Dad. You don't remember? Is it old age?"

"Man," I say, doing my best to act genuinely clueless. "I totally forgot it was my night." I consider, just for a moment, taking the seat across from him at our table so I can tell him everything. Right now. But he does need to eat, and it dawns on me that perhaps a neutral setting might be best for the bomb I'm about to drop on him. "Want to go out?" I ask. "Get a burger at the brewpub? I'm pretty beat, to tell the truth. Let's let someone else cook."

"Sure, I guess." He looks over his homework, as if my dinner suggestion will somehow be confirmed there. "That sounds okay."

We take Christopher's car, and I'm mostly quiet for the trip into town while my son tells me about his after-school activities. He catches me up on working out, student council, and the leadership meetings he's been attending. He's back and forth on culinary school, he says. I'm only half able to listen, because my stomach is in a knot. In the brewpub's parking lot I pause with one foot out of the car to check my phone; there are two texts waiting for me, one from Alan, and one from Lauren. Both of them want to know how things are going with Chris. I don't write anything back.

Inside the restaurant we're greeted warmly by the hostess; she's a former student (whose name I can't remember at all) and she seems to know Chris somehow too. She leads us upstairs to the family seating area, and I'm relieved to see that hardly any of the other tables are occupied. This is good. This vacancy will help. A waiter comes and asks if we'd like anything to drink, suggesting to me a good IPA that they've just put on tap.

"I . . ." It's been a long time since I've had a beer, but I doubt it would help. "I'm okay," I say. "I'll pass."

Chris raises his eyebrows when the guy leaves. "Thought you were about to drink on a school night there, Dad."

"One beer would not be so significant," I say. "Maybe one would help me rest. I didn't get the best sleep last night."

"I didn't either," Chris says, and he laughs. "Maybe I should have gotten one." I shake my head and try to act jovial, but the menu is trembling in my hands. Why does this have to be so hard? Here I am. I am having a fine, happy evening out with my well-adjusted son, knowing quite *unhappily* that it's all going to go to hell in a few minutes when I finally get up the courage to tell him my not-so-good news.

"Did you hear about those sophomores, Dad?" Chris asks as he glances over the menu. Our waiter returns with glasses of water and takes our orders.

"What sophomores?"

"I figured you would have heard about it from Mrs. Mackie already," he says. "Some kid sent out pictures of his girlfriend blowing him or something." This nearly makes me choke on the first sip of my water.

"Chris," I say. My heart, as if it couldn't sink any lower, nearly bottoms out at the thought of the Mastersons getting this news.

"What? I'm just telling you what I heard."

"No, I don't know anything about it." What's another lie? "And even if I did, that stuff is confidential and I couldn't say anything anyway. You shouldn't be spreading stories around. What if it's not even true?"

"You're bullshitting, Dad. Everyone knows about it already. They're *all over* the place. Sparks said two different people tried to show him."

"Jesus. Did he look?"

"No, I don't think so. He's not stupid."

"Good," I say. "I'll say something to Peggy. I have to, now that you've told me about it. And if someone tries to show you—"

"Come on, I'm not stupid either."

This has thrown me. I don't know what to say. What the hell, I think. It's time. How do I even begin? I take a long swallow of my water, I ponder it for a moment, and the idea of framing my news with Christopher's own experience comes to me. This might serve as a good way to bring it up. I take another drink, put down my glass, and rest both my hands flat on the table.

"Chris, I have a question."

"Yeah?"

"Okay, when you and Jill were together . . ."

"Dad!" he says, flushing, and I glance to see if any of the other tables have heard him. "Do you think I'm an idiot? We never did anything like that. Jill would have kicked my ass if I ever asked her for pictures like that."

"That's not . . . that's not what I'm asking." Great, Neil. You're getting off to a *great* start here. "It's not what I'm getting at. At all. But, I am happy to hear the news."

"God, Dad." Now Chris looks around to see if anyone has noticed our conversation. "What are you asking me, then?"

"Okay, so, you and Jill, when you were together. You were close."

"We were super close. You know how much I liked her."

"And you were . . ."

"We were . . . ?"

I force myself to keep my gaze directed at Chris. "Intimate."

My son presses his lips together, and snorts a little like he's trying to not laugh.

"What?" I say. "I'm trying to be serious here."

"I'm sorry." He covers his mouth and laughs. "I'm really sorry, Dad. It's like you're warming up to give me"—he makes air quotes—"the Talk. Do you really need to? Didn't we cover everything pretty well the last time we had it?" He snickers at me, and I think, *This conversation is a complete disaster.*

We did indeed have "the Talk" before. Twice, actually. Once, when he was in the sixth grade, Wendy and I sat Christopher down at the kitchen table and calmly asked him if he knew how babies were made. It was a very clinical discussion then, using words like ova and zygote. The technical aspects of conception were thoroughly covered. Later, having to deal with it all on my own, I knew—when Chris and Jill Swart started spending most of their free time together—that the topic would need to be broached in a more realistic manner. After what I thought was a reasonable courtship, an adequate amount of time for their relationship to have progressed, I left a box of condoms on Christopher's bed for him to find. A good icebreaker to the subject, I believed. That night when he went back to his room and I braced myself for the questions he'd soon be asking, I was surprised to hear laughter coming from down the hall.

"You're a little late on this, Dad," he called. "My girlfriend is on the pill."

"Are you serious?" I coughed. What did this mean? Jill was smart? Slutty? Both? "Does that mean you guys are doing—"

Chris poked his head back into the living room. "It? No. Not yet, anyway."

"Have you ever? Or with anyone else?" Chris shook his head, and my body sagged into the chair with relief.

"Has she?"

"I don't think so, Dad."

"Just be smart, okay? It's a serious thing. Take it seriously when you guys decide it's time."

"Okay."

"Be sure you're ready. Both of you. You don't need to push it."

"We're taking it slow," he said. "I really like her."

"That's good, Chris. Be respectful. Keep taking it slow."

At the time, I thought it was good advice. Reflecting on it now, I shake my head in amazement at how naive I was in regard to the life of my own son, despite being confronted with the general craziness of teenage life on a daily basis at work. I'm also amazed by how lucky I got with him, even if now he is sitting here snickering at me while he munches on French fries. He is a solid kid, just like Alan says. And knowing this, I draw a breath and open my mouth to tell him what I need to say.

"Chris, I have to—" My phone starts to buzz in my pocket. I'm certain it will be Alan calling to pester me, or Lauren, but when I pull the thing out to check the display, I see Peggy Mackie's name, and I stop myself from silencing the call. "Hang on," I tell Chris, tipping the phone up so he can't see Mackie's name on the screen. "I need to take this." I turn myself away from the table to answer.

"Neil," Peggy says, sounding stern. "Are you going to be in tomorrow?"

"God. Yes. I'll be in. Can I call you back later, though? I'm kind of—"

"You'll be there in the morning?"

"Just let me know when you need me," I say, and Peggy ends the call without saying goodbye.

"Who was that?" Chris asks as I return the phone to my pocket. I shake my head, and try not to appear dejected.

"Work stuff," I say. I can't say anything else. The waiter comes back and asks if everything's okay. I nod yes, absently, and for the rest of our meal and the whole drive home, I am incapable of saying anything about the situation with Lauren.

Later, in bed, I find it impossible to get comfortable. I flop about in the dark, and listen to my son on the other side of the house: rustling around in the bathroom, brushing his teeth, laughing with a friend behind his closed bedroom door on a late-night phone call. *God, the Mastersons,* I'm thinking. How will Jo take it when we tell her? Will Denise be able to get beyond it, somehow? The boyfriend will not be so burdened. That's always the way. Some kids got in trouble for it two years ago, and the girl's family ended up moving away. How fair is that? *Poor Denise.* I can't think about this now. I need to put it out of my mind.

Additional texts come from Lauren and Al, and I ignore them. At eleven I sit up in my bed and see light spilling from below Chris's door across the hallway. I could get up, I *should* get up, and go talk to him. I could sit at the foot of his bed like I did when he was a little boy and tell him everything I need to say. Maybe it won't be so bad. Maybe, like Alan claims, he'll be okay with it.

But I don't. I can't, and after some time the light beneath his door goes out.

Jo Masterson. I haven't seen her or her husband, Frank, in months. We seem to run into each other a couple times a year, at the store, at the dentist. Not much is ever said; pleasantries are exchanged. Jo always smiles the same sad smile that makes me wonder if somehow Wendy's accident affected her more than it did me. I wonder what her expression will be when she gets the news about her daughter. I try not to think about it.

Now the clock shows ten minutes past midnight. I turn and turn within the sheets to try to make myself comfortable, and when I bring myself to glance at the clock again, it's nearly one thirty. Later I get up to go to the bathroom, and I don't allow myself to look at the time when I bed back down. I know it would just be too depressing.

Maybe I *should* have had that beer.

I kick off my comforter; I pull it back up. This is hopeless. I rise from my bed and go to the spare room, where I power up my laptop and try to look at the news. Nothing worth reading. I open my gmail and there's nothing there, but in my school email I discover another fifty or so new spam messages filling my inbox. Most of the subject lines are nonsense, but one appears repeatedly, reading, TeshCo for the lulz!!! As I select them for deletion, I find a message with the subject THIS OKAY? from the district's domain, a student's name that I don't immediately recognize, and I open it. When I do, I reel back in my chair and cringe. The body of the message says, U PROBLY LIKE SEX WITH THIS KIDS. Attached below it is a photograph of three young girls in swimsuits running through a sprinkler. Thankfully, there's nothing else with it.

I quickly hit the Forward button and address it to the network administrator's email address, adding, Cory, what the hell is this?? to the body of the message. After it's sent, I delete it along with the rest of the spam messages. When they're gone, I'm surprised to find a reply from Cory, dated 1:41 a.m. The message says, simply, I WILL LOOK INTO THIS NEIL K.

It's not like that was the first weird email I've received in my school account, so I'm not going to worry about it. I'll follow up with Cory tomorrow. I check my gmail account one last time before snapping the laptop shut and padding back to my room.

I lie across the bed on my back, close my eyes, and breathe. There are times in the dark, when I'm spent, when I'm exhausted, when I'm incapable of thinking more coherent thoughts, that I wonder what it would be like to be, just for a moment, inside Wendy's brain. I know there's nothing going on—and I mean *nothing*—at the higher levels: I've seen the traces from her scans, and it's just a tiny scribble indistinguishable from background noise. But deep inside, in her primitive, limbic core, there is something, *something* that keeps her going.

Breathe in, breathe out.

Breathe in, breathe out.

Breathe, breathe, breathe, breathe. Close your eyes and breathe without thinking; repeat, without question, ad infinitum.

What does that feel like? Does it feel like anything? I keep my eyes closed, and focus on the rush of air in and out of my nose. What would it be like if that was the only thing I could know?

Breathe in, Breathe out.

Indefinite function, until all function ceases.

With my eyes closed, it's nothing more than static.

From: xc.coach.kaz@gmail.com
To: w.kazenzakis@gmail.com
Sent: September 12, 1:01 am
Subject: News

There is something I need to tell you: I've been emotionally and physically involved with one of your mother's nurses, Lauren Downey, for nearly two years. I'm in love with her, and she's pregnant. I want to marry her.

I'm sorry. I needed to tell you this. I hope you understand.

I need to tell Chris. I am not sure how to do it.

I'll always love you, and I'll always take care of you. Really.

-Neil

CHAPTER FOURTEEN

Just when I feel myself finally drifting off to a deep sort of sleep, my phone buzzes with an incoming call. I blink my eyes into focus enough to accept it and see the clock on the screen reads 5:20 a.m.

"Uh-huh?" I mutter, propping my head up on my phone-holding arm.

"How did it go?" It's Alan, and he sounds far too awake for me. And in his question, the events of the previous day—my whole life, really—return to me.

"It . . . it didn't go."

"What the hell do you mean it didn't go? You didn't tell him?"

"I couldn't. I have some other stuff going on. The timing ended up not being right."

"The timing is never going to be right," Alan says. "I am planning to keep bugging you until you do this. Got it?"

"Fine," I say, and I terminate the call. I fall back to my pillow and hold the phone to my chest. I will do it when I'm ready. Really. I hold the phone aloft and press the Power button to turn the thing off for good. I don't need to be pestered.

It's a chilly, foggy morning, and we need to wipe heavy dew from the windows on Christopher's car before we can leave. Little is spoken, and I'm grateful for it. Could I tell him right now? It might ruin his day. I will tell him after school. I am making a mental note to myself to absolutely do it after school.

Chris drops me off at the science wing with a wave, and takes off for the student lot. With my pack and my coffee mug, I shuffle to my classroom and let myself absorb the last minutes of eyes-shut quiet at my desk before my first students show up and take their seats.

"Mr. K. looks tired," I hear one of the kids whisper, and I manage a wan smile.

The first chapter in my morning class text is called "Physics and You." In an effort to show these underclassmen (or upperclass slackers) that the rules governing the physical world do in fact have some bearing on their lives, I like to embrace this opener with gusto, and we spend the morning watching an accompanying video that seems to consist mostly of trippy footage of soccer balls in parabolic flight along with—in an obvious nod to the delinquents found in every classroom—twenty minutes of slow-motion explosions and ballistics tests. I sit at the back of the room in the dark and try to rest my mind.

"All right," I say as the end credits go blank and I click the room back into light. The kids seem somewhat more attentive today than they were yesterday; maybe the explosions have perked them up a bit. "Do any of you snowboard?" A smattering of hands show across the room. Eyes blink, adjusting to the brightness. "Question: how rad would snowboarding be if there was no gravity? How fast would you go down the hill if the mass of your body was not attracted to the much greater mass of the Earth?" Empty stares. "But if you didn't have any friction," I continue, "it might get scary. Friction between the snow and the base of the snowboard provides negative acceleration to keep you from going too fast." My example doesn't have much of an effect. "Okay, anybody play the guitar?" More hands, more blinking eyes. "So, when you tune up, say, your low E string, and you pluck that string, if it's tuned right, it will vibrate a little more than eighty-two times a second." Brows furrow as they process this. "That's called the frequency of that string. The frequency is eighty-two hertz. Piano players?" No hands this time; the dedicated piano players in the room are most likely freshman girls too shy to admit it. "Middle C is about two hundred and sixty-one hertz. See? This stuff is all around you. So what I want you to do for me tonight, as we wrap up this chapter, is write one paragraph about how physics affects your life. Doesn't have to be typed, you can rip a page out of a notebook if you want, just give me a paragraph. Okay? Questions?"

A shaggy-haired kid by the door raises his hand.

"How many sentences does it have to be to make a paragraph?" he asks.

I'd like to reply with, "Are you kidding me?" but I decide instead to be charitable. "Let's say more than one. Anything else?"

A wannabe jock's hand shoots up in the back of the room.

"Yes?"

"Why'd you have to be so harsh on Cody Tate?"

The reactions in the room to this question vary from nervous laughter to gasps of shock or looks of confusion. I'd put myself in the third group.

"Who is Cody Tate?" I ask. The name resonates somewhere in my foggy head, but I can't recall if he's on any of my current or past rosters. I don't get an answer, though, because the bell rings and all in the room is abandoned. Peggy Mackie is waiting outside my classroom door, and I nod hello to her as the class rises and begins to file out of the room, and call out, "One paragraph, guys, more than one sentence!" Peggy enters when the last kid has gone. The look on her face is serious.

"I heard the pictures were pretty bad," I say.

"Neil, we need you, right now."

I look to the hall for Denise Masterson's parents, but no one else is out there.

"In Karen's office," Peggy says. Karen Harmon is our principal. "Come on." I follow Peggy down the hall. She's walking at a good clip.

"Wendy used to work with Jo Masterson," I say. "Chris knows about it; he mentioned it last night. So I'm guessing it's getting around the school this week." Peggy shakes her head, and we go through the front office back to the principal's office. This is Karen's second year at the helm, and by all accounts she's doing a pretty good job in the post. She's in there, seated at her conference table, along with the school district's attorney whose name I can't remember, and Gracie Adams, the cold and childless president of the school board. The Mastersons are not present, and Peggy makes introductions.

"Neil, you know Ms. Adams, and this is Stu Lepinski, our attorney." Stu rises to reach over an open laptop on the table and we shake hands.

"It's awful," I say, taking a seat between Gracie and Karen. "Do Jo and Frank know yet?"

"Neil," Karen says, looking up from a notepad in front of her. "What happened after school last Friday?"

"What happened? You mean . . ." I look around the room. "This isn't about Denise Masterson?"

"It's not," Karen says softly.

"Are you asking about . . . the fight I broke up?" They remain silent. "Or the ride I took in Cassie Jennings's car? I . . . I was injured, I needed a ride home, I had Amy Vandekemp come so it wouldn't seem inappropriate."

Peggy stares at my lip, and I touch my fingertips to the tiny scab there. "How did you get injured, Neil?" she asks.

"I broke up a fight. We were just wrapping up after practice, and these kids in the parking lot started going at it—"

Stu Lepinski clears his throat. "Would you take a look at this?" he says, spinning his laptop toward me. "Watch this."

He leans over and taps the touchpad, and a video begins to play full screen on the display. The footage is shaky, and in it a form runs toward the camera. I see that *I* am the form, that it's me running, and I hear my own voice call, "Hey!" The screen is a jumble as I come closer, it steadies again, and I watch myself—time expanding like I'm seeing a car accident as it unfolds—I watch myself grab a boy by the shoulders, shake him, and hurl him to the ground. The video cuts abruptly, and now the boy's face is in close-up as blood runs from a cut over his eye and the bridge of his nose.

"I had to like, fight him off me," the boy says in a nasal, pubescent voice, and the video ends.

"Wait a minute," I say. I feel, as I say it, like I'm standing behind myself, watching all this unfold over my own shoulder. "That didn't . . ." I take a deep breath and look around the room. "It didn't happen that way. That has to be fake. It didn't . . ."

They all stare at me.

"Was that Cody Tate?" I manage to ask.

Stu Lepinski raises his eyebrows. "So you do know him?"

"I don't know him at all!" I say, and they continue to stare. "But a student mentioned his name last period. That video is not real."

Stu pulls the laptop back, and types and clicks. "That's what we thought." He glances up at me. "At first. But this was posted online also—"

"Also?" I say.

"It's since been removed," Stu goes on, "but someone emailed Karen a copy last night." He turns the laptop once again, and now I see the same thing happen from a different angle. Run—*hey!*—shake and throw to the ground. *I had to like, fight him off me.* A different cell phone camera, a different angle. A secondary source. I'm incapable of saying anything after the video ends.

"Do you want to see it one more time?" Stu asks. Karen won't lift her eyes from her notepad, and Gracie looks furious.

I shake my head. "It didn't happen that way," I say, but suddenly I doubt my own memory, and the feeling is beyond unsettling. If anything, I feel like I'm going to throw up.

Stu Lepinski points at his laptop with his pen. "Did you have some reason to be angry with Cody Tate?"

"Neil," Peggy says, leaning close to speak into my ear. "Do you have a lawyer?"

"Why would I need a lawyer?" I ask, my voice rising, quavering. I look around the room. "That . . . it didn't happen like that! Have you talked to any of the kids who were there? Did you talk to Amy Vandekemp?"

"We talked to them, Neil," Karen says, without looking up. "They didn't see what happened. They only found you afterwards."

"We have to ask you to leave the building," Peggy says.

"You're firing me?"

"No, it's a suspension—"

"Standard," Stu Lipinski cuts in.

"—while we investigate." Peggy finishes. "Administrative leave while we sort it all out."

"But . . . this afternoon," I stammer. "Justin Samples is radioactive, and the girls are running to the river . . ."

Peggy puts her hand on my shoulder. "I need to escort you off campus now, Neil."

I'm far too stunned to even try to run home, so Peggy, who knows my routine, quietly offers me a ride once I gather up my things from my classroom. I'm shaking as we leave the building, knees wobbly, surprised I can even walk, and it's all I can do to climb up into her Suburban and slump into the passenger seat. My elbow rests on the windowsill as she takes me north out of town, my forehead cradled in my hand. Peggy says nothing as she drives.

This is bad. As if the situation with Lauren wasn't bad enough. This is very, very bad.

"I didn't do that, Peggy," I bring myself to say. "I didn't—"

"I cannot fucking believe this," she snaps. "You, Neil! You, of all people!"

"It didn't happen that way, though."

"Taking matters into your own hands like that—"

"What are you talking about?"

"—when we had everything under control. You didn't even know the details! Do you even have a clue how much you have screwed things up for me? Not to mention the family—"

"Peggy, what the hell? What family?"

Peggy turns her gaze from the road just long enough to give me a withering stare. "How could you in a thousand years have thought punishing Cody Tate on your own would make anything right or easier for the Mastersons?"

"What? Peggy, who is Cody Tate?"

"The boyfriend," Peggy hisses.

"Boyfriend?" My mouth hangs open for a moment. "Denise Masterson's boyfriend? And you think . . . are you saying you think I did that because I was trying to punish some kid I don't even know? I didn't even know about the pictures until you told me Monday!"

"I've *seen* the videos, Neil. From two different phones, and they both show me the same thing. I've talked to the students involved. There's only one story that doesn't line up with the others. You know which one that is? Yours!"

"Fine," I say, holding off panic. "Fine. Just go. Drive."

"What the hell, Neil. I've known you for so long. How—"

"No, really," I say, interrupting her. "Just drive." I rub my face with my hands. "Oh, oh, wait a minute. I need to tell you something. I need to tell you about Sparks. Timothy Sparks. Senior. Friend of

Christopher. Someone tried to show him one of the Masterson pictures. There. You can ask him about it. I needed to tell you, and now I've told you. I'm relieved of my burden."

"Why are you talking about this right now?"

"Isn't it a felony if I don't? If I know that's going on and I fail to report it? Oh, wait, wait, I guess beating a kid up is probably pretty serious too. Assault can be a felony, right?"

"Christ, Neil," she says, shaking her head as we slow to stop at a red light. "Are you cracking up?"

"The video . . . I didn't do that!"

The signal changes to green, but instead of accelerating, Peggy turns to me with narrowed eyes. "You are seriously, *seriously* telling me you didn't do that to Cody Tate," she says slowly.

"I can't believe you'd ever have thought I would in the first place. I broke up a fight, and the kid hit me with his elbow."

"He says he punched you because you were on top of him. He says he was trying to get away."

"Why would I do that?" I ask. "How could I do that? I didn't. But I saw the video too, and now I have to ask myself, did I? Am I going crazy?"

"It doesn't look good. I'll say that."

I have to laugh at this. "Well, how the hell is it supposed to look? It looks terrible. I'm going to lose my job."

"Don't jump to any conclusions yet. You're a well-liked, well-respected teacher. Which makes this so strange to me."

"Wait, wait." I sit up as the Suburban takes off again. "You're telling me not to jump to conclusions? Who just suspended me from my job? What about due process, or benefit of the doubt? Good reputation? Well liked? Who's jumping to conclusions, here?"

"The district's getting slammed with calls about it, Neil. Not just local callers, either. Nasty reactions and emails from all over. We have to respond to them. I hate to say it's PR, but, it's PR. A big part of it, anyway. And you're getting your due process. It's a leave with pay."

I rub my eyes with my thumb and index finger. "I'm going to get canned for this. How can that video be possible? If it is, I'm going crazy—"

Peggy shakes her head. "Maybe don't say anything else about it until you talk to a lawyer. Not to me or anyone else. And the hidden message in that is, you better call your lawyer as soon as you get home."

"Is there going to be a lawsuit?"

"Jesus, I shouldn't be talking to you about this. I don't even know what to believe here. But we've been friends for a long time. Stu Lepinski thinks the family will sue the district. Along with you."

"Goddammit, Peggy. What the hell?"

"Do you have a lawyer? Even if there's a settlement, you're going to need—"

"I don't care about a fucking lawyer, okay? I don't care about any lawsuit! I'm going to lose my insurance!"

"What? Neil, why are you even worrying about . . ." When the realization hits her, she actually steps on the brakes for a second, and I'm jostled as the car lurches. "Oh no. Wendy."

"Oh no is right."

Peggy turns onto my drive and takes us up to the house. Lauren's car is parked at Carol's, but I do not smile when I see it.

"Neil," Peggy says, leaning over as I step down from the car. "Did you do that to that kid?"

"Do you think I did?"

"I'm conflicted here. The guy I know, and the guy in that video . . ."

"I feel like I don't even know who I am," I say.

"Look. Talk to a lawyer. Have Chris come see me if anything is weird for him at school. Don't sit around and go crazy. Go for a run, or take *Tabby* out if you want. Just give me a heads-up first if you're taking the boat. Steer clear of anybody at the district. Don't be in contact with anyone. I'll check in with you tonight, and I'll let you know if I hear anything. Just keep it between you and me if we talk, all right? Get out for a run."

I slam the door to her Suburban, go inside my house, and drop my bags to the floor. I lean against the wall, and my knees feel wobbly, like I've just returned from a year at sea, or I'm back on Earth after a voyage to the moon. I need something to ground me. Anything. I could go see Lauren, but not yet. Not yet. I could take a slug from the bottle of whiskey in my pantry, but I'd like to keep myself from heading down that path. Instead, I go to the living room, drop to my big chair, and tap Michael's name in my phone's contact list. Mike answers on the third ring.

"Got the email, you liked the pho!" he says. "It's pho-fucking-tastic, right? I knew Chris would be stoked to try—"

"Mike, stop, I am in a big, big pile of shit right now."

"What's up?" he asks. I can hear the sounds of his restaurant kitchen behind him: clanking pots, spraying water, his crew shouting this and that. I tell him what's happened, only with the video, not with Lauren, and the sounds go away. I hear a door shut, and I know he's gone into his office.

"Dude," he says after I finish. "Dude. So the thing is online? What is it, YouTube?" I hear him typing at a keyboard. "There's nothing for your name." A pause. "A lot of me on TV . . . a lot of my cooking stuff if I put just Kazenzakis in. But nothing for you."

"Try 'Port Manitou,'" I offer. "Or 'Port Manitou Teacher.'"

"Hang on, I got something." He falls quiet, and I hear my shout of "Hey!" over the line. *I had to like, fight him off me.* I hear the shout again, and know he's watching a second time.

"This is fucked up, Neil. How could you do this?"

"I didn't do it!"

"I'm watching you do it right now."

"I did not do that. But . . . I don't know. I'm going to get canned. I'm going to lose my insurance. I can't move Wendy. Where am I going to put Wendy if I can't keep her there?"

"You are really saying you didn't do this? You're full of shit."

"Mike! I helped the kid up off the ground. That was it."

Michael sighs. He's not buying it. "You should call Kathleen," he says. He's right. Kathleen is always calm in a crisis.

"I know. I'm going to right after this. You don't believe me, do you?"

"It's not that."

"Then what?"

"This just looks really bad, man."

We hang up, and I try the Detroit office of the adoption agency where my sister works. I get the worse of her two assistants and know immediately my call won't be going through.

"I need to talk to Kathleen," I say. "This is her brother Neil. It's urgent."

"Ms. Kazenzakis is with a client right now . . ."

I hang up and go to our spare bedroom and open my laptop. I point my browser to YouTube and search for "Port Manitou Teacher," and there I am, number one in the results. The name of the video is: TEACHER GOES APESHIT ON STUDENT, WTF???!!! and it's already registered more than eighty-five hundred views. I cannot help watching it, once, again, and one more time after that, and each time it's like gravity departs, like I unmoor from the earth and float uncertainly until it ends. I scroll down to skim through the accumulated comments, already eight pages long:

—This is MESSED UP.

—Look lyk roid rage crazy teacher haaaa.

—Both our daughters had Mr. K. for physics, and this seems very out of character.

I highlight the address for the video at the top of the screen, copy it, and paste it into an email addressed to my sister. As a subject, I type:

Watch this and call me immediately.

Two minutes and forty-four seconds pass before my phone rings.

"Neil, it's Kath. What the hell?"

I explain, again, what happened, and I hear my sister scribbling in the background.

"You know," Kathleen says once I finish, "my first impression here is that your version of this story is maybe . . . shaky."

"I'm starting to feel that way about my version of this story too."

"But you're my little brother, and right now you're going to tell me, did you do this or not?"

"I did not. Do you think I'd do something like that?"

"Of course not. I don't think you're capable."

"Exactly. I absolutely did not do that."

"Okay. I believe you," Kathleen says, and for the first time, I feel the pressure of the day lift, just a little. I hear more scribbling. "Do you have a lawyer? Do you even know a lawyer?"

I laugh at this. "Not really. Do you?"

"The only lawyers I really know all work with adoption. But there's a guy I know in Grand Rapids who might be able to help. Let me get in touch with him. Give me a couple hours and keep an eye on your phone, okay? Watch your email too."

In the calmness of my sister's voice, I begin to feel that my greatest fear of this morning may not come to pass. In her reassuring tone, I can start to believe that, at least today, I might not crack.

----- ———————— -----

Lauren, I see when I check through the kitchen window, is still next door. Through the line of trees between my house and Carol's, I can see the red color of her car; it's there each time I check. I could go over there—I almost go over there—but I don't. I'm not ready to explain what's going on. Instead, I consider Peggy Mackie's advice and change into running clothes. And because I'm not ready to tell Lauren what's going on and don't want her to see me running down the drive, I head out my back door, across the field, and through the orchard toward the beach house.

I'm not being deceptive, really. I just don't know how I'm even going to begin telling her.

I am not ready. For any of this.

On this run I push myself. There's a good reason to push, I'd say. The day is cool, the sky a uniform gray, and I run hard. My mouth is dry, I push myself, I breathe in gulps, and through the effort of propelling my body over the earth I'm able to get a small handle on what's going on. I stopped running for months after Wendy's accident, and it just about finished me. Pushing myself here, gasping, I decide that, no matter how far down this video thing sinks, no matter how bad it all gets, I cannot let myself stop running. I can't.

Arthur is up on a ladder at the beach house, pounding beneath the eaves with a hammer. He yells something, probably a greeting, or maybe an invitation to stop and chat, but I wave and keep going. I go north, beyond our beach, beyond Leland's now-busy complex, and back to the sandy ruts I'd discovered back on Sunday. Up through the cedars and left at the highway and, without thinking, onward to Wendy's facility.

I'm winded when I get there, and I need to take a moment out front to catch my breath. The breeze is chilly, almost damp, and I'm wishing I'd thought to bring a light jacket along. When I get too cold outside and my breathing has calmed enough for me to go inside, Shanice seems surprised to see me.

"Take a personal day, Mr. K.?"

"You could say that," I respond, and I manage a smile. It's hard not to smile in the vicinity of Shanice. In Wendy's room, on the table next to her bed, I find a giant arrangement of white carnations. It's huge, like a floral shrub, really, and I duck back into the hall to ask where it came from.

"A little girl passed in hospice last night," Shanice tells me. "Her parents wanted us to have her flowers over here in Long Term. Lord, there were more flower arrangements than people in that room. And there were a lot of people."

"You guys do a good job," I say. "Wendy is pretty lucky."

I go back into my wife's room and take a seat next to her bed. I lean back, close my eyes, and reach through the sheets for her limp, dry hand. I play with her wedding ring and graze my fingertips over her knuckles. There is nothing. No squeeze back, no flinch from my brushing tickle to her palm. I slide my fingers up to her wrist, and press to find her pulse. It takes a moment, but there it is: the barest throb, steady and unstoppable. There's life in there, faded; a facsimile of existence like the carnations in the room.

Your wrist is so tiny, Wen.

So many nights were spent by Wendy's side at first. Nights in recliners, on cots, or on pillows stacked on the floor. Sometimes Chris would be at my side, or sometimes half-asleep he'd make his way into his mother's bed and nestle up beside her among the tubes. It was like he knew, but he didn't know. He'd speak to her; he continued to speak to her, waiting for an answer, long after I'd quit trying. There were flowers in the room back then too.

Only once we returned from Wisconsin, and Wendy was settled into her new home, did Christopher's darkest period begin. Mike was with us most of the time, Kathleen was there a lot of the time, and Carol's presence was continuous and calming. Christopher's first therapist was adamant we get him back into school and return some sort of order to his life. My family agreed with this, and through my fog they encouraged me to agree with it as well. His teachers at the middle school were more than understanding, and his fellow students were beyond sympathetic. Where Chris had never had a girlfriend before (he'd always been more interested in sports than members of the opposite sex), now we had several girls calling the house to speak with him each night. His tragic mantle, obviously unwanted by him, had a sort of mythic appeal, and the girls in his class fought for the chance to bring him saccharine comfort. Allegiances shifted like the dunes, and breakups came every other day.

To the world, my son seemed normal. He carried himself in a way suggesting he handled his burden well. But a rage built inside him, a justifiable anger at the hand he'd been dealt; his mother, who adored him more than anything, and whom he adored in return, was gone, but not really. Alone, there was fury. His guitar was smashed against the floor. Drinking glasses were thrown into the sink with such force that shards flew and scattered into adjacent rooms. He'd hit things, breakable things: walls and mirrors and framed photos hanging in our hallway. And all the time after, eyes filling with tears as he stared down at his sliced-open knuckles or a rip in his shirt, he'd ask:

"What happened?"

"What did I just do?"

Eventually it subsided. The summer after his almost-fight with Steve Dinks, he got beyond his brooding anger and was back to something like his old self. Chris was Chris, older, physically bigger, and with an unfairly earned comprehension of sorrow and loss. And an understanding too that time can be misplaced, rage can cause blank spaces or ellipses in our own personal timelines that only those who were around to see can document for us. Those missing spaces in his memory frightened him, terrified him, and he got himself together to avoid ever having to feel that terror again.

At the time, to be honest, I couldn't relate. At all. I'd comfort him, for sure, saying things like: "Everything's okay, Chris, I understand."

"I understand," I'd say, but I didn't at all.

Now, confronted by my own impossible ellipsis, my own lost time, I finally understand. Confronted by that same terror, I can only ask myself:

"What happened?"

"Mr. Kazenzakis?"

I open my eyes to see Nurse Irina standing over me, the light behind her forming a halo through her bleached-white hair.

"You spoke out loud," she says. "In your sleep. You are having dreams, I think."

"I . . ." I blink and glance around the room. "I must have dozed off," I say. I'm still clutching Wendy's hand.

I make it back home just past three. A drizzle started as I left Wendy's place, and now, shivering in my kitchen, I'm soaked and cold with flecks of sandy mud splattered up my shins. I heat a mug of water in the microwave for tea and peer out the window. Lauren's car is still there. I drop a green tea bag into the mug and take it to my bathroom, leaving it on the edge of the tub while I take a very long, very hot shower. My hands are against the tile wall while the water drums on my head, and I wonder:

Did I do it? Or did I not?

Am I completely crazy, or is someone screwing with me?

In either case, will I keep my job?

I run the shower until the water turns tepid and I have to shut it off, and I take my robe from the hook on the door and go to the guest room. I almost watch the video again, but I stop myself. What purpose will this serve, other than twisting me into an even tighter emotional knot? I check my email, and there are more messages in my school account, hundreds more. Some of the subjects and email addresses are gibberish, letters picked at random, and others have cryptic words. I find one from a Port Manitou student account with a subject of OUCH and click it open. I immediately wish I hadn't; it's a picture of a bloody body in a crumpled car against a tree. "Jesus Christ," I sputter, closing the thing as fast as I can. Who is sending me this? I'll mention it to Peggy when she calls—*if* she calls—as promised, with an update. I'd like to think she's looking out for me. And just as this thought is passing through my head, my cell rings from back in my bedroom where it's still in my pants pocket. I fish it out and see the name on the display reads Hammil the Mammal.

"Kevin, what's up?"

"Coach."

"Did you see the video?"

"Yes, I saw it. Was it real? Please tell me it's not real. That had to be right after I left Friday."

I sigh. "Jesus, Kevin, you know I couldn't have done that, right?"

"They sent out an email saying we shouldn't talk to you."

"What the hell are you doing talking to me, then?"

"They asked us to tell them anything we might know about what happened last Friday. Do you want me to say anything?"

"The only thing I want you to say is the truth, all right? You tell them exactly what happened, the way you remember it."

Kevin pauses. "I don't think you did it. The girls don't think you did it either. They're pretty upset about the whole thing."

"Are you still having practice?"

"We canceled today, but Cassie and Amy went ahead and said we're meeting up tomorrow. What should I have them do, Coach?"

"Take them through Old Town to the river, then along the bike path back to school. Don't tell any of them you talked to me, okay? Don't get yourself in a mess too."

"The kids in my classes can't decide what they think about it. They go back and forth. The freshmen and sophomores . . . I just can't . . ."

"Don't get too worked up about it. Take the girls out tomorrow, give Cassie some room to lead. Keep her in line, though. Don't let her get too pushy with the younger athletes. And don't tell anyone you called me!"

"All right, Coach. We'll talk soon."

I could linger here on my bed and forget about everything, but now I'm ready to tell Lauren what happened, so I find some jeans and a sweatshirt and throw them on. When I go to the kitchen window, though, I see her car is gone, and the rain is coming harder. The world outside is gray, and more leaves seem to be on the ground.

I'll call Lauren tonight, I guess, but this seems like the sort of thing that should be explained in person. As I consider what I'll say to her, Cassie Jennings's Subaru comes up my drive. Behind the sluggish back and forth of the wiper blades, I see Cassie and Amy Vandekemp up front with some unrecognizable silhouettes behind them; the car moves close to the house, where I can't see from this angle, and the grumble of the engine stops. Footsteps on my front porch and my doorbell rings. A knock, and a knock again.

I'd be happy to see them. My spirits would be lifted. Just hearing their chattering, muffled voices out front is uplifting enough.

I keep still, and don't move toward the door. A last knock comes, their footsteps file away, the car coughs to life, and they roll off down the drive.

It would have been nice to chat with them, but they don't need to get themselves involved.

Christopher is gone, at his leadership thing, and the night is mostly quiet. Earlier than I need to, maybe, I start some water for pasta and warm up a loaf of bread in the oven to be ready for Chris when he gets home later. Alan texts me three times, and three times I ignore him. Lauren texts me too, writing: Understand if things are tough, let me know you're okay? I drop to the living room chair and call her back because I need to hear her voice. I need to tell her. Thankfully, she's quick to answer.

"How did it go?" she asks.

"Not so well. It's sort of still going." It's not such an untruth, is it?

"Oh, Neil. I'm sorry."

"It's okay," I say. "How are you feeling?"

"I feel fine. I haven't felt sick once. I do think my boobs are bigger. Have you noticed if my boobs are any bigger?"

I don't have the first idea how to respond to this levity. So I don't.

"I'm just joking around," Lauren says, reacting to my nonreply. "I'm trying to cheer you up." Out in the living room, the landline rings.

"I'm sorry," I say. My eyes are closed, and I'm rubbing my left temple with my fingertips. "Something else happened today—"

"Pregnancy can cause increased libido too," she adds brightly, cutting me off. The answering machine beeps; there's no message, just a click after a long silence.

"Maybe I have noticed that," I say. "A little." My landline rings again.

"Thought so," she says. "It's more than just hormones, you know. You have a little to do with that too."

"Lauren, I—" The answering machine picks up, and I cock an ear to listen.

"Mr. Neil," a monotone voice says. "I need you to pick up, Mr. Neil."

"Do you need to get that?" Lauren asks. I tell her I should, and she says, "Go answer. Everything will be okay." I hang up, and immediately grab my landline handset.

"Hello?"

"Oh, Mr. Neil, you've done something very bad, haven't you?" The voice is choppy, almost robotic, and vaguely accented.

"Who is this? Are you a real person? Who are you?"

"Very, very bad. And who am I? Or who are we? There are many of us. And you'll be hearing from us, Mr. Neil. All of us!" The call ends with a click. I look at the phone's display to see the name BALLS, INC., on the display, with a spoofed number of 000-000-0000. I put the phone back into the charger and cross my arms, staring at it. Assholes.

I keep my arms crossed and stand in a daze. *Everything will be okay*, she said.

God, if only that was true.

From: xc.coach.kaz@gmail.com
To: w.kazenzakis@gmail.com
Sent: September 12, 4:44 pm
Subject: A Thought

So, I've been thinking about this. If we move your mom into the spare bedroom here, we can rent out the farmhouse. It would probably take me a month to get it in shape to rent (probably even less than a month if I'm not going to be at work), and we'd get maybe a third of what we need to pay for you to stay in Long Term. Or, I could spend a couple months and get everything finished here with the remodel, move in with your mom, and rent our place out for a little more (I think it would go for quite a bit more actually with the view from the deck). Conservatively, I'd guess that would cover about half. I've got my savings, and there's also Christopher's college money, which would keep you there for at least the next three years (or maybe even longer if he goes somewhere with a scholarship).

Highest priority is making sure you get to stay there.

I love you, Wen. Please please please don't worry about this.

-N

CHAPTER FIFTEEN

My landline rings again, and this time the name on the ID is not a prank: Kent Hughes, the reporter assigned to covering the school district by our local newspaper, the *Manitou Bugle,* is calling me. The *Bugle* does okay, mostly, though I have a theory that declining revenue from classified ads has pushed it into tabloid journalism over the past few years. Most people I know in town refer to the paper as "the Manitou Bungle."

If ever there was a tabloid story for our local rag to feast on, mine is it.

"Kent," I say plainly when I pick up. "I have no idea why you're calling." I've known Kent Hughes for a long time; he covers high school sports as part of his beat.

"Neil—"

"Wait! I know why you're calling. We are indeed going to win the state cross-country championship this year. Only the Port Manitou girls' squad, though. Boys will come in seventh or eighth."

"Are you okay?"

"What do you want, Hughes?"

"This video."

"No comment."

"You're in it."

"No comment."

"Did you do that?"

I savor a pause, and repeat, "No comment."

"Okay, off the record. What the fuck, Neil?"

"Exactly."

"It doesn't look good. And it doesn't look like . . . well, it doesn't seem like the Coach Kaz I've known for a while."

"Why don't you say so in the paper?"

"That wouldn't be very objective reporting."

I snort at this. "Like the Bungle has ever worried about that before? All right, make it an editorial then."

"Seriously," Kent says, "can you give me anything?"

"No, I can't. I will not comment on any of it. That's your quote. Well, wait, I do have one thing."

"Really?"

"Jennings and Vandekemp are going to deliver an awesome one-two punch at state."

"You are messed up, Kaz."

The conversation with Hughes makes me feel somewhat better, until it hits me that the story will run in Friday's paper, and that the attention I receive from it will probably be awful. But if I really didn't do anything to that kid, and the video is fake, I shouldn't have anything to worry about, right?

BALLS, INC., rings in again on my home phone, and I do not answer. I'm turning down the volume on the answering machine just as Chris comes in through the front door, and the sound of the latch makes me jump. I didn't even hear his car in the drive. He drops his backpack and gym bag with a *whump* in the entryway before joining me in the kitchen where he starts to make a peanut butter, jelly, and banana sandwich. On the stove, the lid on our big pot rattles over rapidly boiling water.

"Hey, Dad," he says with complete nonchalance as he rummages through our pantry.

"Hey?"

"Rough day, huh?"

"You could say that."

My son shakes his head. "That video is so bogus. Don't even worry about it. It's total crap. We were watching it in history."

"Well, I am kind of worrying about it now, to tell you the truth."

"Dad, it's so fake!"

"There are some people who aren't so sure, Chris."

"It was weak that they sent you home. Boys' and girls' cross-country were talking about doing a sit-in in the halls tomorrow—"

"No, no, no," I say, grabbing his arm and turning him so he's facing me. "No way. Absolutely not. You have to tell them they can't."

"Why not? It's bogus what they did."

"A disruption at school is not going to make *anything* easier for me, okay?"

"I can't tell them what to do."

"If it happens, you're not joining in."

"Why not?"

"Seriously? Chris? I am most likely going to be fired, okay? This looks really bad. I'm the one who has to prove it didn't happen, not the other way around."

"You're not going to get fired. No way."

"Christopher."

"All right, Dad, how about this then. I was watching it with Greg and Sparks, and they were trying to figure out who posted it by looking at some stuff on the YouTube account. Greg thinks he knows who put it up."

"Who was it?"

"I can't remember the kid's name. Let me text Sparks—"

"Hold up," I say. "Will you promise me something?"

"Sure. Anything. What's up?"

"If you guys find anything out . . . wait, let me say something first. Greg is really good with computers, right?" Chris nods. "If you guys want to look into it, great. But I don't want you or Greg or Sparks doing anything shady or illegal, okay? No hacking."

"You'd call it cracking in this case, Dad."

I roll my eyes. "Whatever you call it, don't do anything sketchy. If you find something out, let Mrs. Mackie know about it. Have Sparks or Greg tell her, not you. I don't want it to look like you're getting too involved with it. Because if I get sued, my position could be weakened by—"

"Why would you get sued?"

"Chris?" I look at him, and suddenly it's apparent to me that he might not realize the seriousness of the situation at all. "Okay, if you look at the video, it looks like an unprovoked assault. By me, an adult in a position of trust, on a minor child. That's a pretty big deal."

Chris stares at me, furrowing his eyebrows as he processes what I've just told him. The doorbell rings, and it startles both of us. Chris looks out the window, and what he reports makes my skin go cold.

"Two police cars, Dad."

"Oh," I say weakly. "Oh jeez." I go to the door, and waiting there is Peter Tran, a former student of mine now all grown up and in a uniform, along with another cop I recognize from seeing around the school in the Just-Say-No-to-Drugs mobile.

"Officer Pete," I say, and I nod hello to the other one. "Come on in, guys."

"Hello, Mr. K.," Peter says. "Hey, Chris!" My son is peeking out from the kitchen, seemingly transformed back into a little boy by the presence of uniformed authority in our home. I offer the cops a seat in my living room and try not to shake as they remain standing; it has dawned on me that there's a possibility I could be leaving my house in cuffs.

"This is Rick Coombs, our school resource officer—"

"I've seen you on campus," I say, and Officer Coombs smiles stiffly beneath his mustache and nods. He's holding a pen and notepad, and in the leather pouch on his belt on the side opposite his holster I can see a shiny pair of handcuffs.

"I'm guessing you know why we're here," Pete says.

"Probably not to investigate all these prank phone calls I'm getting lately," I say. They glance at each other, expressions unchanging, and I wonder, for a moment, what Chris would do if they take me with them. He'd be fine here alone, I know, but would these guys be okay with that? Maybe I could send him over to Alan and Kristin's house, with a message for Al to come bail me out.

Pete clears his throat. "Can you tell us what happened last Friday?"

I recite the story, as best I remember it, from practice that afternoon to my ride home. Rick Coombs takes notes while I speak. I tell them how I didn't recognize any of the kids, how they seemed nervous about being in trouble, how they all seemed to vanish after I got hit.

"I was a mess," I say, angling my face up to the light and pointing to my lip. "There was blood all over my shirt. I can show you the shirt if you want."

"Maybe later," Pete says. "Why didn't you report the fight to anyone?"

I think about this. "At the time it seemed pretty insignificant."

"Getting hit in the face was insignificant?"

"I mean, I guess I would have said something about it. But I had some other things come up this week."

"What's your history with Cody Tate?"

"I'd never interacted with him until I broke up that fight, and I didn't even know it was him until I was told this morning," I say, and Pete Tran and the other cop look at each other. "I'd never heard his name until a few days ago."

Pete leans toward the kitchen, where Christopher, I'm sure, has been hanging on every word of this exchange. "Chris? Hey bud, can you give us some privacy for a few minutes while we talk with your dad?" Chris scurries off down the hall, and I hear his bedroom door click shut.

Rick Coombs clears his throat. "There are some photos going around," he says, "allegedly of—"

"Denise Masterson," I say. "I know her family. My wife and the mom were close. The kid was a student of mine."

"Have you seen them?" Coombs asks.

"No. My son told me someone offered to show them to one of his friends, but the friend declined." As Coombs scratches out a note, I quickly add, "I reported that to Peggy Mackie, by the way."

He nods as he stares down at the pad. "When did you first learn about them?"

"The pictures? It was the beginning of the week." I tell them about my history with the family, and how Peggy had suggested I help as a liaison with them if necessary. "That was all on Monday."

"Not last week?" Pete asks.

"No. It was Monday of this week. I'm pretty sure." I almost add, "If I can be sure about anything," but I decide that it's probably not a very smart thing to say.

Pete cocks his head, looking like he's searching for just the right words. "Mr. K., would you say you're pretty worked up about these photos?"

"I haven't even seen them, so I couldn't really form any opinion other than feeling pretty bad for her parents. And for her. More like disbelief when I first learned about it, because I know Denise well and it didn't really seem like something she would do. Then when Chris gave me a hint about what they were of, I felt awful. But that was only yesterday."

"Okay," Pete says. "That should do it for now. Rick, you got anything more you need to ask?" Rick Coombs shakes his head. "We'll be in touch if we need to speak to you again."

"Again? You mean . . . you're done? Nothing else? Right now, I mean."

"No, we're all set," Pete says. "Thanks for your time."

"Do you have any questions for us?" Rick Coombs asks, flipping his notepad closed.

"I do, actually," I say. "Does that video seem real to you guys?"

The two of them glance at each other, and Pete Tran hands me his card. "We need to talk to a few more people," he says. "If you think of anything else you may have forgotten to tell us, give me a call, okay?"

I follow them to the door, and watch them through the screen as they return to their cars and drive away through the rain. Chris slinks back to the living room, and when I join him, we both collapse next to each other on the couch.

"You look a little pale, Dad."

I let out a small laugh. Our boiling pot still clatters in the kitchen. "To be honest," I say weakly, "so do you."

While Christopher gets started on making pasta, I force myself to go to the spare room and check my email. Sure enough, in my personal account, there's an email from a Barton Garvey, Esquire; the subject reads: VIDEO. Kathleen brought him up to speed, he writes, he works out of Grand Rapids and would be happy to help me out. When I see at the bottom of the message how much he would charge by the hour—even with a discount for being Kathleen's brother—I close the message without responding. A quick mental calculation tells me that roughly two days of my work equal one hour of his.

Maybe I'll write him back later.

More messages are in my school account, and I'm filled with the unpleasant feeling that maybe this flood of electronic abuse is something directed at me specifically rather than the district as a whole. I delete the obviously bad messages, the unknown and random senders, and am left with only a few legitimate-looking ones. One subject says: PHYSICS QUESTION, and I open it. The body of the message says DOES IT SINK, DO YOU THINK NEIL? And when I scroll down . . .

There's a photograph of a log floating in a swimming pool.

I stare at the picture for a long time. This cannot be meaningful. It cannot represent what I think it represents. It cannot.

I will not allow myself to believe this has any sort of meaning.

A little shaken, I delete the message, close the laptop, and tell Chris I'm going to see Alan and I'll be back in a bit. There's an assortment of jackets in our front hall closet and I pull one out at random, realizing, when I'm a few steps out the door in the rain, that it must belong to my son because the sleeves hang past my hands. It will be fine. I flip the hood over my head and my ears fill with the sound of raindrops slapping on nylon.

No one answers when I knock at Alan's door. I let myself in and call his name, and he greets me with a shout from his study.

"Come on in, Neil! I'm back here!"

The room is dark when I enter except for the glow of computer monitors; Alan is flying his make-believe plane in some perfectly rendered make-believe world. He's wearing headphones too, and he holds up his hand to me when I try to talk.

"Less than two minutes, Neil. I'm on final into Heathrow." He turns the steering yoke with small motions and punches buttons on his keyboard, muttering pilot jargon the entire time.

"Flaps at thirty . . . gear down and locked . . . little hot, little hot coming in here . . . there we go." The imaginary plane touches down with a very real-sounding squeal of tires, and a smile spreads across Al's face.

"How about that? Greased her right in."

"Hey, something's up, Al. I have something going on."

"Hang on, I need to taxi to the gate."

"For fuck's sake," I groan, throwing up my hands. "I'll come back later."

"No, come on, here, I paused it. You talking about your video? Your fifteen minutes of fame? God, you look like shit. You haven't been sleeping, I can tell."

"No, I haven't. Not really. And how did you find out about it already?"

Alan shrugs.

"I'm getting weird emails," I say.

"Sure you are. Hate mail. Your contact info is on the school's website. And some people are awfully worked up about this video."

"Do you think it's real?"

"I think . . ." He taps his chin with his fingertips. "It is of questionable reliability." He minimizes the flying program and brings up a browser. The YouTube page with my video is already loaded, and he starts the thing playing full screen. "Okay. Let's see. There's something about the kid that seems odd to me. And there's something about you. I've watched this over and over, and it doesn't smell right to me. I'm a fellow who notices things, as you probably know. Would you agree with me on that?"

"You do notice things," I say. "Your powers of observation may in fact border on the supernatural."

"I appreciate you saying that." Alan pauses the video just at the point where I'm grabbing Cody Tate. "Now look here. What is it about this boy that strikes me as peculiar? I honestly can't put my finger on it. Yet. But your face. Look at it. It's the face of a psychopath."

"Uh . . ."

"No, what I'm saying here is that you are most certainly *not* a psychopath in the real world. I've seen you at your worst, and it was certainly nothing like this. In addition to never once seeing a tendency toward this sort of aggression in you, I have never seen this look of calm, detached determination on your face."

"Is that good or bad?"

"What I'm getting at is that I believe, in these frames, some pixels have been rearranged. There's been some digital manipulation of your image. To make you look crazy. As I think about this, it's not the action of you throwing the boy that makes this video unsettling, it's the expression on your face. It's beyond unsettling, Neil. It's sinister. It's troubling."

"It is!" I say. "Seriously, I think you just put your finger on why I'm so bothered by it."

"But the level of sophistication, that should bother you too. The level of work."

"I don't know, I've seen the kids in Steiner's digital media class do some pretty incredible stuff."

"This Steiner, he's a teacher?"

"She's a teacher. A very good one."

"Maybe you should talk to her. About any of her students who might—"

"I'm not supposed to talk to anyone there," I say. "And they're not supposed to talk to me. But Chris and his friends want to go all Hardy Boys on this, so maybe they could talk to her."

"Find out who she thinks could pull something like this off. In the meantime, I'm going to download a copy of this thing and take a peek at it in some video editing software. Where I can blow it up and see it frame by frame. Oh, and a question for you."

"What?"

"You didn't really do that to that kid, did you?"

"God, no."

"Good. I didn't think so."

"I mean, what the hell? Here's this thing that I'm fairly certain did not happen, but pretty much everyone thinks it did, and now I have to prove it didn't happen."

"What the hell," Alan says, nodding sagely. "Welcome to my life, Neil."

"Jesus," I say, and let out a long sigh.

"You haven't told Chris about Lauren yet, have you?"

I shake my head, and Alan rises to his feet and grabs me by the shoulders. "You need to do this. Not telling isn't fair to Chris, or Lauren."

"But this video thing—"

"This video thing is going to blow over. Your family doesn't go away, though. Here's what you are going to do. Get some sleep tonight, some good sleep, and tell Chris tomorrow after school. He can stew about it over the weekend, maybe he'll be a little pissed, and he'll be over it by Monday. You got it?" I nod. "He'll do his basketball thing, and we'll all still have dinner Saturday night. Now, I told you I can get something from Kris to help you sleep—"

"I don't know," I say, rising from the chair. Alan claps his hand on my shoulder and gives me one more brotherly shake.

"It's there if you need it. So, tomorrow, right? I'm letting you off the hook for one more day."

"Okay."

Alan pats me on the back, and I leave his study, to run into Kristin at the front door just as she's getting home. She drops the bag she's carrying to the floor and gives me a hug.

"Al told me about the video," she says. "Why did they do this? Are you okay?"

"I'm okay," I say, then I laugh. "I'm not really okay." I pause, thinking maybe I *should* ask her for something to help me sleep, but I don't.

"Let us know what we can do," she says. "Anything you need, okay?" She gives me a kiss on the cheek, and I trot back out into the rain.

My phone chirps with a call from Peggy Mackie when I'm almost home, and I run up and duck under Carol's garage roof to answer it.

"Any news?" I ask. "The police came here this afternoon."

"They've been getting statements from everyone," Peggy says. "You know, I had Pete Tran back when I was teaching English. Good kid. What did you tell him?"

"I had him too. Great kid. Maybe not so much when he's in your house with a pistol and cuffs. But I told him everything, just like with you."

"The Tate family is going nuts. Like, out for blood on the district."

"Shit," I sigh.

"Do you have a lawyer lined out?"

"I'm working on that."

"Stu thinks there's no way this will go to trial, but I really think he just wants to reach a quick settlement to get us out of the way of negative publicity. And he wants our discussions with the family and their legal team to exclude you, at least as much as they can. Gracie Adams agrees, and will push the board that way. What she lacks in support she makes up with intimidation. It's pretty obvious she's taking the side of the family. Stu I think is pretty eager, which might mean throwing you under the bus."

"What about the pictures, Peggy? Isn't this kid going to get in some kind of trouble for the pictures?"

"I can't talk to you about the pictures right now, or what might happen with them. So don't ask me about it. I'll tell you something when I can."

"Fine," I say. "Something else. I've been getting . . . some emails. Bad ones. Harrassing."

"Everyone is," she says. "Don't worry about it." My shoulders drop with relief. "But how are you seeing them? You aren't even supposed to have access to your account right now. I'll say something to Cory."

"Great. Is anyone questioning whether or not the video is real?"

"The kids are all sticking to their stories so far. At least the ones we've been able to prove are in the background of the video. The YouTube accounts were made with fake names, and they used a proxy server to hide the Internet address, so we don't have any idea who uploaded them."

"That sounds kind of advanced. Technically, I mean."

"Maybe more sophisticated than you'd expect from a fourteen-year-old, but not really. People are looking into it. The Tate kid is the only one we're absolutely sure about, and he's sticking to his story most of all. He says you threw him down. The parents have pulled him out of school, and they won't let us talk to him without their lawyers present."

"Lawyers, plural?"

"They've got some money."

"Great," I say. "That's just great. Oh, you know what else is great? Kent Hughes—"

"Yeah, he called me too. I told him no comment, I need to talk to our lawyer before I can tell you anything on that, blah, blah, blah. Who knows what Gracie had to say to him, though. Hell, she probably got lit up on bourbon and sent Hughes an email before he even needed to call her. She's not exactly disciplined about messaging. But, whatever the article ends up saying, don't get too bent about it. It's just the Bungle, right?"

I try to laugh at this. "Just the Bungle." I try to laugh again, but it's not really working. "Keep me posted, Peggy."

--------- ———————— -----

Chris and I eat dinner quietly together when I'm back home. It's pretty dull fare: penne pasta, marinara from a jar, salad from a bag, and a loaf of store-bought French bread. In spite of his gourmet proclivities, my son downs two large bowls of the pasta; we're all about carbohydrates in the Kazenzakis household.

Later, as I'm getting ready for bed, Chris appears at my bedroom door, staring at a phone in his palm.

"No luck," he says without looking up. "Sparks says they made a new account just to post the video."

"I heard the same. Don't worry about it too much, okay? I think Mrs. Mackie has a good handle on everything."

"We need to figure this out," he says. "It's like, now I'm kind of mad about the whole thing. Oh, there are like twenty new messages on the machine—"

"Just leave them," I say. "Try not to worry about all this, Chris. Deal with your own stuff. Focus on your schoolwork. I'll see you in the morning."

He nods. "Night, Dad."

Lauren has not called back or sent any texts. I know she's busy, and possibly called out or covering for another nurse, so I'm not too worried about it. It happens. In my bed, I leave Lauren one last message.

"Hey, I need to talk to you. Call me when you can. I'll be up for a little bit." I pause. "And I love you."

There. I said it. I lie across my bed with my phone on my chest, but Lauren does not call back.

Nearly an hour passes and my bedroom is getting too oppressive, so I search through my closet for my thick pullover so I can go out to the fire pit. Maybe staring at a conflagration will calm my head. As I'm looking, though, the shoebox on the upper closet shelf where I keep my old prescriptions catches my eye; I take it down and rummage through. Alan *did* offer me something similar, and I really could use some sleep. I find one of my old Xanax bottles and give it a shake, and it rattles in reply. I shouldn't. I know I shouldn't.

Wasn't my best friend okay with it, though? I need rest, badly, so I press off the top and tap one of the pink pills out into my hand while I work up some spit in my mouth.

The tablet is swallowed. Tonight, maybe I will finally sleep.

Outside in the dusk I pull the tarp from the woodpile and wrestle out some suitable logs. I toss them over the wet, dead ashes in the stone ring, prime them with crumpled newspaper, and before long I have myself a glorious bonfire. I should give Alan a call to let him know, I'm thinking, because he's always up for a fire, but my phone buzzes in my hand with a call from Peggy Mackie just as I'm taking it out of my pocket.

"What have you got for me?" I ask her, poking a stick into the fire.

"I didn't think you'd pick up. I was just going to leave you a message. Not much new. I'm getting the impression the family is stonewalling Pete Tran. Pete let something slip to that effect when I spoke with him after I talked to you, but he backpedaled when I pressed him on it. He's also been talking to someone about the technical side of how the video might have been made and posted."

"Tracy Steiner?"

"No. Some cop computer expert. Also, there's going to be a special board meeting Tuesday night about all this."

"A board meeting that I should attend? With legal counsel?"

"I think your presence will be expected, yes. And all I can say is, if I were in your shoes, I'd probably want a lawyer there. How are you hanging in?"

"I keep moving, Peggy. I just keep myself moving."

"I'll talk to you tomorrow."

After we hang up I check my phone for any messages or emails from Lauren—there's nothing—and I dial Alan's number only to get his voice mail.

"Built a fire," I say after the beep. "Come on over if you want."

Alan calls back in seconds. "Should I bring supplies?" he asks. "I have a pretty nice bottle of Tempranillo downstairs."

"You can bring supplies." Should I mention the Xanax? I only took the smallest dose. I can't even feel it, really. A little wine on top will not hurt.

"I'll be over in a minute."

Finally, before putting my phone away for good, I call Lauren. Straight to voice mail again.

"If you get this, and you're still up, call me," I say, trying to sound more alert than I'm beginning to feel.

I slip the phone back into my pocket, and it isn't long before Alan, wearing a camping headlamp, rolls up to the fire pit on his bicycle. He draws a bottle of wine from a folded blanket in the basket, followed by a pair of travel coffee mugs, both of which he fills nearly to the top. He hands me one of the mugs, tapping his own against mine as he takes a seat next to me in the ring of folding chairs.

We're mostly quiet as we sip good wine from plastic mugs in the early night. My mind goes fuzzy and the fire becomes like something I would see in a dream. I can't look away from the glowing core of it, and other than Alan pointing out flight numbers and destinations of the airliners passing over our heads, not much is said as we sit and watch the fire die before us.

From: xc.coach.kaz@gmail.com
To: w.kazenzakis@gmail.com
Sent: September 13, 7:18 am
Subject: rain

It's been steadily raining for nearly a day now, and I feel like I can't wake up. I feel like I can hardly open my eyes, but I can hear the rain through the roof. I'd be happier if it was snow, but I'm not quite ready for winter yet.

But, now that I think about it, I guess you kind of hated snow sometimes.

I just want all of this to go away. I honestly don't know what's going to happen.

Terrible sleep, but I still feel like I can't wake up.

CHAPTER SIXTEEN

It's still raining as I groggily force myself from my bed to see Chris off to school Thurdsay morning. Brown puddles have spread over my drive and into my yard, rippling with falling rain as I watch my son's car disappear. It's strange to not be going with him.

Outside, the rain falls in sheets, and puddles form along the sides of my house. I decide I should take a run, choosing to wear tights instead of shorts with a rain jacket and a thin Nordic ski cap over my head. The thermometer outside my back door reads forty-four degrees.

Rhythm comes slowly today. I head toward town, giving the high school campus a wide berth, and trot down Purple Street in Old Town. The eponymous house is quiet, the scaffolding is gone, and the work trailer has been pulled away. Only the scuffed-up grass in the yard gives a clue that anything had gone on there.

The sky lightens and the rain eases to a light mist, and I can no longer see my breath. My now-soaked hat feels like too much, so I pull it from my head and stuff it down the front of my shirt. As I do so, a friendly dog, fur wet and tongue lolling out of his mouth, bounds next to me for a moment before getting bored and returning home.

The town is quiet, and I may as well be invisible.

Forty minutes out and a bit south of Port Manitou, I decide it's time to loop back home. This time I do skirt the high school athletic fields, and Kevin Hammil's biology class, it looks like, is out doing some sort of fieldwork by a tree. The kids stand in the drizzle bunched together like penguins, hoods pulled up over their heads and notebooks clutched in cold, sleeve-shrouded hands. Kevin sees me and, hesitating just a moment before letting himself do it, lifts his hand in a silent greeting. Some of his kids call out to me.

"Hey, Mr. K.!"

"Come back to school soon, Mr. K.!"

"Python died, Coach! Giving him a proper burial!"

There will be no discussion of snakeskin boots; that's not enough reason to stop. I don't wave back, either. I run, back out of town and into the farmland, and it feels like nothing before I'm home again. Hands on my hips, breathing deeply, I slow to a walk and come up my drive.

Back inside the house, I fill an old chipped mug with coffee, and wager with myself over who will call first with a report on the certain-to-be-devastating article in today's Bungle. Could be Peggy, could be Alan. I bet it will be Alan. He doesn't really have anything better to do.

The answering machine is flashing, but I don't bother to look at the number on the display.

I put on the same oversized jacket I wore last night, grab my mug, and stand out on the back deck. The field is wet, the ground is saturated, and the line of trees at the back end of the field is softened by a light mist. The trees and grass are still green, mostly, green with splashes of yellow and amber, the dusty colors of early autumn, and so, so pretty through the fog. Whatever happens, I have this. I can always come to look at this.

There's a motion at the edge of the field that makes me freeze: a tortoiseshell tomcat slinks out from the line of brush and sets across the field in a stiff-legged trot. The cat looks just like one Wendy used to have, so much that I actually call out the long-dead pet's name.

"Otto?" I call, my voice lifting at the second syllable, the way Wendy used to say it. "Otto?" The cat pauses and lifts its nose before scurrying away, off through the rain and out of my view.

The Olssons always had barn cats around, and Wendy, through her childhood, usually had one—against the wishes of her father— that she'd adopted to domesticate and spoil. When we moved back to her farm, she resumed the habit, and Otto was the cat she chose when we finished our house and moved over from the basement.

I'd never been much of a cat person; we'd always had dogs when I was a kid. But Otto chose us, I suppose. Barely larger than a kitten, he started hanging around while we were building the house, and it wasn't long before Wendy started letting him in to feed him. Begrudgingly, I became pretty fond of the cat, and over time it seemed to be my lap he found the most comfortable when he needed a place to hang out, or my shoulder the best place for him to curl up against at night.

"See?" Wendy would say. "He likes you. And he wouldn't seek you out if you didn't like him back. They can sense that, you know. So there's no use in you trying to deny it."

She was right, but I kept up my act of grumbling acceptance. Otto went out during the days, we'd call him in at dusk, and while he was usually prompt about coming in, those occasional evenings he was late in coming home, I always seemed to be the one to stay out to wait for him. I'd call his name into the insect-buzzing darkness, and finally he'd gallop out of the night, home from his adventures, and bound up the deck. I'd pick him up and say his name while I scratched his neck, before bringing him inside to deposit him on Wendy's stomach while she read in our bedroom.

One year, during winter break, Otto went missing. Chris was in the first grade, just a little guy then, and we'd gone down to spend

Christmas at my parents' house. I'd arranged for one of my students to house-sit for us and feed the cat, and on Christmas Eve when she showed up, Otto made a break for it. The poor girl called us in tears to let us know; she'd tried and tried to get him back in, she explained, but he wouldn't come back. I told her it was fine, he'd probably spend the night under the deck and be waiting for her when she came the next day. But he wasn't waiting. Not that day, or the day after that, or the next day when we returned home. Chris and I wandered the orchard, calling his name, while Wendy called the animal shelter and all the veterinary clinics in the area.

Chris found Otto's collar in the brush line at the far end of our field, and his chin trembled when he handed it to me.

It had been a mild early winter and the ground was bare; our first significant snowfall was forecast for New Year's Day. I went out by myself on the last day of the year to search, once in the morning, and again in the afternoon, and went over to talk to the workers building a house on the property next door before they knocked off for the holiday.

"You guys see a cat around here? He's big"—I formed a shape with my hands—"and kind of multicolored." They shook their heads. Back home, Christopher's eyes filled with tears, Wendy put up a good front, and I felt sick to my stomach. Outside, the temperature was falling, and the weather service issued a winter storm warning starting noon the next day. Ten to eighteen inches of lake-effect snow were forecast. It wasn't much of a New Year's Eve. Chris couldn't sleep, and he crawled into bed with Wendy and me.

"Will Otto come back home?" he asked us.

"I don't know if he'll come home." I told him. "He might not." I didn't want to lie to him, and tears began to roll down his cheeks. "He's been away for five days now. That's a long time."

"Do you think he's dead?" Chris asked.

Wendy was trying with all her might to keep from breaking down at the sight of our heartbroken son. "It's hard to tell with a cat," she said, her voice quavering. "Sometimes something frightens them and they hide. He could come back after a long time. Or maybe some nice person found him and is taking care of him."

"I want him to come home," Chris said. "I'd give back my Christmas presents if Otto would just come home."

This, of course, put Wendy over the edge, and I followed not long after that.

"I'll go out tomorrow morning," I promised him, wiping my eyes with my thumb. "Before it starts to snow."

I set out the next day after breakfast, walking the orchard once—and one more time again—getting down on my knees and peeking under the bushes where we'd found his collar.

"Otto!" I called. "Otto!"

I walked along the highway in the ditch, to the south and to the north, looking through the frost-covered weeds for any sign of him. If I found him here, I wondered, killed by a car, would I tell Christopher, or Wendy, even? Maybe it would be better for them to think he'd found a new home. That would be an acceptable sort of deception, I thought.

"Otto!"

I reached the fence line at the northern end of the orchard, and turned to walk among the trees for a bit, up along that bank of the Little Jib River. Could he somehow be down in the streambed? Nothing. I didn't think he'd ever even ventured that far before. I returned to the highway, resigned to the loss of the cat, and started home.

When I was just about back to my drive, I heard a shout behind me.

"Hey!" a man called, jogging toward me on the pavement. He was clad in heavy canvas work pants and a paint-splattered jacket;

this is how I first met Alan Massie. "Hey, were you the guy looking for the cat?"

"Yes?"

"I think he's in my house. The one we're building up the road."

This seemed too good to be true, and I tried not to get excited.

"Is he big?" I asked. "Brown and white and orange?"

Alan nodded, and my excitement grew. "I found him upstairs last night," Alan said. "He didn't want to come down; there's been a dog hanging around. I think the dog chased him in."

I followed Alan to the house under construction up the highway, trying to keep my hope in check. It really couldn't be. There was no *way* it could be.

"I was talking with the contractor this morning, I told him about the cat, and he said some guy had been looking . . ."

Inside, the house smelled like raw lumber, just open framing with no drywall hung yet, and Alan pointed up into the rafters.

"He hasn't moved from up there all day." Sure enough, it was Otto, and he let out a pitiful meow when he saw me.

"Otto!" I called, sincerely overjoyed. He was perched on some framing over a window, and he yowled and yowled as I approached him.

"Oh wow, my wife and son . . . thank you!" I shook Alan's hand, and we introduced ourselves to each other. "I'd better . . . I don't think I can carry him back without him flipping out. Let me go get his carrier."

"I'll make sure he doesn't go anywhere," Alan said.

I ran home through spitting flurries, and Wendy met me in the garage. She must have seen my smile as I flew up the driveway.

"You didn't . . . is it Otto? You *found* him? Where was he?"

"I'll tell you when I get back."

I ran back with the little cage, and Alan erected a ladder so I could climb up to reach the cat. He felt skinny under his fur, but he purred and purred, and I gave him a good scratch before putting him into the carrier. Alan walked back to the orchard with me. Chris and Wendy met us in the yard, and Chris practically turned cartwheels with excitement.

"Otto's back! Otto's back!" Chris shouted as he danced around us.

"Let's get him inside, Chris," Wendy said. "He's probably very hungry." She gave Alan a hug. "Thank you so much. Are you the new neighbor-to-be?"

It turned out we had mutual friends, and we made plans to get together sometime. When Wendy learned Alan and Kristin had two daughters, the first thing she asked was if they liked to babysit. We always had a hard time finding good babysitters back then.

That night at bedtime Chris climbed into his bunk, and Otto hopped up via the dresser, curled against our son, and began to purr with a throaty rumble. My wife and I stood in the doorway and watched them for what felt like an hour; Wendy even got her camera to take some pictures. I put the camera on Christopher's dresser and set the timer and jumped up into the bunk with my son and wife. We smiled broadly—Chris holding the cat up under his chin—and the flash popped.

I wish I knew where I'd put any of those photos. It's been a while since I've seen them.

We left Chris and the cat to sleep. In our own room, Wendy propped herself up on some pillows in bed to read while I peered out the window to try to gauge how hard the snow was falling.

"That cat," Wendy said, dropping some papers flat on the down comforter. "I really didn't think we'd see him again."

"I had a feeling," I said.

"What are you talking about? You were ready to give up yesterday."

"I just had a feeling I'd track him down."

"Oh, that's right. I forgot I'm married to Neil Kazenzakis, Indian tracker."

"Stop it," I said. I undressed and got into bed, and Wendy picked up her papers and started looking over them again.

"What are those?" I asked.

"It's from Northern Michigan. The CPA program. I can do it in two years—"

"Do you want to do it?"

"Maybe," she said, and she rolled to face me. "But I'd need your help. I'd need your help with the house. I'd need your help with Chris. I can't run this place and go back to school at the same time."

"Are you saying somehow I don't help out enough?"

Wendy just looked at me.

"Okay," I said, rolling away from her to turn off my lamp. "Whatever. Whatever you need."

"I didn't mean it like that."

I stared at the ceiling, starkly illuminated by the light on Wendy's side of the bed. "Just tell me what to do. You tell me, and I'll do it."

"Dammit, Neil, you should know what to do anyway. Why should I have to ask you to do this stuff?" She clicked out the light and the room went dark. We were silent for a while, feeling the weight of the darkness, then Wendy spoke again.

"I'm sorry," she said. "I just feel overwhelmed sometimes. I know you work hard."

"No, I'm sorry. I want you to get your CPA. If you want to do it, I want to help."

"Thank you. It's just—" Wendy sighed and closed her eyes. "God, that cat."

We said nothing more, and slept soundly for what felt like the first time in days. Dreamless sleep while the snowstorm built outside. But at four in the morning—precisely four-zero-zero, I looked at the clock—I was awakened by a thud and a cry from Christopher's room across the hall. The moonlight, diffused by the heavily falling snow, seeped into our room with a soft blue glow.

"What is it?" Wendy mumbled.

"I'll check on him."

A steady whimper came from Christopher's room. It must have been a bad dream, I thought, a monster not tucked in with the night. Entering his room I was confused by the fact that his crying came from the floor and not from high in his bunk, and by a strange rich smell filling the air. I knelt down and reached through the darkness, and my fingers touched the bumpy curve of his spine.

"Chris, kiddo, are you okay?" I rubbed his back and turned him toward me, and the whimpering didn't stop. A warmth flowed onto my bare chest as I held him to me, and my skin prickled in the instant I realized the warmth and the cuprous smell in the room were from my son's blood.

"Chris, what happened?"

Wendy came to the doorway. "What's going on?" she asked sleepily.

"Don't turn on the light," I said. Thinking about it, I'm not sure why I told her that. I must have been afraid of what I'd see. I helped Chris, still softly blubbering, up to his feet, and guided him out of the room. "Come on, kiddo. Let's go to the bathroom."

"What is going on?" Wendy asked again, her voice a little higher now. "Neil?"

"We're going into the bathroom," I said. Chris and I went in first, and through the flicker of the hallway night-light and my sleep-clouded vision I saw a darkness over my chest and underwear as well as down Christopher's pajama shirt.

"Chris," Wendy said, a flicker of anxiety in her voice. "Are you—"

"Don't turn on the light yet, don't turn on—"

The bathroom filled with harsh brightness, and Wendy gasped while I nearly swooned: blood ran from Christopher's mouth in a continual flow, and his lower lip hung slack from his face like a donkey's.

"Oh my God, what happened?" Wendy cried, rushing forward, putting her hand to her baby's chin. My knees went weak and I eased myself to the edge of the tub. I'd seen people bleed before, profusely, even, but seeing my own son hemorrhaging like this was too much. It was like he was vomiting blood, nonstop, and I looked at my feet and took some deep breaths.

"I feel . . . a flap in my mouth," Chris managed to say.

"You're okay, honey," Wendy said. She pulled a hand towel from the bar on the wall and pressed it to his face. "You're okay you're okay you're okay. Come on, let's go to Mommy and Daddy's room . . ." She took him out of the bathroom, and I stayed behind to regain my composure. As I focused on breathing, I heard Wendy go on: "You're okay you're okay you're okay . . . oh, honey, what happened?"

"I think . . . I hit my face on the floor. But I was asleep."

I went to Chris's room and flipped on the light. What I saw nearly made me feel faint all over again. The carpet was patterned with pools and footprints and handprints of blood, and a sheet hung crazily from the edge of the top bunk. He'd fallen out of bed and hit his face, but it looked like a murder scene. I joined them in our room, and willed myself to keep calm.

"Oh, Chris, you're okay," Wendy whispered, while flashing me a look showing she didn't think he was okay at all. She held the towel to his face with her left hand, and stroked his hair with her right. Otto, the prodigal cat, jumped up to our bed and sniffed at the blood on Christopher's face.

"Get Otto away," Chris said, muffled by the towel. I grabbed the cat and put him on the floor.

"I think we need to get him to the hospital," I said.

"Ambulance?" Wendy asked. "Do we even try to drive in this?"

"I'll call 911." Still in just my bloodied underwear, I went to the kitchen for the phone. Through the window I could barely see the utility light on the Olssons' pole barn, so I knew it had to be snowing very hard. I watched the snow, and marveled at how calm the emergency dispatcher seemed when she answered my call.

"My son . . ." I stammered. "He . . . he fell out of his bed . . . he has an injury to his face. And a lot of blood loss, I think."

"Do you need an ambulance?"

"I think so, yes."

There was a pause. "With this weather it will be at least an hour to your location. Do you have a four-wheel-drive vehicle?"

"Uh, let me, let me call you back." I ran back to the bedroom. "I think we need to drive him in," I said.

"Okay, Chris, sweetie, we're going to drive you to the hospital. Neil, why don't you get dressed."

I pulled on some clothes and traded places with Wendy while she dressed herself. I tried to not press Chris's face too firmly, and the cat jumped back onto the bed and nosed at the towel.

"Otto . . . , stop," Chris said.

"It's just Doctor Otto," I said. "He's giving you an exam. He thinks you need to go to the hospital."

"Go away, Otto."

"I have the keys," Wendy said. I threw our comforter around Chris and lifted him up.

"You're pretty heavy, kiddo. Keep the towel on your face, okay?"

"Don't let Otto get out," Chris mumbled.

Wendy led us through the house, opening the garage door and the backseat door to her old Chevy Blazer for me. It was too awkward to simply deposit Chris into the car, so I eased myself in backward with him on my lap.

"Can you drive?" I asked Wendy as she got in the front seat.

"Yes, I can drive." She backed the car into a world of swirling snow, and crept down the drive to the highway. The road had been plowed at least once already, but about three new inches of snow had accumulated since, and it continued to fall steadily.

"Not too fast," I said.

"I know what I'm doing." The car fishtailed in a turn, and Wendy gasped. "Someone's going to think I'm driving drunk!"

"No one's out here. Just keep going."

"The people at the hospital are going to think we did this to Chris."

"They won't. They can tell those things. They'll ask him, to make sure."

At the main highway, Wendy worked up to almost forty miles per hour, and the snow made a curtain of white in our headlights.

"Turn your brights off," I said. "It will be easier to see."

"I want them on."

"But you'll be—"

"I'm the one driving!"

Chris let out a little moan. "It hurts," he said from my lap. "I can feel a flap with my tongue. In front of my teeth."

"Leave it, Chris," I said. "Don't mess with it." I pressed on the towel, and Chris whimpered.

"I'm sorry," I said. "Hang in there."

We made it to the hospital at twenty 'til six; the emergency staff rushed us in, got Chris in a bed and hooked up to an IV drip. We were lucky in that the plastic surgeon on call was already there for a car accident a couple hours before; he looked Chris over and pulled at his lip. I saw bone glisten white through bloody flesh as the doctor probed with his gloved fingers and I had to look away. Chris didn't make a sound.

"You're pretty tough," the doctor said, and he told the nurses to get Chris ready for surgery. Wendy visibly trembled when she heard him say it, but she kept herself together. The doctor motioned us out of the emergency bay.

"He pulled his gum away from his lower jaw," he explained to us, tugging his own lip down with his fingers to demonstrate. "You said he fell out of a bed? I've seen this before in car accidents.

Not quite so substantial, though. Not so wide a separation. And it's usually associated with more facial trauma. I'll anchor the gum to his teeth with sutures, and within a year the tissue will recontour itself in there so you won't even be able to tell anything happened."

The doctor left us to get ready, and we watched the nurses prepare our son. They joked with him, and told him how brave he was. When the anesthetist came to put him under, they told him he'd start to feel sleepy.

"To be honest, Chris," one of the nurses said with a wink as she leaned over him, "it feels pretty nice."

We walked with him as far as we could to the doors of the operating room. Wendy said bye and covered her mouth with her hand, and I told him we'd see him in a little bit. He was already out of it. Once they pushed him through and the doors swung shut, Wendy fell apart sobbing. The nurses swarmed around her, embracing her, and I stepped back.

"You did a good job, Mom . . ."

"He'll be fine, Doctor Fenton is the best . . ."

"When my son cut his forehead I was the same way . . ."

I stepped away while the nurses comforted my wife. I felt, in a way, inadequate. More than inadequate. I found a waiting area to sit and think, and enumerate my inadequacies:

I'd nearly fainted when I saw how Chris was hurt.

I'd bickered with my wife on the drive.

I couldn't support her when they took our son away.

I sat with my eyes closed, and some time later I felt someone sit down next to me. It was Wendy, and she took my hand. Her eyes were red and she put her head on my shoulder.

"Thank you," she told me.

"For what?"

"For being here. For being so brave. I couldn't have handled this by myself."

"I wasn't so brave," I said. "Chris is braver than both of us."

We waited. The surgery wasn't long, only an hour or so, and Christopher came out with strips of tape up under his chin to support the sutures inside his mouth. They made sure he was alert and okay, and let us go home that afternoon. The roads were plowed when we drove back.

Chris stayed in our bed for the first few days after the fall. We fed him chicken broth from an eyedropper, and later, mashed potatoes when he was ready to chew. We read him books and he played with his new Christmas toys. Otto stayed at his side. After a week, if it weren't for the tape, you wouldn't have known anything had happened to him.

I remember at the time thinking: wow, that's it, that was *it*, that was our big parental test. Everybody gets one. That was really something. I'm glad we made it through with a passing grade.

Now of course, in hindsight, I know it was hardly anything at all.

From: xc.coach.kaz@gmail.com
To: w.kazenzakis@gmail.com
Sent: September 13, 8:50 pm
Subject: otto the cat

Wen-

It broke my heart when we lost that cat. A couple years ago
I was coming back from a run and I found him on the side
of the road, right there before the bridge over Little Jib. I
saw him from a distance, not moving, and I knew it was him
and that he was gone, even when I was a long way away. He
wasn't that far from our house either. I don't know if he was
coming or going when he got hit.

I picked him up and carried him home, and Chris and I buried
him near the fire pit, right by that big rock he liked to sit on in
the sun. The next summer, Chris chiseled OTTO in the rock,
and I added A GOOD CAT under that. The chiseling jobs we
did were sort of crude, but you get the idea.

Fifteen years, though, that's a pretty good run for a cat.
Especially one that was outdoors so much. He was so big and
tough I didn't think anything would ever get him.

I'm sort of glad you never had to know that it happened.

-N

CHAPTER SEVENTEEN

The first call I receive Friday morning about the article in the weekly paper does not come from Alan or Peggy Mackie, but from Lauren. I'm standing by the big living room window, watching the rain, when I answer her call.

"Hey, busy night?"

"Um, Neil?" she says. "Were you not planning to tell me about this? What the hell is going on?"

"Are you talking about—"

"The paper? The front page? Possible assault charges?"

My stomach seems to fall away, like I've just gone over the big drop of an amusement park ride. I brace myself with a hand to the window frame.

"Charges?"

"Do I even know you? Hello? You're going around beating up kids?"

"Have you seen the video?" I ask.

"I don't want to see the video! What is going on?"

"Lauren, calm down."

"Don't talk to me like that! I'm not one of your students. Or I should say, ex-students, by the look of—"

"Lauren!" I snap, and she goes silent. "Will you let me talk?"

"How long have you . . . when did this happen?"

"You're not letting me talk."

"Neil, I'm really, really, really stressed, I'm freaking out about *everything*, then I see this—"

"Calm down, okay?"

"Why didn't you tell me, though?"

"I wanted to tell you when I could actually talk to you. Not in a message. I tried to tell you last night, but you had to go and you never called back. I don't even know what's going on myself. Alan thinks someone put a lot of effort into that video to make me look bad."

"Apparently it's working," Lauren says with a sniffle.

"Are you calmed down?"

"A little."

"Can you come over?"

"No, I can't. Work. You didn't do this, did you?"

"Did you honestly think I did?"

"God, Neil." She takes a long breath. "Stressing, okay?"

"I know."

"I don't know if you do. What is going to happen? The family says you were in a rage. The boy is too traumatized to talk about it. You've been targeting him at school—"

"What? I only just heard this kid's name for the first time Monday morning!"

"Well, that's what it says. Here's a quote: 'The Port Manitou School District has zero tolerance for emotional and/or physical intimidation and abuse of students by staff—'"

"Did Gracie Adams say that?"

"How did you know?"

"Fuck." I sit on my couch and drum my fingers on my knee. "You really can't come over?"

"No. Like I said, work. Why didn't you just tell me? Were you home yesterday afternoon? Or the day before? I was here, you had to see I was here."

"It was my turn to freak out."

"You're not the only one freaking out," Lauren says. She sighs. "What are you going to do?"

"My sister put me in touch with a lawyer, but he's expensive. Insanely expensive. The cops are looking at the video, Alan's looking at it too, and I'm pretty sure I've got the support of at least a couple people in the district."

"What happens if they do charge you with assault?"

"The police were here to talk to me the other day, and they didn't mention anything about any charges. But if it does happen, probably I'll lose my job. If I lose my job, I'll lose my insurance. So in the short term, at least, I'll probably move in with Carol and rent my place out for some income to help cover Wendy's expenses."

"Oh God," she says.

"Yeah. So, there we go. It's not pretty, but at least having a vision of it helps keep me clearheaded about things. But this sucks. That's about the best way I can put it."

Lauren doesn't respond.

"Are you there?" I ask.

"Sorry. Sorry. I'm here. I just . . ."

"Just?"

"I'm going to go. I'll talk to you later." She says these words in nearly a monotone.

"Wait," I say. "It's going to be fine, really. I'll get through this. We'll get through this. I love you, okay?" I'm thinking, right there, the three magic words will snap her out of it. But they don't.

"I'll talk to you later," she repeats. And she goes.

I don't get up from the couch for a while. I stare out the window at the rain dripping from the edge of my roof, and wonder just how bad this will get. I almost call Alan, but I don't; instead I go to the spare room and wake up the laptop. The video is there, maximized in the center of the screen, waiting for me.

Hey!

I had to like, fight him off me.

I watch it once, and one more time after that. I almost start it a third, but stop myself. Can I still get into my work email? Why should I even try? I do, though, against my better judgment, and sure enough I'm able to log in. I skim through the subject lines, and when I see one that says WE ARE WATCHING YOU MISTER NEIL!! I flinch and snap the laptop screen shut maybe a bit too hard. I need to get myself away from this. Running would bleed off some of this feeling; I should go run, but there's still the rain, that damned rain.

A padded manila mailer sits on the table to the left of the laptop, the one I found a few days ago in a box of Wendy's things in the garage attic. The envelope is wrinkled and creased with age; an edge is reinforced with tape, the end is torn open, and the label on the front is addressed to Wendy in the stiff cursive of her grandmother. The label has been crossed out with blue marker, and along the top it says *Property of Wendy Olsson*. Underneath, the words *From Neil K.*—bounded on both ends by a pair of hearts—have been written in a more florid script.

I pick up the mailer by a corner so the contents drop out onto the surface of the table. A bundle of my letters, gathered together with a thick purple rubber band, lies on top of the stack. I pick the letters up and feel their collected heft, the weight of a teen boy's love. I poured myself into every one of them. I'd write them at school on lined notepaper, or at home when Mike thought I was just doing homework. I'd fold the pages into awkward squares and stuff them into envelopes provided by my mother. She'd give me postage too, with a smile and a wink. She knew what was going on with Wendy and me.

I don't unbind my correspondence. I went through them all the other day, and that was enough. Their mass in my hand is the only reminder I need.

Wendy's unsent letter is there on the table too. There's a thickness to the blue envelope, more than a few pages inside, I'm sure. She was always neater than I was with her missives, always using perfect handwriting on her stationery, never sending a page with a word crossed out or even an eraser mark. With my eyes closed, I lift the envelope to my nose; there's nothing there but the dusty scent of paper. I trace my index fingertip over the gummed edge of the flap and imagine Wendy licking it and pressing it shut. But she held on to it. Why didn't she send it? I could open it now, but I don't. I keep my eyes closed and press the envelope to my lips.

My thoughts are broken by my doorbell, followed by a knock. Leaning forward over the computer table so I can look out the window, I see Leland's black truck, panels splattered with mud, parked in front of my home. For a moment I consider ignoring him, but I'm curious why exactly he's here, so I go to the door to greet him. He has a somber look on his face.

"Saw the paper this morning," he says.

"I haven't read it yet. But I heard it's bad. Come on in."

I take his jacket and ask him if he wants any coffee; Leland nods and he follows me to the kitchen.

"You didn't do that, I know," Leland says, taking a seat.

I laugh at this. "You're the first person to say it with any sort of conviction."

"Come on, Neil. That's not you. And Steve knows the kid. Says he's a loser. I know the parents, sort of. Money. Big money from Chicago." He waves his hand when I hold up the sugar jar. "No thanks. A little milk is fine, if you have some."

I bring two mugs to the table and take a seat with him. "So what does it mean, them having money? Does it mean I'm screwed?"

Leland shrugs. "I know a good lawyer."

"So do I. They're not cheap."

"No," Leland says, shaking his head and giving a little laugh through his nose. "They are not cheap. And I'm a guy who's dealt with them enough to know. What are you going to do?"

"I guess I'm waiting for the school or the police to tell me what's going on. It's their move."

"You going to be able to afford this?"

Now I shrug.

"Listen," Leland starts, "I know I'm going to sound like some kind of vulture—"

"Here comes the hard sell," I say.

"—but I think there's an opportunity for you here."

"What, if I sell?"

"You could sell, or"—he looks at me—"you could exchange part of your property for a share in the partnership."

"Leland. Come on."

"I know you don't want to mess with the orchard. I know what it means to you, and I know what it means to your wife's family, okay? You forget I knew Dick Olsson a little bit myself. But I know it can't be making much money for you. I know you're probably just breaking even on the leases."

He's right, and I hope my expression isn't giving it away.

"If you joined in, there wouldn't be any major construction on the Olsson Dunes. It would mostly be golf course and open space. As natural as we can keep it."

"What about the Little Jib River?"

"The river stays untouched, just a pathway on the northern side and a footbridge to the golf course. Your house stays, the farmhouse stays. That place on the beach, though . . ."

"You'd take it down?"

"It's barely standing up on its own, Neil."

He's right about that too.

"What about Alan?" I ask. "Are you going to offer him the same sort of deal?"

"Alan Massie is a stubborn man." I raise my eyebrows, and Leland lifts his hand. "Wait a second, I know you guys are good friends. His property doesn't have the same sort of value to the project. But I'll talk to him. For now, though, I'd appreciate you keeping this discussion between you and—"

My landline rings, cutting Leland off.

"You need to pick that up?"

"Doubtful," I say, reaching over to turn up the volume on the machine so we can hear it. A beep fills the house, followed by a man's voice.

"You sound pretty tough there on your message, Mister Teacher," the voice says. "Maybe you need an ass whipping yourself. You are a pathetic son of a bitch, you hear me?"

Click.

Leland looks shocked.

"Are you . . . does that kind of talk trouble you? That's illegal, harassing someone like that on the phone, you know."

"It troubles me less than the prospect of losing my job."

"You need to tell the police about that call."

I shake my head. "I'll tell them about it when they come to charge me for assault."

Leland rises and takes his coffee cup to the sink. "Think over what I just told you. The character of the orchard will stay. Your house will stay. You'll get some money in the short term, and you'll make more in the long term. You're thinking about it, I can tell."

I say nothing, and get to my feet to walk him to the door. "I'll check in with you later," I say, and I can feel my heart beating in my chest.

"All right. Don't get too shaken up about everything. You're going to come through this just fine. I know it."

"Thanks, Leland."

"I'll see you."

I close the door behind him, and turn back into my house. I haven't taken a step before there's another knock at my door. It's Leland again.

"Let me in," he says in a low voice. "Close the door."

"What's going on?"

"You've got some company."

Leland follows me to the guest room and we peek out the window; behind Leland's truck are a pair of news vans with colorful graphics on their sides and satellite dishes on their roofs.

"Who the fuck are those guys?" I say softly.

"It's a Detroit station," Leland says. We're whispering as if the guys in the van could hear us. "The first one, anyway. I don't know who the other guys are. Why would they make the drive up here? You want me to say something to them?"

"No, just . . . go around them, I guess."

"All right."

Leland heads out again while I stay in the guest room. I watch him beeline for his truck, his head ducking through the rain. The headlights come on, and he swings wide through my yard and past the vans. After he goes, two men jump out of the first van: one with a microphone, and the other with a boxy video camera draped in a clear plastic rain cover-up on his shoulder. Both wear rain jackets with their station logo on the breast, and they come to my house and ring my bell. Instead of answering, I take out my phone and call Alan.

"Neil! So you saw the—"

"Shut up," I say. "There are news vans in my driveway. One's from a TV station downstate."

"For real?"

"Yes, for real!" They ring the doorbell again.

"I'm guessing you don't want them there."

"No."

"Sit tight. I'll be right over to take care of it."

The newsmen ring a final time, wait a minute, and slog back to their vehicle. A couple moments after that Alan, wearing an olive-green rain poncho, rides up my drive on his bike. He stops next to the passenger side of the first van and the window rolls down. They all chat for a bit, Alan points to the road and nods, the window rolls up, and the van drives away. Alan speaks to the guys in the second van, and they drive away too.

Alan comes into my house through the side door without knocking.

"What did they want?" I ask him as he hangs his dripping poncho on the back of a chair. "Why does anyone in Detroit care about this?"

"It's not just Detroit," Alan says. "They're CNN's Lower Michigan affiliate. The other guys are from FOX."

I have to sit down. "You're kidding me."

"You had almost a hundred and fifty thousand views on YouTube this morning," he reports with a smile. "You have gone viral, as they say."

"You're smiling about this? Why the fuck are you smiling?"

"Because when it's revealed that the video is fake, the damages you claim when you sue whoever made it will be, in part, predicated on how frequently the video was viewed. Let's get those numbers up, right?"

My home phone rings again, and I put my head in my hands while I wait for the beep.

"Oh, look at me, I'm big and tough and totally picking on people my own size!" It's a man, speaking like a dopey cartoon character. "Look at me, I'm such a fucking pussy in real life that I have to pick on kids! Bwaaaaa!"

"Unplug that," Alan tells me. "Get dressed for a run."

"Alan, I'm not really—"

"Unplug it now, and get into your running things. I'll ride with you."

"What about the guys in the van?"

"We'll go through the orchard to my house." Alan leans to the wall by my phone as he speaks, reaches down, and straightens back up with my phone's loose power cord dangling from his hand. "We'll duck through the orchard, then we'll go north on the highway. They won't even see us."

"Fine," I say. I change into running clothes, shorts, and a long-sleeved shirt for the chill, and I find a light jacket that actually fits. We go outside, and I look all around for signs of video cameras before trotting off through the cherry trees. Alan rides behind me as I run the wet dirt path. When we get to the highway, he moves to my side, speeding up ahead to go single file when we hear a car behind, and falling back once it's passed. We say nothing for the first mile or so, until Alan finally speaks.

"I feel like you're a prizefighter," he says from beneath the hood of his poncho. His knees rise and fall as he pedals. "And I'm your trainer. Getting you in shape for the big fight."

"It is a big fight," I say. I consider telling him about Leland's visit, but I don't.

"I feel like a prizefighter myself sometimes. A sexual prizefighter."

"God, Al, come on."

"I'm being serious. Kristin would back up my assessment, I believe."

"I don't need to picture this."

"You're almost forty, Neil. I'll be fifty in two more years. Can you believe it? Fifty. I feel like a newlywed, though, when it comes to my sexual prowess."

"Why are you telling me this?"

"I imagine you might be edging me out in frequency, however. Maybe not quality, but you and Lauren, quantity! Putting up big numbers. Like a pair of bunnies."

"Are you jealous?"

"Not at all. But I'm happy for you, young man. You two. You should marry her, you know."

"I think I've got a little more on my plate to worry about right now. And Lauren isn't so happy about the whole thing. I mean, she's really unhappy."

"It will all pass, Neil. And remember, you're telling Christopher tonight. The hardest part will be behind you."

Alan stands up to work his heavy bike to the crest of a hill ahead of me. He stops and slides his poncho off over his head, and I realize for the first time this morning that it's stopped raining. Alan rolls up his poncho and drops it into his handlebar basket. I give him my jacket and he rolls it up too before lifting his head toward the maybe brighter clouds.

"Listen," he says, and I hear the faint rumble of a faraway jet. "United two-twenty-three, out of Chicago bound for Copenhagen."

"You know them all, don't you?" I say, bending to touch my toes.

Alan nods. "Pretty much. Yes, I do."

From: xc.coach.kaz@gmail.com
To: w.kazenzakis@gmail.com
Sent: September 14, 2:45 pm
Subject: dune orchard

If the orchard was preserved as something like, say, a park, do you think your dad would have been okay with it?

Especially if it meant you could stay there and we could send Chris wherever he wanted to go for college?

CHAPTER EIGHTEEN

Back home from my run, I see on my cell that I've missed a call from Uncle Art.

"Hey there, Neil, saw the uh, paper. You want to give me a call when you have a chance?" I start to hit Reply, but I stop myself; I'm still in my running clothes, and after a glass of water and an apple, I go back outside and run over to the beach house. Arthur's out on the deck when I get there, fighting to keep a winter shutter in place as he tries to screw it down with a cordless drill. I grab the splintery thing from beneath and hold it still, and Art takes a screw from his teeth, mates it to the drill bit, and drives it tight.

"Thank you," he says, pulling at the shutter to test how firmly it's anchored. "Not sure how many more holes this old trim is going to take." Art is a fit man, in his midsixties with large, work-worn hands. Over his shoulder, the lake is a storm-driven gray like the clouds.

"All these windows really need to be replaced," I say.

"No kidding," Art says, sending another screw home. "So what in the heck is going on with you?"

"You saw the paper," I say, and he nods. "Did you see the video?" Art smirks.

"Sending email to my kids marks the extent of my computer ability. Penny does the Facebook, she tried to show me all that . . ." He chuckles. "No, I haven't watched the video."

"You don't need to," I say. "I haven't even seen the article yet, to be honest."

Art waves me into the house and points to the chipped Formica kitchen counter. The paper is there, but I spend a moment looking over the interior of the place, the leak-spotted ceiling and worn carpet, trying to recall if it was this shabby when my family was renting it.

"I know," Art says, reading my mind. "Pretty run-down. But it still has its charms."

I grab the paper and sit on a wobbly barstool. The article is about what I'd expected: unbalanced, poorly sourced, and just a little mean. Neil Kazenzakis declined to comment for this story, it says, as did senior school administration officials. Gracie Adams was happy to talk, however. She wants to get beyond this and back to the great work of educating kids and preparing them for careers or higher education. The family comes across as less generous. Though it's not the policy of the paper to report the names of minor victims of crime, it says, it's widely known that Cody Tate was involved, and the Tate family is pursuing all legal avenues against the district and Mr. Kazenzakis.

The Port Manitou Police Department, the article concludes, is continuing its investigation.

"Great," I say. "Terrific."

"How in the world did this happen?" Art asks.

"I thought I was breaking up a fight," I say. "I thought I was doing the right thing. I guess I wasn't. And I tell you, I watch the video sometimes, and I almost believe that's the way it really happened. Not like the way I remember it."

"Memory is a funny thing," Art says. "Just have a conversation with my sister for proof." He smiles sadly as he says it.

I look around the interior of the house again. "How much do you think it would take to spruce this place up?" I ask.

"Oh golly, I . . ." Art taps his finger on his chin. "You mean really do it right? You'd have to gut the place, I'm sure. This main part of the structure is nearly sixty years old, the wiring isn't up to code, and who knows what else you'd find once you really dug into it. And whoever did the addition shouldn't have been allowed to swing a hammer, so that would need a load of work, if not torn down and built back up from scratch. You'd have a crew on this job for the better part of a year, I'd guess. Why are you asking?"

"Just a thought," I say.

-----———————————-----

In my memory, the beach house was never so dilapidated. And of all the times I stayed there, there is one visit, one night that stands out in my head above the rest. The autumn of my junior year in high school, I qualified for the Michigan State Cross-Country Championships in Ann Arbor. Simply competing would have been exciting enough, but even better was the fact that Wendy and Carol drove down from Port Manitou to attend the event and cheer me on. I didn't have a very good race (I finished in eleventh place), but seeing Wendy waiting at the finish made me feel like I was flying. After, we sneaked off into the woods and made out against a tree; my body, skin flushed and raging with teen want, was pressed against hers, and I almost had her shorts unbuttoned before we were caught by one of my coaches.

"Later," she said, giggling as we walked back to her mom's car. "Be patient."

We wrote letters through the winter, we hinted at desire and obliquely referred to our "almosts" by the tree. In the spring we both ran track, and while Wendy did not qualify for state that year, she did suggest I ask my mom and dad if I could drive up to see her run at a district invitational in the early spring. Astonishingly, my parents said yes, maybe persuaded by my argument that it was only fair after Wendy had come to watch me.

My mom let me take her old Honda Accord, and I left early that Saturday morning. Michael had talked about joining me, but thankfully bailed out at the last minute. My plan was to watch Wendy run, join the Olssons for an early dinner, and make the nearly four-hour drive to be home by midnight.

The day was cold, unusually cold, and windy, and I wished I'd brought something other than a light jacket while I watched Wendy compete. She only made it to the semifinals in the four-hundred meter, fifth place in that heat (disappointing because that was her best event), and an unexpected third in the finals of the eight hundred. Seeing her get her little medal while I stood with Carol and Dick made me forget about the cold. She smiled with pure joy on the podium, even with her third-place finish.

Dinner at Wendy's house was a fine time. The Olssons laughed at the table, which surprised me, as I'd always imagined Dick would be dour and imposing in their home. He doted on his daughter, and teased me about how close I was sitting to her. I don't know how his demeanor would have changed had he known that, beneath the table, she'd slipped her foot out of her shoe to rub her toes against my ankle.

Wendy's parents asked me the expected questions: how's your family, how is school, have you given much thought to college? When I told them I was seriously considering Michigan State, Dick looked very pleased.

"Oh, a great school, your dad there and all, and did you know Wendy was planning to apply?"

I acted surprised but of course I knew; we'd been plotting it through the mail since the fall. Destined to be together forever, as all young lovers know they are. Wendy's toes pressed harder and she smiled.

Raindrops streaked the dining room window as we ate. The phone rang, and Carol rose to answer it. She wore a bemused expression on her face when she returned to the table.

"Well," she said. "We may just have ourselves an overnight guest. They're supposed to be getting an ice storm downstate tonight, and your parents aren't too comfortable with the thought of you driving home in it, Neil."

Wendy's foot froze against my leg.

"We could probably put him on the fold-out, Dick—"

"I did just open up the beach house. I think he'd be more comfortable in a bed over there." He gave me a look that even my seventeen-year-old self could not miss; it was one thing for me to sit close to his daughter at the dinner table, but to be in such proximity under cover of darkness was not acceptable at all.

"I think the beach house would be great," I said meekly.

I called my parents back to confirm I'd be staying. Dick made like he was going to drive me over to the cottage right then, but Carol laughed at him.

"For goodness' sake," she said. "It's only six o'clock. Let the kids hang out for a while. They can have a little date."

Alone in the Olssons' living room, Wendy and I watched TV and held hands under a pillow, and grabbed kisses from each other when we could. Wendy was more forward in this pursuit; I couldn't shake the vision of Dick catching us and tearing me limb from limb.

"I can try to sneak over," Wendy whispered, pulling back from my lips after a particularly aggressive kiss. "It will be late, though."

"Are you insane? Your dad will kill you if he catches you. He'll kill both of us."

"He sleeps like a rock. I do it a ton." I gave her a look and she added, "Only for parties! He deadbolts the door, but I just go out the window."

Dick took me to the beach house just before ten. I offered to drive myself there, but he insisted; I think the idea of my complete isolation and immobilization appealed to him. He walked me up the wet gravel path to the back door with a flashlight, and inside, the old light switch in the hall came up with a loud *snap!* It was so cold inside I could see my breath.

"You already know your way around," he said. "I don't think you'll need anything." He took me to the room where Teddy always stayed and pulled some sheets and blankets from the closet; wordlessly we made the bed together.

"There are more blankets at the end of the hall if you get cold," he said. "I'll come and get you for breakfast in the morning." He stopped at the bedroom door to turn up the thermostat, and the baseboard heater creaked and popped. "You and Wendy . . ." he started, trailing off. I braced myself for a talking to, but he just gave a small nod. "You're very nice to her," he said, and left.

The sound of Dick's truck faded as he drove away, and I went to the bathroom and washed my face. I stripped to my underwear, snapped out the lights, and jumped into the cold bed, left only with the rush of waves out on the beach and an occasional *ping* from the heater. It was very hard to sleep. At some point it rained. The sound of it on the roof made me drowsy, and I managed to doze off.

I woke later to one of the heater sounds, and gasped when I saw a silhouette standing over me.

"Holy shit!" I said, springing upright.

"It's just me," Wendy said. "Relax. It's okay." She undressed next to the bed, leaving her underwear on. "Move over. I'm *freezing.*" I shuffled over and she got in next to me. She pressed her little breasts into my side, and I was surprised by how firm and cold they felt. Very quickly I got an erection, and I tried to angle my hips away from her so she wouldn't notice.

"You're so warm in here. Are you hard?" she asked me, almost casually. I couldn't answer.

"I'm serious," she said. "Are you?"

"Yes."

"Can I feel it?"

"Okay." I lay still, almost trembling, while she slid her hand beneath the band of my underwear and hesitantly touched my penis. I tried to reach between her legs, but she quickly let go of me to stop my hand.

"You can't," she said. "I'm on my period. Sorry."

"Oh," I said, and her grasp returned, more confidently now.

"What do you call it?" she asked into my shoulder.

"What, you mean like a name? I don't have a name for it. That's kind of stupid."

"No, I mean when it's hard. Do you call it a boner?"

"That's kind of stupid too. I just call it hard, I guess."

"Do you jack off?" The clumsy way she said it sounded almost like a taunt, and I didn't answer. Wendy rose up and rested her chin in her palm.

"Tell me," she said.

"Yeah. I do."

"Do you think about me while you do it?"

"Yes."

"Masturbate is a weird word."

I laughed, as much as I could given the situation. "I guess it is. Do you?"

"Do I what?"

"Do you . . . you know. Do what we're talking about?" I couldn't say the word myself.

"I never feel like I have any privacy in my house."

"Are you serious? You're an only child."

"My parents are always, I don't know. *Around.* They're overprotective." The motion of Wendy's hand slowed and stopped. "Especially my dad. He's always—"

"Do we have to talk about your dad while we're doing this?"

Wendy giggled, and her hand started moving again. "Sorry."

"So, do you?" I asked.

"Maybe. If I can get to the place where I like to do it. But you'll laugh at me if I tell you."

"I won't," I said. "I promise."

"Well, if the weather's bad, I do it in the basement. Between the water heater and the wall. I put a pillow on the floor." I held my breath as I pictured it. "You said you wouldn't laugh."

"I'm not. I'm sorry. It just seems awkward. What if the weather's good?"

"There's a place," she started, and a splatter of raindrops sounded on the roof. "In the woods. Right up next to the river. It's totally off-limits for me, my dad never let me go there. He was always afraid I would fall in and drown or something. But there's this bent-over tree with some bushes, it's like a shelter, you can't see inside at all. I go in there and do it. Can I tell you something? And really don't laugh?"

"Sure," I said.

"I imagine you are there with me. Doing those things to me. And I'm doing this to you."

I swallowed. "Why would I laugh at that?"

"I don't know. Am I doing a good job? Is this how you do it to yourself?"

"Kind of. But the way you do it feels better."

"Does it make a mess?"

"We should pull down the sheets," I said.

Wendy stroked me, saying nothing more in the cold and the dark, and rested her head on my shoulder. It went on and on, awkwardly and perfectly, and she giggled when I arched my back, held my breath, and came all over my stomach. I felt embarrassed, and ecstatic.

"That's just . . . keep it away from me." She giggled again. "We don't need to make any babies."

"I thought you had your period?"

"That doesn't mean anything. It's never *really* safe. I'll grab some tissues."

We cleaned it up and flushed it away, flipping on the light to check for evidence. I watched her from the bed as she dressed, her small, dark nipples and the curve of her waist above her hip. We turned out the lights and she kissed me, and kissed me again, and left in a way that made me wonder if she'd ever even been there.

In the morning we acted like nothing had happened. I ate breakfast with the Olssons and drove home.

The roads leading home were perfectly dry; there hadn't been an ice storm at all.

--------—————————--------

Back at my house after my visit with Arthur, I reread Barton Garvey's email. From his letter, at least, he seems like a good lawyer. He must be good, if his almost incomprehensibly high hourly rate is an indicator of his stature in the legal world.

I read the email one more time, and tap out this reply:

Bart, do you have time to talk tomorrow?

I know this will set the meter running, so I don't hit Send. Not yet. How many hours of this guy's work would my savings cover? I could pay for my defense now, and hope something comes along to cover Wendy, or I could play it safe and ensure Wendy's care is paid for at least the next few years, and take some punches to the chin.

Is there a chance this will all blow over? Maybe I could simply do nothing, and hope it all just goes away.

Or, there's always Leland.

I do not check my district email. Instead I clean myself up, get into fresh clothes, and walk over to Carol's house. Leaves stick to the wet concrete of the basketball court, blue sky shows through broken clouds, and the breeze seems significantly chillier since the rain stopped. There's a car in Carol's drive, not Lauren's, and I'm not sure which nurse it belongs to. Something on the corner of the house catches my eye: there's an orange bit of color that I first assume to be a leaf stuck to the trim, but it seems too vibrant for that, and when I come around front to investigate, I let out a long sigh. The highway-facing garage wall has been splattered by a dozen or so paintball pellets, and the orange pigment has garishly wept down the siding in the recent rain. I pull a coiled hose from next to the front porch and do my best to spray the house clean.

Carol is in her living room when I finally make it inside, sunk into her recliner with the TV on full blast. The nurse working is not one I recognize, so I introduce myself as Carol's son-in-law and she says, "Oh!" like she's heard about me. I pull a chair from the dining room to Carol's side, and she mutes the volume with a trembling hand on the remote.

"Hi, Neil," she says, smiling. Here's one person, at least, who doesn't seem to know about the video.

"Carol, how are you?" I ask, trying to gauge her state of mind. "I had a nice chat with your brother a little while ago."

"Who?"

"Your brother, Arthur."

"I just got a letter from Arthur," she says, glancing around at the floor. "It's here . . . somewhere. Terrible, just awful for him over there. He's been fighting in the jungle for ten days straight. I don't dare tell our mother what he writes in those letters. She'd go into shock."

There's my answer.

"Carol," I say. "He's home. He made it home safe."

"Oh!" she says, looking like she's going to cry. "He . . . he's home? He's okay?"

"He's just fine. I need to ask you something. Can I ask you something?"

"Of course, Arthur. It's so, so good you're home."

"How do you feel about the orchard?"

Carol sighs. "Dickie is going to work himself to death in this goddamned orchard. I told him he needs a trip away to clear his head. He's a strong man, but financial worry can make a man's heart weak. We thought we'd had the chance to get out from under it, but that son of a bitch pulled out at the last minute."

"Who? What happened?"

"That Lawler, that spineless Lawler from the co-op. Was going to buy the twenty-eight acres on the north end. That was going to be our retirement! Dickie was ready to sign the papers, and that son of a bitch backed out."

"You were going to sell?"

"We were all set to go, then, *psh*. Another fellow came by this spring, but now we're gun-shy, you know. Dick's going to work himself to death."

"What . . ." I start, and I can feel my pulse in my neck. "What if I told you there was a sure thing? Someone who wouldn't back out?"

"Well, Arthur, if you can convince Dick he's not a son of a bitch like that Lawler, I'm all for it. I worry about my husband."

"I'll talk to him."

"All right. If he says fine, you fix it for us."

-----———————-----

Chris has meetings for student government again tonight, and I go back and forth over whether or not I should call him home early or wait until his extracurricular work is complete. Inside our empty house the air seems suffocating, and Lauren hasn't called since I spoke with her this morning, which only makes me feel worse. In the too-quiet space, all I have are my thoughts, my thoughts of my earlier conversation with Carol.

They really tried to sell the orchard?

Really?

Memory, as Arthur said, is a funny thing. Maybe this near-transaction with a shady Mister Lawler is a complete figment of Carol's imagination. Maybe it happened to a friend, and she's absorbed it into her addled brain and made it a memory of her own.

Or maybe it was true, and the Dune Orchard complex is not as sacred as I'd once believed.

My cell rings to break the silence, and I see my brother Teddy's name on the display.

"What the hell?" Teddy says as a greeting. In the years since our childhood, his voice has mellowed to a middle-aged growl. "Haven't you called a lawyer yet? Kath says she hooked you up with a good lawyer and you haven't even talked to him yet."

"I'm going to," I say. "I needed to be ready."

"Ready for what? Ready to be bent over and fucked? You need to get moving on this right now."

"Lawyers aren't exactly cheap, Teddy. I need to be ready to pay for him."

"What are you going to do? Do you have anything saved up?"

"Not a ton," I say. "There is Christopher's money for school. And I might be able to come up with something on top of that."

"Shit. Don't wreck yourself to pay for this. Don't wreck anything for Chris."

"I might have something going with a real estate deal."

"Did you see you were on MSNBC?"

"You're kidding me."

"I'm not!"

I don't speak.

"Neil? Talk to me here."

"I need to go," I say.

"Get back with that lawyer. Like, now. You can figure out how to pay for it later. We'll figure it out somehow, okay?"

———————————

I decide, after an hour of wavering, to call Christopher home after school to get this done with. The last bell, I know, at Port Manitou High rings at three fifteen; I sit, waiting and watching the clock, for that time to come so I can call my son. Christopher's last class of the day is AP European History, and I imagine him there, scribbling his notes and waiting on the clock for the same time I am.

Of course, he's waiting for a very different reason.

Finally it comes. I wait an extra couple minutes because I know he has to get to his locker, and I dial him. Chris answers on the second ring.

"Dad, what's up?"

"I need you to come home right now."

"Is something wrong? Did you hear what I heard about the video?"

"I just need to talk with you about something."

"Is it like, an emergency?"

"No . . ."

"Can it wait, then? I have that student elections planning thing tonight."

"It's pretty important."

"Can you just tell me now?"

"No, I can't."

"But it's not an emergency."

"Chris. Just come home, okay?"

"Fine." He hangs up, and already I feel like this is starting out the wrong way.

I pace in the house while I wait. I go into the bathroom and look at my own face in the mirror. I draw my fingers over my stubbled cheeks, pulling them down to highlight the dark crescents that have formed beneath my eyes.

I'm tired. So damn tired.

Another hour passes before Chris shows up at home. The waiting is terrible; I stand, I sit, I pace, I walk the field. When I finally see him driving up to the house, it feels like I can hardly breathe.

"Dad," he says, looking genuinely aggravated. "If this isn't an emergency, can we make it quick? They're holding everything up for me, so I need to get back soon."

"Sit down," I say. "Let me tell you this, and you can go back after if you feel like it."

"What's going on?"

"You know Grandma's—"

"Is something going on with Grandma?"

"No. Wait. Just let me talk, okay?"

He sits, concern and confusion filling his face, his full, youthful face, where, if I look the right way, I always see his mother.

"You know Grandma's nurse, Lauren."

"Yeah?"

"I'm in love with her."

Chris laughs, an explosive bark of mirth. "Seriously?" He laughs again, and his eyes are wide with an expression somewhere between astonishment and joy. "I've seen how you look at her, Dad. Don't think I haven't noticed, dude. Holy crap, you like Ms. Downey!"

This was not the reaction I was expecting.

"Chris, we've—"

"I mean," he goes on, "she *is* kind of hot." He stares at me in a state of goofy shock, and shakes his head. "Don't worry! She's not really the type I go for." Christopher smiles broadly, almost laughing at the absurdity of the thought of us both being attracted to the same person. "Wow. Go, Dad! Are you going to ask her out or something?"

"Christopher." I sit down across the table from him, and will myself to not look away from his eyes as I speak. "I've been involved with her for almost two years now. I am sorry I didn't tell you. I didn't feel like I could tell you. I didn't know how. I am sorry."

The smile leaves my son's face, and his mouth hangs barely open with jumbled surprise.

"What? You've been . . . what?"

"There's something else. She's pregnant. And we're going to get married. Probably sometime soon."

"What?" His mouth goes wider, and his brows tighten with anger. "Dad . . . what? How could you do this!" He rises to his feet and walks behind me as if he's leaving for his room, but he stops and stomps back and knocks his chair to the floor. "How could you do this?"

Now he goes to his room, and I follow.

"Christopher, I'm sorry."

He crosses the room, grabbing the reading lamp as he passes, flipping it to the floor.

"I can't believe you!" he shouts. He marches down the hall, dragging his hand along the wall, knocking down framed photos one by one.

"Chris, I didn't mean—"

"*Don't fucking talk to me!*" he yells, slamming his door behind him.

The lock to his door clicks loudly.

I stand, for one minute, for another, looking down the hall toward his room. Then I walk to his door, picking my way through the broken glass over the floor. With my ear to the door, I hear him moving around in there.

"Chris?"

"Go away," he says.

"Chris, can we talk?"

"I said go away!" There's a catch in his voice as he says it, and it makes my throat go tight.

"I'll just . . . I'll just be out here."

He doesn't answer.

I go to the kitchen. I bring the chair back to its feet, take a broom from the closet and sweep up the glass in the hall. I pick up the frames and put them in a stack on my desk. I bring the reading lamp back to a standing position and straighten the shade. And I return to Christopher's door.

"Chris, I'll be right out here. If you need to talk."

There's no reply. I lean my back to the wall, and slide myself down to a seat on the floor. For a very long time I stay there.

Chris does not emerge from his room for the rest of the evening. I listen as I sit on the floor, for the shuffling sounds, the bangs and thumps, the occasional evidence of respiration. I give up on saying anything to him; he won't answer. And I finally give up on waiting.

Dinner does not bring him out, so I pour myself a half glass of whiskey over ice and eat alone. My brother on TV does not bring him out either. He's upset, I get it. My glass remains half-filled; sometimes replenished by ice, and other times by spirit.

Alan was right, like he is about everything: I should have told him sooner.

I go outside to take a stroll around the field, the short glass clinking at my side through the dusk. The grass is wet, and my shoes and the lower legs of my jeans are soon soaked. I don't really care. When I'm as far as I could possibly be from the house, my phone rings in my pocket. I fumble as I draw it from my pants, thinking, hoping, it might be Chris, but it's just Peggy Mackie.

"Neil, how are you holding up?"

"You know, this video thing seems relatively minor now, to tell the truth."

"Good, good," she says, completely missing the point. How would she know? "So, do you want the good news or the bad news first?"

"Let's get the bad news out of the way. I'm ready for anything."

"Bad news is, the board will probably recommend that your teaching contract be terminated Tuesday night."

"Oh great," I say. "How about that." It's not like I didn't think it was coming; the revelation seems almost anticlimactic.

"Now," Peggy goes on, "that's just their recommendation to Admin. We'll be expected to follow it, but your lawyer will probably want to contest the terms, and the teachers' union representative will certainly contest the terms. Can you bring your lawyer Tuesday?"

"Uh, sure, I'll get right on that."

"Good. Has the union guy called? He claims he has your number."

"Union guy? No union guy has called."

"Typical. He'll call."

"So what is the good news?"

"First part of the good news is there's precedent in the state for you being terminated with a year of your salary and benefits, and probably some sort of severance. With that to go on, we'll tack it on to the board's recommendation."

"No shit?" I say. In light of everything else, this really is pretty good news.

"No shit. I'm pulling for you to get the best deal here, okay? And you did not hear me say that, ever. If it were up to Gracie, she'd find a reason to have everyone at your pay grade fired. Now, the other part of the good news, maybe the best news; Pete Tran is going to bring two kids in tomorrow for questioning."

"How is that good?"

"He thinks they were involved in the whole Cody Tate thing, and some of the stories aren't lining up. He thinks if he can get them out of school for a day, maybe he can trip them up. I told him they're texting each other twenty-four-seven and it probably wouldn't make any difference, but he seemed to think it would. Maybe he's just trying to scare them into slipping up."

"So again, how exactly is this good?"

"If he's got reason to think something weird is going on, and his computer guy seems to be leaning that way, maybe we can ask the board to wait on a decision. Or get better terms for you. We've been taking a beating on this in the media for sure. Every time something's on the news about it, Gracie calls me in a rage. She's got the rest of the board worked up about it too."

"I thought you were done with the bad news part?"

"Just hang in there," she tells me. "Wait. One more good thing, but not so related. The Masterson pictures."

"Yeah?"

"Both were fake. The kid just got them from a porn site and cropped them down so you couldn't see faces, then told his friends they were of his ex when he sent them around. He's still in big trouble, but it's a different kind of big trouble."

"God, you almost would want to kick the shit out of a kid for doing something like that."

"You did *not* just say that, Neil. I am going to pretend I didn't hear that."

"Right," I say. "Thanks for everything, Peggy."

We hang up and I go back inside; there's evidence in the form of a plate by the sink that Chris ventured out of his room for something to eat. I refill my glass and return to his door.

"Chris, come on. Can we talk?"

Nothing. Complete silence. I'm tempted to get a thin screwdriver to unlock the door, but we made a deal a long time ago that

I'd respect his space when his door was locked, and I feel like today I've burned enough of his trust.

I go to the kitchen and wash my son's dinner plate. That's something. And the potential of a severance package, that's something too. I have received no call from any union rep, though, and it dawns on me that maybe the number they have is my landline, and that maybe I should plug the thing back in and check my messages in the event that he might call, or has called already. The instant I work the phone's plug back into the outlet, the set rings at full volume, nearly making me jump out of my skin; the name on the ID reads TESHCO.

"Is TeshCo the name of the teachers' union?" I say upon accepting the call.

"You are not such a good man, Mr. Neil K." It's the robot voice again.

"Why don't you just leave me alone," I say, not very forcefully.

"I could leave you alone, but the rest of us probably would not. We are so, so many! And our memories are long, Neil K. And our sense of justice is perhaps . . ."

"Perhaps what?" I say. I'm speaking softly. I don't want Christopher to hear, but at the same time, I wish he were out in the room with me. "You're assuming I did something wrong. How do you know—"

"We know, Neil K. We have seen the video. We know what it is like at the hand of a bully. Maybe you now can know this thing too. We are everywhere, and we know." *Click.* The hair on my arms is standing up as the call goes dead. I hang up the phone, and unplug the phone from the wall once more. Screw it, the union guy can track me down some other way if he needs to talk to me so badly.

My hands are shaking. *Who the fuck is that guy?* Is it some student trying to frighten me, or is it something more sinister? If it's a student, he's succeeded, at least in the immediate term. I consider for just a moment calling Pete Tran to tell him about what's going on, but what the hell. I'm fine. I fill my glass once more with whiskey and go around the doors of my house to make sure they're all locked.

With a conspicuous silence hanging over the house, I go to my room to prepare myself for bed, and do my best to purge my head of all thoughts. I stand and look at my still-made bed, and, knowing that sleep will be as hard in coming as it's been all week, I go to my closet and reach for my shoebox. The pill bottle rattles lightly when I test it, and I open it to find only two tablets remaining. One might be enough to get me to sleep, but I want to be *certain*, so I dump both of them into my hand, bring my palm to my mouth, and swallow them with the watery dregs of my drink. The empty glass is as depressing as anything else, so I go to the kitchen for a last refill before slinking back to my spot on the hallway floor.

"Chris?" I say softly. Nothing.

I draw up my knees and rest my head against the wall. I repeat my son's name: two times, three. I say it again, and close my eyes.

From: xc.coach.kaz@gmail.com
To: w.kazenzakis@gmail.com
Sent: September 14, 8:45 pm
Subject: Lauren Downey

I told Chris, and he didn't take it very well. I haven't seen him lose control like that in a long, long time.

Keeping something inside like that for so long can kill you.

CHAPTER NINETEEN

I'm surprised when I wake in my bed the next morning, both at the fact that I am fully clothed beneath my covers, and at the fact that it is ten minutes after eleven o'clock. Have I ever slept this late in my entire life? Chris says nothing when I meet him in the kitchen. His lips remain pressed into a thin line, and he won't meet my eyes. When I stand in the doorway to try to speak with him, he keeps his back to me.

"Christopher, come on." No response. He makes himself a sandwich, and I get myself a glass of water to try to clear out the whiskey-sludge feeling left in my mouth and the hazy feeling up behind my eyes. Just how much did I drink last night?

"You're pissed," I say, trying to find the right words. "Okay. I understand. But this is what's going on. I'm dealing with all this, and I want you to be with me on it, okay?" Nothing. He silently takes a bite of his sandwich and chews. "What if we do an overnight on *Tabby* Sunday night, huh?" I ask, catching the smallest flicker in his eye as a response. "Soon as you get back from basketball camp, we'll get the boat, head out to South Manitou, talk it out. Don't worry about school on Monday. You can take a day or two off. I need you, Christopher. I need you back on the team."

Chris finishes his lunch, drops his plate into the sink, and blows past me to pick up his pack and gym bag on his way out the door.

"Think about it, Chris!" I call from the doorway. "I'll see you tomorrow!"

In that flicker in his eye, there was a hint of détente. I'm sure of it.

I consider a run, but I feel like shit, so I go over to check on Carol. No car is there yet, and when I go in the door, I see that Lauren's name is on the scheduling whiteboard for today beginning at noon. When I see her name there, I almost smile. Maybe, somehow, things will be okay. Just like Alan said, Chris would be mad about it, then he'd get over it. Maybe everything will work out.

A year's pay with benefits, plus a severance? That would buy me some time with Leland, for sure. I could fix up the houses to rent out, or maybe even have the beach house remodeled and tell Leland to forget it. And if we have some income from renting Lauren's condo . . .

Maybe things won't be so bad after all. Maybe.

Carol is seated upright in her bed, with a copy of Friday's Bungle spread out over the quilt before her.

"Neil, what the heck is this business with you in the paper?"

So much for this refuge.

"Some kids have played a pretty mean trick, I think. On me."

"It says you're suspended from your job?"

"I am."

"Damn kids," Carol says.

"You can say that again." I pull a chair next to the bed and sit. "Feeling good today?"

"I'm feeling pretty good. Seems like the mornings can be better. It comes and goes. I can't even explain what it's like when it's not good. I find myself places, Neil, and I don't even know how I got there. I think I see Dick."

"You've called me Arthur," I say.

"Sure I have. You look just like Art when he was a young man."

I consider, just for a second, telling her, in this rare moment while she's clearheaded, about me and Lauren, everything about Lauren and me, but I stop myself. I should talk with Lauren first. She should be here too.

"Did you ever know anyone named Lawler?" I ask instead. "Here in Port Manitou, or somewhere around here?"

"Oh gosh, there was . . . well, Harvey Lawler we knew, from the co-op over in Suttons Bay. A real crack-up, Harvey was. He lost his first wife to . . . well, I can't recall the illness now. But his second wife, Bess, was a crack-up too. We had them over for cards here and there. What in the world made you think about Harvey Lawler?"

"You mentioned that name the other day, it just got me wondering."

"I don't even remember that, Neil. You see what I mean? It used to trouble me. Now I figure, if I worried myself about it, I'd be worrying all the time I was feeling well! I guess you could say I've accepted my position in life."

"Did Harvey Lawler ever have anything to do with the orchard?"

"No, no, not that I recall. We always worked with the Manitou co-op. But what a funny man that Harvey Lawler was."

"Would Dick ever have sold the orchard? Or any part of it?"

"Goodness no. Dick would have had himself buried on the orchard if he could have. He looked into it, you know, when the lawyers were drawing up his will. I told him he should just be cremated and we could toss his ashes out around the cherries, but that idea didn't sit too well with him."

I hear the garage door open, and the sounds of someone in the farmhouse kitchen. Carol can't hear it, but she sees my reaction.

"Nurse is here, I suppose?" I nod. "Did you happen to see who I've got today?"

"Lauren Downey," I say.

"Oh, well then." Carol gives me a sideways glance. "That Lauren's a real sweetie, don't you think?"

"I . . ."

"Come on, Neil. Don't tell me you've never caught one of those looks she gives you from time to time."

"No, uh, I really never . . ."

"Well, look at you, Mister Bashful. A lady can tell these things, you know. I think you should try to get to know Miss Downey a little better."

I cannot believe I'm having this conversation. With my mother-in-law.

"Maybe I'll go say hello to her now," I say.

"You do that," Carol says. I think she actually winks at me as she says it.

Lauren's unpacking some groceries when I find her in the kitchen.

"Oh." she says. "You're here. Hi. How is Chris?"

"He was pretty mad about everything last night, and he left for his basketball camp a bit ago without really saying anything. I might try for some Dad time with him tomorrow night."

"You do Dad time," she says, and she wraps her arms around my waist and buries her face in my shirt so I can't see her. "I don't know about this." She's sobbing, and her shoulders shake beneath my arms. "I just don't know if I can do this."

"We'll be okay," I say, perhaps with desperation. "We will."

By saying it, can I simply make it so?

"You'd better go," Lauren says. She pulls a worn tissue from her pocket and wipes her eyes. "I need to check on Carol. Call me later."

Back home, I clean up the kitchen, deliberately washing and drying Christopher's plate before putting it away in the cabinet. The bottle of whiskey, nearly empty, sits on the counter by the window; the taste of it still lingering in my mouth seems vile, so I pour the last of it down the drain and drop the bottle into the recycling bin beneath the sink.

Chris. Why did he react this way? He's a teen boy, I must remind myself, large in size and tendency toward kindness, but not yet an adult. I forget that sometimes. And I've really been lucky with him, so lucky, especially knowing as well as I do from school how far things can go wrong in some families.

He'll cool down tonight at camp, I know it. He'll have a chance to work out on the court, burn off some steam, and he'll come home tomorrow and we can talk about it.

If anything, I feel relief right now. The greatest burden I've felt over the past two years, the burden of secrecy, the burden of hiding something from my son, is gone. Even as everything falls apart, the heaviest of weights has been lifted.

I go to the spare room and wake up the laptop. YouTube is up; I close it and open my personal email.

And I type a letter:

From: xc.coach.kaz@gmail.com
To: w.kazenzakis@gmail.com
Sent: September 15, 9:12 am
Subject: Chris, and Other

Dear Wendy,

Christopher, as I said, did not take the news about Lauren very
well. He is angry, with a teen boy's sort of rage: he shouted and
knocked things over last night, and locked himself in his room.
He gave me the silent treatment this morning. As unpleasant
as it was, though, and as rotten as I'm feeling right now, I feel
much better getting it out.

There's something I want to tell you. Something, actually, I've
wanted to tell you for a long time. But first, a digression: I
notice, in my life, that the greatest organizer of memories, the
way I file and assign the events of my existence into some sort
of chronological order, is by remembering how old, or what
grade, Chris was at the time. It's odd, because I feel like I'm
a constant in these memories, but Chris is always changing,
getting bigger and bigger. It's like a form of archaeology,
dating my stories by the size of our son.

You are a constant too, with two distinct states, pre- and post-
accident. AM, PM; BC, AD. Wendy Before, and Wendy After.

Anyway, it was late spring, almost the end of the school year.
Chris was in the seventh grade. I attended some conference
in downtown Chicago; I don't even remember what the

conference was about, but I do know Christopher was thirteen and it was the springtime. It was, in fact, unusually warm in Chicago, and I got a sunburn on my face and arms when I walked around the city one day because I was so used to it still being winter at home and forgot to put on sunblock.

I think you remember Anne Vasquez. Maybe she was still Anne Stedman at that point, I don't recall if she was married yet, or if she was still just engaged. I'm pretty sure she was engaged to be married then. You met her at the conference I took you to in Philadelphia, and maybe at another one after that, and you would certainly remember her for the catty nickname you made up for her, "Anne of the Rack," because she had a big chest.

Anne was at that Chicago conference too. Springtime, Chris in seventh grade conference. She and I were friends, you didn't like that, you never liked that, and it made me sad because I think you would have really liked her if you'd ever had the chance to spend time with her. You rolled your eyes when I told you she was going to be at that last one with us in Wisconsin, and you sarcastically told me to have a nice time with Anne of the Rack.

So, to continue the story of Chicago, the story I need to tell you: the last night of the conference, most of the attendees from districts in Michigan met up to go out for dinner. It was a big table, there was drinking, Anne was sitting next to me. To be honest, as I was drinking, maybe I was glancing at the rack a little bit. I think she noticed, and teased me about it.

We settled the bill and a handful of us went to a bar. People were dancing. Not me, you know I'm not a dancer, but Anne danced, she was having fun, and I just stayed back and watched her dance. That was good enough for me. But she kept bugging me, she kept bugging me: "Come on, Neil, come here, come dance with us, it's fun!" and I had been drinking enough that I thought, sure, I'll dance, why not. So I did. I danced, and Anne laughed at me for my stiff dancing, but it was fun.

Things were a little foggy by then, but at some point, maybe it was closing time, the few of us who were still standing made our way back to the hotel. I had the highest floor of all our rooms (floor seventeen, how do I remember that?) and everyone got off one by one, and I noticed when Anne didn't get off at her floor (twelve), but I didn't say anything about it. She stayed on, and when we got to my floor, just her and me, she got off the elevator and walked with me to my room. I didn't say anything about that either.

We kissed in the room. We stood there, barely staying up, we were swaying from drinking so much, and we kissed. I had my hands on her hips, and she untucked my shirt. We kissed, and one of us said "we shouldn't," and the other said "no, we shouldn't," but we kept kissing for a while more, and my hands were inside her shirt, kind of, and everywhere else, kind of. Time passed. Then one of us said "God, we really can't do this," and the other said "you're right," and she left the room, and that was it.

The next morning at the hotel breakfast, she sat down at my table, and when no one else was around she said, "Bad, bad, bad, Neil. Never again." I said, "Never." And that was all we ever said about it.

So, there it is. Springtime, Christopher in seventh grade.

-Neil

CHAPTER TWENTY

My cell phone buzzes in my pocket just before one; I grab for it, hoping it's Chris, hoping he'll say we should go out on *Tabby*, and my spirits lift when I see TC REC CENTER on the display.

"Hello?"

"Hey, Neil, it's Janine." Janine is one of the coordinators for the basketball program. "Was your kiddo planning to show up today?"

"Pardon me?"

"Chris is on the roster, but no one here has seen him."

I don't speak.

"Neil?"

"I'm not sure . . ." I gather my thoughts. "You know, I don't know if you saw what's going on with me, the video—"

"I have. I'm really sorry."

"Thank you. And Chris got some more news last night on top of that." I wonder, for a moment, if he's been in an accident, but stop the thought before it spirals into panic. "I'm going to say he's not going to make it tonight. I'm sorry for the inconvenience."

"Oh, no worry," Janine says. "We'll miss him! The kids are going to miss him. He's such a great guy."

"Thank you," I say. "Do me a favor, okay? If he does show up, will you call and let me know?"

"You got it. Hey, good luck with everything, Neil."

"Thanks." I tap to end the call and rub the back of my neck. I consider for a moment calling Pete Tran to ask if he's heard of any car crashes involving old Volvos, but I don't. Instead I dial the nursing home, and ask to be put through to Wendy's wing.

"Long Term Care, this is Linda."

"Linda, it's Neil Kazenzakis. Wendy's husband. Is Shanice there?"

"Sorry, Mr. K., it's her day off today."

"Oh. Has my son, Christopher, been over there?"

"You just missed him. He left maybe ten minutes ago."

"Really? Did he seem . . . upset?"

"Not that I could tell. We chatted a little bit. He said he wanted to say hi to his mom."

"Thank you. If he comes back, will you call me?"

"Is something wrong, Mr. Kazenzakis?"

"Oh no . . . we're fine. I'll catch up with him soon."

After I hang up, I dial Chris. The call goes right to his voice mail, and I need to pause for a moment to think of what to say.

"Chris, hey. Hey. I know you're upset. Rec Center just called, Janine said you hadn't shown up. So don't worry about that. Just . . . be safe, okay? Don't get mad and go driving around all crazy or anything. Just come home when you're ready, and we can talk."

I orbit the room, pacing, pacing, and make my way out onto the deck. The air is not as cold as it was earlier, and the sky is a crystalline, cloudless blue. I duck inside to grab a pair of shoes, and head back out and over to the basketball court. Three balls rest at the base of the basket on the end of the court closest to the house. I pick one up and take a few clumsy shots, as if that will somehow conjure my son, or induce him to come home.

Years ago, standing where the basketball court is now, Dick Olsson had a red, metal-sided pole barn. I never ever went in there as a kid when we were visiting, and I still felt odd entering as an adult, even when I was invited. It was Dick's hideout, filled with several decades' worth of tools, guns, car parts, disabled tractors, assorted fittings, snowblowers, expired jugs of herbicide, and animal trophy mounts hung in the rafters, staring with their dead glass eyes down on all the detritus—along with the beatific gaze of Ronald Reagan from over the workbench. After Dick's heart attack, it fell on me to clear the space of all his stuff, a job that ultimately took me three and a half years. The roof needed repair, the sliding door didn't work, and we decided the best thing to do would be to clean out the building and raze it to the ground.

After I'd taken away all of the obviously useful things like tools and good lumber and stowed them in my garage, and his friends had stopped by to pick over everything else, I had an auctioneer come to take a look at what was left. Drill presses, metal lathes, fifty-five gallon drums, and more were all carted away and sold downstate.

Still, this left me with a lot. I had the Sanitation Department deposit a full-sized industrial Dumpster outside in the grass, and I built up my arms and strained my back throwing thirty-year-old chrome car bumpers and ripped-up draftsman's chairs in there. Wendy helped too. We spent hours, it seemed, going through his things. Sometimes Chris joined us to search for some new treasure; we just had to be sure to check how potentially lethal any find might be before letting him run off to play with it.

Some things couldn't be just tossed. Practically, I could not in good conscience discard seven pounds of gunpowder, twenty cases of .45-caliber ammunition, or a three-foot sword. Sentimentally, I certainly wasn't going to pitch a lock of hair labeled as coming from Dick's mother, or the box I found of Dick's medals—including a purple heart—from his time in the marines. Those things went over to Carol.

I'd never even known Dick had been in the military. I'd spent an awful lot of time with the man, building our house and doing other things, but he just wasn't the type to talk about his past that way.

As I got the place cleared out, I found myself becoming oddly attached to it. It seemed much larger inside with all the stuff gone; there was a long, solid workbench, and a fridge if I wanted to come have a beer in peace. The roof wouldn't be too hard to fix, I remember thinking. I started to feel the charms of the space, and began to understand why Dick loved it so.

I was almost done with the job when Wendy had her accident, and I didn't go back in there for a while. I couldn't. There were other things to deal with at the time.

Chris is still not home by four in the afternoon. He hasn't called either, and, despite all efforts to keep myself calm, my worry has hardened into something visceral I feel in the center of my body. It's not like him to keep me in the dark about where he is and where he's going, and not having this knowledge is disorienting. I've almost run my phone dead from checking it so frequently, and now I have to keep running into the spare bedroom where I have it plugged into the charger cord next to the laptop.

If he's gone much longer, I'll move the cord to a more convenient location.

I check the phone again, and no there's no text waiting, no missed call. I try Chris, and once again I go direct to voice mail. I don't leave a message, and I call Lauren right after.

"Hey," she says. "Neil, about earlier, I'm sorry, I was—"

"Stop. Chris is sort of missing. He's not where he's supposed to be."

"What do you mean?" I tell her about the call from the rec center, and Lauren is quick to try to reassure me.

"He's . . . he's got to be just wandering around, thinking it all through," she says. "He'll be back, Neil. Let him process it all. This is a big thing we've given him."

"I know. But I feel . . . I should have told him everything a long time ago."

"You didn't want to hurt him. It's okay."

"That seems to have worked out really well, doesn't it? God, this isn't like him at all."

"Oh, Neil. Didn't you ever do something like this when you were younger? Weren't you ever moody? Or brooding?"

"No, not really." The only time I caused my parents any real grief was when they'd found out Mike and I had hosted a party at our house when we were seventeen. Compared to this, that situation seems pretty minor."

"I understand if you don't want me there, but do you want me to come over? I didn't mean what I said. I want this. I want us. You can say no if you want."

"I would like it if you were here."

"Should I bring things to stay the night?"

What would Chris think if he came home and found Lauren here?

"Why don't you bring your stuff," I say, "and we'll see how it goes. I'd like you to stay, but let's see what happens."

"I understand. Why don't I pick up something for us to eat too?"

"You're awesome," I say. Cooking is the last thing I want to deal with right now.

"He'll be back, Neil. He will."

-------- ———————— - - - - -

One year when Chris was in elementary school, on a summer day when I was supposed to be keeping an eye on him, he went missing. Wendy worked as an office manager for a tour boat company then, and I'd watch Chris some days during the summers. It saved us money on day care, and I got to spend time with him, so it was a win all around.

I'd been working that summer on building an extension to our back deck. Dick would come sometimes to help me out, but mostly I was solo. Chris played in the yard while I sawed lumber or screwed down deck boards; sometimes I'd give him a hammer and some scraps of wood to nail together in his own little projects. It was a fun summer.

One morning I was preoccupied with hanging deck joists. I'd mismeasured at some point, my alignment was off, and I had to pull out a bunch of my work to start over. I got absorbed by the job for a couple hours. When I finally looked at my watch, I realized it was well past noon, and I needed to get Chris inside for some lunch. But he wasn't in the yard behind me. His hammer was there, his scraps of lumber were there, but no Chris. I unbuckled my tool bags and dropped them to the ground, and started to call his name. I walked out into the field and called for him, but there was no answer.

"Christopher!" I shouted, maybe louder than I'd ever shouted anything before. "Chris!" I ran around the perimeter of the field, trying to shake off an encroaching feeling of dread. "Christopher!"

Dick heard my shouting, and emerged from his workshop in the barn.

"What is it?" he asked.

"I can't find Chris."

"Oh Jesus," Dick said. "I'll check up by the river."

I ran east into the orchard while Dick went north. I searched, calling and calling, and when it wasn't me hollering Christopher's name, I heard Dick's far-off shouts echoing through the groves of cherry trees. We met back in the field, and I had a sudden horrifying vision of my son drowning; we'd always had a rule that the beach or the Little Jib River were only places to go with a grown-up, and I worried that made it tempting for him. Panic seized my chest, and I took off, full bore, for the dunes, running and shouting his name. From the top of the most beachward dune, I scanned the shoreline, north and south, and out into the water; there was nothing. My heart felt as if it was going to come out of my chest. Then I heard Dick.

"Neil!" he called. "Come on back. I got him."

I raced back to the field, and found my father-in-law smiling as he waited for me.

"Where is he?" I asked, trying to catch my breath.

"Come on," Dick said. "Keep your voice down."

I followed him into the pines, and to a deer blind Dick had built from an old truck bed and some sheets of plywood for a roof. Inside, curled up and fast asleep in a nest of dusty horse blankets, was Chris.

"Oh," I said, trying not to cry with relief. "Oh." Dick smiled, and I smiled too. I didn't want Dick to see me cry. But when I looked, I saw Dick was crying himself, so I stopped worrying about it.

"Chris," I whispered. "Hey, wake up, kiddo."

Chris blinked his eyes open, startled, I'm sure, by the two silently weeping grown men looming over him. He blinked his eyes into focus, took in his surroundings, and gave a sideways smile.

"What happened?" he asked us. "How . . . how did I get in here?"

-------- ———————— ------

Maybe Chris is in the deer blind now, I think. Why not check? I've checked everywhere else. I head off through the field and duck under the heavy boughs of our pine woods; Dick planted these trees with his father, I learned, when he was only ten years old.

The deer blind is not as I remember it. The plywood roof is split and sagging, and the camouflage paint of the old truck bed has completely given way to a scab-colored patina of rust. Everything is thick with pine needles; the rotted horse blankets are completely covered with them.

Chris is not there.

I stand for a bit, wishing it would be as simple as finding him here, knees pulled up and mouth hanging open, a placidly breathing, sleeping little boy. But I can't go back to that. I think of the times I spent in the blind; more of those silent times spent with Dick Olsson. He'd ask me to come and we'd sit for hours, quietly, me with a thermos of coffee and him with a gun across his lap. I remember a time when a massive buck passed not twenty feet in front of us. The creature paused to sniff the air, and I waited, not breathing as Dick raised his gun and sighted down the barrel, bracing myself for the massive report that would send the animal to the ground. Wanting to feel that, but not wanting to at all, I waited for Dick to do something. He didn't though, and the big deer continued on to wherever he was going. The gun went back to Dick's lap.

"Anymore," he said after the deer was gone from our view, "I prefer to just let them wander around."

Northward now, I move toward the river, through the pines and groves, and west along the bank toward the dunes. The lake is peaceful under the faintest breeze; the beach is calm. Chris is not here. Not far away, the beach house is shuttered and silent, and Art's truck is gone.

"Chris!" I shout, but there's no answer.

Lauren waits for me when I return to the house.

"I figured you were out," she says. "Running or something. I got Thai food. Is that okay?"

It is okay, and I tell her so; she hugs me and apologizes for earlier and we sit on the floor to eat. Sometimes Lauren reaches to rub my knee.

"I haven't even asked how you're feeling," I say. "I suck."

"I'm great," she says. "Really. I feel so normal I'm almost having doubts that you knocked me up." She winks at me and I manage a wan smile in return; I'm feeling too sick to my stomach to offer anything else.

"I scheduled my first OB appointment," she goes on. "One week from next Wednesday."

"What time?"

"Eleven thirty. I bet it will run late."

"I don't teach that period," I say. "I'll get someone to cover me if I'm on lunch duty."

"You . . ." Lauren cocks her head. "You think you'll be back at work?" I almost laugh.

"God. No. I forgot."

We finish and clean up, and I find a screwdriver to unlock Christopher's door. Everything seems normal; the bed is made, his homework is on his desk, some clothes are tossed over the back of his chair.

We go outside and walk together down to the highway. I stand and look toward town while Lauren holds my hand and leans into me.

"If he stays away tonight, I think I might really lose it," I say.

"He'll be okay. He's upset. He's a good kid. You've made him a good kid."

The early dusk glows with a pair of headlights in the distance. They approach, slow as they pass us, and drive on down the road.

Back inside, I find the student directory containing the home numbers of almost all of my son's good friends, and I spend an hour and a half calling around to see if anyone has seen Chris. Nope, they all say. Nope, haven't seen him. We'll call you if we do. Lauren is reading a nursing textbook on the couch, a highlighter in her teeth and her legs pulled up to her side.

"You bring an air of calm to the household," I tell her. "By acting so normal, you make me forget anything's going on."

"That's good, right?"

"Maybe. I feel like I should be panicking a little more." I almost tell her about the strange phone calls from the robot voice, but I don't. I don't want her to worry.

"How would panicking help anything?" she asks.

"It might make me feel like I was doing . . ." I think I hear a noise, a car approaching maybe, and I twist my head so my ear is toward the door. It's nothing. "It might make me feel like I was doing something."

"Okay. Let's think about this. Come, sit." Lauren pats the couch next to her and twists to an upright position. She closes her text and flips her notebook open to a clean page. "If he's not back by tomorrow morning, what's the next step?"

"Look at you, so organized. Did I mention the calming effect you seem to have on me?"

"I'm serious. What do we do? Call the police?"

I lean my head back and sigh. "I don't know. I don't want to get the police involved now. He's almost eighteen—"

"But he's not eighteen yet. Think about it this way. If one of your students was missing, and his parents called you for help, what would you tell them to do?"

"Call the cops," I sigh. My head is still back and my eyes are closed, and I hear Lauren's pencil scratching on her notepad.

"Okay. What's our cutoff time to call?"

"Are you always this precise about things?"

"Yes, actually, I am. What time do we call if he's not back?"

"If he's not back by three tomorrow afternoon," I say, picking a number out of thin air, "then let's call."

"If he's gone away somewhere, what are some of the places he might go?"

"Well . . ." I start, and I sit up and pause. "I should call Michael. Jesus Christ, I should have called Michael."

I dial my brother as fast as I can; thankfully he answers right away.

"What do you guys *want*?" he says testily. "I'm kind of in the middle of Saturday night service, here. Why the fuck do you guys keep calling?"

"Has Chris called you?"

"He's tried like three fucking times! What the hell, you guys, can this wait?"

"You've talked to him?"

"No, Neil, I haven't! Maybe because I'm like, running my restaurant on the busiest night of the week?"

"Chris is missing. He didn't go to his basketball camp today and he hasn't come home."

"You're kidding me." It's suddenly silent in the background.

"I'm not. If he calls you, Michael, please talk to him." I'm holding the phone to my ear with both of my hands. "Answer when he calls you the next time. Talk to him. Find out where he is, tell him to stay put, and call me right away, okay?"

"What the hell? What is going on?"

I take a breath. To my side, Lauren is leaning in to me as she listens.

"You know I told you about how I've kind of been hanging out with one of Carol's nurses, right? Lauren."

"I recall you told me about this Lauren."

"I've never told Chris. But I told him last night."

"And he freaked out?"

"Well, Lauren's pregnant, and I told him that too."

"Dude. She's what?"

"Don't worry about that now. We're talking about Chris. I need you to help me with Chris. Just talk to him when he calls, okay? Talk to him and—"

"Calm down, Neil. I'll talk to him. I'll call you back."

We wait for nearly two hours, Lauren with her textbook and me with my phone in my lap. When it rings, I nearly jump. It's Michael.

"No call," he tells me. "He didn't leave me any messages when he called before either. I tried him back, but nothing." I don't respond. I can't. "You okay?" Mike asks.

"Not really. Not at all."

"You want me to come up? I can leave first thing in the morning."

"No," I say quickly. "Stay put. I think he might . . . just stay there, okay?"

We end the call, and I sit, staring at nothing. *Where could he be? Christopher, where are you?*

Lauren touches my arm and it jolts me back into the room.

"Let's go to bed, Neil," she says softly. "Let's get some sleep and be ready for tomorrow."

I wave my hand toward the hall. "You go," I say. "I'm going to wait here on the couch a little while more."

"Okay," Lauren whispers, leaning close and kissing my cheek. "He'll be all right."

I nod, and ask Lauren to turn out the light as she goes. There is no more whiskey, no more sedative; I must face this darkness on my own.

In the unlit room, I sit and listen and wait.

---------———————-------

Sometime in the middle of the night, I wake from my half sleep on the couch to check my phone for missed calls or texts. I open the mobile browser to check my email, draw in my breath, and say, "Holy shit" out loud when I see what's there.

My last email to Wendy, subject "Chris, and Other," has a reply.

From: mailer-daemon@googlemail.com
To: xc.coach.kaz@gmail.com
Sent: September 15, 3:01 am
Subject: RE: Chris, and Other

_____

Delivery to the following recipient failed permanently:

w.kazenzakis@gmail.com

Technical details of permanent failure:

The email account that you tried to reach does not exist.

CHAPTER TWENTY-ONE

When I blink my eyes open, I'm assaulted by a bright blue glow; the full moon is setting over the dunes, and the light of it shines through the living room window and onto my face. I'm still on the couch, I realize, and the clock on the cable box under the TV says four forty-four. I roll to my back and rub my eyes, and remember the email I got in the middle of the night.

Wendy's account has expired, I realize; no more emails to Wendy.

No more.

Then I remember my son has been missing, and I push myself upright. Did he come back home sometime in the night? I jump to my feet and run to his room; the door is closed but unlocked—it's unlocked!—and I go in.

The bed is made, he's not there, and the memory of checking in there last night returns to me.

"Neil?" Wendy calls.

"He's not here," I say.

"Come to bed," the voice says, and I blink and realize I cannot be speaking with Wendy.

"Hold on." I go into the bathroom, relieve my night-filled bladder, and shuffle through the darkness to my room to climb into my bed with Lauren's voice, with Lauren, for real. She's so warm, the real Lauren, it's perfectly warm under the covers with her, and I curl in behind her, tucking my knees against the backs of her legs and sliding my arm up under her shirt and around her waist.

"Is he home?"

"No." I press my lips to her shoulder and neck.

"Did you sleep at all?"

"A little." I say.

Curled together, we rest. Daylight fills the room when I wake again; Lauren remains in heavy slumber. I take my arm from her slowly, slip out from under the covers, and get myself dressed.

There are no messages on my phone. It's ten after seven, and I dial Chris. Nothing. I check my email, and there's nothing there either. I check to see if I can get into my school email account and, sure enough, I can; maybe a student knows something about Christopher's location and will have sent me something, *anything,* to give me a hint of where he could be. The inbox is empty except for one email from the network administrator, Cory, with a subject of: VERY IMPORTANT!! Could he know something? I open it and read:

I DO NOT THINK THIS FLOATS SO VERY WELL, NEIL!!

Below the line of text, I see the beginning of a photograph. I can only see the top: blue sky, white clouds. I scroll down. Tops of trees, summertime green. Scroll some more, and there's damp concrete. White tile. NO DIVING in stenciled letters. Chlorinated blue water. And though I know I shouldn't, *I know I should not do this,* I scroll down to the bottom of the page.

There's a body at the bottom of the pool. A woman's body, lifeless.

I stare at it, and stare; my teeth are clenched, the world goes white, in a rage, a *rage,* my phone is in my hand, the name in my contacts is tapped, and I'm rising to my feet in fury.

"You little fuck!" I nearly scream when the call is accepted. "You weak little piece of shit!"

"No, Mr. K.—"

The world is white with rage, and all I can see is a body at the bottom of a pool.

"You thought this was funny, right? Right? You think this is funny!"

"No, stop, please," Cory says, begging. He sounds pathetic to me. "We were—"

"I want to hurt you right now," I spit. "And it wouldn't be funny. So help me, I want to take my own hands and—"

"—we were hacked! Someone got in, they took over the whole network. I'm sorry, I'm so sorry, the police have been here. We got hacked, it wasn't me, I swear."

"Jesus Christ," I say, feeling sick. Lauren is at the door.

"Neil, what's going on?" she whispers.

"They got in five days ago," Cory goes on, pleading. "They locked me out of my account, out of everything, I don't know how they got in. I tried to call you, I kept trying to call you, I'm sorry, I left messages on your machine—"

My phone shakes in my hand so violently I can barely operate it, but I hang up on Cory and dial Chris again immediately. To my amazement, I get a ring, and to my even greater amazement, the call connects with the sound of fumbling.

"Chris!" I say. "Christopher, where—" Immediately, he hangs up. "Goddammit!" I shout, and I try to call him back. Nothing.

I feel myself beginning to come apart.

"Neil?" Lauren says, her eyes wide. "What's happening?"

I grab a jacket and dash out of the house, and the emptiness of the space to the side of the garage where Christopher parks his car seems like a taunt. "Damn it!" I shout. "Damn it, Chris!" I set off in a run, down the drive and to the path by the highway, all the way to Alan's house. I burst in the door, startling Alan in his kitchen. He's wearing a robe and holding a coffee mug, and he spins his body toward me in surprise as I come in.

"Hey, what's going—"

"You told me to tell him!" I shout. "You told me it would be okay!"

"I did tell you to tell him."

"None of this is okay! You said it would be okay!"

"I never said—"

"You're supposed to know everything! How the fuck could you be so wrong!"

"Neil, you need to calm down if we're going to deal with this in a reasonable way."

I shake my head and leave his house, starting out fast but settling into a jog halfway home. I feel like an idiot. I feel better, maybe, for the outburst, but I still feel like an idiot.

I'm nearly calm when I get back home, but I see Leland's truck parked in front of my driveway, which gets me agitated all over again. I run in through the front door and Lauren jumps up from the couch.

"Is he in here?" I bark. Lauren puts her hand to her chest.

"No, Chris isn't—"

"Not Chris, Leland!" I go back outside, and Leland steps from around the side of my house, staring at an unrolled surveyor's map.

"Hey," he says, glancing up as he notices me. "Just the man I wanted to—"

"Get out of here!" I yell.

"Excuse me?"

"I said get the fuck off my property!"

"Whoa, Neil, what is going on?"

"Get . . . out . . . of here!" I pick up a fist-sized limestone cobble from the landscape border by my garage, and hurl it at his truck. It bounces off the rear quarter panel with a *tunk!* I pick up another rock.

"Settle down, I'm leaving! I'm leaving!" I throw the second rock and miss widely just as Leland jumps into his truck. The wheels spin out and throw gravel as he drives away.

My breath comes heavily as I watch him go, and the inside of my head seems close to crumbling. I do not want to break. I go to the barn slab, pick up a basketball, and squeeze it between my hands. Instead of taking a shot, I rear back and throw the ball off into the brush.

It was two months after Wendy's accident when I finally brought myself to go into the barn again. Everything was there, just as we'd left it: a case of beer in the refrigerator, a last few boxes of Dick's things to be classified on the workbench. A push broom rested against an open stepladder, right where Wendy had placed it, waiting for her return from a weekend trip to Wisconsin. The broom seemed especially hard to take. I held it, thinking how Wendy's hands had gripped it last, how, through the simple act of her using it, it ceased to be inanimate and became an extension of her. A broom! A stupid, fucking broom. I assigned sentimental value to all sorts of things back then, but the broom was, for a while, the most significant.

Being in the barn was not troubling for me. It provided an unusual comfort; it was quiet, it kept me out of the rain, it kept things cold for me to drink. A bottle of gin joined the beer in the fridge, and a bigger bottle joined after that. A pill bottle filled with antianxiety drugs stayed in the cabinet where Dick had kept fishing lures.

With this pharmacopoeia, I kept myself numbed.

Chris went back to school, and I spent more time in the barn. I started accumulating things there, Wendy's things, my own morbid museum dedicated to my almost-late wife. I set a length of rusty salvaged conduit across the peaks of a pair of stepladders, and from it hung every article of Wendy's clothing that had been in our closet. Her toiletries were spread over the workbench. Toothpaste, hairbrushes, facial scrubs. Could I really ever bring myself to throw these things away? Every one of them had been, at some point, an extension of her.

I kept a padlock on the door. I kept it on the outside when I wasn't there, or on the inside when I was; I didn't want anyone to see her things in there, and I certainly didn't want anyone to see me in there with them.

I didn't want anyone to see me falling apart.

Chris spent a lot of time with Carol then. For a period of time after he'd lost his mother, he lost his father as well.

After Leland has gone, back inside my house, Lauren grabs me as I dash through the living room.

"Neil," she says firmly, pressing her hands to the sides of my head as she stares me in the eyes. "You need to calm down."

I try to twist away from her. "But I'm—"

"You are starting to panic. Breathe. Now."

I take a shaking breath, and another, and the whole time she holds my face and looks at me.

"Okay?" she asks. She doesn't blink. "Breathe. Keep breathing for me. Don't break."

I draw air deeply into me, hold it, and exhale. The tremor through my body begins to slow.

"Okay," I say through clenched teeth.

"Good," she says. "I mean it. Don't break. What happened? What set you off?"

"There was a picture in my email," I say.

"What was it?"

I shake my head. I can't bring myself to say. "Then I called Chris. He picked up, but he disconnected as soon as he knew it was me."

"You probably woke him up," Lauren says.

"He's mad at me."

"I can leave if you need me to. If you don't think I should be here."

"Don't leave." My phone rings. It's a local number on my display, not one that I know, and I answer it eagerly. "Hello?"

"Neil." It's Leland. "I need to—"

"You don't need shit right now," I say, feeling myself wind up again. Lauren puts her hand on my arm and whispers, "Easy."

"I need to apologize. I just heard about Christopher."

"What?"

"I just stopped by Massie's place. He filled me in."

"Christ. I'm sorry, Leland." I take a deep, slow breath. "I'm sorry I flipped out on you."

"It's all right. Let me know when he's back, okay?"

"I will," I say. "Hey, wait, will you . . ." Breathe. "Will you do something for me? Ask Steve if he knows anything."

"I'll give you a call if I come up with any news."

I drop to the living room chair and let my shoulders sag. Lauren sits across from me on the couch with her hands on her knees.

"I'm an asshole," I say to the floor.

"You're not. You're worried. It's okay to be worried. Just breathe."

I press my own hands to my face to rub my eyes. "Where the hell is he?"

--------—————————------

We sit, and wait. Time passes and passes; Lauren puts some music on, but I ask her to turn it off. Nothing seems right; there's no appropriate sound track for the situation. I stay calm, mostly, but from time to time, I stand up and begin to pace around, and Lauren has to tell me to relax.

"Easy," she tells me. "Don't break."

I try to call Christopher, again and again, but he doesn't answer.

Lauren gets up to make some tea, and Alan stops by while she's in the kitchen.

"I'm really sorry about this morning," I say as he joins me in the living room.

"Don't even," Alan says. "I understand. Really. I probably never told you about the time Angela stayed out all night." Angela is the younger of the two Massie daughters. "It wasn't the year she had you for AP, no, it must have been the year before. She was a junior. All night she was out, no call, no nothing. Kristin was the calm one. I was just like you! Maybe even worse. Didn't sleep, tore my hair out. She got home the next morning, man, I didn't know whether to get on my knees and thank God, or ground Angie for the next year for giving me a scare like that. And when I found out she was with a boy, whew, I was ready to go wring his neck. But Kristin calmed me down."

"Wait up," I say. Alan's story has reminded me of the possible appeal of old relationships. "Hold on a second." I go to the spare room and find, in my old planner, Jill Swart's family's number. I get her father and explain what's going on, and he in turn gives me my son's ex-girlfriend's cell number. Alan watches from the doorway. She doesn't answer when I call, so I leave a message.

"Hey Jill, it's Christopher's dad, Saturday morning, hope you're doing well in Ithaca, can you give me a call?"

Maybe he's talked to her. Or maybe not. Anything's worth a try at this point.

"Boot up your computer," Alan directs me after I hang up. "Bring up your video. I have something to show you." I go to the page, and I'm not thrilled at all to see it's up to nearly half a million views.

"Oh boy," I say.

"Move over. Let me sit. Now watch." Alan starts the video and allows it to play almost all the way through, pausing it right at the moment Cody Tate says, "I had to like, fight him off me."

"Now, look at this. What do you see about this boy's face?"

"He's . . . he's all scuffed up. A little bloody. Is that what you're talking about?"

"Right. How did that happen? Or, I should ask, how would this video lead you to believe that had happened?"

"From me chucking him to the ground, I'd say."

"Right. Now watch again." Alan starts the video, and pauses it just before I put my hands on Cody's shoulders. "Look, what do you see about his face?"

"He's got the same cut on his nose . . . hey. And his eye. Holy shit."

"How did they get there already if you haven't thrown him?"

"Holy shit."

"Exactly. I'd say we're maybe not getting all of the story here, wouldn't you?"

"Wow" is the only thing I can manage to say. I begin to ask Alan to play the thing again, but the doorbell rings, and when I look out the window, I see a police cruiser parked out front.

"Oh no," I say, my knees feeling wobbly with the sudden, certain vision of my son in the morgue. "No, no, no." He's been killed in a car crash, I'm sure of it, and someone has come to officially notify me.

I didn't have the chance to jinx it.

"Neil?" Lauren calls. "Should I get the door?"

"I'll get it," I say, and it feels like I'm floating down the hall and into the entryway.

Please. Please let this not be what I think it is.

I never got to say goodbye!

I open the door, and Pete Tran is standing on my front porch. At his feet, there's an envelope lying on my doormat. The words *For Neil Kazenzakis* are hand-lettered on it.

"Can I ask you a couple follow-up questions, Mr. K.?"

"It's not Chris?"

"Excuse me? What about Chris?"

"You're not here to . . . ? Sure." I feel like I could collapse. "What do you need? Do you want to come in?" I consider for a moment mentioning Christopher's absence, but I don't want to complicate things. Pete stands ramrod straight on the porch, his expression almost stern. He looks from me to the envelope, and back up again.

"No, I'll be quick," he says. He's holding a notepad, and he scans his eyes over it. "You told us when we spoke to you the first time that you broke up a fight."

"That's right."

"When did you first notice the fight?"

"Practice had ended, and I saw them across the parking lot."

"Practice had ended, or it was still wrapping up?"

"I . . . I think we were done."

"So practice was complete."

"I think so? I mean, I'm pretty sure we were done."

"What was it about the boys that first got your attention?"

"It just seemed odd that there was even a group there."

"This fight you say you broke up, it had already started?"

"I guess I went over there when it was obvious something was going on."

Pete nods. "All right. Thank you. You've still got my card, right?" I nod, and Pete glances at the envelope again. "Anything else going on, Mr. K.? Anything you want to tell me about? Anything unusual?"

"I've . . . been getting some emails," I say, and Pete nods again. "Pretty bad emails."

"We know about the emails," he says. "We're looking into it."

"Some calls too. Pranks, threats." Pete nods and makes a note. "And then"—I go on, poking the envelope with my toe—"who knows what this is."

"Do you want me to open it for you?"

"Maybe you should," I say. Pete picks the thing up, slips his finger under the sealed flap, and draws out and unfolds a piece of paper. I can see through the back that a picture is printed on the sheet. The muscles in Pete's face tighten, and quickly his grasp changes so he's holding only the corner of the page and envelope between his index finger and thumb, like one would hold a dead rodent by the tail.

"I don't think you need to see this, Mr. K."

"You can show me," I say.

"I really don't—"

"Show me."

Pete turns the thing around, and I need to brace myself against the house when I see what it is. It's a picture of Wendy, a real photograph of my debilitated wife, in her bed in Long Term. Above the photo are the handwritten words: *Why don't u email me n e more Neil?? Why not??*

Pete turns the photo so I can't see it anymore and holds it—still pinching it by the corner—away from his body. "I'm sorry," he says.

"That's recent," I say softly. "The picture. She only got that quilt in the past week."

Pete makes a note, thanks me, and apologizes again, and lets me know that regular patrols will be coming by the house to keep an eye on things. I stay at the open door and watch him as he returns to his cruiser and drives away, and I realize Alan has come to stand behind me in the entryway.

"What was that all about?" he asks.

"I wish I knew," I say. *I wish I knew.*

CHAPTER TWENTY-TWO

I don't tell anyone about the photo. They don't need to know, and maybe if I say nothing about it, I can make myself think it never existed. Lauren gets called out to one of her patients just before noon, and Alan suggests we take a drive to look for Christopher.

"He probably stayed over at a friend's house," he says. "We'll do some drive-bys and look for his car. I bet we'll see it parked somewhere."

"That's good," I say. "Good idea."

"Are you okay to drive?"

I laugh and say I'm fine, which is a complete lie.

"No, you're not. I'll drive us."

"Do you even have a license anymore?" I ask.

"These are special circumstances," Alan says. "Where are your keys?"

We load into my truck and Alan takes us toward town. It feels strange to not be in the driver's seat, but Alan is in full control, and he seems to be savoring the experience of being back behind the wheel of something moving through real, and not virtual, space.

"You're not going to have another seizure, are you?" I manage to joke.

"Keep in mind I never had one in the first place. Your rig drives pretty nice for being so old."

"Thanks. I think?"

We start outside of town, through both of Port Manitou's quasi suburbs. I try to remember every haunt, every home of every one of Christopher's childhood friends, and I direct Alan around accordingly. He keeps a running commentary going the entire time.

"Oh, Smithfields' house, Angela got busted at a huge party there . . ."

We loop south of town, by a farm I know Chris has been to, by the state park.

"Kids have a kegger down here every weekend . . ."

We go up the national lakeshore; Alan explains what's going on to the ranger at the entrance to the parking area, and she waves us through without having us pay. I spy a cream-colored Volvo wagon, just like Christopher's, but Alan discounts it as I'm pointing it out.

"That car is missing the middle rail on the roof rack. Your son's car has all of them."

After the residential areas, I point Alan east, toward Wendy's facility. He knows where we're going without me having to say it, and he drives us there without direction.

"I'll wait out here," he says as he pulls into a space in the Long Term lot.

Shanice is here and she greets me warmly, obviously having no idea what's going on with me or Chris. It's jarring, her happiness, but maybe good for me.

"No Christopher today?" she asks.

"Nope. I'm guessing he hasn't stopped by?"

She smiles. "Sounds like you two men have a little bit of a communication problem. Typical, typical."

Oh, Shanice, if you only knew.

"If he stops by, will you call me? I'm thinking he might . . . well, he's got a pretty busy day today; he gets distracted. He might forget he needs to call me. Or his phone might be dead. Will you call me if you see him?"

"Sure thing, Mister K."

"By the way, you haven't noticed anyone strange visiting my wife, have you?" Shanice shakes her head no, and I thank her.

I enter Wendy's darkened room and take a seat next to her bed. She's there, no different than she ever is. Air goes in, air goes out. I take her hand in both of mine and lean close to her ear.

"Where is he?" I whisper. "Do you know? Can you tell me?"

Nothing. Her mouth hangs open, her eyes stare without seeing.

"I need him to come home."

I close my eyes and press my face to her shoulder. I remain still, this way, and in the stillness is something close to calm. I raise my head and kiss Wendy's cheek.

"I'll find him," I tell her.

--------———-----

On the highway again, Alan points us back toward town and drives at a pace that seems maybe a little too leisurely for the situation.

"Well," he says, rolling down the window, "at least we've got ourselves a pretty nice day. Maybe a little cool, but still very nice. Breezy!"

"That's great," I say, staring at the passing landscape. "Isn't that great?"

"Just making an observation, Neil."

My phone rings in my hand—I've stopped bothering to put it into my pocket—with an out-of-state number.

"Mr. K.?" a girl's voice says when I answer. "Hey, it's Jill Swart."

"Jill! How are you?"

"Is something going on with Chris?"

"Have you talked to him? Yes, something is going on with Chris. Please tell me you've talked to him?"

"Um. He kind of told me not to tell you that he called. He said he figured you would call me. But he was acting weird, so I wanted to tell you."

"Do you know where he is?" I wave at Alan and whisper, "Stop the car, stop the car!" Back to the phone I say, "What do you mean, 'acting weird'?"

"He told me he wasn't at home. And maybe weird isn't the right word. He was just really, really mad."

"Did he tell you why?"

"Yeah. He's . . . um."

"He's what? Jill, please, I am so worried, you can't even understand how worried I am. This is not like him. Is he coming to see you?"

"God, no. His car wouldn't make the trip here, I don't think. But he talked about . . ."

"But he talked about what? Jill, tell me, please."

"He talked about like . . . well, maybe this is the weird part. He talked about being a chef? I mean, he was really upset and rambling and he talked about that and he said he hates Western Michigan and he feels like you keep pressuring him to go there. But mostly he was really upset about you. And that was it. I swear."

"Do you have any idea where he is? Or was?"

"No, it was really noisy. It was kind of hard to hear him. And he was sort of rambling."

"Okay, Jill. Thank you. If you talk to him again, please tell him to call me. Tell him I'm not angry with him, I just want him to call me so I know he's okay."

"I will, Mr. K. I think he's all right. Just mad."

We hang up, and I stare at my phone.

"What's up?" Alan asks.

"Hold on," I say. I dial Michael, and he answers breathlessly.

"Dude, I was seriously starting to call you right this second. I just got off the phone with Chris."

"Where is he?"

"He wouldn't tell me. And he pretty much commanded me not to talk to you. So don't tell him we talked."

"Fine, fine! Mike, what did he say?"

"He said he thinks he wants to go to culinary school—"

"That's great, he can do that, where *is* he, though?"

"Wait a second, he said he wants to start right away. I told him he needs a high school diploma or at least a GED—"

"What is he doing, Mike? Is he driving to Chicago?"

"I asked him, and he wouldn't say. He asked me if he could crash on my couch, I told him he could but we needed to talk to you about it first."

I feel panic rising through me again.

"Okay, Michael. If he just . . . shows up or something, keep him there, okay?"

"You got it."

Mike clicks off, and I think I'm starting to hyperventilate.

"Neil," Alan says.

"Hold on, hold on." I feel like I can't swallow, and I dial Lauren, but get her voice mail. "He's going to Chicago," I say after the beep. "I think he's running away to Chicago!" I turn to Alan after ending the call. "Let's go back to the orchard. Maybe I do need to call the cops. Oh Christ."

Alan puts the truck into gear, and we start back toward Port Manitou. We go through Old Town, past the commercial docks and municipal marina, and Alan slows. He's looking at something to our right, the side of the street opposite the waterfront and Lauren's condo complex.

"There's his car," Alan says with complete nonchalance, pointing as he turns into a parking lot. Chris's Volvo is parked at the back of the lot, behind a Dumpster. I have no idea how Alan managed to spy it back there, but I have the truck door open and I'm out on the pavement before we come to a stop.

"Come on, come on, Chris, where are you?" His car is locked, and I press my hands to the glass to look inside. It's clean, like it always is, and nothing seems amiss. It's then that I notice the pair of signs high on the building we're next to. Two signs, one over the other. A thousand times or more I've driven past here, and I've never noticed these dingy signs before. The upper one says WESTERN UNION MONEY GRAMS.

The lower one says GREYHOUND BUS.

My jaw hangs slack. "He took . . . he took the bus?"

I dash to the front of the building and inside the terminal. "Hey," I shout, and the two people inside, plus the woman behind the counter, look at me like I am clinically insane.

"Have you . . . have any of you seen a kid? A tall kid? My son . . . he's . . ."

They all shake their heads, staring at me. Alan comes in and grabs me by the shoulders.

"Come on," he tells me. "Let's get back home and we'll figure this out."

I don't speak at all during the drive home. I can't speak. I'm not sure what troubles me more: the fact that my son has run away, or the fact that my son has possibly run away on a Greyhound bus.

"We'll call the bus line," Alan says as we turn onto my drive. Possibly he's reading my mind. "We'll see if he got a ticket somewhere."

"They don't just tell people that stuff. They only tell those things to the police."

"We'll call the police then."

Inside, I go to the kitchen and drop into my normal seat. Chris should be here; he should be *right here*, talking to me, joking with me, home from basketball camp with stories from the night before.

But he's not, and the weight of his absence is oppressive.

I'm glad Alan's here. It would be too much for me to be alone right now. He works about the kitchen, tidying things up, continually moving around.

"You want some coffee?" he asks me.

"I'm wound up enough already."

"How about some tea, then? Herbal tea."

"Sure. Fine." I accept his offer because it's easier than not accepting. Alan takes the kettle from the stove, fills it, and returns it to a lit burner.

"Where do you keep your tea?"

"It's in the pantry." Alan opens the door and looks around. "On the middle shelf," I add. "Waist high."

"Not seeing it, Neil."

I sigh, and get to my feet. I tell Alan to look out, and peer inside the pantry door. And what I see, or rather, what I fail to see, makes my skin feel cold and my stomach drop. Christopher's milk crate, usually there on the shelf, usually filled with bottles and jars of Asian spices, is gone. A great empty space is in the middle of our pantry. I see this space, and it's too much: my son is gone, I fall apart.

In seeing this void, I break.

My knees buckle, and tears begin to roll down my face. I ease down to my knees, bring my hands to my face, and sob.

"Christopher," I say through choking breaths. "Chris!"

------ ————————— -----

This has happened to me. Once before.

In the months after Wendy's accident, as the winter months crawled by, I retreated more and more into the old barn. I had a chair in there and glasses for my drinks; tonic had been abandoned for nothing but Xanax and gin. Hours were spent in thought. I'd bring a bound journal along with me, and when Carol gently asked me what I spent so much time doing in the barn, when my brother Mike came up and asked me not so gently what the fuck I was doing in there all the time, I replied that I was gathering my thoughts and writing them down. It was therapeutic, I told them. This was for my own good.

I was not really writing down my thoughts.

Sometimes Chris would knock at the door. "Dad?" he'd say through the metal door. "Grandma's got dinner ready. Dad? Are you coming out soon?"

Sometimes I'd come out. Eventually. A lot of times I wouldn't. My brother, when in town, would bang on the door, on the corrugated metal sides of the building. I was too numb to be startled by it, too numb to really care.

"Get out of there," Michael would shout, when Christopher wasn't there with him. "I swear to fucking God, Neil, you need help! You're going to wither up and die if you don't come out of there!"

I did have help, though. I was seeing someone, weekly; I told her things were great, and she gave me refills for Xanax. I was coping, I thought, in my own way.

At night, when everyone was sleeping, I'd bring Wendy's things over to the barn. Entire drawers from our shared dresser. Files from her desk. Pay stubs, canceled checks, tee shirts from a 10K charity race, splattered recipes scrawled in her hand and stuffed inside a cookbook. All of these things had some connection to her; all of them had been an extension.

I curated these things. I catalogued them in my journal; I jotted down each memory associated with them.

I found, one day, a shoebox in the house. It had been under the bed; I must have missed it the first time I'd searched under there. Chris was reading in his room when I discovered it, and when I peeked inside, I found it to be stuffed with photos Wendy had been intending to file into albums. A treasure trove! I scurried over to the barn through melting spring slush, and eagerly spilled it out over the workbench and began to look through the pictures. They were random, insignificant: pictures of the field, an apple tree, some holiday party at her office.

Many pictures of our cat. I ducked out the door to scoop snow into my glass and came back inside to pour gin over it, and I drank and tried to assign some chronological order to the images.

I came to an envelope fat with processed pictures and I turned up the flap and spilled them into my hand to shuffle through them. Again, nothing of significance.

Until the end of the stack.

The last seven pictures were from the night we'd found Otto. Chris was in bed with the cat, I was next to him in some, Wendy by the bed in others. And the last one, the very last one—I remember us trying to take it—we'd used the timer on the camera so we could get a picture of all of us. Chris held the cat, and my wife and I leaned in close. We all smiled.

Click.

We were complete. In my hands, I held evidence, photographic proof, that we had once been complete.

And at that moment I broke down.

I fell to the floor, sobbing, holding the picture to my chest, pressing it to my face. It was the time I thought things couldn't get any worse. I don't know how long I was like that, maybe an hour, maybe less; I stayed that way until I was interrupted by the squeak of the door. I'd forgotten to padlock it from the inside, and my son stood there, staring at his lost and inconsolable father.

"Dad?" he said. "What are you doing, Dad?"

I froze. The picture was on the concrete floor.

"Dad, it's okay," he said. He came and put his arms around me. "Come inside. It's not good for you to be out here."

"I miss her, Chris," I said, tears spilling down my face. "I miss her so much."

"I do too, Dad. Please come back to the house."

I left the picture on the floor, and followed my son back home.

CHAPTER TWENTY-THREE

Here I am, kneeling before my pantry, staring at a void on the shelf that represents most accurately the void in my life.

"Neil," Alan says, touching his hand to my shoulder. "Come on, stand up."

"Damn it," I say, rising and wiping my eyes with my sleeve. "I'm sorry."

"This is understandable, the way you feel."

"He ran away with a box of condiments, for fuck's sake." I can't help but laugh at the absurdity of it. I wipe my eyes again. "He's the only thing I've got."

"You love him," Alan says. "And that's important. But you're not alone. Not at all."

I nod, because he's right.

Alan calls Lauren, who was already on her way, and he calls Kristin after that. I wait on the couch and get myself back together. In an odd way, though I shouldn't be surprised, falling apart has made me feel much calmer.

"Oh, Neil," Lauren says as she comes in and sits next to me. "Are you okay? Alan told me."

"I'm fine," I say. "Really. I do feel better."

"Good," she says. My phone rings with a call from Michael.

"Anything?" I ask.

"Haven't seen him or heard from him. I stationed one of my prep cooks at my apartment in case he shows up there."

"You're awesome," I say. "Keep me posted."

Kristin arrives, and she joins us in the living room as the light begins to fade outside. Someone turns on a lamp and for what feels like a long time no one in the room can speak.

My phone rings, and they all turn toward me expectantly. It's only Peggy Mackie, not Chris; I look at them and shake my head.

"What's up?" I ask.

"Neil," she says urgently in a low voice. "Neil, Jesus Christ, all bets are off, they're going to charge you with assault!"

"You're kidding me."

"I'm not. I'm not! I didn't tell you this, okay? You did *not* talk to me, you understand? The family's been pushing, they're connected, you are going to be screwed. They're going to have you arrested."

"Do . . . do you know when?"

"I have no idea. Maybe tomorrow? Sometime before the board meeting, I would guess."

"Okay," I say. "Thanks for letting me know." I hang up and nod to my friends in the room. "I'm going to be charged with assault," I tell them calmly. "I guess I'm going to be arrested."

They stare at me, stunned. Lauren puts her hand over her mouth.

I have been broken before. I have fallen apart. But out of this, I learned that, in spite of the damage I'd sustained, I was able to put myself back together.

Even with entropy entering the system, some order was restored. I didn't know it the first time I was broken, but I can understand it now.

After Chris found me that night, I didn't go back to the barn for a long time. I did, at Michael's urging, find a new therapist. And I started running again.

We opened up the barn and cleaned it out once more. Wendy's clothes were donated away, her friends picked over her leftover nothings, and I kept a few items for myself and brought them back home. A few mementos, I knew, would be okay.

I had the building knocked down. There was a guy I knew, the guy who had dug out the foundation of my home, good old Karl from Karl's Excavation & Hauling. I asked him if he knew anyone who could demolish a structure. He said he could do it himself, for cheap, and he showed up one day in the late spring with his big yellow excavator and a dump truck. I watched while he smashed the barn apart, bashing his shovel against the sides to knock the walls in, then scooping the splintered and torn remains into the bed of the truck. A cigarette dangled from the corner of his mouth the entire time.

After watching for an hour or so, I called up to Karl in the cab of his machine. "Hey! Can you show me how to do that? I want to take a couple swings at it."

"Get your ass up here!" he growled. He showed me how the hand controls worked, and let me give it a try. I only needed to take a couple shots at it. That was satisfying enough for me.

"You done okay!" Karl shouted over the rumble of the machine as I stepped down. "A natural!" He slapped me on the back hard enough to make me cough. "You ever hard up for work, you give me a call! Ha-ha!"

It only took two-and-a-half days to cart the place entirely away, leaving behind a perfectly flat concrete slab. Perfectly flat and, as we discovered a few weeks later with a long measuring tape, only three feet shorter than a regulation basketball court.

-----————————-----

I have been here before.

"Neil," Alan says. "Are you okay?"

"I'm fine." I say. I have been broken before, and I ended up okay. I came out of it okay.

"What are you going to do?" Lauren asks.

"If they're going to arrest me, I won't be able to look for Chris. So here's what we're going to do. Together. If it's okay with you guys"—I look at Alan and Kris—"we're going to go over to your house. Lauren and I will spend the night. Alan, you can call Greyhound and see if you can get anything out of them. We can make dinner. We missed dinner last night."

"Are you sure you're okay?" Alan asks. His eyes, unblinking, convey a seriousness I don't often see in him.

"I'm fine. We'll leave my truck here and take Lauren's car—"

"I need to check in on Carol," she says.

"Okay. You do that; I'll just run over. Can you guys pick up some stuff for us to cook? I'll give you some money to pick—"

"We'll get it," Kristin says.

I go to my room to get some things together to spend the night. Alan sticks his head in as I'm stuffing clothes into my pack.

"You're sure you're okay?" he asks. "You know . . ." He cocks an eyebrow. "You're kind of going on the lam here."

"I'm not going on the lam," I say. "I just want to get Chris home. After that, you know, whatever. Whatever. They can fire me, they can arrest me. But right now I want him back home."

"This is the Neil I'm used to," Alan says.

"That's right. I'll see you over at your place." He and Kristin leave, and I give Lauren a quick kiss.

"I'm sorry," I say, and she tilts her head. "For losing it earlier."

"I understand," she says. "I do."

"Go do your thing with Carol," I say. "I'll see you over at Kris and Al's."

Lauren gathers up her things to go. As she does so, I leave a message for my son on the whiteboard in the kitchen:

Gone to Alan's house Sun. Eve. Call me when you get home.

I underline the word *home,* and leave.

----- ———————————— -----

When Lauren returns to Al and Kristin's an hour later, she wears a bemused expression.

"Carol!" she says. "She asked me how far along I was. It came out of nowhere!"

"My mother knew both times we were pregnant well before I told her," Kristin says from the kitchen. "It's a generational thing, I think."

Lauren leans close to me. "You didn't say anything, did you?" I shake my head no and she adds, "You swear?"

Alan has been on the phone with Greyhound, at the dining room table, and he rises to his feet with an exasperated look on his face upon finishing a call.

"Nothing," he says. "I thought I was getting somewhere when I called the depot in Chicago and said I needed to know when Chris was getting in so I could come pick him up. They said they had no record of him. I asked if maybe he was arriving at a different terminal, and she checked the whole system, but nothing. At least I got the impression she checked the system."

"Could he have given them a fake name?" Kristin asks.

"I think even buses need identification now to get a ticket," Alan says. "He doesn't have a fake ID, does he?"

It just doesn't seem like something my son would do. "I don't think so," I say. "I really don't."

----- ———————————— -----

Where the barn had stood, a hard dirt perimeter framed the concrete slab. The week after the demolished structure had been carted away,

Christopher and I loosened the earth around the site with rakes and scattered grass seed over the freshly turned soil. We chalked out the lines for a basketball court on the slab, filling in and defining the boundaries with a dark blue enamel. Posts were set into concrete at either end, and regulation backboards were erected.

The following summer, platoons of children ran back and forth over the slab. Two-on-two, three-on-three, and so on. Christopher's friends, mostly boys, sometimes a girl or two, would play.

Through the summer they played there, hollering and laughing. Sometimes they'd argue, contesting a foul or pointing out some perceived sleight. It never lasted long, and they'd go back to playing, running back and forth. Toward the end of the summer, I erected lights around the court so they could play into the night.

Sometimes while they played, I'd go out for a run.

------ ———————— -----

After we finish eating at the Massies' house, I realize I've left my cell phone charger back at my own home. I start to put on my shoes to run over and get it.

"I can take you," Lauren says. "Or you can tell me where it is and I can just grab it."

"That's okay. I'll be right back."

A gibbous moon is rising over the trees as I dash off to my house; it's cool and pleasant outside, and my crisply defined shadow chases me over the ground.

Christopher's parking space remains empty.

------ ———————— -----

Michael calls at ten with an update as Lauren and I are getting ready for bed in the Massies' guest room.

"I talked to him twenty minutes ago," Mike tells me. "The connection was shitty, but he's fine. He sounded sad more than anything."

I feel this news as a squeeze in the chest.

"I think . . . I don't know, I think he's feeling bad, and homesick, wherever he is. Maybe you'll find him home in bed tomorrow morning."

"Maybe," I say. "I'm steering clear of my house right now." I tell him the news of my impending arrest.

"Seriously?" Mike says. "Your shit keeps piling up." I'm sitting at the foot of the bed, and behind me Lauren climbs in and pulls the covers up under her chin.

"It is piling up," I say. "Higher and higher."

"You know what, dude?" Mike says. "It's going to be okay. Do you really have a problem with him going to cook school?"

"No. I don't know where anyone got this idea I didn't want him going to culinary school. He can go anywhere he wants, Mike. I really just want him to come home."

We hang up and I slip into bed. I lie there silently for who knows how long, staring at the ceiling until Lauren turns out the light and rolls over to me. She runs her hand over my chest and, in spite of myself, I slide my hand up under the front of Lauren's shirt and down her underwear; she's perfectly warm and soft and surprisingly wet.

"Really?" she says, teasing me with a warm, breathy voice. "Now?"

"Maybe this is not the best time," I say, but I keep my hand there. I slide my finger against her, and she sighs as she lifts her knee and rolls her hips upward to facilitate the motion.

"You have a lot on your mind," she murmurs, throwing an arm around my neck. "Will you even be able to?"

"I don't know if I'll be able to."

"We could give it a try." I can hear her smiling in the dark.

We give it a try. Somehow, even with everything going on, I manage.

I also manage to sleep, in fits and starts, through the night. Sometimes I wake confused, unsure of where I am. Other times I wake with total clarity, along with frustration that I can't check to see if Chris is home. Every time I wake I reach for my phone to see if he's called. He hasn't.

Lauren drives over to check if Chris has returned and check on Carol. She's probably the last person my son wants to see, but we can't ignore Carol. Alan insists I play Mega-Putt with him while Lauren is away.

"You can't throw any clubs this time," he tells me. "I wasn't kidding when I said you ruined that putter."

"I won't throw any clubs."

We've made our way into the back nine holes, this time featuring the Natural Wonders of the World, when Lauren returns. I'm just about to putt into the Grand Canyon when she stops her car in the drive and rolls down the window.

"Nothing going on," she shouts. "No Chris."

"Any sign of the police?" Alan asks.

"No police either." The window goes back up, and the Prius continues onward to the house.

Alan and I have reached Mount Everest when Lauren hollers to us again, this time from the front porch.

"You just missed a call from Peggy Mackie. Your phone says there's a voice mail."

Any news from Peggy is probably news I don't need to hear, and I don't want to give her any clues to my whereabouts, so I'm not too worried about missing the call.

"I'll listen to it in a bit," I say. "We're just about done here." Lauren nods and goes back inside.

"You played much more calmly this time," Alan says. "I still beat you, though."

Back inside, in the spare room with my phone still plugged into its charger, I listen to Peggy's message.

"Come on, Neil, you guys really had to take *Tabby* out today? With everything going on? And without calling me? I have to say I'm not very happy about this. Fine, whatever, bring her back in later, but call me when you're back. I need to talk to you. It's important."

I nearly drop the phone. The instant I hear her say the name of the boat, I know.

I know exactly where Chris has gone.

CHAPTER TWENTY-FOUR

He took the boat!" I shout as I run to the front of the house. "He took the boat!"

"Who took what?" Alan asks as I clatter into the kitchen.

"Get a map," I say. "Chris took Peggy Mackie's sailboat. He's sailing to Chicago, I know it."

"What kind of map?" Kristin asks, rifling through a drawer.

"Any type. Anything that shows the coast."

Kris produces a AAA road map, which we unfold and spread over the kitchen table.

"How fast can that boat go?" Alan asks. He's thinking exactly the same thing I am. "I don't have anything to plot this out. Kris, sweetie, can you grab a ruler for me?"

"We've hit seven knots on an unusually fast day. Six, six and a half if we're doing really well. Maybe a little lower than that if you were averaging it."

"Let's say he does six miles an hour," Alan says. I shake my head. "Okay, let's say . . . five?" I shake my head again. "Four and a half." He runs his finger over the map's legend. "So, what's the earliest he could have left?"

"I told him everything Friday after school. He stayed home that night, and I saw him in the morning when he left. But he never ended up on campus, so I guess he could have gone straight to the . . . no, wait, he went to see Wendy too. So the earliest he could have left would have been maybe noon Saturday. Maybe more like one." Alan and I lean over the map with Kristin and Lauren pressed in at our sides.

"So, that puts us . . . maybe forty hours out? Which would give him a max range of, what, a hundred and eighty miles or so." Alan traces a rough circle out over Lake Michigan on the map with Port Manitou at the center. "That's a pretty huge area he could be in. He could be all the way over in Wisconsin."

Lauren shakes her head. "That's assuming he went nonstop. Would he have stopped, Neil?"

"I don't know," I say. "He might have worried about getting caught or something. We're also assuming he made perfect time. I don't think he would have gone across the lake. He'd stay close to the coast. God, he's got to be exhausted if he's been under way the whole time."

Alan traces another circle, a little smaller this time. "Even if he wasn't going as fast as he could, that's still a huge area."

"My brother talked to him last night," I say. "So even if he was under way, he had to be close enough to shore to get a signal on his phone. Wouldn't that narrow it down?" Alan shrugs, and we all lean back, as if by some silent command, from crowding in over the map.

"How are you going to find him in an area that size?" Kristin asks. "It's big."

"I know a guy with a speedboat we could borrow," I say. "We could head down the coast and try to catch up with him."

"I know a guy," Alan says. "With a plane."

We scramble out to the Prius, Alan, Lauren, and I, and tear off up the road toward Leland's resort. Kristin has stayed behind, promising to make regular checks at my house to see if Christopher has returned. We find the resort office empty, so we jump back into the car and head back toward town, where Leland lives.

"So," I ask, "do people really just loan their planes out like this?"

"Oh sure. It happens all the time. You need to get somewhere, you borrow your buddy's plane if you—"

"I wouldn't exactly call you guys buddies."

"He'll recognize the need."

"Does Leland even have a license to fly?"

"I understand he's working on getting his ticket. But," Alan says, "Leland's not going to fly the plane."

We tear into Leland's drive, an incongruously funny maneuver considering the lack of noise made by the hybrid car. Lauren stays behind while Alan and I run up to the house. Sherry Dinks answers our knock at the door.

"Neil Kazenzakis!" she says. "How are you? I'm so sorry; I heard what's going on. But it sure is nice to see you."

"Hi, Sherry. Is Leland here?"

"He's working on something out back. Go right around. You'll see him."

We run around the garage and find Leland bent over the open engine compartment of a riding mower. He's holding a rag and a dipstick, and seems startled by our sudden appearance.

"What in the world are you two doing here?"

"Leland, my son ran away in a stolen boat. He's sailing it to Chicago and we need your plane to go find him."

"He what?"

"We need to borrow your plane, Leland," Alan says.

"Well . . . I . . . I mean, sure, you can use the plane, I don't even know if Curtis is around to fly the thing . . . let me give him a call. He might be teaching a lesson this morning."

Alan shakes his head. "Don't call him. I can fly the plane."

"Are you kidding me?"

"Please, Leland," I say. "Anything, I mean it. Help us. We can talk about selling my place, whatever. Please just let us use the plane."

"Whoa, hold up here. Let me get this straight. Your son ran away, stole a boat, and now you're going to borrow my plane so an epileptic man can fly it so you two can go look for the kid and the boat."

"That's it," Alan says. "That's pretty much it. Oh, and his girl-friend is coming with us."

"Christopher's girlfriend?"

Alan shakes his head. "Neil's girlfriend," he says. "She's preg-nant with his child." Leland stares at me, his mouth slightly agape.

"It's a long story," I say.

Leland blinks, regaining his composure. "Well," he says, wip-ing his hands and tossing the rag onto the mower's engine. "Let's go, then."

I drive the four of us back up to the resort, back past the main guest areas and toward a less-finished area with heavy equipment parked about. Leland points for me to stop next to a trailer; his white-and-blue airplane is parked just beyond that. As Leland runs into the trailer, Alan goes to the plane and starts to undo a set of webbing straps stretching from the undersides of the wings to some concrete anchors in the ground.

"Give me a hand here, Neil."

I go over and help him with the tie-downs, and as I coil up the last one, Leland joins us with five big headsets looped over his arm.

"Are you coming with us?" Alan asks, nodding to the headsets.

"Of course I am. You think I'm going to let you trash this plane?"

"What's the fifth headset for?" I ask.

"We'll keep this one onboard," Leland says, matter-of-factly. "Chris will need one for the ride home, won't he?"

----- ——————————— -----

Alan, I can tell, is trying not to grin as he taxis the plane out to the end of the mowed strip. He and Leland sit up front, Alan in the left seat, Leland in the right. I'm sitting behind Leland with Lauren next to me, clutching my hand. Her eyes are wide with apprehension as we bounce over the field to the end of the runway, but she doesn't say a word.

"You're really okay to fly this thing?" Leland asks over the headset.

"Sure am. I know this machine inside and out. I actually got my instrument rating in a 210, you know? Love this plane—"

"No, I am talking about your health! You're not going to slump over in midair, are you?"

"I'm fine," he says as he gathers a book of charts and a notepad from between the front seats and places them in his lap. "I mean it. All right, gang, here we go." He pulls at a knob in the panel and the engine revs up; I feel the brakes release with a jolt, and the plane starts to gently lurch as it rolls forward and gathers speed down the grass airstrip. Al pulls back on the control yoke, and the plane takes one last bounce before lifting smoothly into the air; the ground seems to drop away.

"And we're up," Alan says.

We rise over the dunes to see Lake Michigan, the vast land-locked sea stretching blue to a hazy line at the edge of the earth. Alan climbs straight until the trees seem small below us, and banks the plane to turn us out over the shimmering water. We're all craning forward to scan out the windows. I look back as we turn and see the orchard, the rows of trees, the farmhouse, and my own home.

"There's a sailboat," Lauren says, pointing off to the north. Her voice is small and clipped over the headset. "It's quite a ways out there."

"I don't think that's him," I say. "Too close, wrong direction, and the boat doesn't look right."

"We'll check anyway," Alan says. He levels out in the direction of the boat, and dips down as we approach it. The boat is small, a little sailing dory, and the man and woman down in the cockpit shield their eyes to watch us as we fly by.

"That's not him," I say. Alan banks the plane as we buzz over the boat, and the man in the boat gives us a slow wave. "Head south. I don't think he's gone north."

"Heading south," Alan says. He turns back and flies along the sandy shoreline, and I get a good view of the beach house as we pass the orchard again. It doesn't look too bad from up here.

"So why exactly did Christopher steal a boat, Neil?" Leland asks. I start to answer, but my voice sounds choppy in my own ears, and Alan looks back over his shoulder at me.

"Put the microphone closer to your mouth," he says, pointing to his own mic. "So it's almost touching your lips."

I push it close to my mouth. "Like this?" Lauren does the same.

"There you go."

"Okay, so," I go on, "Chris is running away to Chicago to go to culinary school."

Leland shakes his head. "Does Chris realize there's a series of paved roads to Chicago that would have gotten him there in a few hours?"

"He likes sailing too."

"This doesn't make too much sense to me," Leland says.

"There's more to it than just that. He's very angry with me right now too."

Alan points to the water. "There's another sailboat."

We dip down again, and I know it's not *Tabby* well before we're there.

"Not him," I say, but Alan makes a close pass just to be sure.

We check out two more boats, and still no luck. As we rise back up into the air after our last pass, I'm struck by the horrifying thought of us finding *Tabby* empty, listlessly bobbing with no Chris aboard.

How would I react to that? Could I bear such a loss?

I put it out of my head.

After a while of flying, droning on and on, Alan says, "We're at about a hundred and ten miles out of Port Manitou."

We check another boat, the occupants of which seem irritated by our close pass. They may be irritated, but I'm shaken; Alan seemed to zip uncomfortably close to the wave tops on this last dip down. His flying has grabbed Leland's attention as well.

"Hey, uh, do you need to get so close to them to tell? Neil, you can tell if it's him from higher up, right?"

"Come on, you guys," Alan says. "Don't be wusses. We're fine. You think I want to stack us in? I like living too." Lauren clutches my hand more tightly, and her complexion seems to have paled. I catch her eyes and force a smile, but it doesn't seem to reassure her any.

We fly along, farther south, and see nothing more than powerboats dotting the water here and there, and a regatta of small sailboats in a race just offshore from the port town of Manistee. I shake my head as we pass over the little boats, and we continue on, all of us knowing that we're at about the limit of Christopher's possible range.

"Is that a sailboat?" Leland asks, almost pressing his face to the glass of his window. "Way out there?"

"Way out where?" Alan asks, craning his neck to scan the horizon. "Give me a bearing."

"Two o'clock."

"I see it," I say, leaning forward. A sail shows white against the glimmer of the horizon, and as I keep looking, I think I can see the telltale stripes of *Tabby's* foresail. As we approach, I feel a lump in my throat.

"I think that's him," I say. "Yes, I think that's Peggy Mackie's boat."

Alan descends, not so severely this time. He flies so the boat passes us on the right side, my side of the plane. To my great relief, I see Christopher in the cockpit, alone, wearing a ball cap and sunglasses, and when he turns his head up toward us, I can tell by the way his shoulders fall that he realizes his adventure is over. I wave to him, but I don't think he can see me.

"It's him," I say. "It's him! Can you, is there any way you can call him?"

"We can do marine radio," Leland says. He turns a knob in the cockpit, and I hear him speaking over the headset.

"Christopher K., Christopher K., this is Leland Dinks in the plane passing over you, I'm here with your father . . ."

Chris just stares up at the plane.

"Christopher K., Christopher K., please respond . . ."

"Either he's ignoring us," Alan says, "or he doesn't have his radio on."

"Get a waypoint," Leland says. "Mark where he is, then take us back to Manistee. There's a little airport northeast of the city."

Alan writes something on the notepad in his lap, and circles *Tabby* in one last pass.

"What are you thinking, Leland?"

"Just hang on. I'm pretty sure I can get us out to Chris."

Alan completes his circle and starts back toward the mainland, and I twist to watch Chris and *Tabby* recede in the distance behind us.

- - - - - ——————————— - - - - -

We land at a paved airstrip, and taxi to a building at the end. Lauren, looking positively green, has her hand to her forehead. A kid in a blue polo shirt dashes out from the building to meet us.

"Mr. Dinks!" he says. "I'm sorry, we didn't realize you were coming."

"No problem, Jimbo, it was kind of a last-minute thing. Can we grab the crew car? We'll only be a couple hours, tops."

"Sure thing, Mr. Dinks. I'll bring it right over."

The kid sprints off, returning a few moments later in a black Lincoln Navigator. He hops out and runs around the big car, opening the doors for us.

"Here you go, Mr. Dinks."

We climb into the car, Leland taking the driver's seat, me up front, and Alan and Lauren in back. Leland accelerates off across the taxiway, only slowing to let a security gate open to let us through.

"Oh man," Alan says, raising his arms to lace his fingers behind his head. "I forgot how plush the world of private aviation can be."

Leland has his cell phone to his ear. "Hey, Mark, yeah, been good, you? Listen . . . huh? No, I came to town last minute with some clients; you mind if I grab the boat? Just going to take them out for a quick joyride, nothing too long. You sure? Great, great, I owe you one!"

Leland ends the call and throws the phone into the center console.

"I've been working on a development down here for the past eighteen months," he says. "One of the investors lets me use his boat. Nice boat. Fishing boat. I don't really like to fish." We pass a speed limit sign reading forty-five; Leland is going close to eighty. Alan leans forward between the front seats while Lauren leans back and clutches the armrest on the door. We skirt past town and into a marina parking lot, and Leland doesn't even bother to park in any sort of designated space, simply skidding to a stop diagonally in the middle of the lot. He leaves the door open after he runs out.

"I need to sit still for a little bit," Lauren says weakly. I point after Leland and Alan running down to the docks.

"You don't want to come?" I ask, and she shakes her head. I give her a kiss. "I'll be back," I say. "With Chris."

"Come on, come on!" Leland calls. Just as I catch up to them another earnest kid, this time in a buttoned-up polo shirt, greets us.

"Hello, Mr. Dinks!" he says as we run past. Leland ignores him as he leads us onward. "Mr. Reeves called to say you were coming; the boat's almost all set," the kid calls after us. "She's over at the gas dock."

We stand and wait for the marina crew to finish fueling the fly-bridged fishing boat with a pair of massive engines mounted on the stern. Leland, surprisingly, seems to be chafing at the holdup more than I am. When they finally withdraw the fuel line from the fitting on the deck, Leland springs aboard and starts working at the boat's wheel.

"Cast us off, guys," he says, turning a key to start the motors rumbling. Alan unties a line at the front and I do the same in the back, and we toss them aboard and follow them in. Leland pulls us away from the dock and out into the marina channel, waving at some men outside a bait and tackle shop as we pass.

"So you take this boat out a lot?" I ask.

"Here and there. Hang on." We pass the NO WAKE sign at the harbor wall into the swell of the lake, and Leland presses the throttles forward to send the engines into a roar. The boat lunges forward over the waves, and I keep myself up, barely, against the sudden acceleration. Alan tumbles backward onto his ass, and I am suddenly very glad Lauren opted to stay behind.

"Wow!" Alan shouts, clawing his way back up next to me. "Wow!" My eyes tear up at the wind in my face; I wish I had, as Alan and Leland do, a pair of sunglasses. I duck behind Leland to shelter myself behind the Plexiglas windscreen over the steering console.

"You got those coordinates?" Leland shouts to Alan over the din of our very fast motion. The boat slams onward, bashing wave after wave after wave in knee-jarring jolts. "Keep an eye on the GPS, okay?" He points to a screen in front of the steering wheel, and Alan nods. Leland bends down to pull a pair of binoculars from a well under his seat, and hands them to me.

"You look for him," he says. "Tell me when you see him."

It takes a little more than thirty minutes for us to reach *Tabby*. I see the boat first, and watch through the binoculars as we close in on it. At first it seems like Chris doesn't respond to us; we're just another fishing boat blasting out into the lake on a Sunday afternoon. But he starts paying more attention to us as we approach him, glancing in our direction from time to time until he's finally watching us exclusively. When he realizes we're coming for him, he tries to steer *Tabby* away.

"Sorry, kid," Leland mutters as he pulls back on the fishing boat's throttles. "I think we're a little faster."

Our vessel slows and settles down into the waves, and Leland eases us alongside the sailboat. Christopher continues to turn the wheel to steer away, and the mainsail and boom swing wildly above him. He won't look at me as we ease up next to him. He won't look at any of us.

CHAPTER TWENTY-FIVE

The two boats come together in the waves, and I move to the gunwale of the fishing boat, looping my arm around a chromed awning post to keep myself steady. Aboard *Tabby*, Chris has his back to us and continues trying to steer away, even as the sailboat is no longer driven by its crazily flapping sails.

"Hold on, Neil," Leland says as we approach. "Wait up, wait up." The vessels move out of sync with each other; we rise up on the waves as Chris falls, and vice versa. Leland gives the throttle a little surge, and the two boats line up perfectly.

"Now, Neil," Leland says. "It's good, go!"

I jump over *Tabby*'s lifeline and land sprawled over the cabin top, bashing my knee so hard against a cleat that it makes me gasp. I get back to my feet, helping myself up with a hand on one of the mast shrouds, and wave at the fishing boat to let them know I'm okay. Leland backs away to give us some space.

"Chris," I say, staying where I am on the side deck. "You really had me worried." He turns his body to his left so he's not facing me. "I'm not mad. I understand, okay? I understand." I move closer to the cockpit, and I have to duck to miss the swinging, clanking boom. "I should have told you. I should have told you a long time ago. I understand why you're mad."

From the side, I see Chris has his lips pressed tight, and a tear slides down his face from beneath his sunglasses.

"I love your mom, okay? I always will. But she isn't coming back. Ever. She'll never come back to us. I'll take care of her as well as I can. I might even have to sell part of the orchard to take care of her. I've been talking to Leland Dinks about it. I probably should have told you that too."

Chris says nothing, but he sniffs and more tears come down his cheeks. I take another step toward the cockpit.

"Lauren is a good person. She is kind, and funny, and compassionate. She takes good care of your grandma. I've been in love with her for a while. We just . . . I was over there with her a lot when we first brought Grandma back from the hospital. I was lonely, she was breaking up with a guy she'd been seeing, and we liked each other. I didn't even realize at first. She asked me to go to dinner with her, can you believe it? I could have said, let me talk to Chris, why don't I talk to Chris before we go out. Instead, you know what? We went to dinner over in Traverse City. Instead of telling you what was going on, I tried to hide it from you. I know you were younger, but you weren't stupid, you could have dealt with it."

I step down into the cockpit, and Chris makes a little sound as he wipes his nose with his hand.

"You're the only thing I have, Chris. When you left, it was almost too much. I couldn't have taken it if you'd left me. You're my only son. My only family."

"Then why did you almost do the same thing to me?" he screams, his voice breaking. "You don't get it at all, do you? Why did you try to leave?" He turns to the stern of the boat and lunges like he's going to jump overboard, but I'm there, somehow I make it around the wheel to him and get my arms around his strong body to pull him to the bottom of the cockpit. My knee throbs, and the sails flap impotently over our heads.

"No, Christopher. No." I say, the side of my face pressed between his shoulder blades. "Don't leave. Please don't leave."

"Why not?" he says, crying, twisting himself away. "Why not, when you were going to do it again?"

----- ——————————— -----

There are things we make ourselves forget.

What is a memory, anyway? Is it an indelible record, unimpeachable, frozen in some synaptic arrangement and stored away for some moment it might be needed in the future? Or is it subject to editing and revision, something plastic that our brains can shape into another form we can handle, something less toxic than the original, something less able to poison us?

That night Chris found me in the pole barn, a picture of our family had shattered me. This I recall. The photograph was like a live electrical wire; my fingers contracted around it and could not let go no matter how terribly it hurt me. I finally shook it from my hands to let it fall to the floor. It fell faceup, and I stared at it, I kept staring at it, I could not take my eyes from it. My eyes never left the picture—mother, father, son—even as I took drink after drink straight from the bottle of gin. I fell to my knees, bent over the picture, and my tears dripped onto the gloss of the print and merged into blurry dots. My fists squeezed tight and pressed against the sides of my head, I groaned with clenched teeth, I closed my eyes to get away from the image. It was there whether my eyes were open or not. And as I squeezed my eyes shut . . .

The door squeaked.

"Dad? What are you doing, Dad?"

Memory is a funny thing. I was incapable of getting to my feet. I was incapable of living.

I lay on the floor in a heap, shattered, with a crumpled photo before me and a nearly empty bottle of gin by my feet. Incapable. Christopher came and put his arms around me.

"I miss her, Chris." I sobbed.

Just how much have I come apart?

"I miss her so much."

"I missed her so much," I tell my son. "I'm sorry, Chris. I'm so sorry. I didn't . . . I was crazy. I was lost."

I let go of my son, and he sits down in the well of the cockpit with his arms around his drawn-up knees. He looks forward, away from me, and sometimes he wipes up under his sunglasses with his fingers.

"You don't get it," Chris says. "You were a wreck."

"I know. I know I was. When your mom was first in the nursing home—"

"I'm not talking about then, Dad. I'm talking about two nights ago. I'm talking about the night before that."

I stare at him blankly.

"You don't even remember, do you? You don't even know what I'm talking about." He sniffs a couple times, and rubs his nose with the back of his wrist. "Thursday night, okay? I was doing homework, and Sparks texts me this thing about the video. I went to get you so I could show you, right? You weren't in your room, but you weren't in the house, either. Then I found you out by the stupid fire pit asleep in the chair, and it's like, okay, he fell asleep, I'll get the old man in bed. You were just saying weird shit. You even said stuff about Lauren, but it didn't make any sense. And it was like you could barely walk. But whatever, I got you to bed."

"Thank you," I murmur.

"But then Friday night . . ."

"What, Chris. Tell me."

"So, I was mad, okay? I was really angry with you. I went in my room. I was in there for a while, and I cooled off. I thought, well, maybe it's not such a major thing. I mean, it's totally a major thing, but did I really need to lose it like that?" He looks at me, maybe waiting for me to say something, but I don't, and he looks back out to the water. "So I came out. I was going to come into your room and talk to you. Because I knew I was being stupid, and I knew I should talk to you about it. But instead it's like you're passed out on the hallway floor with a bottle between your knees. That's when I really lost it. I was like, really? Seriously? I'm going through this again? I was there once already—"

"Chris, I'm—"

"I was so mad, I was pissed! I just wanted to leave you there. But then I thought I'd better get you in bed at least; I couldn't just leave you on the floor. I wasn't going to leave you like you were leaving me. Somebody had to act like an adult. So I got you up, and you're like 'I'm fine, I'm fine.' And I was not fine. Because I'd heard that once before. The first time, you know, you said the same thing. But you weren't. So I got you to bed, and that's when I decided I needed to leave."

"God, I'm sorry."

"It was just like after Mom's thing. You said everything was fine. You said it over and over. And Mike came up from Chicago, and he told me 'don't worry, we'll get him better.' And I don't know, he talked to you or whatever, and it was like you did get better, and after a while you went back to being my dad. The way you were before, mostly. I thought you were over it, but here it started again. I mean, I know you had a beer here and there, but it was no big deal. You had a grip."

A wave slides under us, rolling the boat in a way that clanks the rigging against the mast.

"When it was happening, you said everything was fine, and I believed you," Chris says. "But I guess it's really easy for you to lie about things, isn't it?"

"God, no, Christopher, it's not."

"You lied to me then, and now, with Lauren Downey, you lied to me for, what, two years? That's what you said. You've been with her for two years."

"I didn't mean—"

"After everything with Mom, after you got back to normal and you were running again and everything, remember the talk we had?"

"We've had a lot of talks," I say. Now I'm the one looking over the water, back toward the hazy shore. A welt is forming on my knee, and I press it with my fingertips.

"It was a big one. At the beginning of the summer. You said, 'no matter what, you be straight with me, and I'll be straight with you. About everything.' Remember that one?"

"I remember."

"I took that seriously, Dad. I've never kept . . . I've never kept anything from you. Ever." My son makes a hiccuping sound and wipes his eyes. When he speaks again, his voice is pitched higher. "But you kept stuff from me. You went and—"

"Stop," I say. "I didn't mean it."

"So you lied about that, you totally lied to me about Lauren, then it's like, well maybe he did lie to me about the way he was after Mom, and what the fuck? What the fuck, Dad? I can't believe you'd"—he sniffs, and wipes his nose on his sleeve—"you'd just tune out like that."

"Christopher," I say, and another big wave throws the boat from side to side. "The time after Mom, I hardly even remember it."

"Well, I do."

"Maybe it happened like you remember it. Maybe it didn't. Maybe I blocked out how bad it was. Did I lie to you about it? Did

- 323 -

I lie to myself? Maybe when things were at their worst I did. I don't want to lie to you, Chris. You are my son, okay? I know I don't always say how I feel, but I know you know it. And when you left me, I was sick with worry, I was crazy. All this other stuff going on, it was like nothing compared to you being gone."

Chris says nothing.

"So, what," I go on, "you were going to stay with Uncle Mike?"

"Why not? At least he never lied to me. I've never seen him get so wasted he passes out."

"Chris, I didn't think I ever lied to you about Lauren, I just never told you."

He laughs, bitterly. "Oh, okay. So you just deceived me instead of lying to me. Thanks. That makes me feel a lot better."

"There's no easy way I can explain it. Maybe when you're older—"

"Don't even try to give me that 'when you're older' crap, Dad."

"Maybe," I say, "maybe someday when you have kids. Maybe you'll have a son. If you have a son, you will love him more than anything. I can't explain the feeling. The only way you can understand it is when you're there. But if you have a son, you'll love him, and you'll do anything to keep him from being hurt. If he takes a tumble on his bike, you'll wish it was you instead. If you see him get shoved on the playground, you'll want to go find the kid who did it and shove him back. Your mom was the one who was hands-off, Chris. She always had to remind me that you needed room, that you needed to learn how to deal with being hurt on your own. That it was okay to have a scraped-up knee, or to get your feelings hurt a little bit. You can't grow up without getting knocked around some. Your mom knew that, and I tried to remember it. I tried. I really did. Do you understand at all what I'm trying to say?"

Chris looks at me without saying a word, and the sailboat bobs in the water.

"But," I go on, "here's the thing, and you can't . . . you can't even know this until you're a parent. You'll do anything to keep your kid from being really hurt. You'd jump in front of a car or run into a burning building or . . . I don't know. I thought somehow that knowing about Lauren and me would really hurt you."

"I don't care if you have a girlfriend, Dad. I don't care if you get married again, even. I've always liked Ms. Downey—"

"All right. I know that now. Maybe I was stupid for not knowing. Or for not trying to know. I just assumed it would hurt you, okay? I didn't give you any credit. I didn't realize it was more like a scraped knee than a burning building. I didn't keep it from you because I was mean, but because I was stupid. I didn't trust that you'd be able to deal with it. I didn't understand that you needed to deal with it, just like I needed to deal with it. I didn't want you to be hurt. Do you understand?"

My son twists farther away from me, resting his chin against the padded lifeline as he stares down at the water.

"Chris, can you understand that, even if it wasn't right, I didn't tell you about Lauren and me because I didn't want to see you hurt?"

His head tilts in a barely perceptible nod.

"I was stupid," I say. "Do you understand how sorry I am?"

Another nod.

"Do you think you can forgive me?"

There is a long pause, and Christopher turns his head away so that he's looking forward along the length of the boat. Seconds pass, and finally he nods again.

"Okay," I say, taking a deep breath. "Let's get back home." I take *Tabby*'s wheel and pull in the mainsheet until it tightens against the wind. The boat picks up headway again, and I turn us back toward shore and let the sheet out as we begin to gather speed.

"I'm sorry, Chris."

"I wish you'd just told me."

"I know," I say. "I wish I had too. I thought I was doing the right thing. I'm sorry."

"Just forget it, okay?"

Pushed by the wind, we begin to roll over the waves toward shore. Alan and Leland watch from the fishing boat about a hundred yards away. Leland starts to come toward us, but I make a broad motion with my arm to the shore and he waves back and throttles the boat up and out of our sight.

I won't ever just forget it. And I know Christopher won't either.

It takes us a couple hours to get back to the marina in Manistee. Alan and Leland are waiting on the docks, and they've arranged a slip for us to tie the boat in. Farther up the shore, Lauren stands by the parking lot, shielding her eyes from the sun with her hand. I wave, and she gives me a little wave back.

As for *Tabby*, I figure I'll call Peggy and explain everything when we're home, and I can come down to return the boat later in the week. I doubt she was planning to use it for anything.

I gather Christopher's things up down below and stuff them into his gym bag. The red milk crate is crammed up in the forward bunk, and I leave it there. Chris doesn't say anything when we're back up on the dock. Leland greets him with a soft hello, and Alan puts his arm over my son's shoulders.

"Bet your legs are a little wobbly, huh? Couple days out on the water, that always did it to me. I bet you're tired too. You look cooked."

He's not the only one feeling cooked. With the relief of having my son next to me, safe, I feel like I could fall over and sleep for a day.

I sit between Chris and Lauren in the backseat of the Navigator while we return to the airport. He says nothing to her. He says nothing to any of us. My son is exhausted; I can see it in his face, but I can see he's curious about how we got down here, and why we're traveling in a giant SUV that obviously does not belong to us. We pile out by Leland's plane, and the same kid who greeted us before takes the car away. The five of us clamber into the Cessna, and Alan shows Chris the proper way to wear his headset.

"You ever flown in a small plane?" Alan asks him as we taxi down to the end of the runway. Chris shakes his head.

"It's pretty fun, Christopher," Leland says. "It's the only way to travel." I turn back to Lauren, alone in the third row of seats, and she weakly laughs and shakes her head with a look that says: *Never again.*

We lift off, gracefully slipping up from the runway, and Alan banks the plane to make a pass over the marina before we head back north.

"There she is, Chris," Alan says. "Your grand getaway."

"Slowest getaway ever," Leland gently teases, and he twists back to smile at Chris. Chris doesn't see, though. He's looking down at the boat.

We don't talk as Alan flies us back up along the beach. The sun is sinking to the west, filling the plane with a deep golden glow. I turn back to check on Lauren, and see that she's dozed off. I think Chris might be asleep too, but then he speaks, and the sound of his voice over our headsets startles us all.

"Mr. Massie?" he asks, furrowing his brow. "Should you be flying this plane?"

Alan drives the Prius to drop Chris and me off at home. I unload his bags while my son goes straight to his room. He lies on his bed, fully clothed, and covers his eyes with his hands. I go outside to get his last duffel, and give Lauren a quick call.

"I told you he'd be home," she says.

"I know," I say. "You were right all along."

"You still have some stuff over here at Al and Kristin's. Should I bring it all back to your house, or do you need me to wait a bit?"

"Hold up on that. Let me talk with Chris a little first."

I head back inside and peek into his room.

"Are you hungry?" I ask.

"More just tired," he says, still covering his eyes. "Really, really tired."

I enter his room and sit on the floor, leaning my back against his bed.

"Am I going to get in trouble for this, Dad?"

"I don't know," I say. "We need to call Mrs. Mackie to let her know where her boat is. I'll call her in a little while."

"Maybe I should call her. I'm the one who took the boat."

"How about I'll call first, tell her what happened, and you can talk to her after that. Okay?"

"Okay." Chris doesn't say anything for a long time. After a while I hear him sigh.

"Am I in trouble with you?" he asks.

"God, no." I shake my head. "You're not in trouble with me." I consider this for a moment, this whole concept of "trouble," and I let out a laugh. "What about me? Am I in trouble with you?"

"How could you be?" Chris asks.

"I lied to you," I say. "Or, okay, I deceived you. You deserve to be angry. But," I add, "if I'm in trouble, I think you punished me enough. Let's call it even." Chris laughs through his nose. I look at him and see his eyes are still shut. "Lauren has some of my stuff over at Alan's house. She was going to bring it over here, but I understand if you—"

"Dad, I don't care about Lauren. I mean, I told you, I don't care if you have a girlfriend, okay? I wasn't even that pissed because you lied to me. It was finding you passed out. That's why I blew up. I thought I was losing you. I guess I panicked. That's why I was mad."

"Never again, Christopher. I swear."

"Okay." A pause. "Lauren's really pregnant?"

"She really is."

"Man. Are you going to get married?"

"At some point," I say. "I'd like to, yes."

"Okay. That's fine. You should have told me, you know, a lot earlier."

"I know I should have, Chris." I wait, and open my mouth, but what I want to say is hard in coming.

"Chris?"

"Yeah?" he murmurs.

"That time . . ." I lean my head back and look at his ceiling. "That time in the barn. All of that time. I forgot about it. I'm not kidding; I made myself forget about it. God, Chris, never again. I'm ashamed to even think about it now. Did it really happen? Or is it like that video? Did it really happen like that in the barn?"

Are we alive because we remember things, or because we can forget?

"You're my son, Chris," I go on. "You're my son, my family, and I love you." I turn my head to look at him. I want him to know I mean it. He knows nothing though; he breathes deeply with his head turned and his mouth slightly parted, alive and unknowing in the deepest of sleep.

CHAPTER TWENTY-SIX

While Christopher rests, I call Peggy Mackie and explain what happened. She doesn't say anything while I tell the story, just listens, and finally says, "Hm." I think she understands. She's dealt with a lot of teen boys in her career.

"We'll fly down later this week and bring her back, Peggy," I tell her. "Or if you know someone you'd rather have sailing her home, that's fine, I'll pay to get her back up here."

"No, it's okay. I just want you aboard with Chris when you bring the boat back. No solo trips. And I want Chris to call me to tell me all this himself."

"I think he was planning to do that," I say.

"Did Pete Tran stop by to talk with you?"

"Nope. Never saw him." It's not a lie, either; I don't mention that I might have been away from my house.

"I don't know what the hell is going on with this. If you end up not talking to him, just come to the district office tomorrow. Seven o'clock."

"See you then, Peggy. Thanks for being so understanding about this."

Lauren, at my insistence, comes over to spend the night. She was reluctant when I asked, but I told her she should. Chris knows, I explained, he understands. He's okay with it. So she comes. I go into Christopher's darkened room to put a blanket over him before we go to bed, and Lauren stands in his doorway with me and rubs her hand up and down my back while we watch him sleep.

Chris stays home from school on Tuesday. Lauren greets him in the morning and he sheepishly says hi. I'm working on breakfast while they talk out in the living room, and I can't help but listen to them.

"I'm sorry about everything that happened," I hear her say.

"Seriously," he says. "Don't worry about it. I'm over it."

"If you're angry with me, I understand. But I want us to talk about it, because, you know, I'm here."

"I was kind of angry at my dad. But we already talked about it. I know why he didn't tell—"

"It wasn't all him, Chris. I was part of keeping it a secret too."

"I understand," he says. "We talked about it. I'm not angry anymore. It's fine. Are you going to move in?"

"I hope so. But I want to ask you if it's okay. This is your space too."

"There's enough room," Chris says. "And I'll be leaving for school next fall, so, yeah. It's no problem."

"Thank you. I don't want it to be weird. Any weirder than it already was. Or is, I guess."

"So you didn't really spill anything on yourself the other day, did you, Ms. Downey?"

"No," she says. "I didn't. And I want you to call me Lauren."

"It's kind of strange for me to say."

"Well, you aren't going to call me Mom or anything like that instead, I hope."

Chris laughs. "No, I don't think so. I'll stick with Lauren."

Pete Tran does not come by at any point during the day.

------ ——————————— -----

At six I shower and dress; the sport coat I wear, my only sport coat, was last donned a little less than a year ago for the end-of-season cross-country awards banquet. I should at least look presentable for whatever I have coming.

Chris asks if I want him to come, and I reply with an emphatic *No.* Lauren asks me the same thing, and my answer doesn't change. I tell her if I am to be publicly lashed, I'd like to bear the weight of the experience by myself. She shakes her head, goes to my room, and returns in a moment in a dress and sweater.

"I am coming with you," she says. "And that's that."

I'd like to think I've become pretty good at handling these burdens on my own, but, like she says, I guess that's that.

We say little on the drive to the district offices. Lauren holds my hand on the way, and she holds my hand as we walk into the building. The boardroom is not as filled with people as I've seen it in the past, but I am surprised to see a number of teen boys there sitting in two rows of chairs along with a number of adults behind, who I assume to be their parents. I'm also surprised to see Steve and Leland Dinks seated with them. Leland sees me enter and nods, and he gives Lauren a warm smile. I'm suddenly very glad she's there with me. Cody Tate is seated in the room too, his nose and eyebrow clear of any scrapes. He sees me enter and quickly looks away. A stern-looking man sits next to Cody, and next to the man are two more men in suits. Kent Hughes from the paper is in the back of the room, tapping away at an iPad on his knees. Pete Tran, in civilian clothes, is standing by Jo and Frank Masterson. Their daughter is not with them. Pete steps over to greet me just as I'm taking a seat.

"Were you looking for me yesterday?" I ask as we shake hands.

"I was, in fact."

"To cuff me?"

Pete screws up his face. "Why would you think that? We got a little break. You can tell your friend his theory was close, but not quite there."

"My friend? What friend?"

"The pilot. The guy with the miniature golf course."

"Alan," Lauren says.

"*Alan* called you?"

"More than once. I had a feeling this was all crap, but he knew it from the beginning. When he told me how the blood was already on the kid's face, that's when I really understood it was bogus." He nods over to the boys. "These guys are going to explain it. Oh, and those emails . . ."

"Yes?"

Pete draws a notepad from his packet and flips to a page. "Did you ever know someone named . . . Victor Tesh? Former student, maybe, or someone you knew in Lansing?" I shake my head; I've never heard the name before.

"Or what about the Marshall Place Apartments in East Lansing?"

This is a surprise. I haven't heard that name in a long time. "That was . . . I lived there. With my wife. Well, girlfriend, then. My last year in college."

"The guys downstate are on it. I'll keep you posted."

Peggy Mackie enters the room and nods hello when she sees me, and Pete excuses himself to go talk with her. A short man with a mustache scoots over to introduce himself after Pete is gone.

"Mr. Kaz . . . Ka . . ." he tries.

"Kazenzakis," I say.

"I'm Gary Burke from the teachers' union."

"I got your call," I lie.

"Great, great. Listen, I'm here to—"

The official-types start to enter the room, and Gary Burke falls silent along with all the small conversations that had been mumbling through the space. Stu Lepinski comes through the door with an accordion file under his arm, followed by a couple board members I don't really know; Gracie Adams files in last, and they all take seats behind microphones set up at the table at the front of the room. A screen, glowing a washed-out blue from the light of a ceiling-mounted projector, has been pulled down behind the table. Next to me, Lauren leans close and rests her hand on my forearm. Peggy closes the doors to the room, and Gracie clears her throat into her microphone.

"I'd like to get going here," she says. Gracie's face wears a sour expression, and I get the distinct feeling she's avoiding looking at me. "Peggy?" At the mention of her name, the boys all stare into their laps, as if in church.

"So we're here to talk about this business with Mr. K.," Peggy says. "I guess to start, we need to see how this thing was made. Who is going to show us? Why don't you go over to that table; I think you're all ready. It should be all set up for you." Two boys rise from their seats, along with their parents, and shuffle to a laptop set up at the side of the room. Peggy flips out the lights, and the hanging screen is bright with the projection of a computer desktop. Even though the room is dim, I can almost feel how the boy seated at the laptop is shaking.

"So, um," he starts, "we kind of—"

"Can you speak up, please?" Gracie says. "Into the microphone."

"Yeah, um, there was this video, the original video, there were actually two of them."

"Would you show us the videos?" Peggy asks.

"Yeah, sure." The boy clicks away on the laptop, and on the projection screen, the student parking lot of Port Manitou High appears. I am in the distance, frozen midstride. The boy clicks again, and I begin running, growing larger in the screen.

"Hey!" I shout. *Hey!*

I stand in the frame, talking. It's hard to understand what I'm saying. The audio is muffled, scratchy with the sound of the windy day, and my hands are held out. I turn around and speak. At the bottom of the frame is a flicker of white, Cody Tate's shirt, and the camera aims down to show him sprawled over the ground. I reach to pull the boy up, and, with my hands on his shoulders, I speak again. A boy's voice fills the room, loudly, over the speakers:

"Tater's a pussy, that's what."

Laughter rings through the clip, and Cody Tate begins to swing his arms. My head snaps back as his elbow collides with my face, and I fall, careening back and out of the shot gone suddenly mad with a view of shaking pavement and running feet.

"Holy shit, holy shit, dude!"

"Oh holy shit, is he getting up?"

"Cody, you hit that fucking teacher, dude. You laid him out."

"Yeah."

"You got your ass handed to you first though. Gretch kind of kicked your ass."

"No way, dude. I had to like, fight him off me."

I had to like, fight him off me.

When the video is complete, the kid at the laptop clicks and starts a second one. It's the same, almost the same, shot from a different angle. The high school gym can be seen in the background. It begins at nearly the same time as the first, with me running, but it ends sooner, the moment I fall to the ground.

"So," Peggy asks in the dark room, "that was how it really happened?"

There's a reply, but I can't hear it.

"Excuse me?" Peggy says.

"I said yes, ma'am."

"All right. Now, how did you make the version that showed up on the Internet?"

The kid at the laptop gets up to trade places with the second boy.

"Well, Mrs. Mackie, we did some editing—"

"Obviously," Peggy says, and a couple of the parents chuckle. I do not chuckle. I notice in the dimness that Lauren's mouth is slightly agape, and realize for the first time how tightly she's gripping my arm.

"Yeah, so, we did some editing, and it was like, we took the video of the guy, I mean the teacher, running toward us, this part"—he clicks the laptop and I am running toward the camera again—"we stopped it right . . . here. See how he has both of his hands up? If you play through that all the way, you see he's just waving for us to like, cut it out. But we stopped it before that. He's also at the edge of the frame, so you could think that Cody was standing just out of the shot."

"I see." Peggy says. She's turned, like all of the board members, so she can watch the screen up behind her.

"So then, like, if you go forward about four-and-a-half seconds, that's when he picks Cody up off the ground." The boy advances through the video, frame by frame, as I lift Cody Tate from the pavement, up to the moment I have my hands resting on his shoulders. "Watch that . . . it's almost one second of footage in reverse, like this, check it out." He scrubs backward through the frames, I hurl Cody to the pavement, and a mother in the group exclaims *Oh my God*. "It looks like the teacher totally grabs Cody and throws him for real, right? Especially the way he holds his shirt right . . . there. If you speed it up ten percent it seems even more realistic."

"It does," Peggy says.

"So we cut those together this way," the boy says, opening another video file. This one shows me running, spliced together in a jarring cut with the reversed footage of me picking up Cody Tate. "That version is still obviously totally fake. So I put a blur filter over that transition . . . like this . . . then I added shake into the frames, on top of the blur. So you can't even really tell there's a cut there. After that we just took the sound from when Cody hit the teacher, like how you can hear everyone react with surprise, I just laid it over the reversed part so it's like they were reacting to him throwing Cody."

The room is silent for a long moment, and Peggy rises and goes to the door to flip on the lights. "Can I ask one thing?" she says, looking over all of the boys before turning back to the kid at the computer. "One thing. Why? Why in the world did you do this?" He doesn't answer. "No, really, why did you make this video? Did you have any idea what sort of impact it might have on Mr. Kazenzakis?"

"I guess . . . I guess I just wanted to see if I could make it look realistic," the kid says. "It was challenging."

"You made it look very real. Why wasn't that good enough? Did you think at all about the consequences it might have? Do you have something against Mr. Kazenzakis? Do you even know him?"

The kid at the laptop points to the second row of chairs. "Those guys know him," Laptop Kid says, and a number of the boys hang their heads and stare down at their shoes. "They knew I was good with this stuff," the kid adds. "They asked if I could make something like this."

"They asked you to make this," Peggy says, her brows narrowing. "And you did." She turns to the boys. "How do any of you know Mr. Kazenzakis? Is he a teacher of yours?" I can't get a good look at any of their faces, but what I am able to see isn't ringing any bells.

"No," a voice says.

"Then how did this happen? Why did it happen? I want one of you to tell all of us here what you told me and Officer Tran this morning."

"Well . . . there was . . . a fight," a boy's voice says.

"Yes, okay. A fight. Why did this fight happen? Was someone worried about something? Or was someone mad? Maybe both?"

"Both," another voice says.

"Both." Peggy crosses her arms. "Let's start with the worried part. Some of you were pretty worried about something. What was it that you were worried about?"

"Those pictures," a boy says, and I wonder if I am imagining the sound of Denise Masterson's parents shifting in their seats behind me. "Tater showed us all some pictures and we sort of freaked out because . . . I mean, we really freaked out because he sent them around. We thought we would be in trouble for having them. Because we thought they were like illegal."

"So you beat up Tater. You beat up Cody Tate."

"It wasn't like a real beat down. None of us even asked for the pictures. We didn't want to see that stuff in the first place. So we were pissed. And some of us thought it was pretty weak that he would do that to Denise"—another rustling behind me—"and we were pissed about that too."

"But then you found out they weren't even her."

"Yeah. We were really mad when we found that out."

"Okay. You were mad and worried. But why the video, then? Why drag Mr. Kazenzakis into it?"

Another boy raises his hand to speak, a gesture I might find endearing in any other circumstance, and Peggy says, "Go ahead, Drew."

"We made the video after the fight," the boy named Drew says. "Like, the next day, Cody told everyone the pictures weren't real. And he said something about how his dad was going to have everyone prosecuted for beating him up. Because it was an assault or something."

"And you believed him?"

"I mean, it's obviously such B.S. now, but when he said it . . . he's all rich, you know, his parents are totally rich, so, yeah, I guess we believed it. So a bunch of us were hanging out the next night and when we looked at the video, and it was like, I don't even remember who noticed the backwards thing, but we were like holy crap, because we realized . . ."

"What exactly did you realize?"

Drew looks into his lap, and a man sitting next to him, his father I'm assuming, says something softly into his ear. "We realized we could make it look like the teacher did it. And I was like, but why would a teacher do that out of nowhere? Someone remembered that he was tight with Denise somehow, her family, so it would totally make sense that he would be mad at Cody. About the pictures, I mean."

"So you made the video."

"We kind of made one, we tried, but it sucked so bad. It was obvious how fake it was. Somebody called Craig"—he nods to Laptop Kid—"and he came over and made one that was unbelievably perfect. In less than an hour. It blew us away."

"I just wanted to see if I could do it," Laptop Kid adds. "I didn't really have anything against him."

"Then why did you put it online?"

"Everybody puts stuff online," the kid says. "It's just how we show stuff off." Now Steve Dinks raises his hand. When Peggy nods to him, he rises to his feet.

"Mrs. Mackie, I was at that party when the first one got posted. The guys I was with didn't know anything about the fight then, the reason for it I mean. We just thought it would be funny. We didn't think people would believe it. We didn't even think that many people would see. Then it got out of hand, it was just that first night and it was going around like crazy, crazy how many views it was getting. So I made them take it down. I thought if they took it down, it would be over. But then a second video got made, I wasn't around for that one. It was just as bad, I mean, just as bad for how fast people were sending the link around. And the second video looked more real than the first. The second one got way out of control."

"We put the digital shake filter on the second one," Laptop Kid says. He sounds almost proud of it.

"Cody?" Peggy asks. "Did you have anything to do with the video? Other than being in it? You didn't make it, did you?"

Cody Tate shakes his head no.

"Did you have anything to do with actually posting the video online?"

Another shake of the head.

"You told me the video was real. You swore up and down to me that was how things happened that afternoon. More than once. You told the same thing to Officer Tran. Why didn't you speak up about it?" Cody Tate's chin, I can see across the room, is trembling, and his father looks livid. "Can you tell me anything about this?"

"He was going to get a beat down for real if he ratted them out," a teen voice says, and another voice follows, saying, "Dude! Shut up!"

"Wait, who's 'them'?" Peggy asks. "In this room? Cody, did someone threaten you about what the consequences might be if you told the truth?" Cody Tate's father says something too low for the rest of the room to hear, and Cody, really shaking now, looks up at Peggy and nods.

"There was that," Cody says in a barely audible voice. "But they had the real video of me hitting Mr. K. They said if I told anyone what really happened, they'd show the real video and I'd be in—"

"Big trouble," Peggy says in a measured voice. "You think you aren't in big enough trouble now? You could have saved everyone here a ton of trouble if you'd just spoken up." Peggy shakes her head. "Mr. Kazenzakis most of all." Stu Lepinski leans to say something into Peggy's ear, and Peggy rolls her eyes.

"We need a little time to discuss this," Gracie says. "Can you all step out into the hallway? Everyone, please?"

"Neil, stay here," Peggy says. Lauren takes a step toward the door, and I shake my head.

"No," I say. "Don't go." Gracie Adams gives Lauren a look, and I add, "She's here with me."

The kids and parents file out of the room, and one of the Tate family lawyers grabs my elbow and says, "Can we talk with you about this after?" Pete Tran remains behind along with the union guy, and Kent Hughes tries to stay too. Peggy thumbs toward the exit and says, "Out of here, Hughes." Kent leaves, and Peggy closes the doors behind him.

"Neil," Peggy says. "I am very sorry. About all of this." Stu Lepinski whispers something to her again, and Peggy says, "Stu, the guy got screwed over. We can apologize to him, don't you think? We owe him an apology."

"Mr. Kazenzakis," Gracie says, insisting on speaking into her microphone in spite of the fact I'm standing five feet in front of her. "You are aware, I'm sure, that you didn't follow the correct procedure for dealing with a physical altercation between students?"

"Are you kidding me?" I say, and Pete Tran actually laughs.

"Gracie, seriously," Peggy says. "Look, for Mr. Kazenzakis, this is done. Neil, come back to work next week. Take this week off, and come back Monday. If you're going to sue the district, have your lawyer talk to Stu. I really hope you don't sue the district, because we like working with you, and we like having you here. We did what we had to do given the situation. I think you understand that."

"Of course I do," I say.

Gary-whatever, the union rep who up until now has been sitting behind me, gets to his feet. "I think the union's going to want to have some input on—"

"You guys hash it out," I say, cutting him off with a wave of my hand. "I don't need to deal with it. To tell you the truth, I think anything I try to say right now is going to be nonsense, because I am completely exhausted."

"I bet you are," Peggy says.

"Are we done?" I ask. I look at them, and they look at each other. "Keep the substitute for the rest of this week," I say. "I'll be in on Monday. Kevin Hammil can cover girls' cross-country until I'm back. I'm sure he's been doing a fine job at it."

"We'll see you in a week," Peggy says, and I take Lauren's hand and start for the door. "Gracie, do you have anything?"

"Nothing for him. We need to discuss what's going to happen with everyone out in the hall—"

"Wait," I say, stopping at the edge of the chairs. "One thing. Do what you have to do with Cody Tate, but don't expel any of those kids, okay? Especially not the seniors. What they did was stupid, but that's all it was. Most of those guys are going to college; I don't want any of them screwed up just for being stupid. Okay?"

"Mr. Kazenzakis, beyond the video, which was bad enough on its own, there was a fair amount of deceit going on here. Intimidation. They coordinated their stories—"

"Of course they did," I say. "They're kids. They didn't want to get in trouble. They got into their stories, and the longer they went, the deeper it got. Trust me, I understand this. More than you know. I also understand you need to discipline them, but don't expel any of them." I pause. "Here's what you can do. Just have them post the original video with an apology. That's all I want."

"Neil," Peggy says, "you have to remember that some of these kids were physically threatening Cody Tate if he said anything. A threat of violence is something we have to take seriously."

"I understand," I say. "You get to the bottom of that part of it. If they broke the law, do what you need to do. But the ones who were just involved with the video, even that jackass who did the editing, go easy on them, okay? Go easy on Steve Dinks. That's all I'm asking you. Will you consider it while you figure everything out?"

"We will, Mr. Kazenzakis," Gracie Adams says. Strangely, she looks like she means it.

All the kids out in the hallway turn to watch as Lauren and I leave the room. Leland nods, and Steve Dinks approaches us. I'm so drained by exhaustion I feel like I could fall to the floor.

"Mr. K.," he says, keeping his eyes level with mine. "I was telling the truth in there. I didn't mean for it to get out of control like that. I don't think any of us did. I'm really sorry." He holds out his hand—a big move for such a young guy—and I shake it.

"Thank you, Steve," I say. "I appreciate you speaking up."

I really do.

Christopher is in the kitchen when we get home, and he freezes in the middle of whatever it is he's doing over the stove when we enter from the garage.

"Well?" he asks.

"Everything's fine. The video was fake."

"I told you!" Chris says, pumping a fist. "It was so fake. Are the people who did it busted?"

"Pretty much," I say. "I'll tell you about it tomorrow."

"Oh, Neil," Lauren says. "You look so tired. Go sit. Sit. I'll stay and help Chris, if he'd like me to." Christopher nods.

"Sure," I say. "Okay." I hang my jacket on the front closet doorknob and kick off my shoes, then sink into my couch and close my eyes for what feels like an age. I hear low voices from the kitchen; Lauren filling Chris in on the board meeting, I'm imagining. I keep my eyes shut as someone drops to the couch next to me; I can tell by the sound it's my son.

"So they're really busted?" he asks. "Who was it? Do I know any of them?"

"I didn't really know any of them. Well, Steve Dinks was one of them."

"Oh man, that so figures. I should—"

"You should not do anything. Just let it go. I'm sure his dad will deal with it just fine."

"But, Dad—"

"Chris, really. It's done. I'm home, you're home. We're all good here, right?"

"Yeah," he says. "We're good."

"How's it going with Lauren?" I ask, lowering my voice just a little.

"What do you mean?"

"I mean, here she is. In our house. Is it weird?"

"What's weird is how not weird it is. If that makes any sense. I didn't realize she was so cool."

"I should have told you sooner."

"Yeah, you should have. But, whatever. We're all good now. Really."

"What are you making for dinner? It smells good. Spicy maybe?"

"Just wait, Dad. It's a surprise."

My eyes remain closed, and Christopher heads back to the kitchen to resume his work with Lauren. I'm so close to dozing off, *so* close, but my brain is half tuned-in to the banter coming from the other room.

"So next step," my son is saying, "you're supposed to flip it, but I always blow this part."

"Here, watch. You do it like this, back and forward, and the wrist like . . . ta-da."

"Oh my God, how did you do that? How do you make it look so easy?"

"I can do it with my left hand too. Watch."

"How are you so good at that?"

"My little brother is a sous-chef in Cleveland."

"No way?"

My phone rings from the pocket of my hanging sport coat, and I will myself to my feet to grab it. It's Leland.

"Neil," he says.

"Yes?"

"Peggy Mackie told me what you said to them."

I blink. "What I said to them? What I said about what?"

"The board. About not expelling the kids."

"Well, I meant it. I don't think what they did quite rises to the level of expulsion. It was maybe more stupid than malicious. I was kind of surprised to see you guys there—"

"Steve was acting weird all week. Really weird when I asked him if he knew anything about what was going on. When we got back last night, he told me what was up, how he was there when the thing got rolling. I told him he needed to do whatever he could to make it right."

"That was pretty big of him to speak up like he did tonight."

"He did that on his own," Leland says. "I'm surprised you're not more angry about all this, Neil."

"You know, compared to everything else, the video thing is pretty minor. It's just not that big a deal to me at the moment. Chris is okay, he's home. That's all I need to think about. And on top of everything, I'm dead tired. Maybe I'll have some energy to be angry about it after I get some sleep. Let me get back to you later about being angry. Maybe tomorrow I'll find it in me to be pissed."

"I just wanted to say thank you."

"No, shut up. I should be thanking you, Lee. For the plane. For all your help. *That* was a big deal."

"It was nothing. If something was up with Steve, you'd have done the same."

I tell Leland we should talk again soon, and I mean it. Not about real estate, not about bickering. We should catch up. He agrees.

I put the phone on the floor by my feet, and I close my eyes and listen:

"I don't get how you do it."

"Watch me again. Back, forward, flip with the wrist. Here. Do it. Just like . . . you did it! See? Easy."

"Sweet. Let me do it again. Sweet! Dad, I flipped something in a pan!"

With my eyes closed, I smile and nod. They cook together, and they laugh. I cannot help but smile as I hear it. They are together, I am part of them, and in my home something is complete.

I will remember this, precisely as it happened, for a long, long time.

Neil my love,

I was so so so sad you couldn't make it to my graduation party but I understand how that stuff goes. And hey I couldn't get to yours either so I guess we're even right? But it doesn't really matter now because it's only five more weeks (well four weeks and five days but I haven't been counting REALLY) before a certain family comes to stay at a certain beach house and a certain boy will be with that family. Do you have a guess who that boy might be? I bet you do. I think I like being with him very much.

Speaking of the beach house my dad was doing work on it and he offered me five dollars an hour (WOW) to help him paint inside and when I was inside of course I had to think of the times we spent there (like the "ice storm" event HA HA) and when you came up for spring break (I promise promise promise the next time we do that I will be 100% better at it and I will be perfect and wonderful for you like you are perfect and wonderful for me and it will be the most incredible thing either of us have experienced. Okay? It's a deal.) Did your parents even have a clue that you came up here? I was scared my parents would see your mom's car in town and we would get in trouble but I guess I was just being paranoid.

Oh guess what in the news a boat sunk just outside of PM! It was a fishing boat for tourists and it sunk in less than two minutes the paper said but everyone was okay because other boats were close and got everyone out of the water. My dad knows the guy who the boat belongs (belonged?) to and said he wasn't surprised that the boat sunk which I thought was pretty funny.

I am still waiting for MSU to send me the housing stuff for my dorm. Kelly Kramer from track is going there too and we are going to try to be roommates. It's funny because we were never really friends even though I have known her since she moved here in 3rd grade but last year on track we got really close and now I am excited to live with her. CRAZY. Most of all I hope you and I end up in the same dorm complex so I can see you as frequently as possible!

My graduation party was mostly a lot of fun. Again I was SAD that you weren't there but I guess you know that and I don't need to tell you again right? We had the party at the beach house my mom decorated it and Uncle Art and my cousins showed up (surprise!) and Uncle Art gave me a check for $200!!!! My dad had a guy come to play music which is not like him AT ALL but it was really fun. We had a bonfire and things got a little crazy because after the adults went to bed Tim Smith (I told you about him) showed up with a bunch of guys who had all been at another party where there had been drinking and Tim had three cases of beer in his car so everyone on the beach started drinking (yes me included) and things got crazy Tim and these two other boys were trying to jump over the fire and Kelly threw up next to someone's car and I had to find a place for her to lie down. It was like a college party even though I have no idea what one is like but I guess we'll find out soon enough.

Tim kept talking to me which I thought was weird because he's had the same girlfriend for nearly two years and he knows how I feel about you. A couple times he tried to put his arm around me but I asked him "where's your girlfriend Tim?" and he would feel guilty and stop. But then he kept doing it and it was just easier to let him after a while. This is the part I feel really bad about and I am scared you will hate me but I need to write it out and I don't even know if I'll send this but at least I will write it down and see how I feel about it. I walked up the beach with Tim and he kept his arm around me and I didn't tell him to stop. Then when we got to where *the Little Jib River lets out we started kissing and I asked him to stop so we sat down but we started kissing again. I always thought of Little Jib as OUR place but it was so strange and I don't know why I even let us go there or why once we were there I didn't make him stop when he started to kiss me again. I felt so terrible I still feel terrible but I was curious I guess and I didn't stop. He wanted to do some of the other things too and we sort of did but only a couple of them (not any of the bad bad ones those things are ONLY for you) but I felt so horrible I got up and said I had to go home.*

God I feel awful about this I just needed to write it down. I don't know if I ever can send this. I don't even like him and I don't know why I did any of that. I love you so much and the only thing I want is to be with you at MSU and be your girl-friend and have you be my boyfriend and we can do everything and be happy. I'm scared if I send this none of that would hap-pen and my life would be empty and nothing because I know in my heart you are the only one I will ever truly love. I know that sounds ridiculous and some people say you're too young how could you even know? But I do know and the weird part is that what happened with Tim Smith makes me know it even more.

Maybe I will never send this. I don't have the courage. But if I do send it I hope you have the courage to forgive me.

I love you so much. I know I say it so much but I love you. Please please don't hate me if I send this and you read it.

Your love

(and favorite running/sailing/everything else partner sorry I had to say it and if you hate me don't ever forget that part at least)

Wendy

CHAPTER TWENTY-SEVEN

Theodore Hamilton Kazenzakis arrives in the spring, on May 19. Just shy of seven pounds in weight, he mews like a kitten after he's born, and struggles to latch on to his mother's breast.

"What do I do?" Lauren whispers to the midwife, crying in amazement at this thing that's just happened, this tiny life she's just produced and is now holding against her bare chest. She's asking for advice on getting him to nurse, but the midwife takes a broader view.

"First you love him," she says, stroking the back of the newborn's head with her fingers. "And everything else will fall into place."

Like his father, my new son has a mouthful of a name. Hamilton is Lauren's middle name, a family name, and Theodore . . .

Let's just say my father is thrilled.

Still, though, there's that mouthful of a name. I hope he grows to bear it well.

In December, I drove down to Lansing to give a videotaped statement to the Michigan State Police about the threatening emails I'd received in the fall. They'd arrested a graduate student in the Computer Science Department at Michigan State, Viktor Tereshenko—also going by the name of Victor Tesh—who, along with some online associates in a hacking collective known as TeshCo, had admitted to waging an electronic vengeance campaign against me by breaking into the Port Manitou School District's computer network and flooding me with abusive messages.

TeshCo's motivation to harass me was unclear at first. I *had* lived in East Lansing for a great portion of my life and the video had received a lot of press there; Viktor sometimes claimed, according to the police, they'd barraged me with emails and images to rectify a great injustice. Other times, he said they'd acted just for the fun of it, "for the lulz."

When Tereshenko's sister, Irina, was arrested at her job as a certified nursing assistant in Port Manitou, Michigan in January, his true motivation began to make a little more sense.

Their trial is scheduled to start in October.

--- ⸻ ---

The Port Manitou Girls Cross-Country team had a stellar season. Counter to my earlier predictions, however, they did not win the state championship, finishing instead in third place. Cassie Jennings had a personal-best performance, taking first place individually, but Amy Vandekemp, having suffered an ankle injury the week before, was not able to compete, and we lost on points. It will be tough to lose Cassie, but we've got deep talent for next year's squad.

Entropy in the system is constant. But there's always next year.

--- ⸻ ---

A few days after the state championship, while Chris and I were working on installing our fireplace, I got a frantic call from Kristin Massie. "Neil, please, come quick, it's Alan, come quickly!" I ran to their house as fast as I could, certain, for some reason, that my friend had suffered a heart attack. I flew through the front door to find Kristin sitting on the floor cross-legged and crying; Alan, on his side with his knees pulled up, had his head resting in her lap.

"What happened?" I said, kneeling in front of them. Alan blinked and looked at me, and when I saw the absolute sadness in his eyes and the lamp that had been knocked from the end table, I knew my friend had not experienced a cardiac event. I also knew he would never sit in the captain's seat of an airplane—commercial or otherwise—again.

"I had another," he said quietly.

"Oh, Alan," I said, putting my hand on his shoulder. "Jesus. Alan, I'm sorry."

--------- ———————————— -----

Theo is six days old when we bring him to see Carol. It's a gray spring day, and the sky seems low as we arrive at the place we've moved her. My mother-in-law's condition has declined, and her needs have become too great for in-home care. She understands this; the great paradox of her fading life is that as her body has become frailer, her mind has gone the other direction and opened up with clarity. I think she's happy that she's clearheaded as she approaches the end. She has a lot to remember as she goes. The memories keep her company.

I also think she was holding out to see Theo.

We visit her—Chris, Lauren, Theo, and I—at the nursing home, in the hospice wing where she's been living for nearly the past two weeks. The staff, none of whom I know as well as the gang in Long Term, gathers in around the baby's car seat to coo and take in the tiny joyous thing that, for a moment at least, has superseded the usual grim nature of their work. Theo wakes and starts to fuss and squawk at all the attention, and Lauren takes him from his carrier to nurse him in a chair in the corner of Carol's room. After a few rough days of struggling at it, they've both figured out the feeding routine, and Theo calms down quickly. Chris kneels next to Carol's bed.

"How are you, Grandma?" he asks.

"Oh . . ." It takes a moment for her to work up a reply, and her voice has the weak rasp of a dry leaf blown over pavement. "I'm not so bad today, Christopher."

"That's good."

"How do you like that little brother of yours? He's got . . . a strong cry. Have you changed a diaper yet?"

"I changed him just before we came over," Chris says, and I laugh.

"He was scared of that more than anything," I say. "But he did a good job."

"I imagine you might have been a little rusty yourself, Neil. I'd like to see the baby, when you're ready to bring him over."

Lauren buttons herself up and wipes Theo's contented little face with a cloth, and she rises to bring him over to the bed. She holds him over Carol so she can see.

"Bring him here, Lauren. Bring him close to me. Oh, what a fine baby boy. What a good boy. I wish Dick were here to see this baby. You'll show him things, won't you, Chris? You help him grow up the right way, like you have."

"I will, Grandma."

"Show him the orchard. All the good places to run and hide. Take him to the beach. He can play in the sand. You keep a good eye on him when you're with him on the beach. That river in the woods. Your mom played there. You did too, when you were a little guy. Keep a close watch on him there."

"Yes, Grandma."

"You're such a good boy, Christopher. Bring this baby a little closer." Carol lifts her wavering hand, and her fingers brush over

Theo's head on the way to her own face. She tugs at the oxygen line with her crooked fingers.

"Help me with this, Christopher. Bring him closer." Chris helps pull the clear tubes up and out of the way as Lauren holds the sleeping baby up next to Carol's face. She closes her eyes and presses her wrinkled cheek to his head.

"So sweet," she says. "So sweet. Oh, Lauren, I'm so happy for you. What a perfect little boy."

"We're going to see Wendy," I say. "Carol, would you like me to get a nurse so we can bring you over with us?"

Carol is quiet, her eyes closed, as she breathes in the closeness of my infant son.

"No," she finally says. "No, that's okay. I have my memories of my little girl. And that's good. That's how I'd like to keep it now."

The orchard is staying with our family. I told Leland last fall I wasn't sure I was ready to make a decision on selling, and as months passed, he became less interested. I think things have slowed at the resort. People aren't buying; he's given me hints the couple times we've gone out together. We've met up here and there: Leland has a beer, I stay with water, and we catch up on things. He tells me people haven't been able to commit, but he's pretty sure things will pick up someday. Absent his interest, I've looked into having our property protected from development in the future by a conservation easement.

As it is, we aren't so worried about finances. We rented out Lauren's condominium at the beginning of the year, and we've still got my paycheck. Lauren will finish up her studies at the beginning of the summer when I can watch Theo full-time, and she's planning to go back to her job eventually. Most of the farmers working the orchard have renewed their leases too, so we've got some income there. We're doing okay.

On top of all that, the Tate family, possibly overestimating my appetite for litigation, worked out a preemptive settlement with me over the whole mess with their son. Alan thought I could have gotten more, but I didn't really care. They wrote me a check, and I put it straight into Christopher's college fund.

He'll be going to culinary school in the fall.

Theo is a great hit with Shanice and the other nurses over in Long Term, who crowd around Lauren as she brings the infant carrier up to the main desk. I am planning to run home after this visit, and a bag with my things hangs from my shoulder.

"Look at that baby!" Shanice gasps. "That is the most gorgeous little baby I've ever seen!"

It's Saturday, visiting day, and a handful of family members hear the commotion and come from their rooms to see what's going on. Everyone smiles, tired, wistful smiles, reminded perhaps that the ones they've come to visit here were once perfect babies too. Undamaged, and ready for the world. Theo is that. He is perfect, and he carries our hopes.

A man I don't know pats me on the back and shakes his head in a daze.

"Wow," the man says. "Wow."

The attention gets Theo worked up again, and when his little mouth puckers and trembles and finally erupts with an outsized wail, the spell over the gathered group is broken and we emit a collective "Aww!" Everyone laughs after that. Everyone but Chris, that is. My son has fervently embraced his position as elder brother, and he holds out his hands to Lauren.

"Let me take him," Chris says. "I know how to calm him down."

"He can't be hungry again," Lauren says.

Lauren lifts Theo to Christopher's hands, and, cradled there, the baby's crying stops.

"He likes pressure under his feet," Chris tells me as the observers return to whatever they were doing before we interrupted. "I figured it out yesterday. He likes to be held like this." Chris brings Theo close to his chest, and I raise my eyebrows.

"When did you learn so much about babies?" I ask.

"It's not that hard, Dad. You just try whatever and go with what works."

Inside Wendy's darkened room, Chris holds his little brother up to his mother's face. He leans down close to her.

"Mom," he whispers. "This is Theo. He's just a little baby. I never really even held a baby this small before Theo was born. He's so awesome, Mom. He's incredible."

I have to turn away as he says it, and Lauren presses her hand to the small of my back.

"He's like . . . I can't even believe it, Mom. He's my little brother. I love this little guy. Can you believe it?"

This is too much for me, and I go to the restroom to change into my running things. My phone drops out of my pocket as I fold my pants, and when I pick it up and cradle it in my hand, I feel the reflexive urge to tap out a message to my former wife. If Wendy really was somewhere on the other end of the wire, waiting to read and waiting to reply, what would I tell her?

I think I'd just write: We're okay. And I'd mean it.

Everything is okay.

But there will never be a reader, never a reply. I know this now. The phone is stowed in with the rest of my clothes, and Lauren meets me in the hall and takes my bag.

"You all right?" she says. I nod, and she gives me a quick kiss. "Have a good run. I'll see you back home."

I wave goodbye to Shanice and head out into the spring air. A light drizzle has started, but it's warm outside, almost humid. Summer is not far away. I start to run, and my nose fills with the smell of rain and wet earth. I run along the shoulder of the highway in an easy rhythm, and the rain gathers up on my forehead and eyebrows; it flows down my face, it drips from the tip of my nose. There is wet dirt, a puddle in the gravel, new grass pushing through old in the ditch. Violets grow along the edge of the road. To my right, the Little Jib River flows brown and swollen to the lake. The water moves ceaselessly, and I move along with it. To my left, across the road, the rain strips wilted cherry blossoms from the rows and rows of trees, and drops them to the ground. I see all of this. The smell of rain and earth, the smell of growing things, my feet on the pavement, they're the only things I know.

How many times have I known these things?

I know these things. I remember them all.

And able to remember, I know that I'm alive.

ABOUT THE AUTHOR

David Swift, 2014

Born in Michigan, Jon Harrison studied English literature and geo-logical sciences at Ohio University. A lover of the outdoors, he moved to Jackson Hole, Wyoming, in 1994 and has lived there ever since. Read more about him at his website: www.harrisonpages.com.